Hidden Beneath

Amir H. Kasra

Luminari Books

eBook ISBN: 979-8-89795-236-6
Paperback ISBN: 979-8-89795-237-3
Hardcover ISBN: 979-8-89795-238-0

Contents

Prologue

Tears welled in her eyes as she stared at the painting on the wall, a haunting reminder of how deeply she missed her. Curling up beside the empty space where she once slept, she gently ran her palm across the sheets, lowering her nose to inhale the lingering scent woven into the fabric—a hint of her that refused to fade.

Her gaze drifted to the painting: a small boat rocking in the surf, the lighthouse looming ominously in the background. Closing her eyes, she imagined herself on that boat in the dark, a gust of sea spray stinging her face and body.

A shiver ran through her. Turning to the window, she spotted seagulls hovering effortlessly in the wind. Her lips curled into a smile as she approached and opened it wide. A gust of moist sea air rushed in, caressing her face and reminding her of the painting.

She scanned the horizon for any sign of land but found none, only the relentless waves tossing the yacht about.

Stepping into the cabin's bathroom, she stood before the mirror, running her fingers through her wavy blonde hair that spilled over her shoulders. Gazing at her reflection, she contemplated jumping overboard again but quickly dismissed the thought—she knew they'd fish her out in no time.

The sound of footsteps sent her heart racing. Adrenaline pulsed in her veins as she dashed to her nightstand, grabbing a vase. Drawing a deep breath, her lips pressed tight and eyebrows furrowed in determination, she steadied herself. Standing by the door, she held the vase over her head, waiting.

Her eyes locked on the doorknob as it turned, sending chills down her spine.

"Celine, you fuckin' bitch… You in here?" A familiar voice growled, slicing through the tense silence.

All she could hear was the thudding of her heart as the door slowly creaked open.

Amor Omnia Vincit

Love Conquers All

—Virgil

1

A subtle smile tugged at the corner of her lips as the familiar aroma of freshly brewed coffee grazed her nose. Her eyes flew open, and she sprang out of bed, racing to her front door and nearly tripping over her flowing nightgown. Her laptop sat open on her nightstand, but she'd rather see it in print—on the front cover.

She swung her front door open and found the morning paper sitting on the doorstep. As she reached down to pick it up, a familiar voice rang out.

"Good morning, Claire!"

Claire looked up toward the source of the voice and smiled. "Good morning, Mr. Wellington!"

Realizing her gown had flown open in her rush, she quickly tucked the flaps back in, holding them closed with her forearm. Grabbing the paper, she spun around to go back inside.

"I'm really sorry! I was in a hurry and dashed to the front door. I didn't mean to be so indecent!"

Thoroughly amused, Mr. Wellington tipped his bowler hat and laughed. "My dear Claire, there is no need to apologize. I'm half blind in one eye and can hardly see anything out of the other. That's why I'm headed to the Tube—the greatest British invention since the steam engine! And, not to mention, my granddaughter Elizabeth is just about your age. Perhaps you two could meet sometime."

"Of course! I'd love that… Well, I'd better get going. It's lovely seeing you again, Mr. Wellington!"

He smiled and waved as he turned in the opposite direction toward the underground train station, chuckling and mumbling to himself.

Claire waved and ran inside, closing the door behind her. Her heart pounded with excitement as she unfolded the newspaper.

The rich scent of coffee filled the air, but she dismissed it with a wave of her hand. Coffee could wait.

She opened the paper and smoothed out the pages. There it was, glaring in bold type on the front cover:

RARE FIND SHEDS LIGHT ON ROMAN BRITAIN

Archaeological dig at Hadrian's Wall finds that Roman soldiers stayed behind and married local Britannic women after Rome ended its rule in Britain.

She let out a loud gasp, her hand flying to her chest as she continued to read.

The site unearthed a gold Aureus (Roman coin) belonging to a Roman tribune or prefect, along with his skeletal remains and other local artifacts. These latter items might have belonged to a native Britannic noblewoman—presumably from the Carvetti tribe—who was laid to rest beside him. Radiocarbon dating, along with DNA testing, may finally provide the scientific evidence to support the prevailing hypothesis that Roman soldiers stayed behind and integrated with the local population after Roman rule ended in Britain, often marrying local Celtic women. These findings, according to lead archaeologist and historian Claire Langford, could dramatically enhance our understanding of Roman rule in Britain and rekindle interest in further exploration and research in the field.

A ping sounded on her phone, pulling her attention away from the paper. Reluctantly, she glanced at her screen; it was 7:02 a.m., and she had a text message from her assistant, Jane Morgan:

Good morning!! OMG!! I saw the paper. Congrats. You must be thrilled!

Claire smiled as she typed a reply, her excitement bubbling over.

Good morning Jane! I'm very excited. Btw, I'm running a bit late. I'll be in shortly.

No worries, take your time. See you when you get in.

Claire wasn't particularly fond of texting or emailing; she often preferred to keep her responses short and to the point. She wasn't keen on computers either—she cherished the feel of books, newspapers, and tangible objects she could hold in her hands. The older and dustier, the better.

Another text from Jane interrupted her thoughts.

Sorry, I forgot to mention. You have a new applicant for the assistant position. I just emailed you his bio link. I think you'll really like this one!

Claire typed a quick reply and hit send.

Thanks Jane! I'll check it out.

Hurrying to her laptop, she tapped the space bar a few times to wake it up. The screen blinked to life, and she quickly logged in and opened her email. There it was in her inbox, the subject reading "New applicant."

She opened the email and clicked on the link.

Highlights of Achievements

Assistant to Professor Ismail Al Waziri, chief archaeologist, Roman Leptis Magna, Libya.

I assisted Dr. Al Waziri in the excavations and preservation of artifacts unearthed in Leptis Magna.

Hmm... she thought, her eyes hastily scanning the rest of the resume.

Brown University – MA, Anthropology

Impressive! she murmured to herself. *Now, let's see who you are... Stewart Anderson... American... You're hired.*

Eager to jump in the shower and head out the door, she reached to close the laptop but paused. The "Download Images" icon sat on the screen, daring her to click. She did, drumming her fingernails on the nightstand. "Come on now, Betsie! Mummy doesn't have time for fun and games!"

She'd been having internet connection issues, but the image finally loaded.

Oh! ... You're definitely hired.

She loathed wearing makeup—it brought back memories of her dating days and failed relationships—but something compelled her to wear it today. A smile formed on her lips as she applied her lipstick. A touch of blush. A sweep of mascara. Hair pulled back into a messy bun. It was all the effort she could muster to make herself look presentable.

2

Claire was at her breaking point. Jane, her overworked accountant, had been doubling as an assistant, but the cracks were painfully obvious. Between juggling finances and trying to help Claire with archaeological tasks she barely understood, Jane was drowning—and so was Claire.

Her office was a short distance from her flat near Lombard Street, but every morning felt like a race against time. Claire didn't own a car; she relied on taxis or, when she felt a touch of childhood nostalgia, London's iconic double-decker buses. Today, clutching her newspaper and bag, she hurried out the door, arm raised to hail a cab, her mind already buzzing with the endless demands of the day ahead.

When Claire arrived, Jane had her office computer on and was signed in to Zoom.

"Hi, Claire! … Are you ready? I've got Stewart Anderson standing by." Jane smiled with her finger poised to click "Join Meeting."

Claire smiled nervously and nodded as she tossed her newspaper onto the office table.

"Go ahead."

Jane clicked the link and rose to her feet, offering the chair to her boss.

Claire sat and waited for the image to appear on the screen. Glancing at her watch, she realized she was five minutes early. About a minute later, a handsome, smiling face appeared on the monitor.

"Hello, Miss Langford!" he said.

"Hello..." She felt her face flushing. "Please call me Claire. We don't need to be formal."

He nodded and smiled. "Of course, Claire. You can call me Stewart—or Stu."

Claire smiled back. "Stewart it is, then."

"Thank you, Claire."

First impression—check! she thought. *And a nice smile.*

She tried to rein in her feelings and focus.

"So, Stewart, please tell me about your work—your tasks and responsibilities with Dr. Al Waziri at Leptis Magna. To tell the truth, I'm intrigued... I've always found Roman North Africa quite fascinating—the entire Mediterranean basin, in fact—from the Hellenistic period to the rise of Carthage and Rome; a fascinating few centuries, wouldn't you say?"

"Indeed, Miss Langford... I mean, Claire."

Unable to contain her enthusiasm, she continued, "And Cleopatra, Antony… Caesar… they were the real triumvirate, weren't they? They were the true power trio. Cleopatra—now she had vision, ambition. Centuries before Septimius Severus... and your Leptis Magna..."

Stewart remained silent, listening intently. He admired her brilliance and wore a smile, patiently waiting for her to conduct her interview.

She shifted her gaze from her monitor to Jane, who sat at the other end of the table, watching with an amused smile. Jane understood her boss well and recognized how passionate and driven she could be.

Catching herself rambling, Claire sighed and smiled, feeling embarrassed.

"I'm sorry, Stewart... Sometimes, I carry on." She gestured with her hand. "Please go ahead. Tell me about your experience with Dr. Al Waziri."

Stewart knew she came from money, and while he had entertained some preconceived notions about her, he could now clearly see that she had earned her stripes.

"Not at all, Claire," he replied. "I was really enjoying listening to you. I didn't want to interrupt you. I can see you are deeply passionate about the time period."

She tucked away the compliment and smiled. "Thank you. Please do go on."

"Well, to be perfectly honest, I feel I may be a bit underqualified to work for you. You see, my job was to basically take notes for Dr. Al Waziri and archive and document his findings—not much more than that. You have such profound knowledge and grasp of the time period, I'm afraid..."

Claire shook her head and gave a dismissive wave of her hand.

"No, Stewart. You don't understand; you just described the job perfectly: archiving and documenting." She gave him a reassuring smile. "You see? You've got nothing to worry about… and then there's 'on-the-job training,' as they say."

Stewart nodded, lowering his gaze. "Thank you, Claire. That means a lot to me. To be perfectly honest, I almost didn't apply for this position, thinking I may not be able to cut it. I thought the job may be too much of a reach for me."

Claire had already made her decision: she was going to hire him. But she also felt like she'd intimidated him, and that was not her intent. She decided to back off. *First impressions work both ways,* she reminded herself.

"So, why don't you tell me something you liked about Leptis Magna? Was there anything that stood out—something you felt drawn to?" she asked.

"Yes! Definitely," Stewart said enthusiastically, then hesitated.

Noticing his hesitation, she gave him a reassuring smile. "Please, go on."

"Well, I'm afraid it's of no academic importance or significance... It was just..." Stewart trailed off.

"That's quite all right... Please tell me... What was it?" Claire encouraged.

Stewart let out a sigh. "It was the sunrises and sunsets... Standing at the top of the Roman theater, with the Mediterranean Sea just beyond the Baths on one side and the lighthouse on the other... It was the most amazing thing I've ever seen in my life. I mean, I'm just an Indiana farm boy..."

Claire felt a lump in her throat. He'd struck a chord with her. She was accustomed to working at the excavation site from sunup to sundown, watching as the sun pierced through the horizon at dawn and sank beneath it at dusk—her favorite times of the day when she found her inspiration, her zest for life.

She glanced at the resume and stared at his references, thinking she should call them—or at the very least, Dr. Al Waziri—but instead, she placed the resume face down on the table and shifted her gaze to Jane, who was staring at her, grinning and nodding.

Jane knew Stewart had scored big with his story. She'd celebrated a few triumphant moments with Claire at the dig, and she was aware of her obsession with sunrises and sunsets.

Claire's gaze returned to the monitor, where she found Stewart lost in thought, staring at his lap.

"Mr. Anderson… Stewart…" she called.

Stewart looked up, his eyes widening. "Yes, Claire?"

"I would like to offer you the position of my assistant... If you wish to join us, that is."

He nodded enthusiastically. "I do! Thank you very much, Miss Langford… I do!"

She laughed lightly. "Just Claire, please."

"I'm sorry, I mean Claire."

She chuckled at his response, and Jane smiled, giving her a thumbs-up.

Claire took a deep breath and continued, "Welcome to 'Langford Antiquities,' Stewart. We're delighted to have you on board."

"Thank you, Claire. I truly appreciate the opportunity. I'm really looking forward to working with you."

She gave him a warm smile. "My pleasure, Stewart, and likewise."

Jane leaned in from across the table and whispered, "Would you like me to begin onboarding him now?" She held up her arm, pointing to her watch. "Remember, you have another meeting in 15…"

Claire nodded slightly and turned to Stewart. "Well, Stewart, I have to leave for another appointment, but Jane will take over and get you started… Goodbye, and I hope to see you very soon!"

As she stood up to leave, Jane scribbled on a piece of paper and slid it across the table to her.

She placed her fingers on the note and drew it closer—it read:

"Would you like him to attend the fundraising gala next week?"

She met Jane's eyes, smiled, and nodded once more.

As she walked away, she overheard Jane congratulating Stewart, asking, "By the way, do you happen to have a black suit?"

Things had been hectic lately, but Claire could finally relax and let her hair down. Her recent discovery had virtually guaranteed the much-needed financial backing, and she was thrilled about her new assistant.

It had been a productive day, and sitting in the back of the cab on the way home, she fished out her compact mirror from her purse, flipped it open, and swiped on a fresh coat of lipstick. As she studied her reflection, she realized something—her frown lines had smoothed out. A smile tugged at her lips, and she snapped the compact shut.

3

The arrival of spring brought a surge of renewed energy to the dig site. With the earth as solid as a rock during the winter months, excavation had come to a standstill, and Claire had been anxiously awaiting the spring thaw so work could resume.

Before she could return north to Newcastle, she had to deal with her father, Charles Langford, president and senior partner at Langford Equity Capital, one of London's leading private equity firms, specializing in joint ventures and investments. He had provided the financing for his daughter's ambitious project and was patiently waiting, hoping for a worthwhile return on his investment.

Although Claire grew up in a Victorian mansion near Buckingham Palace, she had never had it easy and had to pay her dues. She adored her father but hated dealing with finances and money.

Sitting in her home office chair, she gazed out the window at her backyard and the sycamore tree—its branches, now covered in lush green leaves, tapped against the glass with each gust of wind as if reminding her that spring had arrived.

She took a deep breath, grabbed her phone, and dialed "Daddy."

"Hello, Charles Langford, speaking..."

"Hi, Daddy!"

"Oh, hello, sweetie... How's my precious daughter doing? Still digging around in that frozen muck up in Caledonia's godforsaken hills?"

Claire laughed. "Oh, Daddy, it's in England—just outside of Newcastle, not Scotland."

"I know, sweetie; it might as well be Scotland. It's too far north for me. I don't like traveling beyond Manchester or Leeds."

"Alright, Daddy, but one day, I'll have no choice but to kidnap you and take you to see my work... Anyway, how are you? How's Mummy?"

"We are all in good health, sweetheart, and Mummy is currently shopping at her preferred charity shop, Harrods."

"Mummy, she's a shopaholic. And you enable her, Daddy!" She snorted.

"I suppose so, sweetie, but it keeps her happy."

"... and out of your hair?"

He let out a hearty laugh. "I did not say that." He emphasized, "Not."

She laughed along. "Better a shopaholic than a shoplifter, I suppose."

"Oh, naughty, naughty, girl."

Claire's mother, Margaret Langford, was an avid shopper who spent most of her time browsing the aisles of London's most prestigious department stores.

At home, she drove the housekeeping staff crazy with her infinite energy and boundless zeal for organization. So, when she wanted to go shopping, no one would protest—least of all her husband.

Claire turned her attention to the stack of financial documents Jane had printed for her. She shuffled the papers around on her desk, attempting to make sense of them: *income and expenses, balance sheet, statement of cash flows...*

She let out a frustrated sigh, shaking her head.

"Daddy, I'm going to send you my financial statements, and you can look at them. Okay?"

"Of course, my dear! Did your finance girl take a peek at them and whittle away at your expenses a wee bit?"

"No, Daddy. Jane has been busy with other projects," she replied, sounding frustrated.

"Don't worry, sweetie, I will have my accountant review it all."

"I mean, I can read cuneiform, Latin—even hieroglyphics—but I can't stand finances; my brain flat-out refuses."

"It's all right... I can't stand finances either—why do you think I have my accountants? I've just learned to look at the bottom line." He chuckled. "And if I don't like the bottom line, I call a meeting and let 'em have it."

She laughed. "That's right, Daddy! You let 'em have it—the whole jolly bunch of them!"

He loved hearing her laughter, but sensing her anxiety, he decided to change the subject.

"Why don't you tell me what you've dug up at the site? What's all the hullabaloo in the newspapers about?"

She sighed, her excitement bubbling underneath. "Oh, Daddy... I'm so thrilled! We've unearthed the remains of a high-ranking Roman officer, and buried right next to him is a local Celtic woman. There are artifacts and inscriptions, correspondences with Rome... and..." She stammered. "And love letters."

He cleared his throat. "Did you say love letters?"

"Uh-huh. One of them reads, 'Te amo, Te desidero, Cara, Uxor mea...'"

"It has been decades since I studied Latin, my dear, but let me see if I remember: 'I love you... I miss you, Cara. My wife...'"

She felt tears welling up in her eyes. "Very good, Daddy... Her name was Cara. A Britannic woman—most likely from the Carvetti tribe—married to a Roman officer."

"Oh, darling... That's wonderful! Hadrian's time?"

"Perhaps the Nerva-Antonine dynasty... I'm not sure yet. It's too early to tell. We won't know until we conduct some tests. But what if it's from much later? Roman rule in Britain ended in 409 AD. And until 197, when Septimius Severus relaxed the laws, it was illegal for Roman soldiers to marry local women. So, did they marry in secret?"

"Hmm…" He scratched his head, mumbling to himself. "Yes… yes… this is very, very interesting…"

"This could rewrite the history of Roman Britain, Daddy!"

"I am so proud of you, darling. So, so proud."

Claire couldn't hold back her tears. "Thank you, Daddy." She reached for a tissue box, pulled one out, and blew her nose.

"And, Daddy?"

"Yes, darling?"

She hesitated before continuing. "Um... I had to hire an assistant. I needed one urgently. I had to let my previous assistant go, and Jane was stretched thin, taking on additional responsibilities."

"That's quite all right, my dear. I have an army of assistants; they're quite indispensable. If I had to fire anyone, I'd start with the accountants—beginning with Alfred—and then the solicitors, the entire lot of them." He paused and groaned as if he were contemplating it all. "So, tell me, is this new assistant any good?"

She smiled. "He's perfect, Daddy... Stewart Anderson… He's an American."

A dramatic sigh came through the phone. "Oh, my dear, why did you have to go on and tell me that? Now I can't get the thought out of my head—a Yank!"

She let out a laugh. "I love you, Daddy! I have to go now... Bye, Daddy!"

"I love you, too, darling. Goodbye."

He is perfect. The thought settled in her mind as she let her nightgown slip from her shoulders, pooling at her feet before she turned on the water. She dipped her toe into the water to check the temperature—it was just right.

She deserved a soothing bath before climbing into bed. A smile curled on her lips, realizing everything, even the water temperature, was perfect.

Slowly lowering herself into the tub, she thought about her fundraising event… and him—her new, perfect assistant.

Was it all too good to be true? She swatted away the thought. *No, everything will be great, absolutely exquisite.*

She ran the wet sponge along her thigh, watching the water trickle down her raised leg, goosebumps rising in its wake. Her body shivered slightly as she closed her eyes, fully immersed in her moment of triumph.

4

A singing goldfinch perched on the Sycamore tree brought a smile to Claire's face as she sat curled up on her living room settee, sipping her morning Darjeeling tea—her favorite morning ritual.

She noticed that the outer edges of her painting didn't align with the grooves in the cherry wood-paneled walls. Shaking her head, she rose to her feet and placed her teacup and saucer on the vintage oval-shaped coffee table in front of her.

Gently dragging one of her French country-style antique dining chairs across the Persian silk rug, she positioned it underneath the painting and climbed onto it.

Now, she stood face-to-face with Hannibal, one of the most brilliant generals in ancient history, accompanied by his legion of war elephants as they crossed the Alps into Italy.

She leaned in, inhaling the faint scent of oil paint—her favorite.

Spinning around on the chair, she glanced across the room at her other painting, which depicted Cleopatra standing defiantly at her ship's bow during the Battle of Actium.

She blew her a kiss and muttered, "A true queen."

From her vantage point on the chair, she scanned her modest two-bedroom flat for decorating ideas but found herself at a loss. All the rooms showcased wood-paneled walls, Persian rugs, antique French and English furniture, and curio cabinets filled with Roman coins and artifacts.

Bursting at the seams, there was little else she could cram inside the place. It was evident that she'd outgrown her flat, but it was hers; her mortgage was affordable, and she didn't have to answer to anyone, especially her overbearing mother.

She'd moved out a couple of years ago and never looked back.

Just then, she heard a ping on her phone—it was a text from Jane.

Good Morning! So whatcha planning to wear to the ball?

Lol, ball. I'm not Cinderella, and I genuinely don't know.

She'd thought of everything except what she would wear, and the fundraiser was only three days away.

Watching the message bubble appear as Jane typed, she pressed her index finger against her lips, contemplating her options—perhaps she could ask her mom to accompany her shopping. But she shook her head. *It's a bad idea, Claire. . . Terrible idea.* She let out a giggle at the thought. *Malo me gladio cadere* ("I would rather fall on my sword" in Latin.)

Her phone pinged again, snapping her focus back to the screen.

I'm all caught up. I can take the day off tomorrow and we go shopping!

Claire hesitated; she felt she'd already shared too much about her mom and family and was considering whether it was prudent to socialize with her assistant, but her fingers began typing before she could finish her thoughts.

Sure. Harrods?

Noooo!!! You may run into your mum!!!

Lol, omg, you're right.

And Harrods is for old people. I know a few good swanky boutiques.

Swanky?

Lol. . . posh. . . chic. . . cool. . .

Hahaha. Ok.

Any thoughts at all on what you'd like to wear? Any favorites?

Not a clue.

Hmm. . . evening gown? Floor length or cocktail dress?

They all sound good. Do they come in khaki or mud color?

What???

Lol. I'm an archaeologist, always in the muck and dirt.

OMG!! PLZZZZ!!!. . . you're gorgeous. . . we need to dress you up!!!

Yeah, right. Are you drinking?

Yes you are!!! And you never know. . . you may run into Prince Charming. . . we'll pick up a pair of glass. . . nvm, crystal slippers, and PC will whisk you away.

PC?

Prince charming!

You're funny.

You're beautiful. . . so what time tomorrow?

Morning. 10 am?

You're the boss. I have a smart beautiful boss!!! Are you coming in today?

No. Working from home. Call if you need me.

K. Have fun

K. You too.

Claire walked over to her vanity desk, pulled out the stool, and sat down, gazing at her reflection. She'd never felt particularly beautiful—especially not in the mornings when she hastily threw her hair up in a messy bun, applied a touch of lipstick and mascara, and dashed out the door.

Running the brush through her auburn hair, she studied her face—her hazel eyes, the freckles sprinkled on her nose and cheek—and smiled. Cute, maybe. Pretty at best. But not stunning like Jane, who was blonde with sparkling blue eyes and endowed with all the right curves in the right places.

In comparison, she felt like the flat-chested goldfinch she'd seen perched on her sycamore tree.

She chuckled, thinking, *You're full of crap, Jane!*

5

Shuffling through the clothes rack, Claire couldn't decide: should she go for the elegant and sophisticated look or the sexy and seductive? Which one was more likely to captivate her audience and secure the funding she so desperately needed?

Moving from one rack to the next, she sifted through hanger after hanger, searching for the perfect dress. It was vital for her to project the right image and convey the appropriate message.

She felt she had two major disadvantages: she was too young and too female for her stuffy, old audience.

There was no room for error. Her speech was solid, but her delivery and appearance had to be perfect, and she didn't want to blow it: too casual, and they wouldn't take her seriously; too formal, and they might lose interest. She knew she had to walk a fine line.

Holding a dress up against her body in front of the mirror, she pursed her lips and tilted her head, closely scrutinizing it. She paused, then shook her head and put it back on the rack.

"Here, try this one!" Jane's hand reached out from behind and held a dress in front of her. "This'll look amazing on you."

Claire turned, raising a skeptical brow. "Hmm. . . do you think?"

Jane met her gaze in the mirror, smiling as she gave a slow nod.

"I do! I think it'll knock their socks off!" She lowered her nose to Claire's neck and inhaled deeply, a playful glint in her eyes. "Mmm... and honestly, I'd wear whatever it is that you've got on right now. They'll be throwing wads of cash at you."

Claire's mouth fell open before she burst into laughter. "Jane, I'm not going to strip for them!"

Jane's eyes widened. "Oh my God! I didn't mean it that way... I was just playing!"

Claire waved a hand. "Don't worry about it. I'm playing with you, too. I'm not that uptight."

Jane winked and handed her the dress. "Why don't you try it? Let me see you in it."

Claire took the dress with a grin. "All right. . . let's see. . ."

Jane raised her wrist and glanced at her watch. Claire had been in the dressing room for over twenty minutes. She called out, "Are you okay in there? Need any help?"

Claire didn't respond.

Just as Jane was about to walk up to her stall and knock on the door, she heard the latch click.

Claire stepped out of the changing room, beaming. She looked down and gestured at her dress—a fitted black satin gown with a high slit, V-neck, and a plunging back.

"What do you think?"

Jane gasped, pressing a hand to her chest. "Oh my! You look gorgeous!"

And she meant it. Claire looked stunning with her red hair and fair complexion, which contrasted beautifully against the black satin.

Claire tilted her head in disbelief. "Seriously?"

Jane nodded vigorously. "Yes, seriously! You're beautiful!"

Claire's smile widened. "Thanks, Jane, for bringing me to this place." She glanced around. "I missed the store sign—what's the name of the store?"

With her hand on her chin, Jane studied Claire's dress before replying, "Evening Elegance. . . Glad you like it."

Claire had dropped a small fortune on the outfit, and they were about to leave the store when Jane paused, laying her hand gently on Claire's forearm. Her eyes sparkled with mischief, and a sly grin crept across her face.

"Hey, I've got an idea."

Claire chuckled. "Another one? I'm not sure I can afford anymore..."

"Yeah, but it won't be as expensive as the dress," Jane laughed. "I promise it'll be cheap, but lots of fun—cheap fun!"

"Oh? I wasn't aware of such a thing in London—cheap fun!"

Jane nodded. "There is. . . In fact, it'll be my treat."

Claire folded her arms and shot Jane a skeptical look, a broad grin spreading across her face. "All right. . . Let me hear it."

"Well." Jane drew closer. "You know how we'll soon be knee-deep in dirt and mud?"

"Yeah?"

"And we haven't really celebrated your fantastic discovery..."

"Oh, Jane!" Claire gave a dismissive wave of her hand. "I don't care. . . "

"Wait, just hear me out, please?" Jane pleaded.

"All right, go on." She shook her head, still smiling.

"I was just thinking we could have a girls' night out, that's all. Just a couple of drinks. I know a great spot—pretty please?"

Claire hesitated, then sighed with a playful eye roll. "Fine, but only a couple of drinks."

"Yay!" Jane mimed a clapping gesture. "It'll be lots of fun. . . Say, around eight? I'll pick you up."

Claire nodded. "Just casual, right?"

"Yes! Come in your jammies if you want."

Claire laughed. "Don't tempt me. I might just."

6

"To my boss," Jane toasted, raising her glass.

Claire smiled, lifting her own, and they clinked glasses. They were seated in a dimly lit corner booth, shielded from prying eyes, with a good view of the entire bar.

The place was packed with hip young Londoners huddled around in small groups or sitting at the square-shaped bar at the center of the floor.

Jane raised her empty glass, motioning to the server for refills. She'd been drinking Moscow mules and Claire vodka spritzes.

Jane had chosen a bar because London pubs didn't have servers. She didn't want them to have to walk up to the bar to get their drinks. She was out celebrating with her boss, and the last thing she wanted was to run into a rowdy crowd of locals screaming at a football game on television—or worse, draw unwanted attention, which she detested.

She smiled, bringing two fingers to her lips. "Is it all right if I step out for a smoke?"

"Of course," Claire replied, returning the smile. "Enjoy your cigarette. I'll be fine."

"Thanks, boss," Jane grinned, giving Claire's hand a quick squeeze as she rose to her feet. "I'll be right back. . . I can never finish a full cigarette; just a few puffs and I'm done. . . I'll be back in no time."

Jane wore a silver-tone chainmail top with a draped neckline and crisscross back, paired with designer jeans and silver pumps—her idea of casual.

With her wavy blonde hair spilled carelessly over her shoulders, she leaned against the front of the building with one foot against the wall. Lighting her cigarette, she gazed at the long line of people trying to get inside.

She waved at the bouncer in front, her Jamaican friend, who waved back with a smile.

Savoring her moment of solitude, she took a deep drag with her eyes shut, holding the smoke in for a few seconds before releasing a thin stream of it into the air.

A booming voice shattered her peace.

"Hey, babe, what's happening?" The man's voice was loud and confident. "Can I buy you a drink?"

Her eyes sprang open. Without even glancing his way, she snarled, "No, but you can fuck the fuck off."

She kept her gaze fixed ahead as the man walked away, muttering, "What the fuck's wrong with you, bitch?"

"I have low loser tolerance," she fumed. "Now, fuck off!"

A few drags later, she felt centered enough to return to her table.

"Weren't we supposed to go casual?" Claire teased, gesturing to Jane's outfit. "I mean, look at me." She was wearing her regular everyday jeans, white high-top sneakers, and a black T with white letters that read, "I dig dirt" on the front.

Jane laughed. "I'm so sorry. I completely forgot. Next time, I'll show up with rollers in my hair—promise. . . Okay?"

Claire waved off the remark and laughed. "Don't worry, we'll just stay in next time and get drunk at my place. That way, we don't have to worry about anyone seeing us."

Jane threw her arms up in agreement. "Hey, I'm game. I don't like going to bars anyway—they allow too many idiots in!"

No sooner had she finished her sentence than another ardent admirer appeared in front of their table, wearing a grin.

Jane shot him a warning glare, but he didn't get the message. He'd barely opened his mouth when Jane beat him to the punch. "Fuck off—pretty please?"

Claire smirked, watching the man tuck his tail between his legs and walk away with a vanquished look. She almost felt bad for him—almost, but not entirely. She sympathized with Jane's stance on men, finding most of them dull and uninteresting.

"I'll let you know if I'm interested," Jane mumbled under her breath. "Until then—"

She raised a finger, gesturing for Claire to finish her sentence.

Claire smirked and obliged. "Until then, you can bugger off."

Jane burst out laughing. "You tell 'em, sister."

Claire's fingers twirled the straw in her glass, a remote expression on her face. Already on the edge, Jane followed her gaze to her empty glass and rose to her feet.

"I'm going to go find that waitress; where the hell is she with our drinks?"

"No, Jane! Stay." Claire pleaded, grabbing her arm and trying to keep her from making a scene. "By the way, have you heard back from Stewart? When is he starting?"

Jane reluctantly sat back down. "Mm, sorry. . . I forgot to mention, he's flying out from JFK and will be here for the fundraiser."

"Good. I want the sponsors to meet the entire team—all the staff members, including the supervisors."

"I'm so excited!" Jane beamed. "I can't wait to go back up north. I love getting up early, sipping my coffee, and listening to you rave about the sunrise." She placed her hand on Claire's.

"I really love working for you, Claire! You're the best boss—ever!"

Claire smiled, her face flushing. "Thank you, Jane. . . "

"No, I mean it." Jane released a deep, long sigh. "This is the only job I've ever had where I look forward to coming to work every day. I've learned so much from you—so much about Rome, about archaeology... I mean, I'm just a bean counter."

Claire shook her head, placing her hand over Jane's, and gave it a squeeze. "You're much more than that; you're my right-hand woman."

It was subtle, almost undetectable, but it was there—a hint of an accent slipping through Jane's otherwise crisp English one. It became more noticeable after she'd had a few drinks.

Claire had hired Jane only a few months earlier, but she'd grown to rely heavily on her since then. Jane played a vital role in her operation. She was in charge of Claire's finances and kept her calendar organized.

Even though they'd spent months together at the dig site, often sharing a tent—or a hotel room in Newcastle when they stayed in town—Claire knew very little about Jane, about her private life.

And that was deliberate. Claire had no desire to open the door to any questions about her own private life; she'd already shared enough about her relationship with her mother.

So, she kept Jane at a distance. It was simple to do; after a long day at the dig site, they'd both return to their tent exhausted and ready to retire for the day. After a bit of reading, it was lights out.

Claire stared at her empty glass, her hands wrapped around it, swirling the ice cubes around. She contemplated opening up and letting Jane into her life.

"Penny for your thoughts," Jane said in a gentle voice, eager to rekindle the conversation. She hated the awkward silence.

Claire shifted her gaze away from the glass to Jane's and smiled.

"You can have them for free."

Jane laughed, then hesitated. She didn't want to pry; she only wanted Claire's attention.

With her mind hazy from the alcohol and sitting with her body pressed up against hers, she froze, her eyes riveted on Claire's, thinking how lovely she was. Even in her plain T-shirt and jeans, she looked positively radiant.

"Free, but a limited-time offer," Claire teased, playfully toying with Jane.

Huddled in the dimly lit corner of the bar, they were by far the prettiest women there, despite being older than most of the crowd: Jane was 29 years old, while Claire was 32.

Jane hesitated again.

"All right, I'll start," Claire laughed, her own inhibitions blunted by the vodka. "But first, why do I detect an accent?" She brought her index finger and thumb close together and lowered her voice. "It's a tiny one."

Jane sighed, her demeanor growing somber. "My mom was French. My dad was Welsh. I grew up in Wales… and my mom would speak to me in French."

"Do you ever go back home and see them?" Claire asked, genuinely curious.

Jane shook her head, her gaze dropping as she absently rolled the corner of her cocktail napkin.

"They both passed away: she died of cancer, and he died in a car accident."

Claire arched her brow, her hand instinctively moving to Jane's back. "I'm so sorry. I didn't mean to pry."

Suddenly, it seemed as if Claire was looking at another person entirely—the bold, assertive woman who moments earlier told a man to fuck off had transformed into a vanquished and vulnerable young girl who was about to burst into tears in front of her.

Jane looked up at Claire and smiled, teardrops beading in her eyes.

"It's all right. . . It's…" She stammered. "It's just that it's been rough since I lost both of them."

Claire gave her a reassuring nod. "I get it. Trust me, I do."

Jane's skeptical expression showed she wasn't entirely convinced.

"You do? Really?"

Claire met her gaze. "Tell you what; let's go back to my flat, and I'll tell you all about it—sounds good?"

Jane glanced at her watch. It was already one in the morning.

"Sounds great! But are you sure? It's getting late."

"I'm sure. . . and you can stay the night if you want."

Jane blinked, a single tear slipping down her cheek as she nodded.

"I'd love that!"

Claire pulled a tissue from her purse and gently dabbed the tear away. "I didn't want it to smudge your makeup. Now, let's get out of here."

7

Claire struggled with the corkscrew, her grip slipping as she tried to pop the cork.

Jane giggled and held out her hand.

"Here, let me do that for you," she offered.

Claire laughed and handed her the bottle of Chablis with the corkscrew sticking out of it.

Jane took the bottle, and Claire watched as the muscles in her arms flexed slightly while she popped the cork out with a few effortless twists.

Working alongside each other at the dig site, they'd both become tan and trim—Jane more so than Claire since she also worked out and spent longer hours in the sun. Claire was fairer and burned too easily, so she wasn't nearly as tan as Jane.

Jane smiled and offered the bottle back to Claire.

"Here you go, all done."

Claire raised a hand. "I'll let you do the honors."

Jane poured the drinks, handed Claire a glass, and lifted hers.

"To your amazing discovery," she toasted.

Claire raised her glass. "To our amazing team: We couldn't have done it without them!"

Jane's eyes locked onto Claire's, a warm smile playing on her lips as she sipped her wine. She appreciated how Claire used the words "our and "we," always giving credit where it was due.

As Jane wandered through the living room, her gaze lingered on the carefully arranged artworks and objects adorning the walls and displayed in the cabinets.

"Your place is amazing, Claire," Jane said, shaking her head in amazement.

"Thank you. I'm glad you like it; please make yourself at home. I'll be right back."

Claire went to her bedroom, changed into her pajamas, and returned with a pair for Jane.

"Here. Try these on, see if they're comfy."

Jane reached for the pajamas, her gaze still fixed on the paintings. Without hesitation, she began to remove her clothing right there in front of Claire.

Having spent enough time with Claire in a tent, she felt comfortable undressing in front of her. Slipping into the pajamas, she let out a contented sigh. "Gosh, they're soft!" She smoothed out the wrinkles on her top with her hands and added, "Now, I don't want to take them off!"

"They're silk," Claire giggled. "And you can have them. I have way too many pairs."

"I couldn't possibly," Jane quipped with a snobbish head tilt, flicking her wrist in the air. "But don't mind if I do."

Claire laughed as she adjusted the back of Jane's collar. "They look great on you. The white silk really pops against your tanned skin." She gazed into Jane's eyes. "Seriously, I want you to have these."

Jane threw her arms around Claire, hugging her tightly.

"Thank you so much! I really love them."

Claire sank into the sofa, resting her head on her hand, while Jane sat beside her with her knees pulled up to her chest. They looked at each other and smiled.

"Are you tired?" Claire asked.

Jane shook her head. "Nope. Are you?"

"No. I'm too excited to be tired. Is everything ready for the event? The catering?"

Jane nodded and smiled. "Everything—I promise! Please don't worry."

Claire returned her smile. "Then we can sleep in, can't we?"

Jane laughed. "You're the boss!"

Looking around, Jane shook her head. "So, tell me—how did all of this start?" She gestured at the room. "I mean, it's obviously more than just a job to you. . . "

"It's my obsession." Claire completed her sentence. "It's my lifelong love affair."

"With Rome?"

"With history. Ancient history, to be precise. Initially, I focused on the Mediterranean Basin and the Roman Near East. But since I live here, I felt Roman Britain—its northernmost territories—might be worth exploring."

"And, jackpot!" Jane threw her hands up.

Claire chuckled. "Yes, I suppose I did hit the jackpot. But let's not count our chickens until they hatch. We still need to conduct DNA analysis… radiocarbon dating…"

Jane laughed and raised her hand in a mock salute. "Roger that! I won't count the chickens."

Claire laughed along with Jane, thinking about how much she enjoyed her company and her exuberance. Then it struck her—Jane was her only true friend. The only one who genuinely cared about her.

In contrast, others were just pretenders—fake friends, entitled sorority types who saw life as a popularity contest. But her morning and evening companion, Jane, was always with her, toiling alongside her through thick and thin.

Claire opened up about her upbringing and her relationship with her parents, explaining how close she was to her father and how her controlling mother had practically driven her away from home.

Initially, she pursued her studies at Oxford University, earning her PhD in archaeology, before fleeing to remote regions of the country to distance herself from her mother. "At first, I hated it—the mud and the dirt. I despised being so isolated, so far away from my home, away from my father. But then something happened."

"What happened?" Jane asked, her eyes drawn to Claire's lips.

"I fell in love."

"Let me guess—one of the boys at school?"

Claire shook her head. "I fell in love with the sunsets, the untamed wildflowers… the clean air… and the stories behind the lives. Think about it. Think about the couple we found buried together. Here they are centuries later." She took a deep breath and sighed. "They've come back to life, Jane!"

"It's so romantic," Jane mused, her eyes glistening.

"There," Claire nodded at her. "That's it, right there. You can read about it in a book. . . "

"But it's something else entirely—feeling it, touching it," Jane cut in, sniffling.

Claire smiled and pushed the tissue box toward her. "Now you've got it—it's a two-thousand-year-old love story: 'Te amo, Te desidero, Cara, Uxor mea...'—'I love you, I miss you, Cara, my wife.'"

Jane took a tissue, dabbing her tears, and blew her nose. "And now we know her name: Cara."

Claire smiled softly, motioning towards Jane's eyes.

"You should go wash your face; your mascara is running."

Jane giggled, then gestured toward the window. "And there's your sunrise."

Claire spun around, her hand flying to her chest, and gasped. The deep orange glow of dawn was slowly swallowing the black velvet of night. In the foreground, she saw her morning companion, the goldfinch, perched on her sycamore tree, singing, heralding another sunrise.

"Does your sofa fold out into bed?" Jane yawned, covering her mouth.

"Yes, it does. But my bed is absolutely gigantic—you can sleep with me if you want. . . I promise I don't snore."

Jane laughed and nodded. "I'd love that. . ."

8

Marcel Fornier settled into his chair, gazing out from the small balcony of his Paris condo at the boats drifting along the river Seine. He sipped his morning café au lait—his one true indulgence aside from his Friday night poker games.

His wife's miniature poodle, Titou, trotted up beside him and let out a half-bark.

"Bonjour, Titou! Where is your mommy?" He called out for her. "Madeleine, mon amour, are you home?"

Titou barked again.

"Excusez-moi, Titou. I didn't quite catch that— 'Mommy went out?' All right, back to work."

In the distance, he caught sight of the Pont de L 'Alma Bridge, the infamous site of Princess Diana's car crash on that fateful night. He shook his head and muttered, "What a tragedy. . . What a loss."

He averted his gaze, pushing away the thought.

He'd been investigating a string of kidnappings linked to a human trafficking syndicate operating in Europe and Canada, catering to a global clientele—a case that demanded his full concentration.

The case had been referred to him by his father-in-law, a prominent Parisian who had pulled strings to secure Marcel's job with the police force at the age of twenty-three. Over the years, Marcel had climbed the ranks, eventually becoming an investigator with the Gendarmerie Nationale.

His phone's alarm went off. He sent off a quick text to his wife.

My love, I'm leaving now. Be back on Friday. I love you!

She had been anxiously awaiting his text. With a sigh, she typed out her reply.

Miss you already. Sorry I had to leave for my doctor appt. Just a checkup. Don't worry. Be careful! I love you!!

His flight to Montreal was scheduled to depart in two hours. He grabbed his carry-on suitcase, said goodbye to Titou, and headed to Charles de Gaulle Airport.

Sitting in the back of the taxi, he flipped through his notes, reviewing details of a new lead he had received from his colleague at Interpol. During the interrogation of several suspects apprehended in the Czech Republic, one name kept surfacing: Henri Bouchard, a Canadian national from Montreal.

He underlined the name twice and tucked the notes back into his carry-on.

He sent a text to his superior.

Flight takes off in 2 hrs sir.

The response came quickly.

Be careful inspector! Keep me in the loop.

9

Jane beamed as she welcomed the attendees inside the hall. She could feel their eyes on her as they plodded along, some stopping to get more familiar.

She let out a groan as one of the guest's hands grazed her butt. Her fingers curled into a fist behind her, knuckles whitening, but she kept her composure. She wasn't going to do anything to ruin Claire's big night. She'd grown to love and respect her like an older sister.

Taking a moment for herself, she stepped into the restroom to freshen up and text Claire.

Her fingers swiftly typed the message and hit the send button. *Hi! Where are you? People are starting to show up early.*

Standing in front of the mirror, she gazed at her reflection. The black satin dress hugged her figure, its ruffled halter accentuating her shoulders. A side slit ran up her thigh—a dress she'd poured an entire paycheck into, hoping to impress Claire.

Tilting her head, she sighed, struggling to muster a smile. She had a lot on her mind. She took out her compact from her purse and dabbed some powder on her nose and cheeks.

Then her phone pinged. Seeing Claire's reply, she smiled.

Sorry! Im here. Where are you?

I'm in the loo. Lol.

Stay there. Im coming to you.

The door swung open, and Claire walked in, beaming with her arms outstretched. "Hi, I'm so sorry. I was running late and couldn't find a cab. . ."

Jane stepped into her arms, hugging her tightly. "You're not even late. People just showed up early." She glanced at her watch. "The event doesn't technically start for another hour. We have time."

Claire nodded and drew back, examining Jane's outfit. "Gosh, you look gorgeous, Jane—absolutely stunning!"

Jane giggled. "Thank you. You look mighty fine, yourself, boss. You're gonna knock their old, crusty socks off!" Her delivery of the words "old" and "crusty" was filled with emotion.

"Ew. . . I just visualized that!" Claire made a gagging gesture with her face.

Jane laughed. "I'm sorry. I didn't mean to gross you out." Her hand gently brushed Claire's arm.

But something in Jane's tone had shifted.

"Is something wrong, Jane?" Claire asked, studying her closely.

"Oh, nothing. . . Don't worry about it." Jane replied, her expression suggesting otherwise.

"Go on, please tell me."

Jane quirked her lips and wrinkled her nose. "It's nothing. . . It's just that some of the guests like to get a little handsy."

"Oh, Jane! I'm sorry." Claire hugged her. "Show me who it was, and I'll— "

Jane shook her head. "No, no. That's not necessary. I suppose I'm just too sensitive."

"No! You're not. And that's not okay. I want you to stay away from them, all right?"

Jane nodded and smiled. The tension in her shoulders eased. "Thank you." She exhaled, finally relaxing. "By the way, Stewart is running a bit late. Had to get settled and find his way around. He texted me—he'll be here soon."

Jane had done an excellent job scouting and securing the venue. The historic, renovated 1920s ballroom in South Kensington was the perfect location for the event.

The valet staff moved swiftly, parking the guests' cars while Jane guided them along the red carpet and into the hall, where they were promptly seated at their assigned tables.

Outside, photographers and journalists buzzed, discussing the event's significance—one that could rewrite Britain's ancient history.

Jane looped her arm around Claire's, smiling and nodding at the guests as she accompanied her across the aisle to the podium. It was the moment Claire had been waiting for since graduating from Oxford.

Jane smiled and whispered, "Break a leg." She gave Claire a small wave before returning to the audience. Taking a steadying breath, she flashed a confident smile and began boldly, quoting from Shakespeare's *Julius Caesar*.

"Friends, Romans, countrymen, please listen to me. . ."

The crowd erupted in laughter. A guest at the back shouted, "To be or not to be," referencing *Hamlet*.

Claire chuckled. "I'm only joking. . . I have no plans to recite Shakespeare."

The audience continued to laugh and applaud.

"Although I might," she added with a playful smirk, "Terence: Fortes Fortuna Adiuvat. 'Fortune favors the brave.'"

The laughs continued unabated.

"Or, in my case, she favors the extremely lucky."

As the laughter subsided, Claire's gaze swept across the audience, scanning for familiar faces. When she spotted her parents, her heart swelled.

"And speaking of being extremely lucky…" she pointed toward them. "I was lucky enough to have the greatest parents in the world. I owe them a huge debt of gratitude for their support— both during my years in school and later when I roamed about the country, playing around in the 'muck,' as my father calls it."

Heads turned toward her parents, laughter rippling through the audience. Claire's mother nodded and waved, clearly relishing the attention.

Then Claire gestured toward her team.

"And then, there's my team." She smiled, waving at them. "They're the ones in the muck with me—day in, day out, rain or shine."

They waved back, one member calling out, "We love you, Claire!"

"I love you too," she promptly shot back.

From the corner of her eye, Claire saw Jane standing by the entrance, smiling as she ushered late arrivals to their seats.

She moved her lips closer to the microphone, amplifying her voice.

"And then there's Jane. . . My relentless, untiring Jane. . . my assistant, my right-hand person!"

Hearing her name, Jane turned and faced Claire and smiled.

"I simply wouldn't know what to do without my Jane," Claire went on.

A rush of blood colored Jane's cheeks as all eyes shifted toward her. She wasn't comfortable with attention—especially in a crowd this large. Bowing her head, she blew Claire a small, affectionate kiss.

Claire's gaze lingered on Jane, her expression softening before she turned back to the audience.

Taking a moment to regain her focus, she shifted her gaze towards her potential sponsors.

"And last but not least, I want to thank my alma mater and the university chancellor for gracing our presentation with their presence. It is my sincere hope they will find it somewhat insightful and engaging. I also wish to thank my guests—some of whom I have yet to meet—for their interest in our humble endeavors."

After a brief round of applause from the audience, Claire redirected her focus to the main reason for being there. Although she'd prepared notes, she decided to set them aside; she knew exactly what she wanted to say.

Taking a deep breath, she smiled.

"When Caesar gazed at the white cliffs of Dover in 55 BC, he must have suspected—known in his gut. . ." She placed her hand on her belly. "That the histories of Rome and Britain would inevitably intertwine."

She turned to Jane and saw that she was watching her, smiling and nodding. She returned her smile and continued. "And Caesar's gut feeling would have been spot on since Rome would have some level of presence in Britain until the early fifth century, likely around Anno Domini 409. Or 409 of the Common Era, or CE, if you prefer."

A guest yelled out, "We don't. . . we prefer our Anno Domini." The audience's laughter encouraged him to add, "None of that C.E. nonsense—it's too common!"

Claire laughed. "As you wish."

She adjusted her microphone and nodded to a staff member. A moment later, the first image of the slideshow flashed behind her on a projector screen: a picture of modern-day Newcastle.

She cocked her back, looking at the picture.

"Beautiful, isn't she?"

Silence.

She returned her gaze to the audience and noticed that a few had puzzled expressions on their faces. "I know. . . nothing *new* about Newcastle. I get it. What's Claire doing showing us pictures of Newcastle? Nihil sub sole novum, right? Nothing new under the sun—especially under the Newcastle sun."

The audience laughed.

"But I assure you, there *is* something new—something remarkable—just outside the city, and it lies not under the sun but rather hidden under strata of the earth: an ancient burial site; a high-ranking Roman officer, a tribune or prefect, buried beside his Britannic bride—an Anglo-Roman couple, buried alongside one another. Theirs was a union that was likely forged in secret since, for a time, it was against the law for a Roman officer to marry a native."

A murmur rose in the crowd. From the corner of the room, Jane beamed, flashing Claire two enthusiastic thumbs up.

"And consider this," Claire continued. "There is a treasure. Not just a solitary gold coin, as the newspapers indicated, but a chest full. . . And there may be more that has yet to be unearthed. . ."

The crowd erupted with applause.

"And other artifacts and jewelry—lots of it... and we've only excavated the top strata; this is just the tip of the iceberg. This burial site lies beneath a mound—a lonely hill—that has been overlooked for centuries. Except when I first saw it, I thought, 'Claire, what an odd place for a single, solitary hill sitting alone on a plain with no other mounds or hills around. It was conspicuous in its isolation."

She placed her fingers on her chin. "Hmm. . . "

The crowd chuckled.

"And there was something else. . ." She paused, enjoying interacting with the crowd and watching their faces light up with excitement.

"What was it, Claire?" A man called out. "Come on now, dear; don't keep us hanging."

Claire giggled. "All right, I'll tell you if you promise to keep it a secret."

"I promise, dear!"

Claire laughed and went on.

"All right. I trust you. . . The significance of the mound lies in its close proximity to Hadrian's Wall; it is located less than thirty meters from the wall, and it's not very tall—roughly the height of, say, a small fort."

The crowd murmured with curiosity. She paused, letting it all sink in before going on.

"Furthermore, we won't know to which period our couple belongs—the Nerva-Antonine dynasty or later... Not until we conduct DNA analysis and radiocarbon dating."

Claire switched on her wireless microphone, grabbed a laser pointer, and turned to face the projector screen.

"And this is our wonderful team," she explained, pointing to the image behind her. "In this slide, they are working on small squares that make up a site grid. This next slide shows some of the artifacts stored in boxes. As you can see, we follow strict protocols in the preservation of historical artifacts."

She let out a laugh when the next slide appeared.

"Oh, that's Jane and me... Here we are in our not-so-glamourous khakis, playing around in the dirt." She paused, then added with a grin, "Well, allow me to amend that last statement; Jane always looks glamorous."

Claire turned around and found Jane laughing. From a distance, she couldn't tell if she was blushing. She gave her a wave.

"Hi, Jane!"

With a barely audible voice, Jane waved and said, "Hello."

Claire moved on to the next slide. "Here, we have a Lorica Segmentata—a type of Roman armor used throughout the period in question. As the name implies, it was made of segments or strips of metal, allowing for flexibility and mobility during battle. Given its proximity to the burial site, this particular piece of armor could have belonged to our subject. The Lorica Segmentata was utilized as late as the third century AD, confirming that we're on the right track in terms of the time period—so, putting it plainly, it cannot be confused with the Anglo-Saxon or Viking periods."

The audience erupted into laughter. Claire joined in, adding, "And likewise, we certainly can't confuse a gold aureus with a gold shilling—unless we're planning to melt them."

She paused until the laughter died down before continuing.

"But for me, this is far more than just artifacts and loot. I'm not a pirate or treasure hunter. Instead, this is what captivates and excites me the most..."

She pointed to the next slide, which displayed a letter the Roman officer had written to his wife. "What I love most is the romance—Virgil said it best: 'Amor Omnia Vincit,' or 'Love Conquers All.' Here is a centuries-old love letter written on papyrus from our man to his wife. Part of the letter is missing, and we don't yet know his name, but we do know hers. The letter ends with, 'Te amo, te desidero, Cara, uxor mea.' It means I love you, I miss you, Cara, my wife. . . Her name was Cara!"

She glanced at Jane and saw her head down, fingers brushing away tears.

Claire then heard a woman in the back of the audience sigh and moan.

"I feel the same way," she said, directing her voice toward the sound. "I can't see you, but I sympathize with you!"

A soft voice replied, "Thank you."

"You're welcome," Claire said warmly.

Claire shifted her gaze to the spot where Jane had been standing and saw her speaking with a man. The dimmed lights made it difficult to make out his face. Jane had her arms crossed in front of her chest and seemed to be annoyed.

Claire squinted, trying to make out the details, but she couldn't. Then she thought the man might be Stewart, who had just arrived. That would explain why Jane looked upset.

Jane was now technically his boss, and he was late on his first day—and not just on any day, but the most important day. Claire figured Jane might be giving him a scolding, the first of many he'd get if he continued to be late.

Jane didn't mess around, and some of the other staff had learned that the hard way.

Or it could be something else altogether: she could be telling off a guest who'd gotten overly familiar with her. She imagined Jane's hand delivering a sharp slap across the man's face and had to cover her mouth to stifle a laugh.

Deciding to stop overthinking, she waited until the lights were turned back up to see who Jane was talking to. She glanced at the event itinerary Jane had placed on the podium to keep her on track; it indicated dinner was at 8:00 p.m., only 15 minutes away.

The following slides drew loud gasps from the crowd as they showcased dazzling jewelry that presumably belonged to Cara.

"Here we have a gold serpentine bracelet, which may have belonged to Cara," Claire explained, pointing to the slide. "What distinguishes this item from the rest is that it's Roman, not native." She breezed through the remaining slides. "So is this necklace. . . this emerald ring. . . and this gemstone brooch."

She turned to face the audience and pointed to the final slide. "It looks like our Roman soldier truly adored his wife—he brought her souvenirs every time he traveled to Rome."

"How can you positively state that the jewelry belonged to his wife, not his sweetheart or concubine?" A booming voice from the crowd rang out. "Perhaps he had a few tucked away here and there. We *are* talking about Romans, after all."

The crowd erupted in laughter, clearly enjoying the playful banter.

Claire chuckled and said, "Well, we can't say for certain, but there are subtle clues."

"Like what, dear?" The voice pressed further.

She smiled. "For example, there is an engraving on the back of the brooch that reads, 'Uxori, amori meo, Cara.'"

She paused to see if the mystery man was well-versed in Latin. With the room filled with academics—including from renowned universities like Oxford and Cambridge—she expected many to know their Latin.

"Oh, jolly good… Thank you, my dear. Well done! Very well done, indeed."

She nodded and smiled. "It's absolutely my pleasure. Please feel free to call or email me with any questions in the future. I'll be glad to answer all of them. And for those unfamiliar with Latin, the phrase means, 'To my wife, to my love, Cara.'"

10

Claire hadn't eaten in hours, and she could hear her stomach growling. As she skimmed her notes, she decided it was time to wrap things up. She had covered all her topics and more.

"And with that, esteemed ladies and gentlemen, I shall conclude our presentation. I'm sure you're all starving, and I don't intend to be a poor host. Jane has arranged a wonderful entrée selection for you." She glanced at the event menu and grinned. "Mmm… Lucky you! We have salmon en papillote, lamb shank navarin, chicken confit, and steak frites for those who prefer red meat. Our wonderful staff will guide you to the dining area. Bon appétit!"

The audience erupted into enthusiastic applause, some shouting, "Brava!"

With the lights turned up, she saw Jane, her hand on her chest, shaking her head, fighting back tears of joy.

Claire gave one last bow and smiled. "Thank you… Thank you so very much."

One look at her audience's faces, and she knew she'd done incredibly well—she could see it in their expressions. She made her way to Jane, who was waiting for her with open arms.

Stewart stood alongside her, smiling.

"That was amazing. . ." Jane raved, wrapping her arms around Claire. "Just incredible! I couldn't stop bawling—the part about his letters to his wife. . . I'm glad the lights were dimmed, or they would've seen me sobbing." She let out a gasp. "Uh. . . I must've seen those letters a hundred times, but I still get goosebumps!"

"I know," Claire agreed, hugging her back. "Aren't they romantic?"

Jane nodded enthusiastically. "The way you told their story tonight made it seem like they were written yesterday. I pictured

Cara sitting in her room at night, holding her oil lamp as she read them."

"You're so sweet, Jane. Thank you," Claire said, placing her hand on Jane's shoulder.

Claire felt Stewart's gaze on her as she continued talking to Jane, but she didn't want to acknowledge his presence just yet. She wasn't too pleased about his late arrival and wanted Jane to introduce him when she was good and ready. *Stewart can wait,* she thought. And Jane didn't seem to be in a hurry to introduce Stewart, either.

Tonight was as much Jane's night as it was hers. Claire felt particularly fond of Jane and had gained a lot of respect for her.

"I'm so excited for you," Jane gushed. "I just know these people are going to be tripping over one another to sponsor you—I can see it on their faces."

She gestured toward one of the guests and his wife, a distinguished couple in their late seventies or early eighties. "Do you see that man wearing the top hat?"

Claire nodded. "Yes."

"He couldn't stop talking about you. I overheard him tell his wife, 'This could be the biggest find since the Roman Baths. And I know her father; he is a brilliant businessman.'"

"Do you have any idea who he might be?" Claire asked, her curiosity piqued.

Jane shook her head. "No, but I can find out." She drew closer to Claire and playfully pushed the tip of her nose up with a finger, whispering. "He's got that stuck-up look—definitely an aristocrat."

Claire giggled. "That would be wonderful if you could find out who he is, Jane. Meanwhile, can we join our guests for dinner? I'm starving; how about you?"

Jane winked. "Famished!"

Turning to face Stewart, Jane finally acknowledged him. "I'm sorry, Stewart; I got carried away and forgot you were standing there."

She shifted her gaze back to Claire, winking. "By the way, Claire, this is Stewart..."

Claire struggled to restrain her laughter. "Hello, Stewart; glad to finally meet you in person." She extended her hand out to Stewart, a polite smile on her face. "Welcome aboard!"

Stewart reached out to shake her hand. "It's a pleasure to meet you as well, Miss Langford. I'm really sorry; I've had a heck of a time trying to get settled and make it out here. I promise I won't be late again."

Claire decided she would prefer to keep things formal with him. She had initially told him to use first names during his online interview, but she changed her mind for now. "It's quite all right... It's understandable. We're glad you've made it. Now, let's grab some food, as you Americans would say."

While sitting across from Stewart during dinner, Claire chatted with Jane while subtly observing Stewart's demeanor. When he excused himself to use the restroom, she turned to Jane to inquire about their earlier conversation—something seemed off, and she wanted to understand what was happening.

"What's going on with Stewart?" she asked.

Jane gave a dismissive wave of her hand. "Oh, nothing. I just gave him a hard time for being late."

"Is that it? Is there anything else that's bothering you about him? I mean, if there's anything I should be concerned about, I'd rather know now..."

Jane shook her head. "No, nothing at all. I wanted to let him know that his bullshit won't fly when we get started with work— he's got to show up on time with his big boy pants on. I'm not going to babysit him. He's going to be filling my shoes, so..."

"All right," Claire nodded in agreement.

"And if he doesn't fill my shoes, he's going to be wearing them. . . up his. . ."

Claire squeezed Jane's knee under the table. "Shh. . . he's coming back."

He had a confident stride, Claire thought as he approached the table. A devastatingly handsome man with light brown hair, blue eyes, and a thin frame, he looked fantastic for a man she assumed was likely in his mid-forties—a bit older but more attractive in person than he looked online.

She quickly averted her gaze and turned to Jane, who was scrolling through emails while picking at her chicken confit.

Claire didn't want to get caught staring at Stewart. One word summed up her opinion of him: trouble—trouble for her since she felt instantly drawn to him.

11

Marcel had a name and a location—no pictures, no facial composites, and no additional information. According to Interpol, the suspect was a Canadian national from Montreal, a shadowy figure with an elusive identity.

The location was easy enough to find. The cab driver knew exactly where to take him; he was a regular there.

Flashing a grin in the rearview mirror, he said, "Cupid's Corner... Here we are, Monsieur."

Marcel nodded and smiled back as he handed the driver a tip. "Merci. I'll call you when I'm done so you can pick me up."

He wasn't much of a drinker. He'd occasionally enjoy a glass while entertaining or making a toast. Other than that, alcohol wasn't his thing. Still, the club had a one-drink minimum, so he ordered a Scotch and soda, settled into a seat, and observed the dancers, trying not to look like a cop.

He came armed with a wad of freshly minted Canadian cash—singles, tens, twenties, and a few fifties—enough to loosen some tongues.

"Hi, there…" A delicate hand with long, painted nails draped over his shoulder, caressing his chest. He turned to see the face behind the soft voice.

"You look like you're new around here," she murmured, leaning closer, resting her palms on him.

His body stiffened, and he drew back instinctively. She was just a child. Barely old enough to drive, let alone work in a place like this. Anger flared inside him.

He and Madeleine had tried for two years to get pregnant, spending a fortune on IVF treatments, but they continued to face heart-wrenching disappointment. They decided to take a break, but Madeleine's longing for a child—especially a girl—never faded.

Gazing into the young girl's eyes, he could see the emptiness. Her physical presence was there, but her mind and soul were somewhere far away.

"Here, sweetheart, have a seat," he said, extending his hand. As she took his hand, he slipped a folded hundred-dollar bill into her palm. "Just sit and chat with me. Is that okay?"

Her eyes widened, and a smile spread across her face at the sight of the bill. She nodded, glancing around nervously before sitting down.

"Thank you!"

"You're welcome!"

He studied her closely. Behind the layers of makeup, the false lashes, and her glitter-speckled skin, he could see her for what she was—a child.

With her knees together and arms tucked in, she was trying to keep warm. She wore tall platform heels and a sequined bikini— it was hard to tell if it was pink or purple in the club's dim lighting. Her slim build and chin-length black hair gave her a youthful appearance.

"Are you cold?" he asked, watching goosebumps rise on her arms.

She nodded. "Uh-huh… Would you like a lap dance?"

"Would that make you warmer? If you move around, I mean?" Marcel asked, making circles with his finger.

She nodded again and motioned toward the back of the club. "It's over there… the VIP private room… Would you like to go?"

"All right." He grabbed his drink and rose to his feet. She took his hand, leading him toward the back.

The room was small, with a round table in the middle, surrounded by a red faux leather banquette. A lone chair sat in the corner. "Please sit," she said, pointing to the chair.

He shook his head. "Listen, sweetheart, I just want to talk to you. I'll pay more… Is that okay?"

She smiled and shrugged.

He settled onto the bench seat, lowering his drink onto the table. He gestured for her to sit beside him. "Can I smoke in here?" he asked, maintaining his relaxed demeanor.

She nodded as she sat next to him.

He fished out a pack of cigarettes from his coat pocket and took one out. She shivered, and he instinctively removed his coat, draping it over her shoulders. Her innocent smile made his chest tighten. He wished he could take her home, introduce her to Madeleine, and say, "Mon amour, here is your daughter."

He lit the cigarette and took a deep drag, exhaling a thin stream of smoke into the air above him. "Do you mind if I ask your name, dear?" he asked, keeping his eyes half-closed to appear less imposing.

"No, I don't mind… My name is Aurora."

He smiled, keeping his gaze soft. "Is that your real name?"

She hesitated. "We're not supposed to…"

"It's all right—you don't have to."

"Um… it's Amelie… Saunier."

"Hmm… What a beautiful name… French?"

"Uh-huh."

"Do your parents live here? In Montreal?" His voice was gentle, but his eyes watched her reaction carefully.

She shook her head, her gaze dropping to her lap. "No… in France."

Reaching into his back pocket, he retrieved his wallet, handing her another hundred-dollar bill. He then took out a picture of Madeleine and showed it to her.

"This is my wife, my Madeleine."

Amelie took the picture, tracing her finger over it before looking up with a smile. "She's very pretty!"

"Oui, she is… And so are you."

She giggled, a lightness breaking through the tension.

"Do you speak French?"

She nodded. "Oui."

He laughed. "Très bien... Very good, Amelie! Were you born in France?"

"Oui… in Marseille."

He sighed, memories of warm summers flooding back. "Ah, south of France... Madeleine and I spent our honeymoon there. It's the most beautiful city in the world!"

She giggled again, her shyness fading a little.

He felt the urgency to go on with his questions. "Amelie, dear," he said softly, "I need to ask you something important…"

Her face stiffened. "Are you a policeman?"

"Yes, dear," he replied, watching her closely. He didn't want to lie and risk losing her trust. "I'm with the French police, and we free people from captivity—mostly women."

Her eyebrows knitted together, and her eyes widened with concern.

"Please trust me… Can you do that?" He asked with a reassuring tone.

She nodded slowly, her anxiety easing just a touch.

"Wonderful, Amelie… I'm so proud of you!"

She offered a small smile, albeit cautiously.

"Now, dear… Have you heard the name Henri Bouchard before?"

Her face paled, terror flashing in her eyes. She hesitated, shivering again.

"I promise I'll protect you," he pressed. "Nothing bad will happen to you—I give you my word!"

He reached for another cigarette from the pack, but she spoke before he could light it. "I know him. He's… a very bad man."

He put the cigarette back in the pack, his heart racing. Taking a deep breath to steady himself, he turned to her with a reassuring smile, laying his hand over hers.

"Thank you, Amelie, beautiful Amelie. Don't be afraid... Is he here now?"

She shook her head. "I haven't seen him in a while."

"How long has it been since you last saw him?"

She shrugged. "A few weeks..."

"What does he do here? Is he the owner?"

"Yes, I think so... And when he comes, he always brings new girls with him..."

"Did he bring you here?"

Before she could respond, a voice echoed from behind the curtain.

"Aurora, you've got a customer here..."

Her eyes snapped open, and she sprang to her feet, alarm etched across her face. "Sorry, I have to go!"

Marcel raised his hands, trying to calm her. "It's all right... Please don't worry. I'll come back tomorrow. Are you working tomorrow night?"

She nodded, a glimmer of hope in her smile. "Club opens at three in the afternoon... I get here at six."

"I'll come at eight."

She smiled and waved, her expression brightening.

Marcel waved back and blew her a kiss. "Au revoir... See you tomorrow, Amelie!"

Her hand swept aside the curtain, and she froze as if she'd run into a wall. She found herself face-to-face with Ivan, the club manager. It appeared he'd been standing there, listening to their conversation.

12

With some luck, Marcel thought, Amelie's manager hadn't overheard their conversation. The loud music might have drowned out their earlier exchange. But there was no way to be certain, and that uncertainty filled him with creeping dread. As he walked past the dance floor, he couldn't help but notice that most of the dancers looked underage—something he had overlooked when he first arrived at the club.

Anger surged through him when he saw Amelie sitting with an older man—an affluent-looking man well into his sixties. The sight made his heart beat like a battle drum. His heightened senses made him acutely aware of everything and everyone around him, especially that nearly everyone in the club appeared to be older than fifty and filthy rich.

Standing outside, preparing to call his taxi, he watched as car after car pulled up in front of the club. The valet hurriedly snatched the keys from customers, racing to park the vehicles— all expensive sports or luxury cars: Lamborghinis, Ferraris, Rolls Royces, and a couple of supercars he'd never seen before, even in Paris.

He decided to get a closer look at the cars and take down some license plates. Slipping around the back, he hopped over the fence into the parking lot. Pulling out his nine-millimeter semi-automatic, he chambered a round before returning it to his leg holster.

It took a while, but he managed to jot down all the plate numbers while crouching to evade the valet attendants. When he was finished, he hopped back over the fence and called his cab to take him back to his hotel.

Sleep refused to come.

Tossing and turning in bed, Marcel couldn't shake Amelie's face from his mind. Every imaginable nightmare scenario paraded across his thoughts, tormenting him. When had she been taken? Where were her parents? Were they lying awake right now—sick with worry, just as he was?

He checked the time on his phone; it was 4 a.m. He forced his eyelids shut, hoping to fall asleep, but it didn't come. Finally, exhausted, he dozed off around 6 a.m.

Noticing that no one had their phones out, he kept his in his pocket—likely an agreement among club members to avoid having their pictures taken. He glanced at his watch: a classic Cartier with Roman numerals, an anniversary gift from Madeleine.

He missed her, so he decided to send her a text. It was 8 p.m. local time.

I love you!

Paris was six hours ahead, but she replied almost instantly.

I love you too!

Why are you still awake? It's 2 a.m. over there!

I'm thinking about you.

Me too.

☺

Go to bed.

Can't.

Why?

Horny. For you!

LOL!

Are you coming home?

He'd decided to stay another day or two to get some answers but had forgotten to tell her.

Sorry, I need to stay another couple of days.

But I'm horny ☹

LOL. I'll take care of it when I get back. Go to bed.

Where are you?
I'm at a dance club waiting to talk to a girl.
What??
She's a victim. A French girl.
I bet!
Seriously. She's a baby. 19 years old if that.
I'm sorry. Is she okay?
She will be. I am working on it.
Okay. I love you!
I love you too!
And be careful.
I will.

He checked his watch. It was 8:22 p.m., and Amelie was nowhere in sight. He couldn't risk drawing attention by asking for her.

The club was packed with rich, older men gathered around the dance floor or seated at the bar, talking to the girls. He recognized a few faces from the previous night. His stomach churned, watching the old vultures hover over their prey. He wanted to slam each one to the ground and handcuff them. But, as always, he had to rein in his impulse.

Finally, she emerged from the back of the club. The older man from the prior night trailed behind her, a fat cigar clutched between his fingers.

Amelie saw Marcel and waved. He smiled, giving her a slight nod, trying to avoid drawing attention to himself. She read his thoughts, paused, and gestured for him to follow as she spun around and headed to the VIP room.

Marcel felt a pair of eyes on him as he followed her, but he didn't react.

She waved him into the room, sticking her head out to survey her surroundings before closing the curtains. "Hi… Please sit." She motioned to the bench seat.

He smiled and sat down. "Hi, Amelie! How are you, dear?"

"Fine… Thank you," she beamed, happy to see him.

He noticed she avoided direct eye contact, glancing sidelong and favoring one side of her face. "Will you please sit with me?"

She sat beside him, her head down. He placed a finger beneath her chin, raising it to face him. She didn't resist his touch, leaning into it as a slight smile formed on her lips.

His lips parted to form a sentence, but she raised a hand and mouthed, "Wait," as she began moving her head to the rhythm of the song that came on, her eyes shut.

He recognized the melody but couldn't recall the song's name.

"I like to dance to this song," she murmured, her shoulders swaying to the beat. "It's my favorite."

Gazing at her, his fingers began rapping the table to the music. He noticed tears escaping the corners of her closed eyelids as the song ended. When she opened her eyes, he wiped away her tears and whispered, "Beautiful, Amelie... What's the name of that song?" He looked up, searching the air for it. "It's at the tip of my tongue."

She'd barely opened her mouth to respond when the DJ answered for her: "Ladies and gentlemen... That was 'The Best' by Tina Turner. She's a big favorite around here."

He noticed a dark shadow beneath her right eye—the side of her face she'd been hiding. She tried to turn away.

"Please, Amelie… Let me look at your eye," he insisted.

She hesitated, then relaxed.

Gently, he tilted her face toward his for a closer look. It was a black eye. She'd tried to conceal it with makeup, but Marcel rubbed it off when he wiped away her tears. She smiled weakly.

His heart thundered with rage. Without thinking, he sprinted toward the curtain, yanked it open, and peered out. There was no one out there. "Who did this to you?" he seethed.

She shook her head. "Please don't… He'll…" She stuttered, unable to finish her sentence.

"Was it that man who was listening to our conversation from behind the curtain?"

Silence.

"Amelie, dear…" He took a deep breath and softened his tone. "Would you like to leave this place and return to France with me?"

She lowered her gaze, unsure how to respond. Then she said something that took Marcel by surprise. "I don't want to go back to my parents."

Marcel was suspicious as to why she was reluctant to return to them. He paused to think over his response. "I understand. You don't have to go back to them. I know places that help young women…"

"Uh-uh…" She shook her head. "I don't want to go to those places. I've heard stories about them."

Marcel knew he should call his wife to discuss what he was about to do, but he was running out of time. He had to make a decision—and fast.

"You could stay with Madeleine and me until you get settled... I will... *We* will help you. You can begin a new life—a happy life. I promise you... And I will always be there for you. I will protect you."

"Will you promise me you will not leave me?"

Her words struck a chord. There was something in her voice, in her eyes—a plea. She'd felt abandoned by the whole world, with no one capable of rescuing her. She'd felt powerless.

"I promise—I will not leave you! I will always be there for you... like you're my own daughter." He liked the sound of it: "my own daughter," and he meant it. The entire world may have let her down, but he wouldn't.

She peered into his eyes, searching for deception. Finding none, she nodded vigorously. "I'll come..."

Marcel had dealt with plenty of hard cases, but this one tugged at his heartstrings like none other. He smiled and hugged her.

"Wonderful, Amelie!" He sighed, then went on. "Do you know how we can get out of here without anyone noticing?"

She nodded. "I do—there's a back entrance."

He stood and extended his hand. "All right, let's go. We can't lose another second. Show me the back entrance."

She gave him a smile and clasped his hand. "Turn left when we go out of the room, then right at the end of the hall; it's right there."

"Let's go!"

Marcel pulled the curtain aside just enough to survey the area—no one was around. Then the music started blaring. It was the start of a new song.

"All aboard... All the beautiful ladies to the dance floor," the DJ called out. Depending on club traffic, he'd call all dancers to the dance floor and parade them in front of customers once or twice a night.

"We have to hurry!" She shot a panicked look at Marcel.

He nodded and raised his index finger to his lips, signaling her to stay quiet.

They dashed out of the room and reached the rear entrance before they heard the DJ again. "Aurora, sweetheart, where are you? Come to the dance floor."

Then they heard a menacing voice, thick with an accent, coming down the hall. "Aurora! Where the fuck are you?"

Marcel swung the door open, and they ran out into the street. Amelie struggled to keep up and tripped, but his hand caught hers before she hit the ground. "Please take your heels off and carry them... or throw them away. I'll buy you a new pair," Marcel whispered.

She removed her platform heels and hurled them over a neighbor's hedge as they raced down the sidewalk. He glanced at her to see how she was doing. She grinned at him, already feeling liberated. He flashed a smile back.

"Brave and beautiful."

He removed his coat and held it so she could slip her arms through the sleeves. He then drew his semiautomatic from its holster, chambering a round.

He spotted headlights approaching, so they crouched behind a car as it drove by. He peeked from behind the hood and saw a familiar face in the front passenger seat. It was Ivan—his tattooed arm dangled out the window, clutching a revolver. Three men sat in the back seat, each holding AK-47 fully automatic machine guns.

"These guys aren't fuckin' around," he mumbled to himself, his knuckles white from gripping his gun. *"And neither am I... I saw your face, motherfucker."*

He'd seen Ivan's face enough times to recognize him anywhere. Now, he noted the skull tattoo creeping down beneath his T-shirt sleeve.

They waited until the car turned the corner, then walked a few blocks to make sure they'd lost Ivan and his thugs before he dialed a cab on his phone.

"Look!" Marcel smiled, gesturing toward the iconic Grande Roue de Montreal Ferris wheel as he spoke with the cab company dispatcher.

Amelie was stunned, her eyes wide and mouth open. Confined to a small apartment and only shuttled to and from the club, she'd never laid eyes on any of Montreal's breathtaking sights.

He stood beside her, studying the delighted expression on her face—it made it all worth it for him.

He kept his gun locked and loaded with the safety off in case he had to reach for it quickly, keeping a vigilant eye out while Amelie took in the sights.

He'd been in enough firefights that he wasn't afraid to use his gun. He'd had extensive training with GIGN, an elite tactical police team whose missions included hostage rescue and counterterrorism.

Marcel's hair was completely gray at forty-nine, making him look older than he was. With an athletic build, swarthy complexion, and sharp facial features, he looked menacing to his foes.

But his friendly smile and gentle demeanor betrayed another side—one Amelie instinctively sensed and trusted: a father figure, a trustworthy friend, and a loyal, loving husband.

She gazed fondly at him and took his hand as they stood staring out at St. Helen's Island and the shimmering waters of the St. Lawrence River silhouetted against the dazzling Montreal skyline.

But they didn't have much time to take in the scenery. Soon, the taxi arrived, and they got in. He peered out the rear window to make sure no one was following them before giving the cab driver directions to the hotel.

Back at the hotel, he waited outside the lobby and peeked through the glass door to see if anyone was at the reception desk. It was just past midnight, and he didn't see anyone behind the counter. He took Amelie's hand and hurried across the lobby to the elevator.

Unaware that a pair of eyes were following them on a computer monitor, they got on the elevator, and Marcel pressed the button for the 7th floor.

Peering out of the elevator, he checked the corridor, and they swiftly made their way to his room. He swiped the keycard against the card reader and opened the door.

He gave her a warm smile, waving her inside. "Welcome to 'Chateau Amelie!'"

She giggled and stepped inside.

13

Claire couldn't shake off the dream. She tried to focus on the meeting ahead, but the lurid images flashed before her eyes as she ran lipstick across her tingling lips; her senses heightened with each touch.

She gazed at herself in the mirror, noticing how her pale cheeks had turned a striking shade of crimson before she'd even applied blush.

Rolling her eyes, she muttered, "Really, Claire... I don't think so... Stay focused." It was a mantra she'd repeat throughout the day to still her racing mind.

Suddenly, she felt a pair of hands sidling from behind, across her hips, and down between her legs. She gasped, her heart racing, only to look down and see nothing there.

A ping from her cell phone drew her attention—it was Jane. She read the message.

OMG OMG!!!

Claire laughed. "Oh, Jane!" She typed a response and hit send.

LOL, I'll bite. What?

Do you want me to tell you? Or would you like to see it when you come in? I'd rather not ruin the surprise.

Well, Idk, you tell me.

I'd rather you wait to get here. It's big!

How big?

The biggest.

Ok. I'll be in in about 30 min.

I can't wait!!

She couldn't decide whether to dress up or go casual. She'd always dressed casually at work—whether in the office or at the dig site. Any change from that would draw attention—or worse, gossip.

"Hmm." She eyed herself in the mirror, tilting her head side to side, checking her hair and makeup. "What are you going to do, Claire?"

Pursing her lips, she stared at her reflection. "You're going casual... That's right, you're going to concentrate on the important things—no distractions, no exceptions."

With a triumphant nod, she flicked off the light switch as she exited the bathroom.

In the end, she wore what she had on the last time she went out with Jane: A T-shirt boldly proclaiming, "I dig dirt," her regular jeans, and comfy white sneakers. "Less is more," she thought as she stepped out her front door.

While waiting for a cab, she shot off a text to Jane.

Btw, who's in the office now?

Everyone!

Why? Nervous?

Yeah, just a tiny bit.

But why?

Just am.

Don't be! You're the BOSS! We work for you. We should be nervous, not you.

All right then. I'm on my way. See you shortly.

Yay!

She didn't expect much fanfare, but that's precisely what she got—a huge round of applause from all her staff. Jane led her to the conference room, where balloons and a large cake with "Congratulations!" written in icing greeted her.

Jane pointed to the cake, grinning. "I was going to have them write 'Sub Terra Celata' on it, but I figured 'congratulations' was safer."

Claire laughed. "'Hidden beneath the earth.' And when did you learn Latin?"

Jane chuckled. "I didn't… I asked that man over there to translate for me." She gestured to a solemn-looking elderly man in a black suit and fedora, sitting alone in a chair.

"I was going to have the pastry chef change it, but then I decided to keep 'congratulations.' I'll introduce you to him after you have cake and read these first."

Before Claire could respond, Jane pulled three envelopes from behind her back and handed them over.

"These came for you this morning before I texted you."

With her eyes fixed on Jane's, Claire eagerly took the envelopes from her.

"All right, this one is from my alma mater—that's wonderful!"

She smiled at Jane, placing the envelope beneath the stack. Jane's face beamed with anticipation. Claire checked the next envelope.

"This one is from Cambridge! All right!" She smiled, curling her fingers into a fist and waving it in the air.

"And the third one is… Who is R.A.H?" She turned it over, frowning. "It has no postmark."

Jane nodded toward the man sitting in the reception area, waiting patiently with a stoic gaze fixed ahead.

"He personally delivered it. He's been sitting there all morning to see you. He represents the man we saw at the event—the one I told you was raving that yours may be 'the biggest find since the Roman Baths.'"

Claire cocked an eyebrow as she opened the envelope, pulling out a card that bore the initials "R.A.H." along with the name "Callum Mackenzie."

Turning the card over, she found the words "RELIQVAE ET ARTIFICIA IN HISTORIA" printed in gold foil lettering. She turned her gaze to the man, studying him, and whispered, "Relics and artifacts in history."

Jane quirked her lips and chuckled. "Well, he's in the right place then."

Claire returned her gaze to Jane and laughed. "Oh, Jane. You're so funny!"

"That's me." Jane shot back. "Nothing if not funny… Should I invite Mr. Stiff Pants to have cake with us?"

Claire's cheeks flamed. She pressed her palm to her mouth, trying not to laugh, and nodded.

Claire sensed his presence behind her before she even saw him. Facing Claire, Jane also noticed him approaching over her shoulders.

"Hello, Miss Langford."

Claire recognized his deep, masculine voice. She spun around to greet him, the remnants of her dream flickering in her mind, her heart thumping furiously inside her chest.

"Hello, Stewart… How are you doing on your first official day at the office?" She asked, transfixed by his deep blue eyes.

"I've had him start with the basics: your calendar and appointments," Jane interjected. "You know, walking before running. He's doing fine."

"Well, that's wonderful, Jane," Claire remarked, turning briefly to her before locking eyes with Stewart again. "I'm sure he's coming along quite well."

"Yes, thank you, Jane, for helping me get started," Stewart said, nodding and smiling. "I wouldn't know where to begin without your assistance."

"You're welcome, Stewart," Jane replied, smiling. "Why don't you gather everyone and bring them here so we can eat this cake?"

Stewart nodded and smiled. He'd barely taken a step before Jane added, "And bring Mr. Stiff Pants, too."

Stewart paused. "I'm sorry?"

Jane gestured to the man in the black suit. "*Him*… Please bring him along."

Stewart nodded again and turned to leave. He'd barely made it to the door when he overheard Jane say, "I love his Fedora… I can just tell he's gonna be the life of the party."

He heard Claire let out a faint chuckle as he exited the room.

Even in a crowded conference room, Claire struggled to focus as her heart raced with his every glance. Her gaze unapologetically sought him out among her staff, her mind consumed by the images from her dream.

14

A gentle touch on her shoulder startled her.

"You get the first piece... You're the star of the show," Jane whispered in Claire's ear as she placed a party plate with a thick slice of chocolate truffle cake in front of her and stabbed it with a fork.

Claire laughed as she carved a piece of her cake and put it in her mouth—her eyes widened as she let out a moan. "Mmm... gosh, Jane! This is utterly divine."

Jane shook her head dramatically as she indulged in a bite herself. "No, it's chocolate truffle. They did have divine, but this is much better—it's truffle!" She turned to Claire, scrunching her nose. "Right?"

Claire nodded in agreement as she took another bite. "Yes... righto."

With the party behind them, Jane cleared the conference room for the long-awaited meeting with the R.A.H. representative, who'd been anxiously waiting to speak with Claire.

Jane began with introductions, motioning to Claire as they entered. "Mr. Mackenzie, I'd like to introduce you to my boss, Claire Langford."

Claire stood smiling, offering her hand. "Hello, Mr. Mackenzie; it's a pleasure to meet you."

"Callum, please call me Callum." He smiled, shaking her hand. "It's a Scottish name, a wee bit north of your Roman wall."

Claire giggled. "Of course... Callum. And likewise, please call me Claire."

Jane mouthed, "Should I stay?" Claire nodded, directing her to sit beside her.

Callum wasted no time, eager to get down to business after waiting all morning. "I greatly appreciate you meeting with me today despite the short notice. I'm a senior partner with R.A.H., here to present our proposal, which I hope you'll find quite generous and comprehensive."

"Please, go ahead," Claire said with a smile, gesturing for him to continue. "I'm all ears."

"Thank you. In short, we believe you've made a tremendous discovery," he said, removing his hat and combing his fingers through his silvery hair, matching the full gray mustache. At seventy-two, his weathered face bore the marks of a lifetime spent excavating beneath the harsh sun.

Clearing his throat, he continued, "As you saw in our letter, our expertise lies in archaeological excavations: antiquities, relics, and artifacts. Our company has been involved in numerous digs."

"May I ask which expeditions?" Claire interrupted softly, genuinely curious from an academic standpoint.

"I'm glad you asked that—it shows your scholarly zeal; you're not a trifle treasure hunter."

Claire laughed. "Of course not. This is my life, my passion!"

He smiled and nodded. "I can see that… Please allow me to go on."

She waved him to continue.

"Well, to begin with, I'll tell you about our recent venture in Alexandria, Egypt."

Claire leaned forward, crossing her arms on the table, her interest piqued. Jane stayed close to Claire, observing her body language with keen interest.

He paused, patting his coat pocket. "May I smoke in here?"

Though her building was non-smoking, Claire wasn't about to tell him that. She nodded. "Please…"

He took a cigarette from his vintage case, lit it, and took a deep drag, discreetly exhaling the smoke to the side. "Awful habit, I know." He chuckled, then continued, "So back to Alexandria… We're confident we can locate the sarcophagus belonging to none other than…"

Claire sat up, her eyes widening. "Wait, let me guess… Cleopatra?"

Callum calmly shook his head. "No… Go back… Go back more than two centuries—go back to the beginning."

Claire's gaze lifted as she mentally traced back through history. "Alexander?"

He nodded slowly, grinning.

"Impossible! His…" Claire stammered, shaking her head as if dismissing the idea. "Alexander's tomb… It has eluded the world's leading experts for centuries… How?"

"Caesar—his journal, to be precise," he explained. "An unpublished personal journal."

"From the time he traveled to Alexandria and visited Alexander's tomb, I presume," Claire chimed in.

"You presume correctly, my dear. He likely visited the tomb multiple times, in awe of Alexander. We believe he secretly relocated his sarcophagus to safeguard it… and we may know where he did so."

Claire sank back into her chair, letting out a deep sigh. "Where to?"

He smiled knowingly. "To the temple of Zeus Ammon…"

Claire rolled her eyes. "Of course! Where he was declared the son of a god." She discreetly reached under the table, clasping Jane's hand and giving it a gentle squeeze.

"Our venture began in Alexandria," he said pensively, brow furrowed. "But the evidence, the footprints in the desert sands, if you will, led us to the temple—to the oracle of Zeus Ammon."

Claire fell silent, a faraway look on her face. She pictured Alexander's weary phalanx marching through the scorching desert toward the secluded temple, a melding of Greek and Egyptian deities. Before continuing his campaign through Persia, the oracle would declare him a god.

"What about Pompeii?" Callum asked, bringing Claire back to the present.

"Huh?" she said, snapping out of her daydream. "I'm sorry, I zoned out."

"That's quite all right. I make a habit of zoning out," he chuckled. "Now, what do you know about Pompeii?"

"Which Pompey?" she asked. "Pompeius Magnus or Pompeii, the city beneath the shadow of Vesuvius?"

He burst into laughter, and Claire and Jane joined in. "Oh, Claire, you certainly know your history… Pompeii the city, not the statesman."

"The usual, I suppose," Claire shrugged. "It's one of the most studied sites in the world."

He nodded. "Dear Claire, what would you say if I told you there may be an entirely different city buried under Pompeii? It's quite speculative at present, but who knows what lies hidden beneath the earth?"

"Sub terra celata?" Claire muttered with a sly smile.

"Oh, my dear!" he laughed. "Precisely so… Hidden beneath the earth."

He turned to Jane. "I thought you were going to write the phrase on the cake."

"I really tried," Jane threw up her hands. "But by the time I had you translate it for me, it was too late. I had to go pick up the cake."

"Oh, well… Next time, then," he said, turning back to Claire. "So… a city hidden beneath Pompeii…"

Claire took a wild guess. "Another Roman city?"

He shook his head. "No… Not Roman—perhaps pre-Etruscan. We've also uncovered clay tablets with Linear A and B script, possibly linked to…"

"Minoan civilization!" Claire interjected, her voice brimming with excitement.

"Precisely, my dear… Precisely!"

She let out a long sigh, turning to find Jane completely immersed in the conversation. Jane shrugged and smiled at her.

"Not unlike your very excavation… Who knows what lies beneath it… Sub terra celata," he said, trying to redirect her attention back to the matter at hand. "Have I found in you a believer, Claire?"

Claire nodded enthusiastically. "Yes… Yes, indeed."

He reached inside his briefcase, pulled out a folder, and slid it across the table. "Please review the pro forma I've prepared for your current project. It includes a cost analysis covering anticipated expenses and others you may not have encountered. For instance, if you discover evidence of other civilizations beneath your current excavation, you can rely on us for additional capital for any future ventures. Furthermore, upon completion of your present project—as you will see in my income pro forma—there will, without a doubt, be commercial opportunities for a handsome return on your efforts."

Claire glanced at Jane, expecting her reaction. Jane leaned forward, drawing the folder to herself, her head propped on a hand on the table, reviewing the proposal carefully.

Turning to Mr. Mackenzie, she smiled. "You mentioned commercial opportunities. May I ask what you had in mind?"

He chuckled. "Ah, that's the best part, my dear Jane. Exhibits, academic forums—you name it. There's your cash cow; that's your source of revenue for future explorations and future adventures. How does that suit you, ladies?"

Jane swung her gaze to Claire and nodded. "There's even a category for the return of initial capital to your father, as well as a fair return for R.A.H."

"We chose to make this offer because we find your discovery most intriguing and because of our acquaintance with your father," he added. "Our company president and he are close friends."

He checked his watch, letting out a groan. "Oh dear, I'm running terribly late." He rose to his feet, extending a hand to

Claire. "I'm sorry, I must go. You have my card. Please call me with any questions."

Claire and Jane each shook his hand and walked him to the door. As soon as it closed behind him, Jane pressed her ear against it to ensure he was gone. Then, with wide eyes, she spun around, leaned back against the door, and silently screamed, pumping her fists in the air.

Claire laughed. "What? What am I missing, Jane?"

Jane grabbed her hand, led her back to the conference room and closed the door. She fanned out the other competing offers on the table. "Look at these closely."

Leaning over, Claire reviewed all three offers side by side, squinting as she traced the bottom-line numbers with her fingers. Jane watched as her eyes widened and her mouth opened.

Pointing to R.A.H.'s offer, Claire exclaimed, "This is three times more than the others!"

Jane gave an exaggerated nod, mirroring Claire's enthusiasm. "Exactly—and it's open-ended. It's like they're giving us a credit card with no limits… and more if we find more stuff…"

Claire caught Stewart's gaze from across the office before he quickly looked away. Noticing her shift in expression, Jane followed her eyes but saw nothing that stood out. The staff were busy on the phones, conducting business, or cleaning up after the party.

Claire took Jane's hand. "What do you say we celebrate?"

Jane flashed a smile. "Uh-huh… When?"

"Tonight… I figured we'd be leaving for the site soon… Wanna go dancing?"

Jane cocked a brow, grinning. "Dancing?"

Claire gave a small nod. "Unless you don't…"

Jane shook her head. "No, I do! … I swear I have the best boss in the world." She held up her hand, and Claire laughed as she met her high-five.

"Why don't we take the rest of the day off?" Claire suggested.

"Really? It's too early to go dancing, you know?"

"Not too early for shopping."

"Really?"

"Can you stop saying 'really'? We won't be able to shop until we get back to London. There aren't any swanky boutiques, as you called them, in Newcastle, are there?"

Jane shrugged, grinning. "I don't know. We've never gone exploring."

"So, would you like to go?"

Jane nodded, lips pressed together, suppressing a laugh. "Mm-hmm."

With shopping bags in each arm packed with clothes they'd bought, Claire and Jane rode up and down the mall escalators, exploring every swanky boutique they came across. But they lingered longest in the shoe store, trying on nearly every style: from stilettos to open-toes to lace-up ankle boots.

Famished, they decided to grab something to eat. Strolling along the River Thames, Jane spotted a restaurant with outdoor seating and nodded to it. "Would you like to eat here?"

"Looks great," Claire groaned. "I'll eat anything. I'm starving."

The sun began to sink below the horizon, its pink and golden hues dancing on the shimmering waters of the river, heralding the end of the day. Sitting on the restaurant's terrace, they raised their champagne glasses and toasted their upcoming adventure in the north. With the sunset turning the golden liquid a shade of crimson and effervescent bubbles swirling inside their glasses, they sipped their drinks, warmth glowing on their faces.

15

The room had a balcony with a breathtaking view of downtown Montreal, but Marcel wasn't taking any risks with Amelie. As much as he wanted her to see it, he needed to keep her out of sight and out of harm's way.

He handed her the TV remote. "Would you like to watch some television while I e-mail my boss? I won't be long."

She shook her head. "I haven't seen a television in over a year. 'No phones, no television, no computers.' Those were the rules. They didn't want us to have any connection to the outside. Six of us shared a two-bedroom apartment with only one shower."

Marcel's jaw tightened as he glared out the window at the city lights, his face dark with anger. Then, turning back to her, he forced a reassuring smile. "I'm really sorry, dear. But you don't have to worry about them anymore—not ever again."

"What about my friends?" she asked, sitting cross-legged on the bed and looking down at her fingernails. "The ones back at the club?"

He softened. "They will be taken care of, too. I promise. You have my word."

She looked up and nodded, a broad smile flashing across her face. She had complete faith in him. "Do you mind if I take a shower?"

"Of course not... Please go ahead."

Looking down at her outfit, she threw her arms up and laughed—she was still in her work clothes, a white ruffle bikini skirt and top. And now she was without her heels, which she'd tossed when they fled from Ivan.

"I guess I'm wearing these to bed."

He chuckled. "Don't worry. I'm taking you shopping tomorrow morning. Tomorrow night, we'll fly to Paris. We'll arrive early in the morning, and you'll meet Madeleine. You'll love her. And you'll love her cooking—she's an amazing chef. She learned to cook from her mother."

"That would be wonderful," she beamed. "I haven't had a home-cooked meal in so long... They would only feed us..."

He interrupted, waving a hand. "I don't want you to think about them anymore, Amelie. Forget them—they don't exist anymore. I want you to focus on your future. Once I have you settled, I'll deal with them."

She released a long sigh and nodded. As she headed towards the shower, she paused and turned around. "Thank you, Marcel... for helping me."

He clicked his tongue and winked. "You are so welcome, my dear."

She giggled and headed for the shower. He loved the sound of her laughter and the warmth of her smile.

Restricted to a five-minute shower during her captivity, she'd forgotten how it felt to luxuriate in a long, warm bath. She winced as her fingers brushed against the shaving scars on her legs, some fresh from the day before—she'd never gotten used to washing and shaving all in five minutes, with her roommates banging on the door, yelling at her to hurry.

"Is it all right if I take a little longer?" She called out. "I'm sorry I'm taking so long... I haven't had a bath in forever."

He chuckled. "Take as long as you want... I take my showers in the morning... Don't rush."

"Thank you!"

"You're very welcome!"

She let out a soft moan as she held the open bottle of body wash under her nose, inhaling the freesia and jasmine scent. Her body relaxed, teetering on the edge of dozing off—and that's when all hell broke loose.

Her eyes sprang open.

"Stay in there, Amelie!" Marcel yelled, just as a loud bang shook the door, nearly breaking it off its hinges.

She screamed and jumped out of the bathtub, fumbling for a towel. She'd barely wrapped it around herself when she heard two gunshots, one after another.

Marcel was on his laptop, emailing his superior, when he heard the keycard reader clicking and darted to hide behind the front door as it swung open.

A hand wielding a gun emerged through the door, and Marcel noticed a skull tattoo on the upper arm—the same tattoo he'd seen hours earlier.

He swiftly grabbed the arm and twisted it into an armbar, crashing the intruder against the bathroom door before collapsing him to the ground.

He held the man down, immobilizing him with his arm twisted behind his back, and fired two shots, center-of-mass, into the two armed men who had trailed in behind him, instantly killing both.

Kneeling, he pressed the muzzle of his gun into the base of the man's skull as he lay prone on the ground. With his free hand, he reached for his phone, dialing 911 for a tactical squad and a couple of ambulances. "I'm not sure if any more of them are coming—please hurry!"

Pointing the gun at the man's head, Marcel rolled him onto his back and peeled off his mask. "Well, well, well... It's Igor…"

"Ivan," he groaned. "My name is Ivan."

"I don't give a fuck, Igor, Ivan; it's all the same shit to me— scum of the earth; that's what you are. I'm going to ask you a few questions, and you'll answer. Otherwise, I will end it now. I don't give a fuck, Igor... So, what's it going to be?"

Ivan hesitated, defiance flashing in his eyes.

Marcel pressed the muzzle of the gun into Ivan's mouth, but when he wouldn't open wide, he forced it in, listening to his teeth crack as his mouth filled with blood. Ivan began to choke.

Marcel then cocked the hammer back. "Who do you work for?"

Ivan made a gargling sound, unable to speak. Marcel pulled the gun away from his mouth and pressed it against his forehead. Blood spewed from Ivan's mouth onto the carpet.

"I can't say... They'll kill me."

Marcel pulled the gun away from his forehead and smashed his elbow into the bridge of Ivan's nose, blood spraying from his nostrils. Ivan screamed in agony.

"I'm telling you, Igor," Marcel snarled. "I won't wait for the police—I'll take you out now. I'll tell them you resisted arrest and went for my gun."

Ivan saw the rage flashing in Marcel's blood-red eyes and realized he wasn't fucking around. He nodded. "Okay."

Marcel pressed the muzzle against his forehead once more. "Who do you work for? Who is Henri Bouchard?"

"He is my boss... I work for him."

"Where is he now?"

"I don't know."

"Goodbye, Igor!" Marcel scrunched his face as if bracing himself to pull the trigger.

"No! Wait. I swear, I... I don't know," Ivan stuttered, his broken English thick with fear. "All I know is that he stays on a big yacht somewhere in Europe. He never tells anyone where... I swear, that's all I know. He comes, brings girls, takes cash from the safe, and leaves."

"He's telling the truth."

Marcel turned his head and saw Amelie standing outside the bathroom, her body wrapped in towels, her face pale with horror.

He lowered his gaze to Ivan's battered body beneath him. "I want you to apologize to her... for everything you've ever done to her. She's the reason you're alive."

Ivan turned his head toward Amelie, his eyes swollen shut, blood oozing from his mouth and nostrils. "I'm sorry, Aurora."

"Do you know her real name?" Marcel grunted.

Ivan nodded.

"Call her by her real name!"

"I'm sorry, Amelie… I am very sorry."

Marcel shifted his gaze to Amelie and smiled. She nodded. He rolled Ivan onto his stomach and cuffed him.

A few minutes later, there was a knock on the door. "Police, open the door!"

Marcel gestured for Amelie to stay silent and retreat back into the bathroom. She nodded and dashed inside.

He lowered his lips to Ivan's ears. "Move or open your mouth, and I will blow your fuckin' brains out."

Ivan nodded, fear etched into his features.

Marcel raced to the door, pulling the hammer back on his gun, and looked through the peephole—an entire heavily armed police tactical unit waited, guns drawn. One officer held a battering ram, poised to smash down the door.

"Marcel Fornier, Gendarmerie Nationale," he yelled. "I called you. I'm opening the door."

Marcel held up his badge as the police officers entered, trying not to trip over the dead bodies strewn on the floor. They shook their heads, astounded by the carnage before them.

"You did all this?" one of them asked.

Marcel tilted his head and shrugged dismissively. "I had some training with the GIGN."

"Well, that explains it."

Other first responders arrived shortly after, securing the crime scene while emergency personnel transported the bodies to the medical examiner's office for forensic analysis.

Two police investigators collected statements from Marcel and Amelie as other officers hauled Ivan away for booking and further interrogation.

Marcel got on the phone with his superior and coordinated an emergency rescue operation with Montreal police to extract the girls from the club and capture the rest of Ivan's crew.

He handed his card to the officer in charge and informed him of his ongoing investigation into the human trafficking case.

"Look, I would stay and assist with the operation," he explained, gesturing to Amelie, who was giving her statement to a female investigator—detailing her capture and captivity. "But I've got to bring this young lady to France."

Amelie smiled at Marcel, her warmth shining through as she continued her conversation.

Having wrapped up their initial investigation, the police sealed off the crime scene and escorted Marcel and Amelie to another room on the tenth floor. They left behind four officers—two to stand guard by the door and two at the hotel's entrance.

The police informed Marcel that the rescue operation would commence at "zero one hundred hours," just minutes away.

On their way out, the police arrested the man at the reception desk who had informed Ivan of Marcel and Amelie's whereabouts. He was the only one working the desk and had no alibi.

With police protection now in place, Marcel thought they could finally rest. But Amelie had other plans. She wanted to stay up and talk. He smiled graciously and listened as she told him her life story and how she ended up in Montreal.

"My stepfather would get drunk every night," she explained. "And he… he would come to my room…"

Marcel tensed. "You don't have to…"

"I want to… please."

Marcel exhaled, nodding. "As you wish, Princess Amélie."

She smiled briefly before continuing. "I told my mom about it, but she didn't believe me—no, I know she did, but she didn't want to confront him. He had a job… He was the one supporting us."

Marcel listened intently, shaking his head. He felt the same rage he'd felt earlier when he had Ivan writhing in his clutches, pleading for his life.

Amelie continued. "So, I started to spend nights at my friends' houses or stay out all night, going to clubs with my friends... anything to stay away from my home—from him.

"One night, I was out at a bar… I was waiting to meet my girlfriend. A man approached me and started talking to me. He offered to buy me a drink. I liked him, so I let him—a Martini, I think; I can't remember. But as he sat there talking to me, I started to get dizzy. Things got blurry... And then everything went black."

Marcel leaned in, his voice low. "And when you woke up?"

She swallowed hard. "I was on a bed. I tried to get up, but my body was too weak. When I finally did, I looked around the room, trying to figure out where I was. Then I looked out the window— I was on a big boat in the middle of the water."

"Did you see any other boats, any beaches, or other landmarks?"

She shook her head. "Nothing. There was nothing around but water. I tried to leave the room, but the door was locked. I started to panic. I felt queasy and had to run to the bathroom. I threw up."

"Was the bathroom inside your cabin?"

She nodded. "It was a small bathroom: a small shower, a sink, and a toilet. Everything looked new: wood-paneled walls, brass window frames, and beautiful paintings on the walls. There was one particular painting—a lighthouse on a stormy night with a yellow beam of light pointing to a small boat floating in the middle of the water, but there was no one in the boat."

Marcel noticed a shift in her mood. She grew sullen, wringing her hands. He knew not to interrupt a victim when they recounted their trauma, so he let her continue.

"I keep having nightmares about it—about the picture... In my dream, I'm in the picture, in the small boat, looking at the lighthouse. Out of nowhere, a big wave crashes into the boat and flips it over. I fall into the water and try to get back on the boat, but wave after wave keeps slamming into my face, and I can't breathe. I'm swallowing water, gasping for air. I get tired and let go. I'm starting to sink. I can see the boat above me, but it's getting smaller. It's hazy and dark. I keep sinking until I can't see the boat anymore. It's pitch black."

"Then you wake up?"

"Yes. I wake up..." She hesitated, taking a deep breath, her gaze distant. "I wake up in the same bed with him on top of me."

"By him, you mean Henri…?"

She nodded vigorously, furrowing her brow.

"He woke you up from your dream?"

She shook her head. "No, *in* my dream—he wakes me up *in* my dream; I keep having the same dream over and over again."

Marcel nodded and turned his gaze toward the window, toward the city lights, thinking, *"You're still out there... and I'm going to find you..."*

This was now personal for him.

It was late; he didn't even bother checking the time. He wanted to end the night on a positive note—to blunt some of the trauma she'd endured.

"Guess what?"

"What?"

"We're going shopping tomorrow."

She giggled and gave an enthusiastic nod. "Thank you!"

"You're welcome!"

Marcel took the floor by the door, giving her the bed. Loading a handful of hollow-point bullets into three clips, he slid one inside the handle and tucked the other two into his coat pocket. He cocked the gun and slid it under his pillow.

"Goodnight, Amelie!"

"Bonne nuit, Marcel!"

16

The picturesque landscape whizzed by as the train rolled along, obediently following its tracks and winding through the idyllic countryside. Jane sat by the panoramic window, gazing out, while Claire sat beside her, flipping through her copy of Julius Caesar's *Gallic Wars*. She was reviewing the section detailing his invasion of Britain, searching for any hidden clues that could guide future archaeological expeditions.

Jane glanced at her, grinning, and shook her head. "You know, you're going to have plenty of time alone with your Caesar when we get to the site," Jane teased. "Why don't you check out the scenery? Spring has sprung—everything is so green, and you're missing it all."

Claire laughed and snapped the book shut. "All right, Jane, let me see what you're fussing about."

Raindrops pelted the glass, and the wind quickly whisked them away as they sat looking out the window. Claire leaned in closer to Jane, draping an arm over her shoulder as she stared out the window. She let out a sigh at the sight of green rolling hills and a lone white horse galloping through a flock of sheep grazing on the hillside, sending them scattering.

"Hey, look at that gorgeous white horse."

Jane nodded. "Beautiful, isn't he?"

"Yes, he is… He is magnificent."

Claire lowered her nose to Jane's neck and inhaled deeply. "Mmm… What is that perfume you're wearing?"

Jane chuckled. She reached inside her purse and took out a handful of small bottles. "I got a bunch of samples from the stores when we went shopping; I don't even know which one I'm wearing."

Claire erupted into laughter. "Oh, Jane… I guess we'll have to check out each one of them to find out, won't we?"

Jane grinned and laid the bottles out on the table in front of them. "Be my guest!"

Claire waved a hand. "Thank you, but that'll have to wait… I've got to go to the loo."

"They'll be right here waiting for you when you get back."

"Thanks, Jane." Claire chuckled. "If I'm not back in 20 minutes, come looking for me. I don't know where the loo is," she said, craning her neck and looking around. "But I'm sure I'll run into a good Samaritan who'll point the way."

Jane grinned, tapping her watch face. "20 minutes—counting down. I'll come and get you."

Claire stood and checked both directions. "I think I'll go right. This way, I can say hi to the staff."

Jane nodded and gave a thumbs up.

Claire smiled and waved as she approached her crew, seated a few rows back. They smiled and waved back, excitement lighting up their faces—their eagerness to return to the dig site palpable.

Sharon, the dig supervisor, stood and said, "The excavation team is already at the site and ready to start. James just texted me. I told him to wait until we get there so you can review the excavation map and set up new grids before they start."

"Well done, Sharon!" Claire nodded and pulled her in for a quick hug. "Great thinking."

"Thank you," Sharon said, flashing a smile. "I've also ordered portable bathroom and shower trailers, a private trailer for you, bigger tents, and the rest of the supplies Jane requested."

"Marvelous, Sharon! You've done a wonderful job. Are you excited?"

Sharon nodded enthusiastically. "Very much, Claire... I can't wait. I miss being outdoors. I was going stir-crazy sitting around my bloody flat all day."

Claire gave her another squeeze and whispered, "Thank you for everything, Sharon, but I've got to go—literally—or I'll pee my pants. You wouldn't happen to know where the loo is, would you?"

Sharon giggled and nodded toward the restroom. "I just got back from the loo myself. It's nice and clean."

"Perfect! Thank you, Sharon. We're almost there. I'm so excited."

Claire hurried toward the restroom, her head down, checking her emails on her phone. Her phone pinged, and she swiped out of her email to open her text app.

Then, out of nowhere, she slammed into something—hard. Her phone flew from her hands. For a split second, it felt like she'd hit an invisible wall. Then, she noticed a pair of hands on her shoulders, steadying her.

"I'm so sorry, Claire! Are you all right?" A deep voice rang out—a voice she immediately recognized.

She looked up, startled. Her heart raced, and goosebumps rose on her arm. She quickly smoothed them over with her hand before he could see them.

"I'm…" She stammered. "I'm fine, thank you, Stewart!"

"I'm really sorry, Claire… I wasn't paying attention," Stewart said nervously as he crouched to pick up her phone. He gestured towards the window. "I was checking out the view; I turned and ran into you—I'm so embarrassed."

"It's quite all right," Claire said, smiling. "I wasn't watching where I was going either."

"It's just that it's so beautiful out here… Everything is so green. I was completely distracted."

She forced a smile as she struggled to hold back her pee. "Yes… I imagine it is... I mean, I imagine it's greener here than in Indiana... with all the rain we get."

Stewart nodded, holding her gaze. He drew closer, almost pressing up against her. "You remembered I was from Indiana."

She shrugged and smiled tentatively, averting her gaze. She noticed a change in him—one that both thrilled and terrified her. "Yes… I suppose I did."

He sensed her reticence. "You know, Claire, I'm really looking forward to working with you." He lowered his gaze. "This is the most amazing job I've ever had, and I'm really grateful for the opportunity."

She had been drawn to him from the beginning, but after all her failed relationships, she found the idea of workplace romance unfathomable—just the thought of it filled her with dread.

Even more troubling, she thought, was the fact that he'd managed to get inside her dreams. Or was it even him? She couldn't be sure. She never saw his face.

Not in her dreams.

She was struck by the urgency to get to the restroom—fast. "I am very glad you decided to join us, Stewart," she said with a smile while trying to cut the chitchat. "But I've got to go now…"

Stewart gave a small nod and stepped aside, clearing her path. "Of course… I'm sorry I kept you."

"Not at all… I just have to attend to something."

Claire turned to walk away when she heard another ping. She chuckled and spun around. "May I have my phone back?"

Stewart glanced at her phone, still in his hands. His eyes widened slightly as he handed it over. "Oh—sorry about that."

She smiled. "No worries, Stewart. I get a bit absent-minded myself from time to time. That's why I need an assistant, I suppose… Goodbye for now."

She hurried away before she wet her pants. The restroom was vacant, so she hurried inside, closing and locking the door behind her. She lowered the toilet seat, placed a toilet seat cover on it, and sat down. She let out a big sigh of relief as her bladder released its content—she'd barely made it; a minute longer, and she would have wet herself.

She noticed she'd missed a text from Sharon and swiped her phone screen to open it.

Sorry I forgot to tell you. We have an applicant for the security position. He seems qualified.

That's great, Sharon. Thank you!

Welcome!

"You made it on time... It's been 18 minutes!" Jane sat with one leg tucked in on the seat and grinned, pointing to her watch. "I was getting ready to come looking for you."

Claire laughed and dropped into the seat beside her. "Thank goodness that's done with."

Jane gave her a quizzical look. "Everything okay?"

Claire nodded and smiled; she didn't want to get into it with her. For all Claire knew, Stewart was completely oblivious to her feelings—indifferent, even. Perhaps she'd let her imagination go wild. She started to feel foolish.

Jane wasn't convinced. She placed her hand on Claire's and gave it a slight squeeze, looking into her eyes. "Are you sure you're all right?"

Claire gave a dismissive wave. "Yes, of course." She then quickly changed the subject. "Did I ever tell you about my train trips with my parents when I was younger?"

Jane shook her head. "I don't think so, but I'd love to hear about it." She shifted in her chair and sat cross-legged, facing Claire.

A slight smile spread across Claire's face as she peered out the window. It was now pitch black outside, with the occasional light from villages and towns flashing before her eyes as the train sped by. "I was twelve," she reminisced with a distant expression on her face. "We would take the night train from London to Edinburgh. Those nights on the train—they were some of my best memories… Our cabin had bunk beds, and I used to sleep on the top bunk. Late at night, when my parents were asleep, I'd slide the curtain aside and peek out the window." She paused as if expecting a cue. "Look…" She pointed at lights that flickered randomly in the darkness. "Did you see that?"

Jane wrinkled her brow, following Claire's gaze. "What? The houses?"

Claire's lips curved just slightly. "I love watching houses by the train tracks. Sometimes, you can look inside the houses and get a glimpse—a quick snapshot—of people's lives."

Jane giggled. "Is my boss a peeping tom?"

Claire gasped. "Gosh, Jane... no." She paused, pressing her fingertips to her chin in thought. "It's like archaeology, I suppose—we get to peer into the past, into people's lives. See what I mean?"

"Oh, don't worry, Claire. I'm a voyeur, too," Jane said, scrunching her nose. "I like to watch people make out from my window… I'll have to show you my binoculars."

Claire's eyes widened, and her mouth flew open. "Jane!"

"I'm kidding, come on!"

"Oh, Jane…" Claire rolled her eyes before continuing. "All right, I'll tell you about my other favorite thing to do on a train." She narrowed her eyes at Jane. "And, no, it's not that!"

"What?" Jane scoffed. "I didn't say anything!"

"Yeah, but I know you were thinking it," Claire said, cocking an eyebrow. "Anyway, my other favorite thing to do… is read the classics."

"Let me guess," Jane interrupted. "Shakespeare?"

Claire shook her head.

"Dickens? Or Austen? Come on, Jane Austen?"

Claire shook her head again. "Oh, don't tell me you don't like *Pride and Prejudice* or *Sense and Sensibility*."

"I do... of course, I do. I like them a lot... but I like Cicero, Seneca, or Homer more."

"Oh."

"Yes, oh," Claire chuckled. "You'll find danger, romance…" She deepened her voice and brought her lips close to Jane's ear. "Scandal, even—better than anything you could find in your trashiest tabloids!" She paused for a moment, then continued in a hushed tone. "I would flick on my night lamp and read for hours."

"Which? The tabloids or Cicero?" Jane teased.

Claire pursed her lips and gave her a gentle tap on the arm. "Oh, Jane… you're incorrigible."

Jane sat opposite Claire, hugging a pillow in her lap, grinning mischievously. Claire shook her head, trying to suppress a smile. She had grown increasingly fond of Jane; she found herself wanting to share more and more with her.

"I've got an idea," Claire announced.

"Uh-oh."

"No, you'll like it."

Claire fished out her "Cassius Dio" and thumbed through the pages until she got to the section on Cleopatra. She glanced at Jane and smiled. "Pay attention now."

Jane batted her eyelashes and smiled broadly. Claire chuckled and then began by providing some historical context: first, Egypt's history, then Cleopatra herself.

"She was a smart, ambitious queen—a descendant of one of Alexander the Great's generals. And the most significant aspect of her life may have been the fact that two of Rome's greatest men fell for her."

"My kind of girl," Jane interrupted, giggling.

"Indeed."

Claire took a moment to gaze at Jane. She looked beautiful in the soft cabin lighting, and for a fleeting moment, Claire imagined her as Cleopatra or Helen of Troy.

Jane caught her gaze and smiled. She drew closer and rested her head on Claire's shoulder as she continued to read to her.

"Wait… Which two Romans fell for her?" Jane asked.

Claire smiled; she could tell Jane was as intrigued by Cleopatra as she was. "Julius Caesar," Claire shot back with dramatic flair. "And Mark Anthony, one of Rome's greatest generals."

"Were they having a threesome?"

"Jane!"

"All right, I'm sorry… I'll be quiet."

"Don't you want to hear the story?"

"I do…" Jane turned the book cover to peek at the title. "Who's Cassius Dio?"

"He's a Roman historian; he's one of the historians who wrote about Cleopatra. Can I go on now?"

Jane nodded, smirking. She seemed too restless to sit through Claire's reading.

Claire slammed the book shut, which made Jane jump. "All right, let's instead talk about the week ahead: Sharon said she got everything you'd asked for."

"That's great! But please continue with the story," Jane pleaded, placing her hand on Claire's. "I'll listen."

"Alright, I'll just give it to you in a nutshell," Claire caved. She paused and looked around. "But I'd kill for some alcohol. Let me flag down the attendant…"

"Wait, you don't need to," Jane cut in. She reached inside her travel bag and pulled out an assortment of mini bottles: whiskey, vodka, and gin. "Take your pick."

Claire's eyes grew wide, and she laughed. "Oh, Jane, you're amazing... I'll take a gin!"

Jane smiled and opened a bottle of gin for Claire and a bottle of vodka for herself. She handed the gin to Claire and raised her bottle. "To your success, Claire. You're the best… Cleopatra can't hold a candle to you!"

Claire raised her bottle and tapped Jane's. "Thank you, Jane! You're very sweet."

Jane's words touched Claire deeply, and a lump formed in her throat. Her eyes welled up. Jane took a small packet of tissues from her purse, removed one, and handed it to her. Claire gently dabbed her eyes, trying not to mess up her mascara.

They downed their drinks straight up, scrunching their faces and making guttural noises from the burn.

Feeling warm and fuzzy, Claire returned to her story by describing the relationship between Cleopatra and Julius Caesar, the power dynamics in Rome, and Caesar's subsequent assassination. She then moved on to Cleopatra's relationship with Mark Anthony.

"With those three, it was just as much a political alliance as it was a love affair," she explained. By the time Claire got to the defeat of Anthony and Cleopatra at the battle of Actium and their deaths, they'd each had a few drinks.

Jane was mesmerized by the story. "Did Cleopatra really die from a snake bite?"

Claire nodded. "According to some, she died from the bite of an asp; according to others, poisoning."

Claire had finished drinking, but Jane hadn't; she opened another bottle of vodka and drank it, wrinkling her face as it went down.

"Hey, won't you slow down?" Claire ran her palm along Jane's arm, gently caressing it. She didn't want to come across as if she were mothering her. It was her day off; technically, she wasn't even on the clock.

"I'm all right," Jane said in a reassuring voice. "Can you please tell me another story?" She looked at her watch and held her arm up, tapping the dial. "We've got another hour to go... Please?"

Claire was an only child. She'd grown up without siblings; if she had a sister, she would have wanted her to be just like Jane. She smiled and nodded. "All right, I'll tell you another one, but you have to promise to keep it a secret—deal?"

Jane pumped her fists in the air in excitement. "I promise."

Claire shook her head and laughed. "All right, pay attention now."

Jane mimed her index finger and thumb running across her lips, zipping them shut.

Claire recalled the old black-and-white photographs and archived records she'd recently come across. She couldn't get the haunting images out of her mind.

"Our next story is about a city in the East..."

"Far East?" Jane mumbled through her pretend zipped-up lips.

"No. I'm referring to the Near East, or Roman Near East—a city in ancient Mesopotamia. It's about a Roman frontier city that fell under siege. But what makes this city special are the tunnel systems uncovered beneath the city walls."

Jane raised her hand, pretending to be in class, straining to hold back a smile.

Claire chuckled. "Yes, Jane."

"What's so special about the tunnels?"

"That's a good question. I was about to get to that… What's special is that they found Roman soldiers buried inside these tunnels—perfectly preserved with their armor, their coin bags, and other personal items. And it looks like they all died in an instant; perhaps the tunnel collapsed, or they died in a flash fire: they found traces of bitumen and sulfur, which may have been ingredients in a chemical cocktail that was used in warfare. What's even more fascinating is that many of these frontier soldiers erected temples or shrines in their cities honoring local gods. They may have also married local women, like our Roman soldier in Newcastle. There are unexcavated parts of the city that may yield great treasures."

Claire paused and stared out the window. She let out a sigh. "But you know me; I only care about the people—how they lived, how they loved, how they died—and how they left their legacies behind for us to uncover beneath the earth, dust them off, and hand them down to posterity."

Jane sat with her eyebrows arched, squeezing her pillow tightly as she listened to Claire. There was no hint of a smirk or witty comment; she seemed genuinely captivated—there was only one question on her mind.

"Are we going there next?"

Claire shifted her gaze to Jane. "Would you like us to?"

Jane nodded enthusiastically. "Yes! I would love it; that part of the world has always fascinated me."

"Me, too. I'll be speaking with Callum soon to see if R.A.H. is willing to finance the venture."

"Oh, god, I hope so…" Jane lowered her head and picked at her fake nails. "And I hope I can always... um…" She stammered, unable to finish her sentence.

Claire took Jane's hand in hers. "You'll always be with me, Jane—for as long as you want to… if you want to…"

"I want to!" Jane hurled herself towards Claire and threw her arms around her. "I really want to."

A smile spread across Claire's face as Jane tightened her grip around her, exhaling a big sigh next to her ear.

Jane pulled back, placing her hands on Claire's shoulders and looking at her. "Thank you, Claire... I love you so much!"

"I love you, too, Jane!"

Claire drew Jane close and wrapped her arms around her, sensing Jane's devotion and sincerity but also detecting the smell of vodka hiding beneath her perfume.

The hotel looked out over the River Tyne. The online booking review boasted, "The best view in Newcastle." Claire agreed. Standing at the window, she pictured Roman ships sailing down the river on the way to Roman forts, rowers' oars slicing through the water.

She heard a snore. Jane lay sprawled on the queen-sized bed. She'd managed to shed her clothes before passing out—she'd had a few too many drinks. Claire had booked the room for two; she wanted to keep her close.

She wrote a letter to Callum Mackenzie, informing him that she'd arrived in Newcastle and would be heading out to the site in the morning and outlining her plans for the upcoming week.

She thought about calling him, but it was late, and she didn't think he was the texting type. She stamped the envelope and stuck it in her purse to drop off at the postbox in the morning.

Before going to bed, Claire approached Jane to check on her. She noticed that she'd turned on her side, shifting the blanket and leaving her body partially exposed.

Moving closer to adjust her blanket, she noticed a shadowy shape peeking out from underneath it. She pulled the blanket aside to get a better look and gasped.

What looked to be a shadow was a bruise on her upper arm— a bruise in the shape of fingers.

17

The mall buzzed with activity, just as Marcel had hoped. The more crowded it was, the safer they'd be. Even with two police officers trailing closely behind, he knew he had to stay vigilant.

He scanned the surroundings for anything suspicious; it was ingrained in his training to be ready for anything. His gaze fell upon a man staring at them as they passed, and instinctively, he reached for his gun. But then he noticed the man's attention was fixated solely on Amelie's bare feet. Ever since she had tossed her shoes, she'd been walking around barefoot.

Marcel picked up a pair of silver lace-up heels and held them out to her. "Do you like these? I think they'd look beautiful on you."

She smiled but shook her head. His confusion was evident, prompting her to lean closer and whisper in his ear, "They remind me of work…"

She pulled back slightly, watching his expression.

He rolled his eyes. "Ah… Of course. I'm such an idiot."

"Not at all! You're trying to help me. Please don't feel that way."

He nodded, casting a sideways glance.

She followed his gaze. "I mean it... I'm so grateful to you, Marcel. You've saved my life."

She reached for a pair of pink sneakers adorned with glittering laces. "Can I have these instead?"

He chuckled. "Whatever you want."

"Thank you," she beamed.

Marcel savored Amelie's ecstatic expression as she held a dress against her body, admiring herself in the full-size mirror. She turned to him, her eyes sparkling with joy. "What do you think?"

"I think you make any dress look beautiful, Amelie."

She scoffed, fighting back a smile. "Oh, come on! Seriously! How does the dress look?"

Marcel laughed. "Seriously! I love it."

She rolled her eyes. "Now I don't trust you."

They both burst into laughter. Ultimately, she decided on a pair of jeans and a T-shirt that read, "I love Paris."

After a lively afternoon of shopping, the police escorted them to the airport. With one hand resting inches from his gun holster and the other clutching Amelie's, Marcel kept a sharp eye out until they reached airport security.

Thanks to advance clearance for his firearm, they breezed through screening without incident or delay.

Just as they arrived at their gate, his phone buzzed with a text from the police team captain: The raid on Cupid's Corner was successful, with the remaining kidnappers captured and the girls rescued and transported to a secure location.

For Amelie, it was an exhilarating moment—a real nail-biter as she waited to hear news about her friends.

Marcel checked his watch, anxious to board the plane. To provide backup, one of the police officers would accompany them on the flight. Before long, they settled into their seats, buckled up, and prepared for takeoff.

Amelie struggled with conflicting emotions: part of her felt sad about leaving her friends behind, while another part was thrilled to start a new life. Watching Marcel dismantle Ivan and his goons single-handedly made her feel protected in a way she had never experienced before.

The feeling of impending doom had evaporated; she felt liberated. It was an exhilarating sensation, and the promise of the future sent shivers down her spine.

For Amelie, Marcel had become the ideal role model, the epitome of what a man should be—something she'd been missing her entire life.

As they peered out the window, the dazzling lights of Montreal twinkled below them, partially obscured by the massive wing of the Boeing 787. Gradually, the giant plane banked east, revealing the city's full splendor at night. The St. Lawrence River meandered like an artery across the landscape, reflecting the glittering city lights.

Sitting by the window, Amelie pressed her forehead against the glass. "Look! That's the Ferris wheel we saw."

He nodded in agreement. "It's beautiful at night, isn't it?"

"Yes… very!" She beamed. "I'm going to miss Montreal."

"Don't worry. One day, we'll return."

"Will you bring me?"

"Yes, I will."

"Will I see my friends again?"

"Yes, you will."

Then, as if erased from a page, the city vanished, the plane punching through the gray sky and emerging above it to reveal an altogether different view—a blanket of silvery clouds resembling a bed of cotton, glistening beneath a bright, full moon.

With nothing but time on her hands and too wound up to sleep, Amelie picked up where she had left off with her story.

She glanced at Marcel before beginning. "It was my first night on the yacht…"

Marcel straightened in his seat, his jaw tightening. "I'm listening."

She took a steadying breath. "I'd been locked up all day inside that room... It was nighttime… I heard the doorknob jiggle. I watched it slowly turn, and the door opened. My heart was racing… It was him!"

"Henri?" Marcel asked, his brow furrowing.

She nodded and continued. "I pushed myself back on the bed toward the headboard, trying to get away from him. I started crying. He sat down at the edge of the bed and laid his hand on my foot. I cringed. I pulled my knees in against my chest. He said,

'Don't be afraid. I'm not going to hurt you.' I asked him what he wanted from me. He said, 'I just want you to relax and have fun. I only need you to help me entertain some of our guests. Then, I will take you back home. That's all.' But that was a lie—it was just the beginning of my nightmare!"

As Amelie recounted her story, her agitation grew. Marcel listened intently, searching for clues, no matter how small. She paused, taking a moment to collect herself before continuing.

"I had no choice. I said okay. He brought me a bikini to wear. I said, 'I'm not wearing that.' He said, 'It's warm outside. Everyone's in swimsuits.' So I put on the stupid thing; he took my hand, and we stepped out onto a large deck full of people."

She scoffed, wrinkling her brow. "All I saw was a bunch of old men with young girls in bikinis. I wanted to throw up. I turned to go back, but he grabbed my arm and squeezed really hard."

She lowered her head, visibly distraught. "He kept me on that damn boat for weeks. From there, he took me to Prague and then to Montreal. I was always at some club... or some mansion... surrounded by disgusting, rich, old men."

She paused, burying her face in her hands. Marcel gently patted her on the back, but she winced at his touch, prompting him to withdraw his hand.

"I'm so sorry, Amelie," he said softly, his heart aching for her. A feeling of numbness spread through his fingers as he let go of the armrest, realizing he'd been gripping it with all his strength.

She leaned back, taking a deep breath. "It's all right... I'm just glad I'm out of there."

He let out a long sigh. "And remember what I promised? I will never let you go... I will always protect you. Your old life is over. The new one is ahead of you, and I promise I'll do everything in my power to make sure it's a happy one."

A yawn replaced the smile that had begun to spread across her face.

She lowered her head onto his shoulder, her eyelids heavy, and drifted off to sleep.

He had many more questions, but they'd have to wait—the whole world would have to wait—until she was ready. Logging onto the plane's Wi-Fi, he texted Madeleine.

My love, we took off an hour ago. I'm so sorry I couldn't text you sooner. I'm bringing the young girl I texted you about with me. I have to bring her home, and then I can place her in witness protection and help her get settled. I hope you won't mind. I will make it up to you.

See you in a few hours. I love you!

He aimed his phone camera at Amelie's peaceful face, brought her into focus, and snapped a picture. He texted it to Madeleine.

Within seconds, she replied.

Hi!!

She's beautiful! And no I don't mind. She can stay here. I'll prepare the guest room.

She is a very sweet girl, my love.

I'm sorry I couldn't text earlier. Things have been crazy. Hectic.

She'd never heard her husband say "I'm sorry" twice in a conversation, and he never used the word "hectic." It was just not in his vocabulary. Her worry deepened.

Now you're scaring me. Are you ok?

Yes, no problem.

Please tell me the truth.

They came after her but I took care of it. Don't worry.

Madeleine's heart began to thump furiously inside her chest. She knew what "I took care of it" meant—she knew her husband well. She paused.

???

I'm here. Are you both safe now?

Perfectly safe now. I have a police escort with me. Please don't worry, my love.

But I am worried. Please be careful!

Marcel stood, spinning around. He snapped a picture of the police officer sitting behind him, smiling, and sent it to her.

This is Jean-Philippe with Montreal Police. See? I have backup. Please trust me. I'm fine.

Lol he looks like Mr. Bean! Be safe. See you in a few hours. I love you.

LOL. I'll tell him what you said.

Better not 

Ok, I won't. I love you!!

And don't forget…

What?

I'm horny.

Lol, I'll take care of it tonight.

Love you! I'll pick you up at the airport at 8:15. See you soon.

☺

They had no luggage—only Marcel's carry-on and a backpack Amelie had picked up at the mall—so they swiftly exited the terminal and arrived at the airport entrance, where Madeleine was waiting for them. She dashed toward them, arms open, and hugged Marcel tightly before turning to Amelie and throwing her arms around her in a warm embrace.

"Hello, Amelie… My god! You're gorgeous," Madeleine exclaimed, pulling back to take a better look at her. "You're even prettier in person!"

Amelie gave her a shy smile. "Thank you, Madeleine. You are also very pretty. I told Marcel that when he showed me your picture."

Madeleine turned to Marcel, laughing. "Oh, did he?"

"Yes, I did," he boasted with a grin.

"And thank you for letting me stay at your house for a few days—it's only until I get a job and get my own place…"

"Oh, never mind that, sweetheart," Madeleine interrupted, waving her hand dismissively. "Let's go home now so you can see your room and settle in. I'm sure you're exhausted."

Titou's ears perked up at the sound of keys jingling, and he came running to the door. He sat there, tail wagging, waiting for it to open. Madeleine was the first person through the door, but Titou dashed past her and Marcel, heading straight for Amelie, who crouched down to play with him.

"What's his name?" she asked, looking up at Madeleine.

Madeleine chuckled. "It's Titou… and I've never seen him act like this with anyone. He really likes you."

Titou must have read Madeleine's mind because he rolled on his back, his tongue hanging out the side of his mouth, while Amelie rubbed his belly.

Madeleine exchanged a glance with Marcel, a smile playing on her lips. He smiled back and winked.

Turning to Amelie, she said, "Welcome to your new home, my dear. You can stay with us as long as you want."

"Thank you, Madeleine!" Amelie sprang to her feet and hugged her tightly. "You are very kind."

"You are very welcome, sweetheart. We're glad to have you with us."

Madeleine looked over Amelie's shoulder and caught Marcel standing behind her, grinning. She gave him a nod with her eyes as she held Amelie in her arms and smiled.

Marcel released a heavy sigh. He suspected Madeleine would bond with Amelie, but he hadn't expected her to be so overjoyed—as if she were holding her own biological daughter.

Tears began to pool in his eyes, but he brushed them away with the back of his fingers.

18

Jane burst into the trailer, clutching something in her hand. Her face was radiant, glowing from the sun's embrace. Claire raised a finger and smiled as she sat facing her laptop, conducting an online interview with a prospective security supervisor.

Jane mouthed, "I'm sorry," and settled into a chair opposite her. Unbeknownst to Jane, Claire was in the middle of a meeting scheduled by Sharon, the dig supervisor.

Claire's gaze flitted between her laptop monitor and Jane, struggling to suppress a smile.

Jane looked excited, crossing and uncrossing her legs, adjusting her straw sun hat with an elegant bow at the back or tugging on the hem of her khaki shorts. Claire appreciated Jane's sense of style—she looked fantastic, even after a long day of digging in the dirt.

Claire moved her hand away from the view of the monitor with three fingers extended, signaling she'd be done in three minutes. Jane smiled and nodded in acknowledgment. Claire's curiosity was piqued, wondering what she was holding in her hand.

"All right, Peter, we'll see you tomorrow, then?" Claire hurried to finish her interview, eager to discover what had Jane so animated.

"Yes, Miss Langford. I'll be there first thing in the morning." Jane couldn't see Peter's expression, but she could sense his enthusiasm.

"Thank you. Please follow up with Sharon to finalize your paperwork so you can start immediately."

"Yes, of course, Miss Langford. And thank you!"

"You're quite welcome... and please call me Claire."

"Thank you, Claire."

Claire nodded and smiled before ending the online session. She rushed around her desk, leaning in to see what Jane was holding.

"All right, let's see what you've got." Claire tried to pry her fingers open. "Come on. Open your hand."

Jane looked up at Claire, eager to see her reaction.

She wasn't disappointed—Claire's eyes widened, and she gasped.

"Oh, Jane! Do you know what you're holding in your hand?" Claire held out her palm, and Jane dropped the object into it.

Jane wrinkled her nose and grinned. "No, but it's shiny... and gold."

Claire laughed, her excitement bubbling over. She took Jane by the hand, leading her to the table in the center of the trailer. She pulled out a chair and pointed to it. "Here, sit."

Jane sat down, and Claire took the chair beside her. She reached for a stack of books on the table, tracing her finger down their spines until she found the one she wanted and pulled it out.

Flipping through the pages, she found what she was looking for. "Here," she said, tapping on a picture. "Does this look familiar?"

Jane leaned in, peering at the image, then back at the coin in Claire's palm.

"It's the same coin!"

Claire waved her hand dismissively. "That's unimportant— look at the name... the date."

Jane squinted closer. "393-423 AD... Emperor Honorius." She glanced at Claire, confusion flickering across her face.

"Jane, this coin is a gold Solidus of Emperor Honorius; it dates centuries later than the period we've been covering."

"This means, um..." Jane grew more excited, taking a moment to calm herself. "Wow, this means there could be..."

Claire nodded, beaming, waiting for Jane to finish her thought.

"This means there could be lots more gold out there."

"Jane!"

"I'm only kidding," Jane giggled. "I get it—we're sitting on many years of history."

"Yes, Jane!" Claire raved. "A span of centuries... with many emperors."

"And gold..."

"Yes," Claire chuckled. "And gold."

Jane shrugged, arching her brow. "I'm sorry—I can't help it; I love shiny things."

"Yes, I know." Claire smirked. "There'll be lots and lots of shiny things."

Claire's phone pinged with a text from Sharon.

You may want to come look at this!

Claire slid the phone across the table to Jane. Jane glanced at the screen.

"More shiny things?"

Claire rolled her eyes and laughed. "Let's go!"

"Yeah, let's!"

Claire sent off a quick reply.

Coming!

"Let's make a bet," Jane quipped as they exited the trailer.

"What kind of bet?" Claire chuckled.

"That Sharon found more shiny things."

"All right... I'll take that bet—the loser fixes dinner tonight."

"But you know I can't cook!"

"But I'll have fun watching you try."

"All right," Jane groaned. "I'll take my chances." She paused, then asked, "Wait, what if you lose?"

"I guess I'll be making dinner."

"Yay! I love your cooking."

"I know you do."

Jane giggled. "So, what do you think Sharon found?"

"Nothing shiny."

Jane pouted and scowled. Claire laughed.

The dig site was less than fifty feet away from the crew campsite. Sharon saw them approaching and waved, yelling, "You're going to love this, Claire!"

Jane knew instantly she'd lost the bet: Claire didn't love gold coins and jewels. She treasured sentimental things, like the letters between her Roman officer and his native wife, Cara. She'd been gushing over them all winter. Claire couldn't wait to get back to the site—back to them.

Claire waved back. "Don't tell me… I want to be surprised." She whispered to Jane with a triumphant smirk, "You're most positively cooking tonight."

Jane laughed. "Don't I know it? But don't rub it in. I may undercook the eggs."

Claire burst into laughter. "Don't worry; I'll cook."

"Aw, you're the best."

"You get to clean up after."

Jane groaned, then laughed.

They stood peering over the dig site, where squared areas were marked off with string for excavation. Sharon sat in one of the squares, scraping away the soil around a marble chest with its cover pushed aside. Inside the chest was a wooden box with its lid slightly cracked open. She shielded her face from the sun with a hand, squinting at Claire and Jane.

"Ready?"

Claire nodded enthusiastically. "Yes!"

Sharon slipped on her gloves, took hold of the lid, and slowly opened it. She reached inside the box with both hands and carefully pulled out a square-shaped object, holding it up for Claire to see.

Claire stepped inside the square, which had been dug about a foot deep, taking care not to trip over the framing string. She drew closer and placed her hands on Sharon's, steadying them as she examined the object.

"What is it, Claire?" Jane asked, following her inside the square.

Claire mumbled in Latin, tracing her finger along the thin, wooden tablet. She translated as she went along. "It says here, 'Mi uxor, nunc Romae sum.' It means, 'My wife, I am now in Rome.' It's slightly faded here, then it continues, 'I will be traveling to Naples soon... I wish you were here with me... I miss you, Cara... my love... Lucius!'"

Claire let out a loud gasp, her hand on her chest, tears brimming in her eyes. She turned to face Jane, who stood behind her.

Jane realized the significance of what she'd just heard and threw her arms around Claire. "His name was Lucius!"

Claire nodded, a wave of relief washing over her. "Finally…" She sighed heavily. "Finally, we have his name."

"Why were these letters inscribed on wood?"

"They are postcards—he sent her postcards!"

Jane's eyes welled up, and she fought back tears.

Claire turned to Sharon, whose eyes were also glistening. She smiled and wiped her cheeks. "Sorry… It takes a lot to get me to cry, but you did it, Claire."

Claire smiled back and squeezed Sharon's arm. "You can go ahead and put that back in the box." She paused. "Wait, let me take some pictures; how many tablets are inside the box?"

Sharon shrugged. "I didn't count them, but there are quite a few."

Claire heard Jane sniffling over her shoulder, watching as she framed and shot photos of the tablets. There were 43 in total.

"The marble chest must have belonged to Cara. Some of these tablets are diaries or journals; the rest are postcards," she whispered to Jane. "I'll read these to you at night—they'll be your bedtime stories."

Jane nodded, smiling. "Mm… I'd love to hear their story."

Claire swiped through the photos on her phone, showing them to Jane and Sharon. She heard heavy footsteps approaching from behind and turned to see someone standing over them, his figure shrouded by the sun's glare. He waved.

"Hello, everyone! I didn't mean to startle you."

"Oh, hi, Stewart," Claire said, raising a hand to shield her eyes. "Sorry, I can't see you; you're in the sun."

"Sorry!"

Stewart stepped forward out of the sun's glare. Claire swallowed hard, her gaze unintentionally lingering on his chest, visible through his sweat-soaked tank top. He loomed over them, holding out a leather pouch.

"I didn't mean to startle you... I thought you'd want to see this."

Claire wanted to reach for the bag, but she froze—she couldn't tear her eyes away from the beads of sweat glistening on his muscular arms. She felt her face flush.

A hand stretched out in front of her. "Here, Stewart, let me see that." Jane snatched the pouch from Stewart's hand. "How are things going at grid two?"

"Great! We're taking our time, slowly working our way through the top stratum."

Jane handed the bag to Claire. "That's where we found the later-period coins."

Claire weighed the bag in her hand. "It's heavy—very promising!"

"Take a look inside," Jane said with a smile.

Claire opened the bag and peered inside, arching an eyebrow.

Jane leaned in closer and whispered in her ear, "More shiny things." Then she turned to Stewart. "Thanks, Stewart! Keep up the good work."

Stewart gave a slight nod and smiled before walking away. Claire watched him out of the corner of her eye until he vanished over the top of the mound and headed toward the new dig site.

The sap-laden logs snapped and crackled in the campfire outside their trailer, sending swirling pillars of embers into the night sky. Jane impaled a fat marshmallow on her stick and held it over the flames. Claire followed suit, holding out her own. Jane swung her stick into Claire's, who responded by striking back, sparking a playful sword fight. Their laughter filled the air until they realized they'd lost their marshmallows in the flames.

"Uh-oh!" Jane snorted, and Claire burst into laughter.

Silence fell as they skewered fresh marshmallows and consigned them to the flames.

"Truce?" Jane mumbled, biting into an unroasted marshmallow.

"Truce!" Claire agreed, nodding. She gestured at Jane's marshmallow as it browned on the stick. "Why aren't you waiting for your marshmallow to roast?"

"Because I'm impatient!"

Claire laughed, took a marshmallow from the bag, and stuffed it into her mouth. "Hear, hear."

Claire took a bite of her gooey marshmallow and looked up at the sky.

"It's a Roman sky," Claire said, pointing at the constellations. "There's Canis Major." She traced the shape with her stick. "And there's Sirius—her brightest star."

A gust of wind blew a cluster of embers into the night sky, mingling with the stars and setting the sky ablaze.

"Ooh, that was cool—I want to see that again!" Jane gushed, drawing her blanket over her chest.

Claire smiled. "Do you realize this is the same sky Lucius and Cara sat under, staring at the stars?"

"Hmm… I didn't think about that."

"Probably only a few feet away from where we're sitting."

Jane drew her knees to her chest and reclined on her lounge chair, propping her head on her hand as she watched Claire's auburn hair dance in the wind. Claire's pale skin glowed in the flames as she gazed at the stars with a distant expression.

"You said you were going to read to me," Jane murmured, rousing Claire from her trance.

A smile spread across Claire's face. She grabbed her phone and scrolled through the tablet photos she'd taken earlier until she found one that caught her eye. She expanded it with her fingers and began reading.

"It's Lucius," she beamed. "He writes here, 'I am in Londinium now…'" She began mumbling in Latin, "'Hadrianus imperator hodie adest.' It means, 'Emperor Hadrian is here today.'"

"Wait…" Jane interrupted. "Where is this Londinium place?"

Claire chuckled. "It's the same place we came from."

"London?"

Claire nodded. "That's right—London!" She paused to savor the expression on Jane's face, then continued. "London was originally a Roman settlement."

"Gosh, that's so neat."

"Yes, it is," Claire agreed. "He says here, 'The emperor wants me to accompany him throughout the city... He wants to see the fortifications. He does not want to see a repeat of the past's calamities.'" The text cuts off briefly before resuming in a lower section of the tablet: "The savage barbarian attack..." It cuts off again, then resumes… and here was the most revealing detail—the name.

"What name?" Jane asked, puzzled.

"Boudica!"

"Who?"

"Boudica," Claire repeated, emphasizing the name. "She was a queen—a native queen of the Iceni tribe, who rallied other tribes and led them to attack Londinium."

Claire saw the fire in Jane's eyes. She chuckled. "Yes, Jane! A woman—a fierce queen. A woman not unlike yourself. And not only did she attack the Romans, but she defeated them and destroyed a significant part of the city."

Jane sat up in her chair, visibly moved by the story. "My kind of girl!" She raved.

"I thought so," Claire laughed. "You two have a lot in common."

Jane paused, wrinkling her eyebrows. "Wait… Why did she attack the Romans?"

Claire had hoped to avoid the topic, but despite knowing Jane would react negatively, she felt compelled to answer. "When her husband died, the Romans didn't abide by his wishes—by his will: for the Romans to rule his kingdom jointly with his daughters."

Jane's demeanor shifted. She lowered her voice and narrowed her eyes. "So, what did the Romans do?"

Claire hesitated.

"What did they do?" Jane repeated, her eyes fixed on Claire's.

"They…" Claire stammered. "They beat Boudica, and they... abused her daughters."

"You mean raped?"

Claire nodded. Even with her eyes down, she could hear Jane's heavy breathing.

"I've got an idea. Wait here," Claire said, avoiding eye contact, and stepped inside the trailer.

"Mm-hmm," Jane mumbled.

Claire returned with a bottle and a pair of shot glasses.

"There's nothing a bit of scotch can't fix," she murmured, pouring the whiskey and handing Jane a glass. Claire raised hers. "To Lucius and Cara," she toasted.

Jane raised her glass. "And to Boudica… and her daughters… And may the Romans burn in hell."

Claire sighed as they clinked glasses.

With the flames dwindling, Jane shivered and smoothed the goosebumps on her arm. "Can we go inside? I'm getting cold."

Claire nodded in agreement. "Me, too. I'm freezing."

The trailer was spacious and easily accommodated two people. They'd set up two beds, but Jane climbed in with Claire. Her body had relaxed after the scotch, and she snuggled close, resting her head on Claire's shoulder.

"Brrr... This is much better," Jane said, shivering.

Claire smiled. "Comfy? Should I read more?"

Jane nodded.

"Let's see, where were we?"

"In Londinium… With Lucius… I like Lucius."

Claire chuckled. "Right, he seems to be a good Roman; he loves his wife."

Claire swiped through her photos and found another tablet.

"Here, listen to this one... It's pretty interesting. He writes, 'The Emperor wants me to expand our defenses and build a road south to the river. He wants me to construct additional fortifications on the north side to protect us from marauding Caledonian tribes.'" She turned to Jane. "Do you realize what this means?"

"He gave us a clue."

"Exactly! We have ground-penetrating radar and other tools, but he just gave us additional insight: he told us there's a road connecting the fort to the river below—it makes sense; it was much easier to resupply from the river than through a land route. And he told us there are further fortifications on the north side."

Jane seemed relaxed and receptive. Claire decided to raise the question that had been troubling her since the night at the hotel. She rolled onto her side, facing Jane, and smiled.

"Can I ask you a personal question?"

Jane wrinkled her brow. "Sure… Anything."

Claire hesitated, wanting to tread lightly.

Jane smiled. "What? Did I do something?"

Claire chuckled and shook her head. "It's nothing like that."

"Then what is it?"

Claire took a deep breath and said, "You know I care for you, right?"

Jane nodded. "You're worrying me... What is it?"

"That night at the hotel, when we returned to Newcastle... You were fast asleep, and you'd kicked off your blanket. I came around to adjust your blanket, and... I saw a bruise on your arm."

Jane flinched slightly but quickly covered it with a casual laugh. "Oh, that was nothing." She waved it off dismissively. "I must have run into my bathroom door. It happens all the time. Please don't worry."

Claire smiled and nodded, not wanting to force the issue. But she couldn't shake the image—the unmistakable shape of fingerprints on Jane's arm.

19

Amelie sat anxiously, gazing at the oil painting on the wall as her fingers dug into the soft leather sofa. The painting depicted a man and a woman at dusk in a rowboat near the shore, locked in a kiss. In the background, a lighthouse beacon cut across the horizon as stars slowly emerged against a velvet sky.

A young girl, barely older than Amelie, approached her with a smile. "Bonjour! My name is Jean-Marie; I'm the assistant to Doctor Tussaud. She is ready to see you. Please follow me."

Amelie stood, her eyes still fixed on the painting. When the door to the doctor's office opened, she continued to stare at the artwork, her head cocked to the side.

"It's a beautiful painting, isn't it?" Dr. Tussaud remarked, standing in the doorway, holding it open for her.

Amelie shifted her gaze to face her. "Yes, it is."

"Please come in," Dr. Tussaud said with a warm smile, motioning to the comfortable couch opposite her desk. "You can sit or lie down—whatever makes you comfortable, Amelie."

Amelie smiled back and walked in. She spun around, surveying her surroundings, and sat down on the couch, her hands resting on her knees.

Dressed in a white pantsuit and dress shirt, her prescription glasses perched on the bridge of her nose, Dr. Tussaud looked more like a business professional than a doctor.

A woman in her mid-sixties with sleek, chin-length silver hair, high cheekbones, and a prominent chin, she gave Amelie a warm smile and began reviewing her file notes.

She lowered her glasses onto her nose, her piercing hazel eyes peeking over them, and let out a sigh. "Dear Amelie, welcome. My name is Jacqueline Tussaud. I want you to know that my closest friend, Madeleine Fornier, referred you to me. She's more like a sister to me. And her husband, Marcel… Well, you already know him."

Amelie nodded and smiled.

"Is it all right with you if I share my findings with him?" Dr. Tussaud asked gently. "As you know, he is conducting an ongoing investigation into the people—into the criminals that…"

Amelie nodded once more, agreeing to discuss the findings with Marcel.

Dr. Tussaud set aside her notes. She crossed her legs, leaned forward slightly, and intertwined her fingers. "Now, tell me what you saw in the painting in my front office," she said in a hushed tone as if sharing a secret. "You seemed very intrigued by it."

Amelie lowered her gaze.

"Please, Amelie… Anything you can tell me would be very helpful. When you look at that picture, what do you notice? Please… anything."

Silence hung between them.

Dr. Tussaud sat patiently, waiting for Amelie to open up. There was no rush. Madeleine's words echoed in her head: "Please take care of Amelie—whatever it takes, however long it takes."

It didn't take long for Amelie to begin talking. "There was another painting like it," she murmured. "There was a lighthouse…"

"Yes… a lighthouse… Please go on."

"It was in the room… on the yacht where he…"

"Where he held you," Dr. Tussaud interjected. "You can say it: where he held you against your will."

Amelie gave a small nod and continued. "There was also a boat in that painting, a small one… but it was empty. And I dream about it."

"What kind of dreams?"

"I dream that I'm on the boat. Then a storm comes and flips the boat over."

"Yes, go on."

"I try to swim, but I get tired… I sink... Then I wake up in my room, and he's on top of me."

"In the dream?"

"Yes, in the dream… But then I really wake up and realize I'm in my room... and the door is locked. I can't get out."

"Are you still having the dream?"

She nodded. "But not as often—not since I've been living with Marcel and Madeleine. And when I do dream, he's not in it."

"How does your dream end, then?"

"I sink… and drown."

Amelie went on to describe her room, where she spent most of her time. She talked about her days and nights on the yacht.

She remembered being taken to lavish private mansions, not knowing where she was most of the time—not until she saw or heard something on the local TV or radio.

She described the wealthy, older men who showed up at these places, all speaking different languages.

And then there was the monster who controlled her life, the one haunting her nightmares—Henri Bouchard. "He made my skin crawl."

Amelie sighed deeply and stared at her lap again, signaling she was done for the day.

Dr. Tussaud acknowledged this. "You did great, Amelie. We can stop for today. Frankly, I'm very optimistic that with time, counseling, and support from Marcel and Madeleine, you'll be fine. You're very young." She picked up her notes and looked through them. "Ah, here it is—you're only 19 years old. I believe you will get past all this and lead a wonderful and happy life. You'll just have to take it one day at a time. And speaking of Marcel," she said, checking her watch, "he said you two have plans for lunch after this session."

Amelie's lips curled into a smile at the mention of Marcel's name, and she nodded. She'd been looking forward to going out to lunch with him.

Dr. Tussaud accompanied Amelie to the front office to say goodbye. "Please take care, Amelie… I will see you at our next session."

"Yes… thank you."

Amelie gave her a shy smile before turning to leave. It didn't escape Dr. Tussaud's notice that Amelie didn't once look at the painting on the wall as she walked past it.

Marcel had never heard of the place before—a coworker had recommended the quaint little mom-and-pop restaurant on the Seine. It was a sunny day with barely any clouds in the sky, and a gentle breeze rose from the river, caressing their faces.

Amelie tore a small piece of bread from her baguette and tossed it onto Marcel's lap. Marcel cupped his hand around his lighter, shielding its flame from the wind as he lit his cigarette. He took a long drag, exhaling a thin stream of smoke toward the water. He picked up the piece of bread, popped it into his mouth, and began chewing.

"You know, I was thinking…"

She didn't respond; instead, she tore off another piece of bread and lobbed it at him.

He continued, "I was thinking… I miss sleeping with Titou so much. He's my baby, too, you know."

She gasped, eyes wide.

"I think I'm going to have him sleep with me tonight… What do you think?"

"You wouldn't." She pulled a face, acting shocked.

He raised an eyebrow. "Well, don't you think he misses me? And Madeleine, too? Don't you think he misses sleeping with us? Have you tried asking him?"

Amelie laughed, covering her mouth as she chewed. She mumbled a barely comprehensible "no."

He took another drag and smothered the cigarette in the ashtray in front of him, grinning.

She retracted her arm, poised to throw another piece of bread, but he gave her a stern look. She hesitated.

He laughed. "Gotcha!"

She threw the bread at him, and he ducked, holding up his cloth napkin. "I surrender… I surrender."

He heard the people at the table next to them laughing. He smiled at them, shrugged, and mouthed, "L'enfant."

Amelie scoffed, then laughed. "I'm not a child!" She sprang up, circled around the table to his side, and wrapped her arms around his shoulders from behind. She whispered in his ear, "I'm not a child… and you said you surrendered."

Marcel threw his arms up. "I do… I surrender."

She leaned in and kissed him on the cheek.

"Guess what?" he whispered to her over his shoulder.

"What?"

"You're going to have visitors."

She drew back and swung around to face him. "Who?"

"You have friends in town… and they want to see you."

She stared at him, mouth open, speechless. He gently coaxed her mouth closed with his fingers. "Your friends from Montreal... They are here in town to see you."

Amelie crouched beside him, placing her hand on his knee as her eyes began to fill with tears. "Really?"

"Yes, of course. You will see them very soon, my dear."

She rose up and hugged him tightly.

"I need you to do something," he continued. "But if you're uncomfortable, we won't do it—at least not now."

She nodded. "I will do it. What would you like me to do?"

He hesitated.

She asked again, "What would you like me to do?"

He sighed. "Do you think you can sit down with a police sketch artist and describe what he looked like? Only if you're…"

"Yes," Amelie interrupted, nodding. "Yes… I will do it for you."

"Thank you, Amelie. I know how difficult it is for you…"

"Could Titou still sleep with me? I sleep better with him."

Marcel grinned. "You know, Titou loves you even more than me. He's *your* baby now."

Amelie sprang up and hugged him again.

20

Titou kept barking at Amelie as she put on her makeup. It wasn't a full bark—more of a tentative half-bark. He knew she was going out. He sat beside her, staring at her. Perhaps he just wanted to come along; she couldn't tell.

She looked at him and blew him a kiss. "I promise I won't be long."

He wasn't satisfied; he barked again.

She giggled. "I'll be gone no more than a couple of hours, Titou. And when I come back, we'll go for a walk, okay?"

Titou let out a low, rumbling growl. It was a protest growl, but he wagged his tail. That was a positive sign; she knew she was making progress. Scooping him up, she pressed a kiss to his soft belly. He growled again. She chuckled.

Marcel heard the commotion from his bedroom and laughed. "You spoil him too much," he yelled out.

"I don't spoil him enough… I love him," Amelie yelled back.

He heard Madeleine in the kitchen, laughing. He cocked his semiautomatic, chambering a round, and flipped the safety on. He slipped the gun into his leg holster and drew his trousers over it.

"Are you ready?" he called out.

"One sec!" Amelie giggled.

Shaking his head, he followed the voice into the kitchen, where he found Titou sandwiched between Amelie and Madeleine, getting kisses and treats.

He shook his head. "Oh, I'm so jealous!"

Madeleine flashed a smile at him, then gave him a look—a look he'd only seen on his honeymoon or anniversary. It was a look brimming with promise. He walked up to her and kissed her, whispering in her ear, "I'll see you later, my love."

Madeleine let out a soft moan. "Mmm…"

He turned his gaze to Amelie and smiled.

"Are you two ready to go?"

Amelie returned his smile and nodded. She then hesitated and raised her eyebrows.

"Wait... What did you just say?"

Marcel shrugged. "I just asked if you two were ready to go."

"Do you mean Madeleine and me?"

He shook his head. "You and Titou."

Amelie's face lit up. "Really? He can come with me?"

He winked and nodded. From behind his back, he produced a leash and held it out to her. Titou recognized it instantly and barked. He nearly bolted out of Amelie's grasp, but she lowered him to the ground just in time.

Marcel had decided to return to the same mom-and-pop restaurant on the Seine. Flanked on one side by the river and with his backup officers covering the area's remaining perimeter, he knew he could quickly secure the spot for the girls.

He lowered his lips to the microphone hidden in his shirt collar.

"How're we looking, team? Is everything secured?"

"Yes, Inspector."

A few seconds later, another reply: "All clear, Inspector."

Amelie waved for him to join her at the table, but he waved back and said, "You have fun with your friends, dear. I need to check my emails."

She pouted her lips but eventually gave a resigned smile.

He sat at a nearby table, watching them closely. He lowered his shades to shield his eyes from the glare rising from the river. Pulling out his phone, he opened an email from Montreal police— the report from earlier that morning. It stated that the interrogation of the apprehended suspects from Cupid's Corner had yielded nothing. All the suspects mentioned a yacht and communications from Eastern Europe, but no one seemed to know anything more.

Ivan, the club manager, had been the only one with direct contact with Henri Bouchard. Marcel wished he could've been there to interrogate him. He had a strong suspicion he could've gotten more out of him. It all made sense to Marcel: keeping the crew in the dark protected the higher-ups from betrayal; if any of them were arrested, they couldn't say much if they didn't know much.

The whole thing reeked of organized crime—a well-capitalized international crime syndicate. Equally disheartening was Interpol's investigation: the license plates he'd sent them identified some of Europe and North America's most prominent politicians and businessmen, who instantly lawyered up when questioned. He felt his case slipping away from him—going cold.

His finger tapped frantically on the pack, trying to coax out a cigarette. When one finally poked out, he quickly snatched it and placed it between his lips. But when he flicked his lighter, the wind conspired and blew out the flame. He shook his head, muttering a string of profanities beneath his breath.

He felt a hand on his shoulder from behind as Amelie leaned in, her other hand setting down a plate of hors d'oeuvres in front of him.

He looked up and saw Amelie's smiling face, silhouetted by the sun, as she took the lighter from him, lit it effortlessly, and brought the flame to his cigarette. He took a drag from the cigarette, cupping her hand to shield the flame from the wind.

"Thank you, my dear."

She sat in the chair beside him, her hand on his.

"You're welcome!"

She grabbed a piece of steak and held it near the ground. He heard lapping of the tongue and the sound of chewing.

He chuckled. "Titou... You're spoiling him."

She shrugged. "I love him."

Marcel heard a murmur of giggles behind him.

Amelie chuckled and nodded at the girls. "They want to meet you."

Marcel gave a confused look, pointing to himself. "Me? Why would they want to meet me?"

"Oh, I don't know; maybe they want to thank you for rescuing them."

He tried shrugging off the compliment. "But I..."

She cut him off. "What do you think we've been sitting there talking about?"

"What? You were talking about me?"

"Yes... you. You're all we've talked about." She made a twirling motion with her fingers. "Turn around."

He lifted his glasses over his head and reluctantly spun around in his chair to look behind him. His face flushed, and he smiled and waved.

He'd been so intensely focused on protecting them that he'd never stopped to see them—and now that he had, he was struck by how beautiful and courageous they were.

After everything they'd been through, they seemed as calm and collected as anyone. They seemed content and playful, not cynical or bitter.

They waved him over, but he stayed seated in his chair, smiling and waving. One girl—a stunning redhead with pale skin and freckles—stood and walked toward him while the others giggled and whispered to each other.

"Oh, you're so done," Amelie teased. "That's Ava... You're not getting out of this now—she's Scottish!"

Ava approached Marcel with a wide smile and extended her hand without saying a word.

"You better go," Amelie cautioned. "... before the rest of them come after you."

"Alright," he said, resigned to his fate, and took Ava's hand. Without hesitation, she turned around and led him to their table as the rest of the girls pumped their fists or clapped, chanting, "Marcel... Marcel... Marcel."

He laughed and tilted his head back toward Amelie. "Are you coming?"

Amelie rose to her feet and followed, laughing. "I was having fun watching you be helpless."

Marcel frowned at her, then smiled and wagged a finger. She gave a shy giggle with her palm pressed to her mouth.

Ava sat at the table and patted the seat, gesturing for him to sit beside her. He nodded and smiled as Amelie introduced each of the girls; there were twelve, including herself. Most were European, with a couple from Asian countries—he couldn't immediately place which ones.

Only three were French; the rest were from Eastern Europe or the British Isles. Despite their smiles and cheerful façade, he knew they'd been through a nightmare.

All of them, ranging in age from nineteen to twenty-nine, were now under police protection and undergoing therapy to help them on their long road to recovery.

Taking out another cigarette, Marcel lit it, inhaling deeply. As he exhaled, his eyes narrowed at a shadowy figure through the rising smoke. A man with a pair of binoculars—watching them.

He shifted his focus away, keeping an eye on him out of the corner of his eye—he wanted to wait and make sure the man wasn't just a nature enthusiast trying to capture a pair of ducks through his lens.

But he became alarmed when a flock of geese flew by him while his binoculars remained fixed on them.

Marcel's jaw tightened. Without alarming the girls, he rose and walked to the river's edge, speaking into his microphone.

"I've got a suspicious-looking male at my 10 o'clock. He's wearing a light blue Polo shirt and jeans. He has a white hat on. He's been checking us out through his binoculars."

"I have eyes on him, Inspector. I'm heading out that way to check him out," a crackly voice rang out through his earpiece.

"That's fine. Just don't spook him, André. Get close, but don't let him see you. I'll approach him; I want to see if he runs—if he does, then take him down."

"Understood, Inspector," André replied.

"I'm heading over, too, Inspector," Claude chimed in; he and André were rookie officers recently assigned to Marcel for training.

"No, Claude! I want you to come here and stay with the girls—do not take your eyes off them! Do you understand?"

"Yes, Inspector. I'm heading to your location now. I have a visual of you now."

Marcel saw Claude running across the nearby bridge, heading toward them.

He drew Amelie aside.

"Please wait here with Claude. I'll be right back. I need to check something out. Please don't leave Claude's side—do you understand, dear?"

Amelie smiled and nodded. She appeared calm, unfazed; she'd watched him in action. She knew what he was capable of.

"My brave Amelie!" He shook his head and smiled, his arm resting on her shoulder. "And don't let this interrupt your lunch with your friends. I'll be back before you know it. I promise… and please don't worry!"

"I'm not worried," she said with a confident smile.

Marcel waited until Claude walked up, then drew him close.

"Call for backup, now! Don't wait. Tell them to dispatch a tactical team. And remember: do not take your eyes off the girls."

"Yes, Inspector."

Marcel darted a sideways glance and noticed that the man was still there, watching them. He decided to circle around and approach him from behind as André walked up in front of him.

He slowly walked off with his phone to his ear, pretending to make a call. He then turned a corner and disappeared behind the restaurant, out of his line of sight.

He'd followed the girls to the restaurant, keeping a safe distance away and monitoring their movements with his high-powered binoculars.

Suddenly, he felt anxious. He sensed something was missing from the picture—or someone. Then, it struck him that the police officer in charge had disappeared from view.

The hairs on his neck stood up. His vision suddenly got blurry. He pulled his eyes away from his binoculars and rubbed them to bring them into focus.

It took a few seconds for his eyes to adjust, and he discovered André standing directly in front of his lens. His eyes flew open, and he dropped his binoculars.

He turned to run and found himself face-to-face with Marcel. He gave Marcel a powerful shove, knocking the breath out of him, and started running across the street.

"Go after him, and I'll try to flank him," Marcel yelled. "Stay on your radio and let me know which way he's headed."

André nodded and took off after him while Marcel ran along the frontage road that followed the Seine. He had a strong feeling the suspect would head toward populated areas and try to disappear in the crowd.

Marcel was gasping for breath when André's voice crackled in his earpiece.

"Inspector, he just turned on Rue de la Huchette, heading toward Rue Xavier Privas."

"That's what I thought he'd do," he replied, panting and struggling for breath. "I'm on Rue Xavier Privas now."

The suspect was sprinting through the crowd when a woman exited one of the stores, pushing a stroller.

His eyes sprang open, and he stretched out his legs as he vaulted over the stroller, the woman's shrieks filling the air.

He cocked his head back to catch a glimpse of the woman who was still screaming at him. He'd barely turned his head back around when another obstacle appeared before him—a sweeping arm across his chest that sent him flying through the air.

He felt the barrel of the gun inside his mouth before his eyes opened. A look of horror spread across his face as he heard the hammer cock back. He could smell and taste the gunpowder residue, a telltale sign that the gun had recently fired.

Then he saw the eyes—and that's when his bladder released its contents.

"You have three seconds," Marcel growled, shoving the barrel deeper inside his mouth. "I'm only going to ask once—then you die… Who sent you?"

The man groaned, unable to speak. Marcel withdrew the barrel of the gun from his mouth and pointed it to his forehead. He didn't have to wait long for an answer.

"They called me…" He stammered. "They wanted me to follow the girls…"

"And?"

"And to…" He was unable to finish his sentence.

"Slow down… And what? What else did they want you to do?"

He paused and took a deep breath. "To report where they go… where they stay… and if there's a police escort."

Marcel instinctively knew he was telling the truth. He looked young. He'd wet his pants and was shivering—he was clearly in shock. He holstered his gun, grabbed his hands, and helped him to his feet.

"What's your name, and how old are you?" Marcel questioned him as he patted him down.

"My name is Luc… I'm twenty."

"Luc, you said you were to report to someone—how?"

"I have a phone…" He reached inside his back pocket, pulled out a flip phone, and handed it to Marcel. "They gave me this phone. They said only to use this phone."

"Who are *they*?"

Silence.

Marcel heard rapid footsteps. He turned and saw André approaching fast with his gun drawn. He raised his hand and motioned for him to slow down.

"Put the gun away," he quietly told him. "Take him to the station and book him. Let me know if he's got a record, and keep him isolated until I come in. I want to interrogate him myself." He gave the phone to André and said, "Get me the call records on this. I want to know who he's been calling."

André nodded. "Yes, inspector. Also, backup just arrived—they've secured the restaurant."

"That's a relief…" Marcel let out a sigh. "Listen, take it easy on the kid; he looks more like a victim than a perp. Stay here with him until a squad car arrives. I'm going back to check on the girls."

"Understood, sir."

Marcel patted André on the shoulder and headed back to the restaurant. He started with a slow walk but sped up to a steady jog as his imagination got the best of him—what if they attacked and overwhelmed the backup? He'd seen firsthand how organized and efficient Ivan's crew had been.

He knew the ordinary police force didn't stand a chance against them, certainly not the rookies.

He began to sprint, but his lungs started to burn. He took his pack of cigarettes from his pocket and aimed for a nearby trash can, ready to toss them. *"This isn't working out,"* he muttered to it. *"You're no good for me."*

Humor always took the edge off when he felt anxious. But then the restaurant came into view, and he saw the police cars. They'd surrounded the building. A look of relief washed over his face.

He was struck by instant remorse. *"I'm so sorry, baby..."* He looked at his cigarette pack and took one out to light it. *"I didn't mean what I said. Please forgive me!"* He kissed the pack and shoved it in his coat pocket.

Amelie spotted him and raced over. She threw her arms around him, holding him tight. Letting out a deep sigh, she pulled back and studied his face, "Did I see you talking to your cigarettes?"

Marcel shrugged. There was no sense in denying it.

"Hmm... I suppose Jaqueline can fit you into her schedule. She can always use another patient."

He laughed. "Yes, I'm sure she can."

Amelie's smile faded as the squad car slowly drove by. She slowly raised her hand to wave. Marcel followed her gaze and saw who she was waving at.

"Do you know that young man?"

She gave a slow nod and watched as the car turned the corner, then turned to face him.

"That's Luc... I do know him..."

"From where?" Marcel interrupted. "How do you know him?"

She lowered her eyes. "From..." She stammered. "From the yacht."

"Was he one of the men holding you?" Marcel asked, placing his hands on her shoulders.

She shook her head, looking distraught. "He was one of us... He was also a..."

He wrapped his arms around her. "It's all right."

"Why was he in a police car?" Amelie asked, burying her face in his chest.

He paused, then said, "He was watching you... He was watching you and your friends with his binoculars."

"They must've forced him to do it. They're..." She choked. Her eyes filled with tears.

A female police officer approached; he waved her off.

"Was he your friend?" Marcel asked.

She nodded, sniffling. "He was very nice to me... He had a drug problem... He was addicted to heroin and other drugs. They gave him drugs in exchange for..." She couldn't finish.

"Listen to me," Marcel cut in. "You don't have to worry about him. We'll get him some help."

"Can I see him?"

"Yes, of course you can," Marcel replied without hesitation.

His gut feeling was right: Luc was a victim, not a perp. He was just a kid—just like Amelie.

21

After dropping Amelie off at his place, Marcel drove to the police station to interrogate Luc. He needed more information but regretted roughing him up. Dialing the station, he asked André to remove Luc from isolation and bring him to his office.

"By the way, he has no criminal history, no prior arrests… no run-ins with the law," André added.

"How about his phone? Did you get his call records?" Marcel inquired.

"No, sir… It's a burner phone—can't trace it and no records."

"All right. I just pulled into the station. I'll talk to him."

Marcel caught a glimpse of Luc through the large glass window of his office, sitting with his head bowed. He knocked as he entered, not wanting to startle him.

"Hello, Luc," he said with a smile before taking a seat across from him.

Luc offered a slight wave but didn't smile or speak.

"I have some good news for you, Luc."

Luc nodded tentatively. "I'm not going to prison?"

"No, I don't think so… and that's not the good news."

Silence. Luc simply stared at him.

"Do you know a girl named Amelie?"

Luc's eyes widened. "Saunier? Amelie Saunier?"

"Yes. Do you know her?"

Luc's face softened. "She's a good friend—why?"

"She's looking forward to seeing you."

"Really? Where is she?"

"At home."

Luc's eyebrows furrowed. "At her parents'?"

"At mine."

Luc hesitated, studying Marcel as if waiting for the punchline.

"She's staying with my wife and me," Marcel explained, watching as a small smile broke across Luc's face.

"If it's all right, I'll ask you a few questions, and then we can leave."

"Leave?" Luc echoed.

"To go see Amelie."

Marcel had seen it all before. He watched Luc nervously shake his legs, his fingers tugging at the corners of a newspaper on the sofa beside him—clear signs of drug withdrawal.

"Do you like to read the newspaper?" Marcel asked.

Luc shook his head. "I just like the puzzles."

"You do?" Marcel leaned in, intrigued.

Luc nodded. "I noticed someone started the puzzle in this newspaper but stopped."

Marcel raised his hand. "That was me. I love puzzles, but some of them are tough."

"Mm-hmm… This one wasn't easy."

Marcel stood and walked over to him. "May I see the paper?"

Luc tilted his head and nodded at the paper. "It's your paper."

Marcel picked it up, his eyes fixed on Luc. He smiled as he thumbed through the pages until he reached the puzzle. His eyebrows shot up as he studied it, shooting a skeptical look at Luc.

"Did you finish this puzzle?"

Luc nodded. "I did, but like I said, it wasn't easy."

"Yet you finished it in minutes."

Luc shrugged dismissively. "I do them all the time. You get good after a while."

Marcel shook his head. "I've been doing them for years, but I could never finish one this fast."

"Well, you'd already done some of it."

Marcel chuckled, having barely made a dent before giving up. He sat beside Luc, crossed his legs, and began questioning him.

It quickly became clear that Luc was gay. He revealed that as an orphan, he'd bounced from one foster home to another until he could live independently. Eventually, he made a living through modeling, often nude for gay magazines.

Luc was strikingly handsome and intelligent—blonde with hazel eyes, a slim physique, high cheekbones, a square jaw, and a perfectly straight nose. However, red spots dotted his veins—clear signs he'd been shooting up.

He recounted a night at a gay bar where he met a man who invited him to a party on his yacht.

"He was nice at first. I stayed with him for a few months," Luc recalled. "But later... he became a monster."

"Monster, how?" Marcel pressed.

"He became mean. I needed..." Luc hesitated, reluctant to incriminate himself further.

"Needed what? Drugs?" Marcel prodded. "Don't worry. You can tell me—I'm only trying to help you."

Luc nodded. "By the time I met him, I was hooked on heroin. I needed regular fixes." He began to pace, glancing at Marcel for a read.

"Go on."

"He knew I needed my fix... and he'd play games with me. He asked me to do things... and when I didn't, he'd get mad—real mad. He'd hurt me." He stopped pacing and sank into the sofa. "When I threatened to leave, he pointed to the door and yelled, 'Go! Get out of here.' He knew I wouldn't go... I couldn't."

Marcel inhaled deeply. "So now, he expects you to follow people and spy on them?"

Luc rubbed his arm. "Not him. I haven't seen him in months. He kicked me out. He has other people running his circus."

"Do you know where the yacht is?"

Luc shook his head. "They take people out at night. The yacht is always anchored miles offshore. You can't even see the shore."

Marcel studied him. "Why do you keep helping them?

Luc shrugged. "Because they hook me up."

Marcel apologized to Luc after the questioning. "I didn't mean to be so aggressive. The last people who showed up looking for Amelie had semiautomatic guns and…"

"Don't worry about it, I get it." Luc paused, then added, "But I could use a shower and a fresh pair of pants." He lowered his eyes, gesturing to his bottoms. "They gave me this to wear when I was in the cell—I wouldn't want to be seen dead in these!"

Marcel pressed his lips together, suppressing a smile. "I'll take you home to shower and get your clothes."

"Get my clothes?"

Marcel nodded. "They'll come looking for you. I'll take you to where the rest of the girls are."

"The rest of the girls?"

Marcel described his ongoing investigation into human trafficking and efforts to capture those involved and dismantle their operation. He told Luc about the other girls in Montreal—how they'd been rescued and were housed in a secure location under police protection.

"Those were the girls you saw today. Did you know any of them?"

Luc shook his head. "Only Amelie. I met her on the yacht." He paused, looking away. "He was so mean to her... He was mean to all the girls... but particularly to Amelie because she wouldn't…"

Marcel's jaw clenched. "Did he have a name?"

Luc saw the look on Marcel's face—the same one he'd seen hours earlier when a gun barrel was jammed in his mouth.

"His name was Henri... Henri Bouchard."

22

He parked his car a quarter mile away and hiked up the mound to avoid contaminating the soil or impacting the terrain. His rigid posture and sharp movements screamed military, while his red hair and mustache lent him the rugged charm of a Highland Scot.

He was the first to arrive at the site; his years in the service had ingrained punctuality in him. Growing up in Newcastle, he knew the area like the back of his hand, and after retiring from the army, he had worked in security. Out of all the candidates Claire had interviewed, he was by far the most qualified for the job.

He stood at the edge of the excavation site, studying every visible entry and exit point, marking the coordinates on his GPS device. The sun had barely peeked over the horizon when he heard the trailer door creak open behind him and footsteps approaching.

"You must be Peter," a soft voice called out.

He turned around with a smile. "Good morning!" He extended a hand. "Yes, I'm Peter... Peter Jenkins... and you must be Claire. I recognize you from our Zoom meeting."

"Guilty as charged." Claire smiled and shook his hand. "Welcome aboard, Peter."

"Thank you, Claire. It's a pleasure to meet you in person."

Another voice chimed in. "Good morning!" Jane approached, a coffee mug in one hand and a cigarette between her lips.

"Good morning, Jane," Claire replied, smiling. "Please meet Peter."

With a nod, Jane exhaled a thin stream of smoke. "Hello, Peter."

Peter waved and smiled. "Hello, Jane. It's nice to meet you."

"Jane is my right-hand person," Claire said, turning to Peter. "When I'm not around, she can help you with anything."

"Absolutely, I understand," Peter acknowledged, continuing to survey his surroundings.

Claire gestured toward the excavation site.

"So, what do you think, Peter? Can we secure this place?"

"It looks very manageable... May I explore and catch up with you later?"

"Yes—please take your time and let me know your recommendations."

Jane sat at her laptop, wearing earphones and swaying her shoulders to the music as she entered budget data into her spreadsheet. Claire watched her out of the corner of her eye while slipping on her jeans and T-shirt, preparing to head out to the dig site. She couldn't shake the thought of the bruise on Jane's arm—she considered bringing it up again but hesitated. Jane caught her gaze and smiled.

Claire mouthed, "Hi."

Jane yelled back, "Hi."

Claire laughed.

With music blasting in her ears, Jane seemed oblivious to her own volume.

She removed her earphones, grinning.

"What's so funny?"

"You were yelling."

Jane laughed. "I'm sorry." She motioned to her ears. "I couldn't hear myself."

Claire waved. "Don't worry. Go back to your music."

"All right... Have fun out there... Bring back lots of shiny things."

Claire chuckled. "I will."

Jane put her earphones back on, quirking her lips and swaying her shoulders as she waved goodbye to Claire.

Claire heard a commotion outside. She waved to Jane and exited the trailer.

Sharon saw her approach and nodded.

"Great timing! I think we've got something."

As Claire got closer, she saw Sharon crouched over something protruding from the ground as the excavation crew cleared the soil around it. Sharon noticed the puzzled expression on Claire's face and smiled.

She grabbed a brush and began sweeping the residual debris away from the object. It took a few meticulous strokes of a toothbrush before Claire could clearly see what she was looking at—the mouth of a large earthen vessel.

Her heart raced. She took a trowel and started to scrape away the dirt covering its opening. A lump of earth fell to the floor and rolled on the ground, all eyes following it until it came to rest on its side, flashing a golden glow.

Claire gasped. She bent down, picked up the object, and turned it over in her palm, examining it closely.

"What is it, Claire?" Sharon asked.

"Yeah, what is it?" Jane echoed, having heard the ruckus, and ran over to see what was happening.

Claire freed the coin from its clay bed and held it up. It read, "IMP... CAESAR... HADRIANVS... AVG."

"It's a gold aureus," Claire beamed. "It's a coin of Emperor Hadrian."

Sharon removed the remaining soil from the amphora's opening. She reached inside and scooped a handful of coins, jiggling them in her palm.

"Correction," she said triumphantly. "It's a jar full of gold coins."

"It's party time!" Jane raved.

"Maybe for you, Jane," Sharon shot back, shifting to one side and motioning to an amphora handle sticking out of the ground behind her.

Jane's eyes widened, and her mouth fell open.

"I'm going to be here all night," Sharon continued. "I'm not leaving this site until we've scoped everything out and removed all these jars." She nodded at Eve, her assistant, who was also her niece. "Hey, sweetheart, would you text Arnold and tell him to hop on over here and bring his GPR?"

"GPR?" Eve asked, puzzled.

Sharon chuckled. "I'm sorry, my fault; I forgot to mention some of our cool toys: GPR stands for Ground Penetrating Radar—that's how we take a peek underground before we start digging."

Eve nodded and smiled as she typed the message to Arnold. She hit "Send" and turned the screen toward Sharon.

"Done!"

"Good job! Now, let's bring out the work lights," Sharon said, clapping her hands. "We're going to need them tonight… Let's get ahead of the game."

"And if we get everything dug up before the weekend, we're going to town to celebrate," Claire added. "I'm so proud of you all."

"Yay!" Jane pumped her fists in the air. "We love going to town, don't we, ladies?"

Sharon laughed and gave a lukewarm nod. Eve kept her head down; she'd only recently started working and didn't want to seem too eager for time off.

Claire chuckled. "Don't worry, Jane; I love going to town myself. I'm sure it'll be well earned by the weekend."

Jane flashed a smile and wrinkled her nose.

Arnold shook his head in disbelief as he stared at the GPR display unit, sweat droplets falling onto the screen. He wiped his brow with his hand towel and sank into the lawn chair Eve had brought out for him. She handed him a water bottle; he unscrewed the top and gulped it down in one go.

Jane stepped in and tried to make out the shapes on the GPR screen. She wrinkled her brow and shot a quizzical look at Arnold.

He smirked. "It's a confusing mess, ain't it?"

Jane nodded. She pointed to the screen. "What are all these squiggly lines?"

Arnold laughed. "Those squiggly things are called hyperbolas... They're generated when the GPR detects an object."

"There are lots of hyper... hyperboles."

"Hyperbolas," Arnold corrected her. "And yes, that's because there are many objects under the ground—at least that's what the GPR is telling us."

"You know what that means, Jane?" Sharon asked.

"It means y'all are going to be very busy," Arnold interjected.

Sharon nodded at Arnold. "What he said."

Arnold stood and gestured for Jane to take his seat. "Please, sit... Let me explain."

Jane smiled and took a seat. "You're a gentleman. Thank you, Arnold."

Sharon and Claire huddled around as Arnold gave Jane a detailed interpretation of what the GPR was indicating. "I'm seeing objects... different-sized objects in tightly packed clusters as if they were arranged or stored. Then there are intersecting walls—rooms, perhaps."

He ran his fingers through his long, black hair and took a deep breath with his eyes shut. He pulled a rubber band from his pocket and tied his hair into a ponytail. Letting out a sigh, he continued.

"Ladies... I see a settlement here." He stamped his foot on the ground. "Right beneath our feet... and it's a large one. This isn't just a fort... or a solitary outpost... This is a massive settlement."

"How massive?" Jane asked.

Arnold arched his brow and shrugged. "Let's put it this way." He nodded at the river below. "It seems to extend off your grid here... all the way down to the river."

"Wow!" Jane exclaimed. "That's big."

"Yeah, wow... It's the biggest I've ever come across."

"And it's consistent with what Lucius wrote in his postcard to Cara," Claire added excitedly.

Jane gave a skeptical look. "But he only mentioned a road."

"Hang on. I have it right here." Claire pulled up a photo of the tablet on her phone.

"Here, I've got it... It says, 'The Emperor wants me to expand our defenses... and build a road south to the river... He wants me to construct additional fortifications on the north side to protect us from marauding Caledonian tribes.'"

"Hmm..." Jane pressed a finger against her lips, furrowing her brow as she searched for answers. "I see... He meant to say, expand the defenses and build a road."

Claire snapped her fingers. "Precisely, Jane! And that's exactly what he did."

"Aren't you all getting ahead of yourselves?" Sharon interrupted. "I mean, you're reaching all these conclusions from a silly scanner."

Arnold arched his brow and scoffed. "Silly scanner? This machine is a..."

"I'm just messing with you, Arnold." Sharon chuckled, waving a hand. "I didn't mean it like that. I'm just old school. I think we need to confirm by putting the shovel to the dirt."

Arnold waved back. "Ah, don't worry about it. I know what you meant... But let's put it this way, whatever it is..." He shook his head. "It's big... It's damn big... It's the largest thing I've ever scoped out with my silly scanner."

Sharon laughed. "You're never going to let me live my silly scanner comment down, are you?"

"Nope." Arnold chuckled.

The diesel generator rumbled in the darkness, powering the work lights illuminating the area. The crew worked tirelessly through the night, extracting the last of the visible amphorae.

Jane had retired for the night, exhausted from the day's excitement. Claire and Sharon stood by, supervising to ensure the artifacts were protected as they were lowered into crates lined with thick bubble wrap and foam or stored in acid-free archival boxes and envelopes.

A shadowy figure emerged on top of the mound. Blinded by the lights, Sharon raised her hand to her brow, squinting to see who was approaching.

"Who is that?" she yelled out.

The figure waved. "It's me, Peter. Sorry, I didn't mean to startle you."

Peter smiled as he drew closer. He nodded at the crates.

"I see you've been busy."

"Terribly!" Claire shot back. "How about you?"

"Busy."

Claire raised a brow. "You were out there for quite a while."

Peter nodded. "I surveyed the entire perimeter—from the river in the south to the northern boundary of your gridlines. I think I covered the whole area."

Claire shook her head and folded her arms across her chest.

"You're going to need to expand your perimeter." She motioned toward the GPR, sitting idly beside a mound of earth. "You see that odd-looking machine over there?"

Peter cocked his head to look. "Yes."

"That's ground penetrating radar." She motioned to Arnold, who was nodding off in a chair. "And he's our radar expert. He's been pushing that thing around all day, scanning the terrain. He tells us there are many more objects underground, including artifacts and structures like walls or rooms. He believes this is a large settlement, not just an outpost or fort. We also have corroborating correspondences from that period indicating that the site went through a period of expansion.”

“That’s wonderful; you must be excited.”

Claire gave a half-smile. “Excited and concerned. These are precious artifacts, but I worry more about my staff’s safety.”

“Of course. I understand. I'll bring in a couple more guards—former military personnel like myself. I’m confident we’ll be fine.”

Claire turned to Sharon; she nodded. “I think that’ll work.”

“Thanks, Sharon!” Claire smiled and ran her palm down Sharon’s arm. “Let’s get these crates over to the warehouse and call it a day; I’m sure you’re exhausted.”

Claire directed her attention to Peter. “You can follow Sharon to our warehouse in Newcastle. There’s an office and a separate room with a lavatory and shower for overnight stays. We also have a nightwatchman, but he’s not armed. With all the precious artifacts, we’ll need at least one armed guard staying the night.”

“Absolutely! I wouldn’t have it any other way.”

“Do you need us to provide any, um…”

Peter chuckled. “No, thank you, ma’am.” He drew his coat flap to one side, revealing his gun holster. “You can’t be in this business without proper equipment.”

23

With the constant hum of generators finally silenced and the staff retired to their trailers for the night, Claire closed her eyes and took a deep breath, a smile creeping across her face. Opening her eyes, she saw the moon peeking from behind the clouds, bathing the landscape in light.

She felt transported back in time, imagining the settlement at night, with the Roman garrison huddled around campfires and oil lamps burning inside homes as families gathered for dinner. Another light flickered before her eyes, pulling her back to the present—the light from her trailer.

Claire knocked before entering, not wanting to startle Jane. She turned the knob and entered quietly.

"Hey, you! Why aren't you sleeping?"

Jane shrugged her shoulders and grinned as she lay sprawled on her belly, scrolling through her phone.

"Can't."

Claire chuckled. "Why can't you?"

Jane giggled. "Because I need you to read to me."

Claire had grown fond of Jane's playful antics. She had secretly hoped to be awake when she returned to the trailer. She smiled as she flung herself onto her bed. Jane lay on the bed opposite hers.

"Come on, then," she motioned with a finger for Jane to come to her.

Jane dashed over and hurled herself on Claire's bed, almost knocking her off. She threw her arms around her, catching her just in time.

"I'm so sorry!" She gasped. "I didn't mean to bounce you off the bed."

Claire burst into hysterical laughter.

"Oh, Jane… That's not the immediate problem." Still laughing, she darted toward the restroom. "I think I tinkled. Stay right there. I'll be right back."

When Claire returned, she avoided eye contact with Jane—she knew she'd laugh uncontrollably if she looked at her. She grabbed her phone and reclined on the bed beside her, scrolling through her photos of the tablets. She found one that indicated Lucius was in Egypt.

She began reading. "The Emperor has sent me to Alexandria… I am to report to him about the grain harvest."

Claire paused to explain the importance of Egyptian grain to Rome. "Egypt was a vital grain supplier to Rome, so much so that it was considered Rome's breadbasket."

"Mmm… I love bread," Jane interrupted, grinning. "I've got massive munchies. Do we have any?"

Claire laughed. "Yes, we do. Would you like some?"

Jane gave an enthusiastic nod.

"Fine… Let's turn this into a learning opportunity."

Claire got up from the bed and strolled over to the makeshift kitchen they'd set up inside the trailer. Jane heard the sounds of cabinets opening and closing. A few minutes later, Claire returned with a plate of sliced bread and butter.

Jane sat up with an eager grin.

"Yum! A breadbasket—that looks so good; I'm starving."

"Wait, recline on your side," Claire said, gesturing with a finger. "On your left side."

Jane reclined on her side, smiling.

Claire placed the plate on the bed and lay down, facing her.

"This is how Roman ate. They reclined on their left side."

"Why did they lie on their left side?" Jane bit into a slice of bread, closing her eyes as she let out a moan. "Mmm… This is the best bread I've ever tasted."

Claire chuckled. She picked up a slice of bread and sniffed it. "And it smells so good." She took a bite before answering. "The

Romans laid on their left side because they believed it helped their digestion. They'd recline on couches in their dining room, known as a Triclinium, as their servants—mostly slaves—brought them multiple food courses."

Jane rolled her eyes. "God… to lay there and have slaves dote on you—it's disgusting!"

"Yes, but bear in mind that life was harsh and brutal back then. Roman soldiers served 25 years in the military and were often away from their families for years. So, when they could, they indulged themselves."

"Yeah, I'm sure they did." She shook her head and furrowed her brow. "That's a long time for a man to be away—I bet they cheated on their wives, came home, beat them up, knocked them up, and then left again for a few more years."

Claire noticed a sudden shift in Jane—a change in her demeanor and facial expression. Her brow wrinkled as she spoke in a low, deep voice. Claire had witnessed Jane react with hostility towards men, but there had always been a reason: a provocation, usually by some drunk at a bar, someone who couldn't take no for an answer.

Something had struck a nerve. Claire wanted to ask but knew now wasn't the time. She picked up her phone and continued where she'd left off, trying to change the subject.

"'The grain harvest has been bountiful this year,' Lucius writes. 'The gods favor us.'"

She continued to read the Latin text. She paused and placed her hand on Jane's. "Listen to this: 'We captured a grave robber... In his possession, we found a likeness of Queen Cleopatra made of gold. I shall bring it home when I return from Alexandria... a gift for you, my love. I adore you. I miss you terribly."

Jane stopped chewing and swallowed. She placed the bread plate on the nightstand and nuzzled Claire's shoulder.

"I like this part... a lot... Will you please read more?"

"All right… Give us a sec.," Claire said with a playful tone, sifting through the photos on her phone.

Jane giggled.

Claire's lips curled into a smile at Jane's laugh. She continued scrolling until she came across something that captured her attention.

"Gosh, this is so interesting!"

Jane peeked over Claire's shoulder to catch a glimpse of her phone screen.

"What's interesting? Will you please translate the scribbles?"

Claire laughed. "All right, here's what the scribbles say: 'My beloved, today I stood and gazed at the great lighthouse…' He means the Pharos lighthouse in Alexandria."

"That's sweet… He calls her his beloved," Jane cut in, ignoring the Seventh Wonder of the Ancient World.

Claire didn't mind—anything to get her out of her dark place and into the light. She smiled and nodded. "His wife's name, Cara, means beloved or dear in Latin. He begins his letter with 'Cara mea.' It could mean, 'My Cara' or 'My beloved.'"

"I think he means both," Jane said in a soft tone brimming with emotion.

"Why do you think that?"

"Because it's obvious he's crazy about her. He writes to her every chance he gets. He brings her gifts."

Claire felt a wave of warmth wash over her. She was ecstatic that Jane had come around. She couldn't bear to see her so consumed by cynicism.

"You know, Jane, there are decent men out there," she said reassuringly.

Jane nodded. "I know… I just wish there were more of them out there—more men like Lucius."

Claire smiled and continued reading to Jane. "'I watched the great flame guide the ships into the harbor…' He's writing about the lighthouse beacon guiding ships into the harbor of Alexandria.

He goes on to describe the types of vessels: 'I can see warships, merchant ships, and cargo ships. They sail in and out of the harbor day and night.'"

She paused and pinched the screen, zooming in on the text.

"Huh," she murmured.

"Huh, what?"

"Naves Piraticae…"

"English, please."

"Pirate ships—he says the prefect of Egypt has asked him to hunt down the Cilician pirates that were disrupting commerce in the region."

Claire stood and paced, reading and mumbling in Latin. Jane tried to ask a question, but Claire raised a finger to hush her. Jane grabbed her cigarette pack, flicked it with a finger, and coaxed one out.

She took the cigarette and placed it between her lips. She brought the lighter to her lips but then froze.

"Uh-uh," Claire said, wagging a finger. She nodded at the door. "Do that outside."

Jane laughed and flung the cigarette in the air.

"I don't wanna go outside. How about a drink? Will you drink with me?"

Claire absentmindedly nodded, her eyes still glued to her phone.

Jane hopped out of bed and hurried to the kitchen. She took a bottle of vodka from the cabinet but spotted another bottle with a pirate image on the label. She wasn't crazy about rum, but she liked the bottle.

She put away the vodka, grabbed the new bottle, and strolled back, humming, "Yo ho, ho, and a bottle of rum."

She returned to find Claire engrossed in her reading. She held the bottle beside her face, with the label facing out, singing, "Fifteen men on a dead man's chest…"

Claire broke out into hysterical laughter.

"Oh, Jane!"

"What? I'm a pirate."

With a belly full of bread soaking up the alcohol, Jane needed a couple more shots to calm herself enough to sit still and listen to Claire. Claire didn't want to keep up with Jane, so she limited herself to one drink. She continued to pace, with her gaze fixed on her phone screen.

Jane tried to give her a refill, but Claire covered the shot glass with her palm and, with a smile, said, "No, thank you."

Jane twisted the cap back on the bottle and pouted. When that didn't get a reaction, she let out a sigh, letting Claire know she could no longer be ignored.

"So, tell me, whatcha been reading about? You've been pacing back and forth for a bit now. What did Lucius do?"

Claire sank into the bed beside her.

"Well, he followed his orders; he set out with three Roman warships in the middle of the night and hunted down the pirates."

"Ooh… That sounds exciting!"

Claire chuckled. "I'm sure it was... It didn't take long for him to find the pirates; they were sheltering in a nearby cove. Lucius ordered his men to row quietly until they got close and then ordered them to speed up and ram the pirate ships."

"Ram them? How?"

"Roman ships had protruding rams covered in bronze on the bow of their warships. When the rowers were given the signal, they'd row hard and fast and ram into the sides of enemy ships, disabling or sinking them. But on this night, they didn't have to destroy all the ships—only one. The rest surrendered."

"So what happened to them?"

Claire shrugged. "Who knows? They would have been enslaved or executed. Lucius doesn't say anything about that in his writing. Remember, he's writing to his wife; I'm sure he left out the gory details."

"Hmm… You're right."

"But that's not the end of the story."

Jane gazed at her with curiosity. "There's more?"

Claire nodded. "Lot's more… What are pirates known for?"

"Arrgh?"

Claire laughed. "Cute—what else?"

Jane shrugged.

Claire scoffed. "Booty, Jane!"

Jane giggled. "They like butts?"

"Treasure, Jane! Treasure!"

"Oh my god! Lucius found treasure?"

"Lucius *confiscated* the treasure... from the pirates."

Jane laughed. "I know… I'm only teasing. So how much shiny stuff did he confiscate?"

"A ton… Let me have him tell you himself."

Jane nodded. She sat up and hugged a pillow, grinning. "I'm ready. Go ahead."

Claire opened the photo app on her phone and found the tablet.

"… The pirates did not put up any resistance. The cove and our ships hemmed them in. One of the ships was filled with gold coins and statues... golden busts of Greek rulers of Alexandria... a magnificent golden bust of Serapis wearing a crown."

"Oh my god, this is so fascinating," Jane gushed. "I wish I were there to see it all."

Claire smiled. "And you still may, Jane."

Jane's eyes widened. "What do you mean?"

"Let me finish the story, and you'll find out—we haven't gotten to the best part yet."

Jane nodded, clutching her pillow tighter.

Claire winked at Jane and continued. "... When I interrogated the ship's captain, he revealed that they had looted the treasures from the royal tomb of..."

She paused and glanced up from her phone. "You ready?"

Jane nodded vigorously. "Yes!"

Claire flashed a sly grin as she widened the image on her phone with her fingers and turned the screen towards her.

"What does this say?"

Jane drew close and squinted. She gasped, and her jaw dropped. She flung the pillow, took the phone from Claire's hand, and stared at it in disbelief.

"What does it say?" Claire asked once more, grinning.

"Alexa…" Jane stammered. "It says, 'Alexandri.'"

"Sepulcrum Alexandri… Alexander's tomb!" Claire said with a triumphant smile. "Under interrogation, the pirate captain revealed he'd taken the treasure from Alexander's tomb."

"Did he find his..."

Claire shook her head and reached for her phone. "Here, let me read it to you."

Jane handed Claire her phone, and she continued reading.

"The captain insisted that the tomb was empty when he found it. I believe him. He was very convincing, as was I. He told tales of an oasis in the desert... a bearded god with horns... and a temple... the true burial place of Alexander."

Jane tilted her and gave a confused look. "Bearded god with horns?"

Claire nodded. "Do you remember the conversation with Callum?"

"Yes—which part?"

"The part about the temple of Zeus Ammon."

"Yes—vaguely. But what does that have to do with a bearded god with horns?"

"Well, the pirate captain seems to be talking about a temple in the desert and a bearded god with horns..."

"Yeah, okay…"

"Jane, he's most likely talking about Zeus Ammon, which depicts Zeus, a Greek god, as the bearded man with the horns of the Egyptian deity, Ammon… Perhaps someone saw a bust or statue of Zeus Ammon at the temple, and the oasis must be the

Siwa Oasis in the desert. Maybe it's all tall tales from drunken pirates; maybe it's not."

Jane's face lit up. "Does this mean Callum..."

Claire nodded vigorously. "Callum will definitely want to know about this. It could confirm his theory that Alexander is, in fact, buried in the temple of Zeus Ammon."

Jane felt overwhelmed. It'd been a long day. She reached for the bread plate, grabbed a piece of bread, and began chewing.

"And that's not all," Claire went on. "The treasure... all the gold... it was all shipped here."

Jane paused mid-chew. "What?"

Claire nodded. "You heard me right. According to these writings, he shipped everything home to Cara. It's all buried here. It's all around us."

Jane swallowed. "Was he allowed to do that?"

"I doubt it… He could've faced severe punishment or even death if he took all that treasure and didn't report it to the Emperor."

"All those blips Arnold picked up on his radar—that's all buried treasure?"

"We'll soon find out, won't we?"

Claire couldn't shut off her brain. A smile formed on her lips as she lay in bed, reading Lucius' correspondence—his intimate letters, his postcards to Cara.

She glanced at Jane lying beside her; she'd dozed off with a half-eaten slice of bread in her hand and crumbs on her lips. A chill wind blew through a crack in the window, and Claire spotted goosebumps on Jane's arm.

She got up, closed the window, and came around to Jane's side of bed. She took the bread from Jane's hand and noticed that the bruise on her arm had healed. She drew the blanket over her.

Claire didn't believe Jane when she said she got the bruise from running into her bathroom door—the bathroom door wouldn't leave finger marks. But she didn't want to pry; Jane would have to tell her what really happened if and when she was ready.

She sat at her desk and wrote a letter to Callum detailing the recent events and findings, including the artifacts they'd dug up at the site and the revelations about Alexander's final resting place.

She decided she'd call him in the morning, but phone reception was spotty at best at the dig site, so she opened her laptop and emailed him the same information. It was overkill, but she wanted to make sure he got the information.

She closed her laptop and returned to bed, yawning. She gave a slight chuckle when she heard Jane snoring and slowly drifted off to sleep.

When Claire heard the sound, it was still pitch-black outside. In the dark, she reached for her phone on the nightstand and tapped the screen to bring it to life. She checked the time: it was 3 a.m. It was too early, and she was too tired.

She thought she'd imagined the sound or perhaps dreamt it. Shaking off the unease, she set her phone back down and turned over in bed. She felt Jane's warm breath on her face and smiled. She'd barely drifted off to sleep when she heard it again. This time, it was right in front of her; Jane was whimpering in her sleep.

Claire wanted to wake her up, but then Jane stopped. She thought she heard her utter a name, but she couldn't be sure—she was too tired, and things were too hazy.

24

"Stop... lay down," Amelie pleaded as Titou's wet tongue painted her face, though she secretly enjoyed the licks. She stuck her hand out from beneath the blanket and grabbed him, pulling him under. "Now, you're done. You're going to stay with me for a bit; I have another thirty minutes before I have to get up." Titou didn't mind; he now had her entire face and neck to lick. Thirty minutes flew by quickly—a knock on the door.

"Bonjour, princess! Are you awake?" Marcel called out.

Her eyes darted at Titou, wagging his tail.

"Don't tell Marcel I'm in here."

"Princess?" Marcel knocked again.

Titou tilted his head and let out a single "woof."

"All right, I'm getting up," she giggled and pointed a finger at Titou. "But it's your fault; you couldn't keep quiet."

Titou gave another head tilt and wagged his tail. Amelie laughed and yelled, "I'm up. I'll be ready in a few minutes."

"Fantastic! We'll go to lunch after the appointment, okay?"

"Okay!"

She slipped on the customized black T-shirt Madeleine had bought her, with "I love Titou" written in rhinestones on the front. She then squeezed into the ripped jeans, put on her high-tops, and hopped in front of the mirror.

She applied some mascara and lipstick and ran out of her room with Titou trailing behind. Stopping at the kitchen entrance, she stretched out her arms and said, "Voila!"

Madeleine was busy gathering her cake ingredients and measuring the flour and sugar when she spotted Amelie. She held out her arms, grinning, and Amelie walked into them.

Madeleine kissed her on the cheek. Marcel was on the balcony, gazing at the Paris skyline. He spun around, took the cigarette from his lips, and stubbed it in the ashtray. He clapped and said, "Beautiful! I love that shirt."

Madeleine brought her lips to Amelie's ear and whispered, "I don't want you to be nervous about this, all right?" She drew back to make sure Amelie acknowledged her words by looking into her eyes. "Everything will be fine."

Amelie smiled and nodded. Madeleine kissed her again. "See you when you get back. I'm baking your favorite cake!"

"Mille-feuille?"

Madeleine nodded.

"Yay!" Amelie threw her arms around Madeleine. "Thank you, Madeleine... and thank you so much for the blingy shirt. I love it!"

Madeleine winked and smiled. "You're so welcome!"

It was a short drive across the Seine to the police station. Marcel noticed Amelie wringing her hands and clutching her knees.

"Don't worry, sweetheart. This'll be quick."

Amelie kept her eyes fixed ahead, her lips slightly curled into a forced smile. She nodded.

Marcel pulled into his parking spot at the police station and shut off the engine. "Just take deep breaths and relax. If this upsets you, we can stop. I'll be sitting right next to you. The lady you're going to meet is a friend of mine. She's wonderful and super talented—you'll see."

Amelie took a deep breath and let out a sigh. "All right."

Inside the station, a woman in her mid-thirties sat in the waiting room. She had black hair with a pixie cut and wore a black pantsuit over a white V-neck blouse and black pumps—she looked like an older version of Amelie.

When she saw Marcel, she stood and extended a hand, smiling.

"Hello, Inspector!"

Marcel shook her hand, then hugged her. "Come on—call me by my name; we've only known each other for how long?"

Sophie blushed and nodded. "I'm sorry, Marcel... I didn't mean to be so formal."

Marcel winked at her, then turned to Amelie. "Amelie, please meet Sophie," he said, motioning to her. "Her father is a dear friend of mine. When I started this job, he taught me everything I know."

Sophie turned her attention to Amelie and smiled. "It's wonderful to meet you, Amelie. I've heard a lot about you." She offered her hand, and Amelie smiled as she shook it.

Sophie could sense Amelie's nervousness; her reticence and shy smile spoke volumes.

"Look, Amelie, I know this is uncomfortable for you, but we're just going to sit and draw a picture together," she said, trying to soothe Amelie's anxiety. "You've drawn pictures before, haven't you?"

"I have," Amelie replied.

"Well, a composite sketch is just like drawing a picture—the same idea, I mean. But the difference is that you'll tell me what to draw, and I'll draw it. See what I mean?"

Amelie gave a nod.

The room was windowless and overly bright, with fluorescent lighting and bare walls, giving it a cold, impersonal feel. A drawing pad, a pencil, and three bottles of water sat on the table. Sophie took a chair opposite Amelie and Marcel, grabbed her pencil, and smiled.

"Let's start with the outline of the face... Did he have a square or rounded jawline?"

"Square, I guess," Amelie replied, trying to visualize the face. She watched as Sophie's pencil glided effortlessly across the blank page.

"What about the nose? Was it straight or curved? ... narrow or wide?"

"Straight... and narrow."

"The ears—did they look normal or stick out?"

"Normal..."

"How about the lips? Did he have thin or full lips?"

"Normal... Thin, not full."

Amelie watched the broad outlines of a face appear on the page—then, with swift and precise strokes of the pencil, a nose, ears, and lips. Sophie turned the pad around and showed it to Amelie.

"How does this look so far?"

Amelie gazed at the sketch and nodded. "It's good."

"What about the hair length: short, medium, or long?"

"Short..."

"Above the ears or longer?"

"Above the ears."

"What about the eyes? The eyes are very important, Amelie; please focus."

Marcel kept his gaze fixed on Amelie, watching her grow agitated as she shifted in her chair and clutched the armrest tightly, trying to answer the question. He opened a bottle of water and handed it to her.

"Take slow, deep breaths."

Amelie smiled at Marcel, took the bottle, and sipped it. She inhaled deeply and exhaled.

"Would you like to stop or take a break?" He asked.

She shook her head. She then shifted her gaze to Sophie.

"Let's finish this."

"Brave Amelie!" Marcel muttered. "I'm so proud of you!"

Amelie took another deep breath and exhaled slowly. She then went on to describe the eyes. "He had a stare... a wide-eyed stare... He didn't blink much." She raised a finger to her brow. "And he had a thin scar across his left eyebrow... He had thick eyebrows."

Sophie nodded as she listened to Amelie and added the final touches to the picture.

"You're doing great, Amelie. This is very helpful. Anything else you can think of?"

Amelie paused to recall the image in her mind, then added, "He always wore ear hoops."

"Small ear hoops or large?"

"Small... small, thin ones."

"On one ear or both?"

"Both."

When Sophie finished, she spun her sketchpad around and slid it across the table to Amelie.

"Does this look close?"

Amelie's eyebrows knitted into a frown as she stared at the picture, her fingers clawing at the armrest. She looked up at Sophie and nodded.

"That's him."

Marcel drew the sketchbook close and stared at the image—it was a face he'd never forget.

Amelie was silent during lunch, picking at her food and gazing aimlessly out the window at people strolling by. She took out her phone and scrolled through her photos, pausing to smile.

She expanded a photo with her fingers and held up the phone with the screen facing Marcel.

"I love him!"

Marcel smiled. "I know... Titou loves you, too."

A pair of hands reached out from behind Amelie, covering her eyes. She grinned and placed her hands on them, trying to identify who they belonged to. She then tilted her head up and sniffed the air.

She recognized the scent—a hint of rose imbued with jasmine. She grinned widely and yelled, "Madeleine!"

Madeleine leaned in and kissed her cheek.

"May I join you two?"

Amelie nodded enthusiastically, her face lighting up with surprise and joy.

Madeleine swung around and sat beside her. She placed her hand on Amelie's shoulder.

"I missed you."

At that moment, something warm and furry pushed between her legs and let out a "woof."

Amelie threw her arms up and shrieked. She reached below and grabbed Titou, bringing him into her lap with his tail wagging and tongue lapping her face.

She shot a wide-eyed look at Madeleine with her mouth open.

Madeleine shrugged, grinning. "He missed you, too!"

Madeleine had grown increasingly close to Amelie. She'd been worried, texting Marcel all morning, asking him how things were going—she knew it wouldn't be easy for Amelie to sit and describe the monster haunting her dreams.

"I hope I'm not intruding," she added. "I was worried about you. I texted Marcel and asked if I could join you two for lunch. He thought it was a good idea."

"I'm glad you came," Amelie beamed. She lowered Titou to the ground and hugged Madeleine. "And thank you for bringing Titou!"

"Well, you know Titou…. He insisted on coming."

Amelie laughed and gave Titou a piece of chicken. "Yes, I know him."

Madeleine ordered an entrée for herself and a plate of diced filet mignon for Titou, and they began to eat. Marcel noticed Amelie was devouring her food; her appetite had returned with a vengeance.

Marcel heard a ping. He took out his phone and saw he had a text from his associate at Interpol. Madeleine looked at him and frowned. She shook her head.

"I'm sorry, I have to take this," he said.

Amelie looked up from her plate and smiled. She nodded; she'd been around Marcel long enough to understand the demands of his job.

He blew them a kiss, then stepped away from the table and opened his text.

Hello Inspector,

I ran the picture through our database. Nothing came up.

It's uploaded into the system. Hopefully we get a hit soon.

Lars.

Marcel shook his head; he hoped he'd get an immediate hit. He sent a reply.

Thanks Lars. Please make some calls and keep me in the loop.

I need to get this guy off the streets.

Madeleine shot a wary glance at him as he returned to the table. He gave her a disarming smile and a wink.

"So, what are we going to order for dessert?"

"Mille-feuille," Madeleine replied. "And it's ready for you at home. I've been working on it all morning!"

25

Claire peered out the trailer window at the clouds, soaking up the pinkish hue from the sun emerging over the horizon, heralding the arrival of dawn. Her gaze swept across the landscape from the Roman wall to the River Tyne, picturing the terrain as it had existed for centuries, witnessing the same sunrise.

She heard a snore. It was still early, and Jane was fast asleep. A faint smile spread across her face as she poured her coffee into her travel mug and twisted the lid. She wanted to let Jane sleep in; she'd been up late working on the budget.

She stole a glance at her before quietly opening the trailer door. As she was about to close the door, she heard, "I'm up... I'm getting up."

"Don't worry. You can sleep in; you were up late," Claire said.

"Uh-uh," Jane moaned groggily. "I'm getting up."

"All right, suit yourself. I'm heading down to the new site. I need to check on their progress."

"I'll see you down there."

"As you wish. Ta-ta for now."

The new dig site was located on the opposite side of the mound from the primary site.

Claire didn't expect anyone at either site for another half hour. But when she reached the top of the mound, she spotted a man at the bottom, with his back turned to her.

Clutching her coffee mug, she strolled down towards him. As she approached, he turned to face her.

"Good morning, Claire!"

Her heart raced. A lump formed in her throat, and she swallowed hard.

"Good morning, Stewart! What are you doing here so early?"

Stewart smiled and shrugged. "I like to get an early start. There's nothing else for me to do."

"I appreciate your commitment," Claire said, grinning. "How're things going?"

"Well, you saw the Honorius coins... Hopefully, we'll find lots more."

Claire smiled and nodded, her gaze lowered as she avoided his eyes. Stewart followed her as she turned and began to walk towards the excavated square.

"You know, I have higher expectations for this site," she confessed.

"Really? More than the primary site?"

"Yes. If this site was settled during the fourth and fifth centuries, as indicated by the Honorius coins, I expect we'll find early Christian artifacts... or evidence of Saxon presence."

Stewart cocked his eyebrow. "That's above my pay grade, Claire. I know nothing about that period."

"Don't worry about that," she said, waving a hand. "I had to brush up on it myself... Rome was in turmoil during that period... divided into the western and eastern Roman empires, and under pressure from invasions."

Stewart shook his head. "I don't know how you keep up!"

Claire smiled. "Like you said yourself, there's nothing else for me to do—this is my life."

Stewart chuckled. "Fair enough."

Claire slumped into a canvas chair at the edge of the excavation. Crossing her legs, she gestured toward another chair nearby.

"Why don't you pull up a chair?"

Stewart brought the chair over and sat close beside her.

"Look, there are centuries between the two sites..." Claire explained. She nodded at the partially excavated square in the ground before her. "Centuries of human settlement. Who knows, you may even come across Viking relics."

"Viking?"

Claire nodded, keeping her eyes fixed ahead. "Have you ever heard of Lindisfarne?"

"No, I haven't."

"It's an old monastery... on an island off the coast, not far north from Newcastle. It was the site of one of England's earliest Viking raids," Claire went on. She made a sweeping motion with her hand. "This entire area is steeped in history."

"Incredible!" Stewart shook his head in amazement. "Not in a million years did I think..."

"Not a million, Stewart; only a few centuries," Claire interrupted, laughing.

Stewart chuckled. "Thanks for correcting me… I guess this is my on-the-job training."

"Perfect… I like that!" Claire said. She paused, then added, "By the way, it's all on-the-job training. You can't learn this in a classroom."

"Hmm… Isn't that a fact?"

Claire inhaled deeply and closed her eyes, feeling the warmth of the morning sun on her face. She still avoided eye contact with Stewart; either his cologne or aftershave—she couldn't tell which—was driving her mad, and her heart thumped riotously inside her chest.

The conversation had stalled, and she couldn't fill the awkward void. She wanted to ask him about his life story but couldn't find the words. She tried to stand up and walk away, but she found herself glued to her chair.

She enjoyed the exhilarating rush—the intense sensation of adrenaline coursing through her veins. Her hands gripped the armrests, pressing down to lift herself out of the chair, but she froze. Her entire body seemed to defy her.

A pair of hands glided over her shoulders from behind, sending shivers down her spine. Tipping her head back, she saw a face obscured by the sun above; for an instant, she thought it was him.

"Hey, boss! … How's it going down here?" Jane teased.

"Oh, hi, Jane!" Claire breathed a sigh of relief, grateful that Jane had shown up. Finally, she felt able to break the spell.

She felt foolish for allowing herself to be alone with Stewart. Once again, she tried to get up, but her legs felt like jelly. She held out her hand, smiling helplessly at Jane.

"Help me up?"

Slumped in her green canvas chair, she looked like a Venus flytrap had swallowed her. Jane took her hand and hoisted her to her feet.

Jane sensed something—she picked up a vibe lingering in the air. She could see it plastered on Claire's flushed face. She reacted quickly.

"Um… Could you come up and take a look at my balance sheet? I know we've got the meeting with Callum; I just wanted to ensure the numbers look okay. I know he's going to ask to see them."

Claire nodded as she smoothed out her clothing. "Of course… I've got to talk to Sharon as well."

"Great," Jane shot back. "She's up there with her trowel, scraping away at the jugs."

"Amphorae," Claire corrected with a grin.

"Yes, sorry... the amphorae."

Claire struggled not to laugh; Jane always had a knack for lightening her mood. She directed her attention to Stewart.

"Keep up the excellent work, Stewart... This could be big."

"Yeah, and I'll text Arnold and have him come over with his radar and run a few laps for you," Jane said, smirking. "I'm sure the two of you will dig something up."

Claire had to look away, or she'd burst out laughing. Without saying another word, Jane turned around and started heading back up the mound with Claire trailing behind.

As they walked away from Stewart, Jane asked, "Is everything okay? You seemed a little..."

"Yeah, everything is fine," Claire cut in. "I was just reassuring him... and I ran out of words... You know? That awkward silence when you don't know what else to say?"

"Yeah—I don't have that problem," Jane shot back.

Claire burst out laughing. "I know you don't."

As they neared the top of the mound, Claire could feel Stewart's gaze on them. She fought the urge to look back but couldn't. She cocked her head back and saw him staring at them. He waved. She waved back.

"Couldn't resist, could you?" Jane giggled.

"I don't know what you're talking about."

Sharon was anxiously waiting for Claire to return. She spotted her walking up with Jane and yelled out, "Guess what?"

"What?" Claire yelled back, smiling.

"I'm sorry!" Sharon grinned as Claire drew closer. "I lose my manners when I'm excited... Good morning!"

"Good morning!" Claire chuckled. "What's got you so excited?"

"See for yourselves!" Sharon turned and nodded at the excavation site. "Notice anything different?"

Claire gasped when she saw what lay before her—small marker flags dotted the entire grid.

"We've marked every single blip on Arnold's radar..."

"I can see that," Claire beamed.

"You're going to need to expand the grid."

Claire nodded. "Why are there flags going all the way down to the river?"

"Why do you think?"

It took Claire only a moment to figure out why. Her eyes grew wide. "Is it a Roman road?"

Sharon gave a big nod.

Claire pressed a finger to her lips, deep in thought. "It makes sense that they'd be resupplied from the river. The land route would be far more arduous."

"Hey, Jane!" Sharon nodded at her. "Sorry, I didn't mean to ignore you."

"No worries, Shar." Jane winked. "I ignore people all the time—I get it."

Sharon chuckled.

Claire laughed, keeping her gaze fixed ahead. She stepped forward to the edge of the grid, picturing what the road might have looked like as Jane and Sharon stood behind her.

They watched her finger trace the path of the ancient road in the air, following the fluttering flags as they revealed its every curve, winding its way toward the settlement.

A moment later, she turned and faced Sharon and Jane.

"I wonder… if…."

"You wonder what?" Sharon asked with a curious expression.

"Hmm… Do we know how far underground the road is?"

"Just a few feet," a male voice answered behind them. "Inches in some areas."

Claire recognized the voice. "Hi, Arnold!"

"Hi Claire… I can see the wheels turning inside your head," Arnold chuckled. "What are you thinking?"

"Do you have a pick and shovel?"

"Are you kidding?"

Claire shook her head. "No… I'm dead serious... Grab them and follow me."

Before Arnold could respond, Claire took off towards the marked areas in the field, with Jane and Sharon following behind. When she got to a straight, level area along the flagged path, she paused and stomped her feet. "Right here… Let's dig right here."

Jane nodded in agreement as Arnold plodded toward them, panting in exhaustion.

"I think we need to wait for shovel boy."

Sharon reached for the shovel as Arnold drew near. "Let me," she said with a smile. "I've got this."

Overweight and out of shape, Arnold was the least fit among them for manual labor. He was excellent at operating the ground-penetrating radar, which was all that mattered to Claire.

"I can do this," he insisted. "I don't want to stand and watch a girl—I mean, a lady—do the digging."

Standing closer to Arnold, Jane snatched the shovel from his hand. "Listen, big boy, we appreciate the chivalry, but..." She shook her head. "Let's get rid of the gender clichés."

Arnold worshipped Jane. He smiled sheepishly and stepped aside. After getting to know him, she understood him well; she knew he'd been bullied all his life for his weight and had a soft spot for him.

She smiled and winked at Arnold before handing the shovel to Sharon. "I'll let you get the next one... Cool?"

He nodded. "Cool!"

It didn't take long for Sharon's shovel to hit something solid. She heard a clink and paused. She gently scooped away a few more layers of dirt and glanced up at Claire.

"Here's your road!"

Claire crouched down at the spot where Sharon had dug. The stone blocks were clearly visible. She used her hands to scoop out more soil, revealing deep grooves in the stones. She glanced up and said, "Raise your hands if you can tell me what these grooves are."

Sharon raised her hand.

Claire chuckled. "I know you know the answer, Sharon."

Jane shrugged, and Arnold threw up his hands.

Claire turned to Sharon. "Go ahead and tell them—I know you want to!"

Sharon kneeled beside Claire. She ran her fingers through the deep grooves. "These grooves are called cart ruts... or wheel ruts. They are carved into the stone by carts running over them."

"Heavy carts..." Claire added. She looked at Jane and smiled. "Possibly carrying pirate loot."

Jane gasped. "You don't mean..."

"I do," Claire said. "Remember when Lucius said he would ship all the treasure to her—to Cara?"

Jane nodded with her eyes wide. Claire smiled at her and continued. "And these ruts... they weren't carved into these stones overnight. It took many years." She gestured to the trail of tiny red flags snaking toward the excavation site.

"Long after Lucius and Cara died, wagons continued up this road to the settlement."

She closed her eyes and let her mind do the seeing. Taking a deep breath, she let a pensive smile curl across her lips. "I can see it... Many generations lived here." She opened her eyes, releasing the tears that had collected in them. "I bet their children and grandchildren grew up here."

It had been a long day. Claire sat cross-legged on the bed, nursing a glass of Chablis, as she scrolled through the photos of the tablets on her phone in search of clues about Lucius and Cara—how they lived and raised their family.

She wanted to learn how they had met; she was a native Briton, and he was a Roman officer. They couldn't have been a more unlikely couple, and that fascinated her far more than the treasure ever could.

She heard a fluttering sound. She glanced up and saw Jane fanning two halves of a card deck, shuffling them.

"Poker, anyone?" Jane said, grinning.

Claire chuckled. "Maybe later..."

Jane pouted and continued shuffling the cards, fanning them louder.

"All right, I'll play, but first listen to this..."

Jane nodded and smiled.

"These are letters or postcards Lucius and Cara wrote to each other. Others are journals or diaries," Claire continued. "The Emperor had commissioned Lucius to make an alliance with the local Carvetti chieftain—Cara's father. The Carvetti tribe inhabited what we today call Cumbria. He may have met Cara when he went to visit her father. He wrote to her, 'I am looking forward to seeing you again... and riding horses together.' He must have taken her horseback riding."

"Aw…" Jane gushed, flashing a smile. She tucked away the cards and lay beside Claire, propping her head on her hand.

"It appears he took her for a ride on the beach. She mentions an island... It must be the Isle of Man. On a clear day, it's visible from the Cumbrian coast. She mentions green hills and tall cliffs." Claire hesitated. "Hmm… They…"

"They what?"

"They lay together on the grassy hilltop... She uses a word here that could mean..."

"Mean what?"

Claire's cheeks flushed as a slow smile spread across her face.

"Oh, come on!" Jane laughed, placing her hand on Claire's knee. "Tell me! Does he screw her right there on a patch of grass?"

Claire's jaw dropped. "Or... maybe he was a gentleman, and they had a picnic... Maybe they just lay together and kissed."

"Right!" Jane snorted. "And you know what they say about kissing..."

Claire scoffed. "No, Jane, I don't know what they say about kissing. What do they say?"

"That it can lead to sex, Claire, sex! ... and unwanted pregnancies." Jane laughed. "I bet he knocked her up."

Claire rolled her eyes. "Oh, Jane! … I thought you liked Lucius!"

"I do… I like him a lot… but he's still a man."

"Therefore inherently flawed?"

"That's right! But I still like him… He always brings her shiny things, and he marries her. But I also think they did a lot more than kissing up there on that hilltop."

Claire shook her head, suppressing a laugh, and continued reading. "All right, let's see... She says here, 'My father has requested to see you. He wishes that you would join us at our celebration. There will be a feast... and great fire...'"

"Sounds like she's asking him to come to her party," Jane said, smirking.

"She is... It sounds like a Celtic festival. She mentions a harvest, a large fire or bonfire... and offerings to their ancestors." Claire paused, then said, "The more I think about it, the more this sounds like the Celtic festival of Samhain—the inspiration for Halloween!"

"She invited him to a Halloween party! I love Halloween!" Jane blurted.

Claire laughed. "I do, too... We'll have a big Halloween party in October." She continued to read. "Cara describes the festival in great detail: 'We wore masks and gathered around the great fire, and he laid his head on my shoulder.' She goes on about their feast: 'A stew of lamb with carrots and turnips, onions... and barley... After we feasted, I took him to my house, and we...'"

"We what?" Jane glared playfully at Claire. "Go on, we what?"

"Well, she uses the same verb, which means to lie together."

Jane threw her hands into the air. "See? I told you... they were having sex!"

Claire rolled her eyes. "Fine! They're having sex! Lots of sex! You happy now?"

Jane laughed. "Yes, I'm happy. I'm happy for them."

Claire struggled to hold back her laughter. "All right, I'm almost done reading… Cara finishes by saying, 'After the feast, he met privately with my father. I do not know what they spoke about.'"

"Yeah, I'm sure it was a big men's club," Jane quipped. "With a sign on the door: women not allowed… Can we play some poker now?"

"Sure," Claire said. "But there's a problem."

Jane narrowed her eyes. "What now?"

Claire shrugged and said, "I don't know how to play poker!"

"Hmm," Jane fumed. "You're not getting out of this!" She began to deal out cards. "The classroom is in session. Today's lesson: Texas Hold'em!"

26

Madeleine slept with blackout shades; she couldn't fall asleep with the slightest bit of light. Marcel reached towards the nightstand and pulled off the hand towel he'd draped over the alarm clock. Even the red LED light from the digital clock kept Madeleine awake. For her to fall asleep, the room had to be cool and pitch-black.

It was 1:00 am—time for him to get up.

It didn't take long for him to get dressed. He slipped his assault rifle into its case and was about to head out the door when he heard a quiet rumble that sounded like a growl. The sound was coming from Amelie's room. He pressed his ear against her door and listened.

There it was again—this time louder. He smiled and whispered, "Go to sleep, Titou! Don't wake her up! I'll be back soon." He paused for a moment, listening, but heard nothing.

Stealthily, he opened the front door and slipped out. A squad car was parked in front of his building, waiting for him. He opened the car door and climbed in.

"Good morning, Inspector," Claude said, smiling at him in the rearview mirror.

"Good morning, Claude! … Thank you for doing this. I'm sure your wife probably hates me."

"Not at all, sir… She was fast asleep when I left… Are we going to the airport?"

"Yes. Thank you, Claude."

"You're welcome, sir."

Marcel caught Claude staring at his gun case in the mirror.

"It's not a guitar," he quipped, grinning.

Claude laughed. "I didn't think so, sir... Do you mind if I ask what's inside?"

"Not at all… It's an MXG 19 assault rifle."

Claude's eyebrows shot up. "Wow, sir... I don't believe that's a standard-issue rifle."

"It's not. It's a custom job. I got it when I was training with our special operations unit."

"So, the rumors are true... Was it the GIGN?"

Marcel curled his lip and nodded.

Claude remained silent for the rest of the drive to the airport, occasionally sneaking glances in the mirror. Marcel was a hero among the police force, and his exploits were legendary. He'd dismantled more criminal networks than the rest of his unit combined.

Pulling up to the curb at the airport, Claude got out to open the door for Marcel.

"I wish I could be there with you, sir," Claude said, his voice tinged with longing.

"No, you don't... Go back to your cozy bed before your wife finds out you're gone. Trust me, there's no one scarier than a pissed-off wife."

Claude smiled and nodded. "Will do, sir."

Marcel paused, studying him closely. "Do you have any children, Claude?"

"Yes, sir... one... on the way."

Marcel sighed. "Go home, Claude. Go home and get some sleep. I will text you when I'm ready to be picked up."

"Do you have any idea how long, sir?"

Marcel shook his head. "It's a hunt... It's a waiting game."

Marcel couldn't identify the plane parked on the tarmac, and he couldn't care less. It was a prop job arranged by the police force, ferrying his team of nine to Marseille—their ultimate destination. That was all that mattered. From there, the real mission would launch on a helicopter.

He knew his crew intimately. They'd been on several missions together, mostly hostage rescues and support for drug enforcement agencies. But, for Marcel, this mission was different. This time, it was personal.

Strapping into his seat, he took a deep breath to center himself. He wasn't afraid of flying—he was solely focused on the mission objectives. Opening his eyes, he found others watching him. He nodded and smiled. He'd already reviewed his mission briefing at the airport and had tons of confidence in it.

The flight was short but long enough for his mind to conjure his demons. He recalled a recent conversation with Amelie about one of her friends, a girl with a fiery spirit she'd met during her time in captivity aboard the yacht—someone around her age with whom she'd formed a close bond. Her name was Celine.

"Celine was a rebel," Amelie had said. "She hated Henri... She didn't follow his rules like the other girls, and she always paid the price for it. She would ridicule him or spit on him. Once, she even jumped overboard, trying to get away from him. She jumped into the sea and started swimming, but there was no land in sight. They threw her a line, but she wouldn't take it. They finally dropped a small boat into the water and chased her down. When they brought her back on board the yacht, she was kicking and screaming... She always stood up for me... She always protected me. During their parties, she'd help me find a hiding place... We'd hide together from the creepy old men. And when Henri found us... Celine always got the worst of it."

Marcel felt a hand on his shoulder. "Hey, chief... you awake?" A voice roused him from his thoughts.

He smiled and opened his eyes. "Yeah, Jean... I was awake... just thinking..."

"You think too much, chief!" His partner Jean smiled and patted him on the arm. "We're landing in 10 minutes... Leave the thinking for when you get back to Madeleine! It's time to go to work."

To avoid radar detection, the flight plan had them following the coastline, heading east at an altitude of 500 feet AGL (above ground level). This was essentially a military operation cloaked as a civilian one.

The mission was so clandestine that only one person at the air traffic control tower knew about it.

It was just before daybreak when the helicopter reached the coastline and descended to its designated altitude. The operatives deployed their night vision goggles and began scouring the water's surface.

Their intelligence indicated that a yacht resembling the description witnesses had provided was sighted off the coast of Toulon, approximately 42 miles southeast of Marseille.

"These boats are too small... mostly fishing or recreational vessels," Marcel said over the communications radio.

"Yeah, you're right, chief," Jean said. "I suggest we go further offshore... A big yacht like the one we're looking for will probably stay as far away from shore as possible."

"Agreed. Let's head further out... Keep your eyes peeled, team!"

"Copy that, captain," the pilot responded. "Heading 155 degrees south-southeast."

Marcel took off his night vision goggles and rubbed his tired, stinging eyes. He wanted to get this mission over with and get back home. He didn't particularly enjoy going on missions like this, but he wouldn't have missed this one for the world.

He pulled a folded copy of the composite sketch from his jacket pocket and stared at it, seething. His pulse quickened, adrenaline flooding his system. He clenched his jaw, then shoved the sketch back into his pocket.

"I think I got it," Jean yelled out. "It's right off our 3 o'clock... It's a big one."

"Dropping down to 100 feet," the pilot announced. "Be ready to rappel down in about 60 seconds."

"We haven't been spotted," Jean said, scoping the stern of the yacht below with his binoculars. "Let's egress now!"

Suddenly, a series of loud pops erupted, followed by pinging sounds against the helicopter's hull.

"I guess I spoke too soon," Jean yelled out. "I have eyes on a suspect on the stern... It looks like he's got an AK-47... I'm taking him out."

Marcel heard two muffled pops and saw the blinding muzzle flash from Jean's silencer. "Suspect's down, gents, but let's not loiter up here... Let's go!" He yelled, his voice muffled by the whirring of the helicopter rotors.

It had been a few years since Marcel rappelled down a rope— he gripped it tightly, feeling the burn in his palms all the way down to the yacht's deck. "Let's do this quick. I'm sure the welcome committee's on its way."

He barely finished his sentence when two more suspects came around the cabin superstructure on the main deck. Marcel had his gun trained on them when they rounded the corner and fired two shots, hitting the first suspect in the chest. Jean, trailing behind him, took out the second suspect.

Marcel saw the muzzle flash through the windows as the rest of his team made their way inside, breaching each cabin, neutralizing suspects, and executing a full sweep of the entire yacht.

"Don't fire unless it's necessary—we need them alive for interrogation," Marcel instructed his team over the radio. "And be careful you don't accidentally shoot the girls... Let's do this quickly and efficiently; I don't want to end up in a hostage situation."

Minutes later, all three decks were secured, and the remaining suspects had surrendered. Alone on the bridge, Marcel studied the vessel's travel plan, departure, and arrival times when he received the bad news. "Chief, we can't find any girls—only crew members and six other suspects," Jean reported over the radio.

Moments later, Marcel dashed through the main cabin entrance and found Jean pressing down his mic key, about to call him again.

"There you are! Where have you been? I've been trying to find you!"

Marcel didn't respond; his eyes were fixed on the suspects zip-tied and on their knees before him.

"What do you mean there are no girls? Did you run a full sweep?" he asked, his bloodshot eyes betraying confusion. "They probably escaped on a small boat and took the girls…"

Jean shook his head. "I don't think so…"

Marcel didn't hear a word Jean said; his attention was fixed on one suspect who dared to meet his gaze. "Who are you?" he snapped. "Are you in charge here?" The man averted his gaze, refusing to answer.

Marcel let out a frustrated exhale, chewing on his lip as he stared at the suspect. He turned to Jean. "Take everyone out to the stern deck. Call for backup and have them transported back to shore. Make sure they go straight to my station for interrogation." He shifted his gaze back to the main suspect. "Leave this one here; I need to speak with him."

"Are you sure, chief?" Jean asked.

Marcel scowled at Jean.

"Understood," Jean said as he and the rest of the team escorted the suspects onto the stern deck, leaving Marcel alone with the one he'd singled out.

Marcel stepped forward. "What's your name?" His voice was low, dangerous.

Silence.

Marcel took out his handgun, cocked it, and pressed the nozzle against the suspect's forehead.

The suspect stared back at him, terror filling his eyes as he muttered something in a language Marcel didn't understand.

Then he heard Jean's voice on the radio.

"Chief, you need to see this... I think we've got the wrong boat!"

Marcel folded his arms across his chest as he gazed at the giant pile of foil-wrapped packages.

"What am I looking at?"

"Fentanyl, heroin, cocaine... You name it," Jean said, nodding at the pile. "The guys found this stuff hidden inside seat cushions on the third deck... We've got the wrong yacht! These people have nothing to do with our suspect—they're part of a Serbian drug cartel. Most of them don't speak any French or English."

"What about these two women?" Marcel asked, gazing at two young women.

"They're the crew," Jean replied. He nodded at two other uniformed men. "Along with these two... The yacht's chartered. They're Greek." He paused, then added, "Backup is on the way. Do you still want them transported back to your station?"

Marcel shook his head. "No… but they're in French territorial waters, so have them transported to Marseille and let them deal with it."

Marcel stood on the stern deck with a vanquished expression, watching as the suspects were loaded onto the French maritime patrol boat. A young Greek girl from the crew with dark hair smiled at him, reminding him of Amelie. He smiled back and waved.

Jean approached from behind and stood beside him, nodding at the crew as they boarded the patrol boat. "Do you think the crew is in any trouble?" Marcel shook his head. "No… I don't think so. The drugs were found in private cabins; the crew likely had no idea they were stuffing drugs inside the furniture cushions... I don't see any culpability."

"I'm glad. They don't look like drug dealers..."

Marcel took his cigarette pack from his coat pocket and raised it to his mouth, pulling one out with his lips. He lit the cigarette and took a long drag, feeling the cool sea spray on his face. He handed Jean the composite sketch.

"We need to track this guy down."

Jean studied the sketch, then nodded. "We will, chief—we will!"

Marcel nodded as he took another drag from his cigarette.

"Chopper is en route for our extraction."

"Good," Marcel muttered.

On the flight home, Marcel typed a text to Madeleine and hit send.

On my way back. Taking you and Amelie out to dinner tonight. I love you both!

Madeleine's response came instantly.

Good!! Been worried sick!! I don't want you to go on these missions anymore. I can't lose you!

You won't lose me. I promise.

No! I don't want to hear that! I want to hear you won't take these risks anymore! Or quit this job!

Marcel didn't know how to respond. He was too tired to get into it. They'd had this conversation before, and he knew sooner or later, he'd have to cave.

Especially now, with Amelie in their lives, he couldn't take any more chances—he didn't want to.

???

Let's talk about it when I get back.

Fine. I love you!

I love you too!

Be ready by 7.

Ok 😊

27

"Will you come sit down, please? You're making me dizzy," Claire said playfully. "Stop pacing back and forth... and as long as you're up, bring me a glass of wine."

Jane threw her hand up in a military salute. "Yes, ma'am! Glass of vino coming right up!"

Claire heard clattering in the kitchen, followed by the unmistakable sound of glass shattering.

"Oops! … Sorry!"

"What did you do?"

"Um... Nothing at all!"

"Jane…" Claire sighed. "What did you do?"

"Oh, nothing…"

"Well, don't cut yourself on that 'nothing' I just heard shatter!"

Jane let out a faint giggle. "It's only three pieces. I'm picking it up—just give me a sec!"

"I don't care about the glass... I would prefer not to have to rush you to the hospital at... um, let's see, what time is it?" Claire glanced at her watch. "At 12:30 in the morning!"

"Don't worry!"

A few moments later, Jane walked into the bedroom with a platter of cheese and cold cuts in one hand and a glass of wine in the other. She curtsied as she approached the bed.

"Voila!"

'Gosh, Jane," Claire beamed. "This looks scrumptious!" She took a slice of dry salami and bit into it. "Mmm," she moaned. "This is better than..."

"Sex?" Jane giggled. "I know! It totally is!"

"Jane!"

"What? It is…"

"I meant to say it's better than what they serve at a gourmet restaurant," Claire corrected, shaking her head with a laugh. "Furthermore…"

A knock on the door cut off Claire's words. Jane handed her the platter and the wine glass, then raised her finger to her nose. "Shhh." She walked up to the light switch and turned it off, snickering.

"Jane!" Claire whispered. "That's not nice... What if it's an emergency? Who is it?"

Jane peeked through the gap in the curtain and let out a muffled giggle.

"It's Sharon."

"You're so naughty... Let her in!"

"Mistress Claire is not home; please return in the morning!" Jane yelled out.

Sharon laughed from the other side. "Hahaha! Open the door, Jane!"

Jane grinned as she swung it open. "Oh, hi, Sharon! How the heck are you?"

"I'm fine. Thank you," Sharon said as she stepped inside the trailer. "How the heck are you?"

"Oh, just groovy!"

"Hi, Sharon," Claire said, waving her over. "Come have some wine and cheese with us!"

"Don't mind if I do," Sharon said, sitting on the edge of the bed.

"What are you drinking, Shar?" Jane asked as she moseyed back into the kitchen.

"Oh... whatever you're having."

"Chablis?"

"Sounds great, Jane! Thank you!"

Sharon reached for a slice of apple-smoked cheddar, sniffing it before taking a bite. "Stinky." She took a bite. "Mmm… and yummy!"

"Ew! Don't smell it—eat it! ... You're not supposed to smell cheese," Jane said, handing Sharon a glass of wine. She scrunched her face and said, "I hate the stinky smell, but I love the taste!"

"So, what are we doing tonight?" Sharon mumbled, her mouth stuffed with cheese.

Claire shrugged. "I was watching Jane pace back and forth before you came, but if you both want, I can read from some of the tablets. I transferred the pictures to my laptop and can now expand the images or enhance their resolution—it's made a big difference; I can see much more detail."

Sharon shot a glance at Jane, and they both nodded.

"I just love these stories," Jane raved. "She's been reading them to me almost every night."

A smile spread across Claire's face as she pulled up the images. She'd created a shortcut for their folder on her desktop, enabling her to open the images swiftly.

"Here's one you'll like," Claire said, her excitement evident. "It may resonate with you—it's close to home."

Jane climbed onto the bed and sat cross-legged beside Claire, glass of wine in hand. "What do you mean, 'It's close to home?'" She asked.

Claire gestured towards the dig site. "It happened right here... The settlement came under attack by Caledonian tribes."

"Wait..." Jane interrupted. "Who are Caledonians?"

"Scottish, dear," Sharon clarified. "Caledonia is another name—a Roman name—for Scotland."

Claire nodded in agreement. "That's right... On this specific occasion, they carried out a nighttime raid on the settlement. Let me find it..." With her mouse, she expanded the tablet's image on her monitor. "Here it is... Cara writes, 'They attacked us in the middle of the night. They breached the northern wall, killing two of our legionnaires in the process. They also set fire to several houses. Lucius hurried out with his men to intercept them."

Claire paused to provide some background information on the Caledonian tribes: "They wore woolen cloaks or animal skins, according to historians, and painted or tattooed their bodies. They were fiercely independent warriors... They mostly farmed or raised cattle."

"So what happened next?" Jane cut in impatiently.

Claire yawned. She covered her mouth and laughed. "Oh, excuse me... I must be getting tired... All right... She says, 'We repelled the raiding party with considerable losses. Lucius and many of the garrison legionnaires gave chase. They pursued them in the hills for days. He sent messengers carrying letters. One day, I received a letter informing me that he was wounded in a skirmish.'"

"Oh no," Jane said, her face filled with worry. "What happened?"

Claire smiled and raised a finger. "Let me finish. 'They loaded him onto a wagon and delivered him to me. I was devastated. He had a grievous wound on his upper thigh—a gash from a spear or sword. The doctor treated him for days. I offered prayers at the altar, pleading with the gods for his healing. I offered prayers to Apollo and his son Asclepius.'"

Claire closed her laptop and yawned again. "I'm sorry... We can continue this tomorrow night if you want. I've got a busy day ahead and need to get some shut-eye, or I'll be worthless in the morning." She turned to Sharon. "You can sleep here if you want. Jane and I can share this bed, and you can sleep in Jane's bed."

"Thanks, Claire! I'd love to," Sharon said with a smile. "But I've got Evie, and I don't want to leave her alone."

"Why don't you text her and have her come? Tell her we're having a slumber party!"

"All right... Let me see if she wants to come." Sharon's fingers swiftly typed the text and hit send.

A few minutes later, Eve knocked on the trailer door. Jane opened it. "Well, look who's here—the prettiest girl in town… Hi, Evie!" She exclaimed, smiling.

Eve waved, blushing. "Hi, Jane!"

"Well, come on in," Jane said, motioning for her to enter.

Eve was always shy, but she seemed particularly distant and didn't speak much. She sat stiffly in a chair in the corner, her color a tad pale. Sharon noticed her demeanor and drew her aside.

"Are you all right, sweetie?"

Eve hesitated, then nodded.

"Are you sure?"

Eve sighed. "I think…" She stammered. "I thought I saw something."

"What did you see?"

"I thought I saw someone... I thought I saw eyes staring at me."

"Eyes? Where?"

"My window… I thought I saw someone staring at me through my window."

Jane heard the conversation and walked over. "I'm sorry, I couldn't help but overhear the conversation." She turned to Eve, placing a hand on her shoulder. "Did you happen to see who it was, dear?"

Eve shook her head, her fingers tugging nervously at the hem of her shirt.

"Did you see anyone walking or hanging around earlier?"

Eve paused and furrowed her brow, her eyes scanning the air for an answer.

"I did. I saw the new security guy."

"Peter?"

Eve nodded. "He waved and said hi to me. He was walking around our trailers, checking things."

Jane offered a reassuring smile. "Don't worry, dear. I'm sure it's nothing. Stay here tonight, and I'll look into it the morning."

28

The moon's rays slipped through a gap in the curtain, casting a soft glow on Jane's face as she lay facing Claire. Her mind raced, deeply disturbed by what she'd heard from Eve.

She considered stepping outside to check things out, but she dismissed the idea; they were miles from Newcastle, and cell reception was shoddy at best.

Still, she couldn't shake the thought.

Her stomach growled. She'd barely eaten earlier and was suddenly famished.

Claire partially opened her eyes and noticed Jane wide awake, staring at her. "Was that your stomach?" she asked.

Jane nodded, grinning.

"Go to sleep. You need some rest," Claire urged.

"I can't," Jane replied.

"Why not?"

Jane sat up and peeked at Sharon and Eve, who were sound asleep after a long day at the dig site. She lay back down, whispering, "I'm worried."

"Why are you worried?" Claire asked, her eyelids heavy with sleep.

Jane sighed. "Because someone is creeping around the camp at night, looking through our windows."

"Mm," Claire murmured, still drowsy. "I'll talk to Peter tomorrow. Maybe it was him doing a security check."

"And then what? He just stopped to peek through Evie's window? I doubt that."

"All right, let's get some sleep. We can figure it out tomorrow. Good night!"

"Okay. Goodnight!"

Minutes later, Claire opened one eye and found Jane still awake, grinning at her. She tried hard not to laugh.

"I thought you were going to sleep," she said drowsily.

"I'm hungry."

Claire buried her face in her pillow and let out a giggle.

"Oh, Jane… Fine, let's get something to eat. But you have to keep it quiet."

Jane nodded, murmuring, "Yay!"

Jane smiled as she slathered mayonnaise and mustard on sandwich bread while Claire arranged the meat slices and chopped the tomato and lettuce.

Claire shook her head, forcing herself not to smile.

"I can't believe we're still up. You know we've got work tomorrow, right?"

Jane nodded as she took a big bite of her sandwich. "Mmm... this is so good!"

Claire bit into her sandwich and let out a satisfied moan.

"It's pretty good, right?" Jane said.

Claire nodded enthusiastically as she took another bite.

"Guilty pleasures!" Jane chuckled.

Claire pressed a finger to her lips.

"Shush! They're asleep!"

A rustling sound outside caught their attention. They paused and exchanged glances.

Jane turned off the kitchen light and peeked through the curtain.

"What was it?" Claire asked.

Jane shrugged and continued to look out the window. "Can we go outside and take a look?"

"What? Are you crazy?"

"Come one! Let's do it! I'm sure it was nothing—maybe a deer or something... Maybe we'll catch a peeping Tom!"

"Or a murderer!" Claire grabbed her phone and started typing a text. "Here, let's get a hold of Peter."

She sent the text and crossed her arms, tapping her foot, waiting for a response. Minutes passed. No reply. Jane grabbed a large kitchen knife off the table and waved it in the air.

"Come on! Let's just go around our trailer—I'll protect you!"

Claire rolled her eyes. "All right… but we're just walking around our trailer—not going any further!"

Jane nodded, her eyes wide with excitement. "Agreed!"

The trailer door creaked open, letting in a blast of cold air. Claire closed the door and gave Jane a questioning look. Jane raised a hand, gesturing for her to wait, and quietly walked up to the closet. She grabbed a pair of jackets off the hangers and tiptoed back with a triumphant smile. She handed one to Claire and slipped on hers.

"Ready?" Jane asked.

Claire shook her head. "No."

Jane smirked and opened the trailer door.

"Remember, we're only going around our trailer," Claire murmured.

"All right."

Holding Claire's hand in one hand and the knife in the other, Jane walked alongside the trailer. As they turned the corner, they both froze. In the distance, the waters of the River Tyne shimmered under the moonlight, and blades of grass swayed in a gentle breeze.

The Roman wall stretched atop rolling hills like a seam holding the land together. Jane let out a sigh, her eyes fixed on the breathtaking landscape.

Claire nodded at Jane to keep moving. "It's beautiful… I know. But we've got to get back inside."

"Beautiful doesn't do this justice. This place is…"

"Magical?"

"Yeah… Magical…"

Less than fifty feet away, the other trailers were parked near the excavation site, their lights off.

"As long as we're out here, let's take a quick peek over there," Jane said, motioning towards the trailers. "We might as well…"

Claire narrowed her eyes at Jane. "I thought we agreed we'd take a quick look around our trailer and then get back inside!"

Jane scrunched her nose. "Please?"

Claire rolled her eyes. "All right, but let's do it quickly."

"Fine! We'll race around them and come right back."

"Yeah, but not too fast!" Claire motioned to the knife in Jane's hand. "You wouldn't want to trip and fall with that thing!"

"Right-o!"

Jane sprinted ahead, pulling Claire along. They reached the first trailer, bodies colliding with it from the force of their momentum. Jane let out a loud giggle.

"Shhh," Claire laughed. "You're too loud!"

"Me?" Jane scoffed. "You're just as loud…" She paused mid-sentence at the sound of a snapping twig and squeezed Claire's hand. "What was that?"

"A murderer!" Claire murmured.

"Oh my god!"

"What? You're the one who insisted on coming out here in the middle of the night."

"All right… Should I scream? That way, everyone will come running out and…"

"What? No! We won't be able to look them in the eye tomorrow from embarrassment…"

"What about that sound we heard?"

"Probably a deer… or a rabbit."

"I don't know; it was a loud snap."

The sound of gravel crunching beneath approaching footsteps sent a chill down their spines. Suddenly, a bright light flooded the area, blinding them.

Jane raised the hand holding the knife, and Claire opened her mouth, about to scream, when the beam of light shifted from their faces.

They saw the silhouette of a man standing before them.

"Hello! I'm so sorry I startled you!"

Jane squinted at the shadowy figure. "Peter?"

"Yes… I'm truly sorry I gave you a start, ma'am!"

"Fuck, Peter! … What are you trying to do? Give us a heart attack and get yourself killed?" Jane snapped.

"No, ma'am. I'm very sorry. I saw someone earlier, and…"

"You did? Who was it?" Claire interrupted.

Peter turned to Claire. "I'm not entirely certain, ma'am. I only caught a glimpse as he disappeared behind the trailer."

Claire shot a glance at Jane, raising an eyebrow before returning her gaze to Peter.

"Which trailer?"

Peter tapped the side of the trailer they were standing in front of. "This one right here, ma'am."

Claire drew her wristwatch close to her face, squinting to read the time. It was almost 3 a.m. She smiled at Peter and said, "Thank you, Peter. You're doing a great job. Let's talk later. It's late, and we should get back to bed. We heard a noise and decided to check it out. I did text you earlier…"

Peter looked puzzled as he took his phone from his pocket and stared at the screen.

"You're right, ma'am. I'm very sorry… I had my phone on silent mode. The ring is a bit loud, so I keep it silent at night." He paused, then said. "I won't do that anymore."

"No worries, Peter. No harm done. I'll see you later… Goodnight!"

Peter tipped his hat. "Goodnight, ma'am!"

"That's Sharon's trailer," Jane said as they walked back to their trailer. "Evie was alone in that trailer when…"

Claire wrinkled her brow. "I know."

29

She felt the cool breeze flutter her nightgown, its gentle touch sending a shiver down her spine. She opened her eyes and saw the window ajar, with the soft glow of moonlight spilling through.

She turned her head and found Jane fast asleep beside her. A shadow flickered past the window, momentarily blocking the moonlight. Claire's heart slammed against her ribcage, a tight knot forming in her throat. She froze, her eyes glued to the window.

A gust of wind blew in, raising goosebumps on her skin. She cocked her head to the side; Jane was still asleep and unfazed.

The shadow glided by once more, drawing her attention back to the window. Her eyes grew wide, and her heart thumped faster. Then, the shadow reappeared, unmoving in the center of the window. It was a man's shadow.

He stood there, his face obscured by the moon's glare, staring at her, his chest rising and falling with every breath. His hands reached through the window, his fingers curling around the frame.

Silent and snakelike, he crawled through the window and rose to his feet in front of her bed.

Claire sat up, her breath hitching, but before she could move, he climbed onto the bed and pressed his palm against her breast, gently pushing her back down.

She didn't resist—her body was filled with anticipation, and her veins flooded with adrenaline as she grappled with her fears and desires. She still couldn't see his face as he lowered himself on top of her, his hot breath on her neck.

His hand reached beneath her lower back, drawing her closer as his lips glided from her neck to her lips. Her body quivered beneath him, a moan escaping her lips.

A familiar smell grazed her nose—the scent of freesia and Jasmine. Her eyes fluttered open. Jane sat beside her, smiling, her fingers gently caressing Claire's arm.

"Hey, you! Are you all right? What was that all about?"

"Mmm… Nothing…" Claire murmured, heat rushing to her cheeks.

Jane chuckled. "Well, it seemed pretty intense for 'nothing.' What were you dreaming about? Come on, now... Share! Was it pleasure or pain?"

Claire laughed, shaking her head. "Definitely not pleasure! I just had a little dream about our camp stalker."

"Gosh… Is that what you were moaning about?"

Claire nodded. "I dreamt he came through our window... I got scared, and then you woke me up."

"Wait! Who was the stalker?"

Claire shrugged. "I couldn't see his face."

"So, what did he do?" Jane pressed.

Just then, Claire's phone pinged. "Saved by the bell," she thought. She wasn't good at making up stories, and she certainly wasn't about to tell Jane about her erotic dream.

She glanced at the screen and saw a text from Sharon, but she didn't open it.

When she noticed the time, she gasped. "It's almost noon! Why did you let me sleep in so late?"

Jane shrugged. "We were up so late, and I thought you needed the rest. I was up on time—I've been working on the budget." She gestured to a plate on the coffee table covered with foil.

"I even made eggs."

Claire smiled. "You're so sweet! But please never let me sleep so late."

"You got it. I'm sorry!"

"No, don't apologize," Claire said with a smile, placing a reassuring hand on Jane's shoulder. "It's just that we've got so much going on…"

Jane nodded. "I get it." She hurried to the table, grabbed the plate with a fork, and brought it to Claire. "Here, have a bite. You'll need your energy."

"All right. I can't argue with breakfast in bed," Claire beamed.

"It's a little dry... and burnt," Jane admitted with a sheepish smile. "I forgot to put oil in the pan."

Claire smiled, taking a bite. "Mmm... It's really good!"

"No, it's not... but thank you!"

"You're welcome! And it's perfectly fine, Jane!"

Claire opened the text from Sharon.

You're not going to believe this!

"Oh, come on, Shar, why are you being so cryptic?" She murmured as she typed a reply.

Tell me. What is it? I'm running late.

Sharon didn't text a response—instead, she sent a picture.

Claire's mouth fell open, and she dropped her fork. She expanded the photo with her fingers and froze.

"What is it?" Jane asked, leaning over Claire's shoulder at her phone screen.

Claire continued to stare at the image on her phone screen, speechless.

Her phone pinged again with another text from Sharon.

Cleopatra, right? It's solid gold.

Claire called Sharon and put the phone on speaker. She answered on the first ring.

"Well... Is it?" Sharon's voice was brimming with anticipation.

With a calm voice, Claire replied, "No... You're off by almost three centuries. Would you like to try again?"

"Um... no clue... Tell me!"

Claire paused and showed the image to Jane. With a secretive tone, she brought the phone close to her lips and whispered, "What you have in your hand, Sharon, is one of the rarest artifacts in the world... Put it this way: there are others like it, but none are made of solid gold as far as I know. I hope Peter is there to guard it—that thing is priceless!"

"Yes," Sharon said. "He's standing right beside me... but you haven't told me what it is yet."

Shifting her gaze back to Jane, Claire explained, "You're holding a golden bust of Olympias, the mother of Alexander the Great... Lucius mistakenly thought he'd seized a golden bust of Cleopatra from the grave robber in Alexandria. This bust is probably what he was referring to in his letter to Cara."

"Wow, Claire! I would've never guessed that!" Sharon exclaimed.

"We're heading over there now!" Claire said. She looked at Jane, who stood speechless, and said, "Let's go. You don't want to miss this!"

Claire sank to her knees as she took hold of the golden bust, which was inlaid with turquoise, obsidian, and other precious stones. Cradling it in her arms, she let out a deep sigh.

"This must weigh at least..."

"25 pounds… Over 11 kilos," Sharon interjected. "I weighed it."

Claire turned to Jane. "Would you like to hold it?"

Jane gave an enthusiastic nod. Claire carefully handed the bust to Jane and then returned her gaze to Sharon.

"So far as I know—and if it's truly solid gold—this could be one of the rarest artifacts in the world." She paused, shaking her head in amazement. "This could rival the Golden Mask of Tutankhamun in its rarity."

"It's certainly magnificent," Jane commented. "I've never seen anything like it."

"Nor have I," Claire echoed. She paused for a moment, then said, "This was crafted for someone royal—for a queen... perhaps a gift from Alexander the Great to his mother, Queen Olympias!"

"My god!" Jane exclaimed.

"I need to call Callum," Claire said. She looked him up in her contacts and was about to dial his number when Sharon raised her hand. "You may want to wait before calling him." She gestured toward the benches set up by her trailer.

"There's more?" Claire asked, wide-eyed.

Sharon nodded. "Mm-hmm… Follow me!"

30

Even from a distance, Claire knew what she was looking at—the shape was unmistakable. Her pulse quickened as she approached the centuries-old breastplate armor, watching Eve meticulously clear away the dirt and debris with a small brush.

Claire drew closer, peering over Eve's shoulder and marveling at the magnificence of the object. Eve shot a glance at her and smiled. Claire returned her smile but didn't say anything; she didn't want to interrupt her flow.

Though the breastplate was an extraordinary find, it didn't intrigue her as much as the golden bust of Olympias. Just as she was about to leave, she paused, her gaze drawn to the emblem at the breastplate's center.

She stepped forward, placed a hand on Eve's shoulder, and continued staring at it. Without saying a word, she reached for the brush in Eve's hand, her eyes fixed on the breastplate. Eve handed her the brush and stepped aside.

It only took a few swipes of the brush to confirm Claire's suspicion.

"Would you like to tell us what we're looking at?" Jane asked, standing beside Claire.

"It's a breastplate," Sharon replied.

"Mm… But not just any breastplate," Claire said, stepping back to shift her perspective.

Jane cleared her throat. "Well?"

Claire turned to Jane and smiled. "You are looking at Alexander the Great's breastplate armor... with a singular, one-of-a-kind feature."

Jane's eyebrows shot up. "What singular feature? Don't make me try and guess!"

Claire took a deep breath and then exhaled. She looked at Sharon and then back at Jane. "Ladies, this is probably the only breastplate in existence belonging to Alexander that has a horned Zeus Ammon emblem."

"Wait!" Sharon exclaimed, brimming with enthusiasm. "The others have a Medusa emblem, right?"

"Smart girl," Claire said, pointing a finger at her. "This breastplate was made after Alexander was proclaimed son of Ammon—son of Zeus. The same image of the ram's horns appears on his coins." With her hands on her hips, she turned and looked out across the excavation site. Jane and Sharon followed her line of sight as she continued.

"Lucius likely traveled all across the Roman Empire. I expect we'll find artifacts from all over the Roman provinces. According to his correspondences, he traveled to mainland Italy, North Africa, and Scotland... Who knows what the remaining letters will reveal?"

"I suppose we'll have to keep on reading his letters," Jane chimed in.

"And hers," Claire added. "Don't forget Cara's letters—or her diaries. They lend a different perspective—her viewpoint from the home front. Remember, she was nursing Lucius when we left her last, tending to his injuries."

A deep voice interrupted the moment, reverberating through Claire's body, sending a shiver down her spine. Her heart skipped a beat. She hated feeling this vulnerable, so completely at the mercy of her own reaction.

Turning around, she saw him standing beside Eve, watching her work. She nodded at the breastplate on the table, trying to ignore the urge to stare at him. "I expect we'll dig up more artifacts like that—more relics from Egypt's Greek dynasty, down to her last ruler... Cleopatra!"

Stewart glanced over at them and waived. "Hi, everyone!"

Claire waved back. "Hi, Stewart! What are you doing here?" The words came out sharper than she intended, almost accusatory.

"I'm sorry! I was just taking a break and wanted to stop by and say hi." He raised his hands, palms facing out. "I've been getting some serious callouses... We've been digging hard all day, every day."

"I'm sorry, Stewart! That came out wrong... I meant to ask…" Claire stammered. "What I meant was, what brings you here? Any good news?"

Stewart shook his head. "Unfortunately, not yet... but we're making great progress. The Solidus coins we found earlier are promising, aren't they?"

"Absolutely! Keep your chin up," Claire said with a reassuring tone. "I'm sure you're going to come across a big find. I have a lot of faith in you... and the new site."

Stewart nodded sheepishly. "Thank you. I appreciate your support."

"You're welcome!"

Stewart motioned to the breastplate on the table. "Roman?"

Claire smiled and shook her head. "Greek!"

Stewart drew closer to the bench and ran his fingers across the emblem.

"It's beautiful! I've never seen anything like it."

Claire wanted to step close to him—to point out the detailed markings on the breastplate and explain the emblem's significance—but she hesitated. Instead, she stayed at a safe distance and said, "That's because there are no others like it."

"Oh?" Stewart said with a quizzical expression. "How so?"

"Well, because it belonged to Alexander the Great."

Stewart arched his brow in surprise. "Wow! Really?"

Claire nodded. "Yes, and it was crafted after he was declared the son of God by the oracle of Zeus Ammon in Egypt. Alexander's regular breastplates had a Medusa emblem in the center of the breastplate," she explained, making circles on her chest with her finger. "That one has a ram's horn design, making it a unique piece."

"And it needs to be cataloged and sent to the lab for conservation," Jane interjected. "You know what to do. Coordinate with Peter—we can't afford any mistakes. Same goes for the gold bust. That thing is studded with precious stones. Please follow proper protocols for shipment and storage."

Stewart nodded and waived. "See you all later."

"Wait!" Claire called out. "Next weekend, we're going to the city. I think we could all use a little break." She motioned to his hands. "And let your callouses heal a bit."

Stewart's face lit up. "That's wonderful! Thank you, Claire."

Claire raised her hand to wave goodbye, but Stewart had already turned to walk away.

"Are we really going to the city next weekend?" Jane asked, curious why Claire hadn't mentioned anything to her.

"Yeah, are we?" Sharon asked, beaming.

Claire smiled and nodded. "I think we could all use a break... It'll be fun."

Claire had written a letter and tried emailing Callum to inform him of the progress she'd made. But he never opened the email. She knew this because she'd sent it requesting a read-receipt and never got confirmation that he'd read it.

However, it didn't matter since he needed to be updated on the latest and far more significant discoveries.

She was pleasantly surprised when he answered the phone.

"Good evening, Callum... This is Claire Langford."

"I know who it is, my dear!" Callum chuckled heartily. "I've got caller identification, you know! It says, 'My favorite girl!'"

Claire turned to Jane. "That's sweet. I'm putting you on speaker, Callum, so Jane can hear you... You remember Jane, don't you?"

"Your beautiful assistant! Of course, I do. How could I forget?"

Claire winked at Jane. "Yes, she's definitely the one!"

"Hello, Callum!" Jane said.

"Hello, Jane… How are you?"

"I'm fine, thank you!"

"Callum, we have wonderful news for you," Claire said.

"That's good to hear. I'm all ears, dear."

"Did you get the email and letter I sent you?"

"I got your letter, dear. I'm not very good at that electronic mail nonsense. I prefer a proper letter. My secretary checks my emails, and I've been trying to avoid her. She always comes at me with a stack of papers. I was planning on calling you, but I've been busy lately. I had a doctor's appointment, et cetera, et cetera, et cetera. I don't wish to bore you. Getting old is a pain, my dear. Never get old. Stay young and beautiful. Both of you."

"Gosh, I hope you're all right!"

"Yes, yes, don't worry. All routine stuff."

"Well, I'm glad. Here's some news that may cheer you up… Can you hear me all right?"

"Yes, I can, dear."

"We have unearthed a golden bust... I believe it's a gold bust of Olympias.

Silence.

Claire continued. "And a Macedonian breastplate... one that likely belonged to Alexander. But instead of a Medusa emblem, this one bears the image of a horned Zeus Ammon."

"Good God!"

Claire glanced at Jane. She shrugged. They heard Callum breathing, but he didn't say another word. There was a flicking sound, followed by a deep inhale and then an exhale.

"Callum?"

"Yes, dear."

"Are you all right?"

Another deep inhalation and long exhalation followed. "Yes, dear… I'm smoking, trying to calm myself down. The doctor said I shouldn't get too excited."

Claire's expression changed to one of concern. "I'm sorry. Should I call you another time?"

"No, that's not necessary…" Callum paused to take another drag of his cigarette. He exhaled slowly and added, "Your discoveries... are truly monumental."

"I realize that."

"And I suspect you've only scratched the surface... Perhaps you could stop here, and we can discuss things in person."

"Of course, where?"

"Edinburgh... It's beautiful up here this time of year. Bring Jane along."

31

The painting in Dr. Tussaud's waiting room no longer stirred the same intense emotions it once had in Amelie. She imagined herself on the small boat, swaying back and forth in the surf as the lighthouse beacon swung around, flashing a bright beam of light at her.

Yet, even against the background of a dark, menacing sky, she felt nothing—no sense of dread, no impending doom. Her fingers brushed against the heart-shaped pendant around her neck. She brought it close to her face and stared at it. A smile formed on her lips, and she whispered, "Titou."

Suddenly, a figure appeared in front of her, grabbing her attention.

"Good morning, Amelie! Dr. Tussaud is ready to see you. Please follow me."

Amelie rose from the couch and followed Dr. Tussaud's assistant to her office.

Dr. Tussaud looked up from her notes and smiled. "Hello, Amelie! It's nice to see you." She gestured toward the chair opposite her. "Please have a seat."

Amelie smiled shyly and sat down. "Hello, Dr. Tussaud."

Dr. Tussaud put aside her notes and crossed her legs, interlocking her fingers around them.

"So, Amelie, how are you?"

"I'm fine… Thank you."

"It has been a while since I saw you."

Amelie smiled and nodded. "Yes, I've been busy."

Dr. Tussaud paused, studying Amelie closely.

"I'm very happy to hear that. How about your nightmares? Are you still having them?"

Amelie shook her head but hesitated before replying, "Well… not exactly."

Dr. Tussaud wrinkled her brow. "Hmm… Please go on."

"I do have nightmares, but they're not about the same thing."

Dr. Tussaud motioned to Amelie's pendant. "That's a beautiful necklace."

Amelie took the pendant between her fingers and gently stroked it.

"Madeleine got it for me," she beamed. "It says, 'Titou' on it… He's my dog."

"Ah… I see… Well, it's beautiful."

Dr. Tussaud was quick to notice the change in Amelie; she was no longer the same patient she'd last seen—she'd transformed. She seemed happy.

"I'd like to know about your dreams." Dr. Tussaud went on. "Explain what you meant by 'not exactly.'"

Amelie lowered her gaze and began fiddling with her pendant. She let out a sigh.

"I meant I don't dream about Henri anymore."

"Mm-hmm, please go on."

"I dream about a girl I knew."

"A girl?"

Amelie nodded. "She was on the yacht with me. Henri was very cruel to her… I have nightmares about that. But I became friends with her; she always protected me… Her name was Celine… I dream about her."

Dr. Tussaud nodded as she jotted down notes. "Please continue… What do you dream about?"

"She used to sneak out at night... and she'd come to my cabin and climb into bed with me… I dream about her sleeping next to me. Then I wake up, and she's not there."

Dr. Tussaud lowered her glasses onto her nose and gazed at Amelie.

Amelie rolled her eyes. "It wasn't like that! I used to cry a lot, and she used to come and lie with me... to comfort me."

Dr. Tussaud chuckled softly. "That's not what I was thinking. I was thinking about a phenomenon called collective trauma or collective trauma bonding—it's when people who have shared a traumatic event develop a bond with each other. It can be a coping mechanism."

Amelie turned toward the window and let out a deep sigh. "I miss her... I'm worried about her."

Her voice carried a sense of sadness. Dr. Tussaud paused to let it linger in the air. She didn't want to cloud the moment with words; she knew she couldn't provide an immediate solution.

Instead, she lent a sympathetic ear, allowing the words to resonate. The feelings of helplessness and the inability to provide a solution were all too familiar to her.

She often felt powerless, listening to her patients while watching the hands on her clock stay stubbornly frozen as if time stood still, unable to help.

There were other times when she knew her words had averted disaster. She knew her voice had reached over the phone like an invisible hand, preventing a desperate soul from jumping off a bridge.

In those moments, she felt triumphant, omnipotent, even. It was these moments that made it all worthwhile.

Amelie shifted her gaze back to Dr. Tussaud. She blinked, releasing the tears that had collected in her eyes. A smile broke through as she wiped the tears from her cheek with the back of her fingers. Taking a long breath, she said, "But I have hope."

"Oh? Tell me about it," Dr. Tussaud encouraged.

"Marcel told me—he promised me—he'd find her... soon."

"Well, that's wonderful, Amelie! That should give you plenty of comfort and reassurance."

Amelie nodded. "It does... I know Celine... She's very strong. I know she'll be all right." She placed a hand over her heart. "I feel it in here."

Amelie's inspiring words filled Dr. Tussaud with joy and relief. Suddenly, she felt like the roles had been reversed: Amelie was offering consolation, and she was receiving it.

She smiled and shook her head. "Dear, you make my job easy. I wish all my patients were like you!"

32

Jane had shot down two would-be suitors before their server even brought their first drinks. Right from the start, they were shooting themselves in the foot with their cheesy approaches and corny one-liners.

She was turning heads, and men were practically tripping over themselves as they passed by their table, too intimidated to approach her. Claire and Sharon snickered as they watched her hapless admirers crash and burn.

Jane wore a red button-front vest blazer, casual jeans, and matching stilettos. Her hair was in a ponytail, and she'd applied just enough makeup to look effortlessly polished. Claire and Sharon watched heads turn as she got up and walked to the powder room.

"She's amazing, isn't she?" Claire mused, her lips curling into a smile.

"She is!" Sharon agreed. "She's the best!"

"And she's not even trying."

"I Know… She's doing everything she can to repel them, not attract them... I have a story to tell you, but you can't say anything, okay?"

"Sure—promise!"

"When she first started working with us, I went out with her once. We'd gone out to a bar, and some guy got a little handsy…"

"Uh-oh!" Claire's eyes widened.

"Yeah, uh-oh… She punches the guy in the face. I grab her around the waist and peel her off him." Sharon shook her head. "You don't mess with that girl... Not unless you want to get your face rearranged."

"Gosh! Was she all right?"

"Yeah! And the funny thing is, the guys in the bar were actually rooting for her... She's one tough cookie!"

"Who's a tough cookie?" Jane asked as she circled the table and took her seat beside Claire.

"Oh, no one... You don't know her. She's a friend of mine from college," Sharon quickly shot back.

"How was she tough?"

"She…" Sharon stammered. "She…"

Jane nudged Sharon playfully, grinning. "She, what?"

"She'd get into fights with other girls."

"Oh!"

"Yeah, she was a great girl, though."

"Mm."

Jane smiled, knowing Sharon was talking about her, but she didn't mind. She knew she was among friends who cared deeply for her.

The club, one of the few places Jane approved of, was a cozy little spot near downtown Newcastle. It was frequented by a few regulars and located near the hotel where they were staying.

Claire smiled and waved at her crew as they entered the bar and sat at tables near her booth. She and Jane always preferred a booth in a secluded corner of the bar, away from prying eyes.

When Eve walked in, Jane waved her over to their table.

She patted the seat beside her and said, "Hey, Evie! Why don't you come sit here with us? Plenty of room here, and it's pretty comfy!"

Eve smiled and waved back. She glanced at Sharon and then at Claire. "Hi, Aunt Sharon... Hi Claire."

Eve sat beside Jane and whispered, "Thanks for inviting me to your table, Jane!"

Jane wrapped an arm around her and pulled her close. "You're so welcome, sweetie! We girls have to look out for each other, right?"

Eve smiled and nodded. "That's right."

Just then, Stewart and Arnold walked in. Stewart headed straight to the bar; he hadn't spotted anyone yet. Arnold stood in one spot, awkwardly craning his neck, looking for familiar faces.

Jane motioned to Arnold and whispered, "Look out! Radar man is here."

Claire and Sharon erupted into laughter. Arnold heard them. He turned and waved.

"Hi, ladies!" he called out.

To Claire and Sharon's utter amazement, Jane waved Arnold over. As far as they knew, it was a girl's night out, and Jane only wanted to hang out with them.

Arnold approached, his nervous smile revealing just how out of place he felt.

Jane was going to ask him to sit at the table with them, but then she came up with another idea: she stood up and walked over to him.

"Hey, Arnold, how's it going?"

Arnold shrugged. "It could be better; I guess... The GPR was glitching. It wasn't reading the ground right. But I think I've figured it out..."

Jane cut him short. "Do you know how to play darts?"

Arnold chuckled. "Yeah, it's about the only thing I know."

"Good, let's go." She turned and headed toward the dartboard in a corner opposite the bar, with Arnold following behind.

Claire and Sharon watched Jane gleefully hurl darts at the dartboard without appearing to care if she hit a bullseye. Arnold clapped for her, no matter if she missed.

Jane would throw a dart, miss the dartboard entirely, and then pump her fists in the air, laughing.

Claire turned to Sharon and motioned toward Jane. "Let's go play darts. It looks like Jane is having lots of fun... Would you like to?"

Sharon gave a big nod. "I love darts!"

Claire pressed a finger to her lips, silently telling Arnold to stay quiet as she approached Jane from behind. She stealthily walked up and covered Jane's eyes with her hands.

Jane placed her hands over Claire's and took a long sniff. "Mmm… You wore my perfume!" She spun around and faced Claire with a big smile on her face. She held up a dart.

"Wanna play?"

Claire laughed and nodded. "Sharon, too. She wants to play."

Sharon chuckled. "I do… If I'm not crowding you all."

"Oh, you're crowding... But I love you, Shar, so you can play… Loser buys drinks!"

From the corner of her eye, Claire noticed Stewart sitting at the bar, watching them and looking glum as if he were being ignored. She leaned in and whispered to Jane, "Hey, should we invite Stewart over? He's been sitting there by himself all night."

Jane gave a shrug while aiming for another throw. "I'm getting tired... I want to go sit back down and chitchat." She threw her dart and missed. She spun around to face Claire. "Arnold told me Stewart's being an asshole to him at work. I may need to have a talk with him at some point… but not tonight."

"All right. Whatever you want to do."

For the rest of the night, Claire kept a close eye on Stewart, watching how he interacted with the team.

She wanted to speak with him privately, but she didn't want to overstep Jane's authority; Jane was his immediate supervisor, and Claire didn't want to cause any tension.

She knew if it came down to a choice between Stewart and Jane, she'd have to let Stewart go, despite her strong feelings for him that had bubbled up since he started working for her— feelings that may have been simmering beneath the surface and spilling into her dreams.

33

While walking around the city, Claire felt proud of her accomplishments. She was overseeing one of the most promising excavation sites in England, and her team had grown by six employees, bringing the total number to 17, not including the excavation operators.

Her team followed behind her as she led the way, accompanied by Jane and Sharon. They strolled along the streets, admiring the remnants of the Roman ruins in front of them.

Claire felt relieved to see Arnold and Stewart behind her, laughing and chatting together. They seemed to be getting along with each other.

Pausing to admire a section of Hadrian's Wall that ran alongside the street, she sensed Stewart standing beside her.

"Does any of this remind you of what you saw in North Africa?" She asked, keeping her eyes fixed ahead.

"I'm sorry?" Stewart said, seeming confused.

Claire turned to face him. "Your experience at Leptis Magna—does this bring back any memories?"

"Oh, I'm sorry... Yes and no. Yes, because all Roman structures have similarities, but no, because Leptis Magna was on the Mediterranean Sea, and—"

Claire interrupted him, completing his thought. "And Hadrian's Wall is in the frozen North?"

Stewart laughed. "No, I didn't mean that... It just feels different here..."

"I know, I'm only teasing, Stewart," Claire grinned, playfully patting his arm. "I wasn't being serious."

Stewart smiled sheepishly and lowered his head.

On Claire's left, Jane stood, looking straight ahead.

Claire leaned in and whispered, "You hungry?"

Jane perked up and nodded. "Famished!"

"Fish and chips?"

"Mmm… Sounds great!"

In her late thirties and with a full, curvy figure, Sharon was a classic beauty who hardly needed any makeup.

With pale skin and green eyes framed by thick lashes and long, wavy black hair, she knew she was beautiful but chose to downplay her physical appearance.

Working in the "dirt pit" all day, as she described it, she didn't want to hassle with makeup. Following in her aunt's footsteps, her niece, Eve, was a carbon copy of Sharon in demeanor and appearance.

Sharon and Eve sat opposite Claire and Jane, eyeing their large baskets of fresh fish with crispy batter and chips. Sharon playfully nudged Eve's arm. "Eat up, sweetie! Your mom's going to kill me if I send you back skinny as a twig… so eat up!"

Eve gave a shy smile and picked up a piece of fish, dipping it into tartar sauce. She bit into it, making a crunchy sound that caught Jane's attention.

"Mmm… That looks so good! Where the heck is our waitress with our food?" She spun around to catch the server's attention. She pointed to her watch, then threw her hands up in protest.

The waitress called back, "I'm so sorry, love! Be right with you!"

Jane rolled her eyes but turned back to Eve with a grin. "I'm only playing… not trying to be mean to her."

Eve pushed her basket of fish toward Jane. "Please have some of mine; there's no way I can finish all this."

Jane leaned in, placing her hand on Eve's. "I love you, Evie! You're so sweet! ... I can wait. I'm not even that hungry." She scrunched her nose at Eve and added, "I just like to make a scene!"

Claire erupted into laughter, and Sharon nearly spewed out the food in her mouth.

Jane shrugged and grinned. "Hey, at least I'm being honest!"

A moment later, the server arrived with Claire and Jane's food. She caught Jane glaring at her as she placed a steaming basket of fish and chips in front of her.

Leaning closer, she cupped her hand around her mouth and whispered to Jane, "Thanks, pet, for your patience! I'm so sorry; I'm running behind. Don't tell anyone, but I brought you some extra pieces at no charge."

Jane smiled and winked at her as she reached for a piece of fish.

"No worries, pet! It's all right... And thank you for the extra pieces!"

The restaurant was packed, and Arnold and Stewart were having trouble finding an open table. Claire saw them and waved them over.

"We've got a couple of empty chairs."

"Thank you, Claire," Arnold said, taking the chair beside her. Stewart sat next to Eve and Sharon, facing Claire and Jane. He gave a polite nod. "Thank you, Claire... for lunch and inviting us over!"

Claire smiled in response. "You're welcome, Stewart!"

The waitress came over to take Stewart and Arnold's order.

"I'll rush your orders, love," she said, flashing a big smile at Stewart. She leaned in, resting her hand on his shoulder, and whispered, "And I'll get you both extra pieces for your trouble!"

Stewart smiled back at her. "Thank you, dear. I appreciate it."

"So, Stewart, tell us about your home state, Indiana," Claire said. "I've never been to America. What was it like where you grew up?"

Stewart set down the piece of fish he was holding and wiped his fingers with a napkin.

"Well, it was a small town called Fair Oaks," he said with a nostalgic smile. "You could hardly find it on the map. I grew up on a farm—I'd wake up before sunrise, drive with my father in his truck, and take hay bales to feed the cows. Then, come back and clean the horse stalls… Not very glamorous work."

"That sounds amazing! I've never been horseback riding. I love animals... I bet it was lots of fun living on a farm."

Stewart shook his head. "You'd get tired of it pretty quickly. It's really hard work: lots of long days. Some days, you work until dark."

Sharon laughed. "You mean just like we do in archaeology every day?"

Stewart chuckled. "Yeah, right! Life's funny that way, isn't it?"

Sharon nodded as she took a bite of her chips.

"I'd never even done a day's labor," Arnold chimed in. "I started out as a computer programmer."

"And I started as a runway model, then became an accountant," Jane interrupted, smirking.

"Did you, Jane? Really?" Eve asked, her eyes wide. "Were you a model?"

Jane shook her head and laughed. "No, sweetie. I'm joking. I got a degree in business administration and got a job at an accounting firm as an assistant. I slowly learned the business, and a couple of years later, I became an accountant."

Eve sighed. "You're beautiful, Jane! You could've easily been a model."

"Maybe in another life, dear... I got into a shitty relationship with a horrible man, and it sucked the life out of me." Jane leaned forward and curled her index finger, gesturing for Eve to come closer. Eve leaned in, and Jane took her hand. "Promise me you won't get into a crappy relationship."

Eve nodded, her voice firm. "I won't. I promise! I'm only 18. I don't even want to be in a relationship right now. I'm perfectly happy working with Aunt Sharon and Claire."

Jane paused momentarily as if trying to read Eve's thoughts to see if she meant what she said. She then smiled and said, "Me too, sweetie… I'm perfectly happy working with Aunt Sharon and Claire."

34

Claire sat in the armchair in their hotel room, sipping her Darjeeling tea and reading her book on Roman Britain. She glanced up and saw Jane pacing back and forth. She'd seemed agitated all night. Every time Claire tried to ask her what was bothering her, she'd change the subject.

Jane opened the sliding glass door and stepped out onto the balcony. She lit a cigarette, took a deep drag, then released a thin stream of smoke into the night. Claire kept a watchful eye on her as she smoked and gazed up at the sparkling stars.

Moments later, she returned inside, stubbed out the cigarette in the ashtray, and sank into a chair opposite Claire. She crossed her legs and let out deep a sigh.

Claire chuckled, closing her book and setting it aside. "Yes, Jane?"

"Can we go out? Just you and me?" Jane let out an exasperated sigh.

"But…" Claire started to say.

"Please?"

Claire studied her for a moment, then agreed. "Sure! Where would you like to go?"

"Dancing! … Just you and me."

"Yes, but can you tell me why you want it to be just the two of us?"

Jane sighed again. "I just do…"

"All right, where should we go?"

'Anywhere! Anywhere there's a dance floor… I don't care… I'll jump on a bar top if I have to."

Claire laughed, then paused and gazed at her. "Will you at least tell me what's bothering you?"

Jane rolled her eyes and looked away.

"All that, huh?"

"Mm-hmm."

Claire stood up and extended her hand. "All right... Let's go!"

Jane took Claire's hand and sprang out of her chair, smiling. "Really? You mean it?"

"Uh-huh... We need to get it out of your system—whatever it is—before we go back to work."

Jane flung herself at Claire, almost knocking the breath out of her, and threw her arms around her.

"I love you, Claire. Thank you!"

Claire smiled, wrapping her arms around her. "I love you, too."

The pulsating strobe lights flashed on Jane's face in sync with the beat of the song as her body swayed from side to side, arms above her head, and eyes closed. She looked like she was in a trance, completely lost in herself.

Claire drew closer, watching Jane and trying to keep up. She caught others staring at her—both men and women—watching her every move as she glided gracefully in her fitted one-piece dress, oblivious to their gazes.

Suddenly, Jane paused and looked at Claire. She took Claire's hand.

"Can we go somewhere quiet? ... Get a drink, maybe?"

"Sure!" Claire nodded.

Claire wanted to ask again what was wrong but held back. She didn't want to meddle or pry; she only wanted to help. She'd tried earlier but hit a wall with her, so she decided to wait and go with the flow.

She knew that, in time, Jane would open up to her. For now, it seemed she just needed someone to be with—someone she trusted.

All the bars were packed with people, and Jane seemed eager to roam freely; she didn't want to linger in any one spot. Holding

Claire's hand, they dashed down the cobblestone sidewalk, their laughter filling the air.

When Jane finally spotted a bar that didn't seem too crowded, she stopped and spun around, grinning widely. She nodded toward the neon sign that read "The Wet Whistle."

Claire chuckled, shaking her head in amusement before following her inside.

"Let's sit at the bar. Do you mind?" Jane smiled and scrunched her nose.

"Not at all," Claire replied.

"Vodka shots?"

"Why not?"

Jane caught the bartender's eye and raised two fingers.

"Vodka shots… Straight!"

The bartender, a young woman in her early twenties, smiled. "Two vodka shots coming up!"

Shifting on her bar stool, Jane faced Claire with a bright smile.

"Thank you for doing this, Claire... You're so good to me!"

Claire returned the smile and placed her hand on Jane's. "You're welcome!"

The bartender set down two shot glasses and poured the drinks.

"Any special occasion, ladies?" She asked with a soft, youthful tone.

Jane smiled at her and said, "No, dear... Just blowing off some steam."

"I'm sorry; I didn't mean to get personal. I'm new… They told me I've got to..."

"It's all right... Don't worry about it," Jane reassured her. "You're doing great! This is the social hour—you're supposed to get personal!"

The bartender smiled sheepishly and nodded as she walked away to serve another customer.

Jane turned to Claire. "I'm sorry… I can't help myself…"

"It's all right…" Claire chuckled. "I get it. You're a people person."

Jane's expression changed abruptly when she heard a commotion.

"What the hell!" A voice shouted. "You're supposed to serve drinks, not tell stories! Now get me a beer!"

Claire saw Jane's smile vanish. Her jaw clenched.

She quickly took Jane's hand. "Hey… Don't worry about it. She can handle herself. She just needs to learn how to deal with jerks."

Jane shut her eyes and nodded, seething.

"Remember, you can't fix everything… Let it go!"

Claire kept her gaze locked on Jane, talking about work, keeping her distracted until the obnoxious customer left. Once Jane saw that the man was gone, she caught the bartender's attention and waved her over.

When the bartender approached, Jane said, "You don't have to take that crap from men—or anyone, for that matter. You need to tell them they can't talk to you that way!"

The bartender nodded. She lowered her eyes; she was taken aback by Jane's intensity.

"I know."

"How often do you get jerks like that in here?"

"Not often," the bartender muttered.

"Do you mind if I ask your name?"

"My name is Isabel."

Jane took a moment to calm herself, then said, "My name is Jane." She gestured to Claire. "And this beautiful lady is my boss, Claire."

Isabel turned to Claire and smiled. "Hi, Claire."

Claire returned the smile. "Hi, Isabel… You have a beautiful name."

"Thank you," Isabel said, lowering her eyes.

Isabel grabbed a bar towel and started to wipe the counter, occasionally glancing up at Jane and Claire, smiling. Then she paused and said, "I'm sorry, but you both look very familiar. Have I seen you somewhere?"

Jane knitted her brow. "I don't know... Have you?"

Isabel looked at Claire, then turned back to Jane and nodded. "Yes, I think so…" She pressed a finger to her lips, gazing at them. "Hmm… Have you been to this bar before?"

Jane shook her head. "I'm sorry, no. We haven't... But we work nearby, just outside of town."

"What do you do, if I may ask?"

"We are working on an archaeological dig," Claire answered. "We come to town for supplies... or some relaxation…"

"Wait!" Isabel pointed at Claire. "I know where I've seen you!"

Jane was about to sip her drink but lowered her glass, her curiosity piqued. "Where? You've got me curious now."

"It was in the papers. I saw you in the papers... You had an event not too long ago, right?"

"That's right," Claire said. "It was an event to showcase our recent discoveries. Our goal was to attract sponsors."

"Did you find one?"

"Yes! We've got a great sponsor."

"That's great. I'm happy for you."

Isabel smiled at Claire and Jane before wandering off to attend to a couple sitting at a nearby table.

"She's really sweet," Jane commented, her eyes following Isabel.

"Yes, she is," Claire agreed.

"I was thinking…"

"Yeah?"

"Maybe we could invite her to the site and let her look around. I think she'd enjoy that."

"I think it's a great idea!" Claire exclaimed.

A few moments later, Isabel returned with a bottle of vodka. "Can I pour you another?"

"No, thank you, dear," Jane replied. "But we were wondering if you'd like to visit the site sometime."

Isabel's eyes grew wide. "You mean at your...?"

Jane smiled and nodded. "That's right! You can look around and see what we do."

Isabel beamed. "I would seriously love that!"

Jane laughed. "Then consider it a serious invitation!" She grabbed her phone and opened her contacts. "Give me your number. I'll text you."

Before leaving, Jane reached into her purse and took out a wad of cash. She put the money on the counter and placed her shot glass on top.

Claire and Jane waved as they walked past Isabel, who was attending to another customer.

"Bye, Isabel! We hope to see you soon!" Claire said with a smile.

Isabel waved back, beaming. "It was great meeting you both! And I'll definitely call you and stop by!"

Back at the hotel, Claire noticed Jane's entire demeanor had changed. She lay on the bed, her head propped on her hand, thumbing through the pages of a magazine.

A calmness had washed over Jane, and Claire didn't know why. She didn't care—she welcomed it.

<h1 style="text-align:center">35</h1>

Madeleine stared at herself in the mirror and grimaced at her reflection. She leaned in and traced her fingers along the bags under her amber eyes, which sparkled beneath softly arched eyebrows.

She glanced at her wedding picture on the dresser and shook her head. Her dishwater-blonde hair had streaks of gray peeking through at the roots. She combed her fingers through her hair, trying to brush the grays aside, revealing more of the blonde.

She had grown up playing tennis and maintained her slim figure by regularly playing with Marcel. Returning her gaze to the mirror, she picked up her makeup brush and began applying foundation.

Another picture on the dresser caught her eye: it was an image of her and Marcel, with Amelie standing between them. A smile appeared on her lips.

She heard the front door open, but Titou didn't bark; instead, his nails clicked against the wood floor as he bolted toward the entrance. She immediately knew Amelie was home. Hurrying out of her bedroom to meet her, she found Amelie on her knees, cradling Titou in her arms, her face buried in his belly.

Madeleine laughed as she wrapped her arms around both of them, squeezing them into an embrace.

"You know, you're the only one who can do that?"

Amelie pulled her face away from Tiou's belly, grinning. She nodded and said, "I know."

"So, how was your session with Jacqueline?"

Amelie lowered Titou to the ground. "It was great."

"You know, she's a very good friend of mine."

"I know… She's very nice," Amelie said, her eyes darting around the room. "Where's Marcel?"

"He left earlier. He didn't want to interrupt your session with Jacqueline. He won't be gone long; he'll be back tomorrow night," Madeleine replied, gently brushing a strand of hair away from Amelie's face. "He wants to take us out to dinner when he returns. In the meantime, you and I are heading to the salon, and then we'll go shopping. How does that sound?" Amelie furrowed her brow, alarm washing over her face. "It sounds good... But where did he go?"

"He had an assignment."

"Where?"

"Somewhere in Prague, I think."

Amelie fell silent. Titou stood on his hind legs, looking to be picked up. She lifted him and took him to the living room couch, sitting with him on her lap.

Madeleine strolled over and sat beside her. Gently running her fingers along Amelie's arm, she said in a comforting tone, "Please don't worry. He'll be back before you know it."

Amelie let out a deep sigh. "You haven't seen what he does, have you?"

Madeleine shook her head. She put her arm around Amelie and drew her closer. "I haven't... I don't know if I could..." She hesitated, her voice faltering. "I don't think I could handle it."

36

Marcel had never been to Prague; he'd only heard stories from his colleagues at Interpol.

Standing on the Charles Bridge, he gazed across the Vltava River and spotted his target.

He pressed the mic button on his radio and said, "Marek, I have eyes on the suspect. He just crossed over the bridge. I'm following him. Don't get too close; I don't want to spook him... He's our only lead."

"Copy that, Inspector," Marek's voice crackled over the radio. "My team is tracking him."

Marcel had fought hard to deploy his own team for the mission, but he ran into a bureaucratic maze of red tape. In the end, the answer he got was a definitive "No."

However, he was pleasantly surprised by Marek, an experienced and meticulous operator who'd gotten a mission briefing just a few hours earlier and had his team ready for action by the time Marcel's plane landed.

Marcel watched his suspect enter the club. After a few moments, he followed him inside and reached for his mic.

"I'm inside now. Have your team secure the perimeter. I'll flush him out, and you can arrest him."

"Copy that, Inspector."

"Oh, one more thing... Remember, I need him alive to interrogate him."

"Understood, Inspector."

Marcel was engulfed by a wave of sound the moment he stepped onto the dance floor. He'd heard the rhythmic booming of the rave music from the outside, but he wasn't prepared for how loud it was.

He pressed his mic button and called out to Marek, but he couldn't hear anything; he could barely hear his own voice.

His eyes scoured the dance floor, searching for his suspect, but he couldn't spot him among the large crowd of young people packed tightly together, moving in waves like a massive school of sardines.

He heard clicking sounds over his radio, but no audible voice came through. Pushing through the writhing crowd, his gaze shifted from one end of the dance floor to the other.

Suddenly, he heard the familiar popping sound and the bright muzzle flash of a gun lit up the dimly lit dance floor. Screams erupted as people dove to the floor or bolted toward the exits.

As the crowd scattered, a shadowy figure emerged in the middle of the dance floor.

Marcel stood face-to-face with the panicked suspect, holding his gun over his head, poised to fire another round.

He saw the glint of steel as the suspect lowered his pistol, aiming it directly at him. Instinct took over, and he fired two shots—one at the suspect's shoulder, the other at his thigh.

The suspect let out a shriek as his gun flew out of his hand, and he collapsed to the floor.

He kneeled beside the suspect and checked his pulse; the man was still alive.

Hearing the pounding of boots, Marcel looked up and saw Marek and his team approaching with their guns drawn. He raised a hand and shouted, "It's all right... He's down, but he's breathing."

Marek holstered his pistol and crouched beside Marcel. "I'm sorry, Inspector! I tried to reach you, but all I heard was the background noise... We ran into him in the back... He saw us and ran back towards you."

"Don't worry about it, Marek, I understand… These things never go as planned." Marcel patted Marek on the back. "Look, we got our guy, and no one got hurt."

Marek nodded at the suspect sprawled on the floor. "Except him."

"Except him," Marcel echoed. He looked down and noticed the suspect's eyes were open. "But he'll live." He paused, then added, "I'm afraid I must return to Paris. Please let me know how the interrogation goes when he gets out of surgery."

Marek nodded. "Don't worry, Inspector. I'll handle that myself and call you as soon as possible."

Marcel had heard a lot about Prague, the City of a Hundred Spires, and its rich medieval history. Marek took the scenic route to the airport, allowing Marcel to take in some of the sites.

He sighed, gazing at the city's gothic architecture, especially St. Vitus Cathedral and Old Town Square. He wished he could stay and explore the city, but there was a dinner date waiting for him in Paris—one he wouldn't miss for the world.

He grabbed his phone, swiftly typed a text, and hit "send."

I will be there in 3 hours. Looking forward to dinner tonight. Love you both!

Madeleine breathed a sigh of relief when she saw the message appear on her phone. She showed it to Amelie and quickly typed a response.

We love you too! Someone has been anxiously waiting for you to get back home.

Give her a hug and a kiss for me! I'll see you soon!

37

Jane leaned over the counter, squinting as she tried to read her texts while struggling to twist the corkscrew into the wine bottle.

Claire chuckled. "You know, it'll be a lot easier if you put the bottle down first."

Jane huffed, walked over, handed the bottle to Claire, and stuck out her tongue.

Claire laughed as she pulled the cork out. "So, are you going to tell me what's going on?"

"I've got two texts—one from Isabel, asking if she can stop by to visit us, and another from Peter. He wants to know if he can hire another armed guard. He says he's been struggling to secure both the warehouse and the dig site. He says we need at least one more guard so he can cover the site and the warehouse effectively."

Jane looked up from her phone, waiting for a response.

Claire gave a wave and said, "Tell him, yes, he can hire another guard."

"And what about Isabel?" Jane asked as she typed a text to Peter.

"By all means, have her stop by. Tell her to come early so she can spend the day here."

"She says she's off tomorrow."

"Then tell her to come tomorrow."

"Yay!" Jane exclaimed as she sent the text to Isabel. She grinned and said, "Done!"

Claire's eyes followed Jane as she placed her phone on the nightstand, grabbed two wine glasses, and sank onto the bed beside her.

"Story time!" Jane exclaimed, pouring a glass for both herself and Claire.

Claire laughed as she took the glass from Jane. "What would you like to hear?"

Jane sat up cross-legged, facing Claire, and asked, "How's Lucius doing? He was wounded when we last read about him... Remember?"

"Hmm... You're right... Let's see..."

Claire opened her laptop and searched through her folders until she found an image titled "Skirmish in Caledonia."

"Here we go... Here's Lucius... He was brought home to Cara, wounded.

Jane nestled close to Claire and sipped her wine; her eyebrows furrowed in concentration.

"Did he make it?"

Claire began to read the Latin text, quietly muttering under her breath. "'Apollo eum sanavit... It means, 'Apollo healed him.'" Claire continued with Jane's eyes glued to her lips. "Cara then makes a sacrifice to Apollo, thanking him for saving her husband's life." She paused and knitted her brow. "Hmm..."

"What is it?" Jane asked.

"This is interesting," Claire replied, pressing her finger to her lips. "Cara makes a sacrifice to Apollo, but her ritual seems more Celtic. This is a prime example of the melding of cultures, a mix of Roman and Celtic rituals and practices."

"Mm... She must have really loved him," Jane whispered softly, resting her head on Claire's shoulder and peering at her computer screen. "I want to hear more about them—about their personal relationship."

A slight smile spread on Claire's face as she enlarged the image of the tablet. She loved seeing Jane's softer, more vulnerable side—her calm, sweet side.

She recalled when Jane was about to unleash her fury on the customer at the bar who'd been harsh with Isabel. Now, sat curled against her, blissfully immersed in a 1900-year-old love story.

Here was the duality of Jane's personality—of her essence—on full display.

"Here's your answer," Claire murmured. "This will tell you more about her feelings for him: 'I did not leave his side for a month, tending to his injury as he slowly recovered. I bathed him and cleaned his wound. I slept beside him, holding his hand, and I prayed to Brigid.

"Wait... Brigid? Who's Brigid?" Jane interrupted.

"Brigid is a Celtic god associated with healing and fertility, among other things."

"So she prayed to her Celtic gods, too?"

"Yes, she kept her own heritage and her customs... But as you can see, she was completely devoted to him."

Jane downed the rest of her wine and set her glass on the nightstand. She flopped onto the bed, hands behind her head, and let out a sigh.

"I wonder what they looked like."

Claire put away her glass and lay beside her. "You may soon find out."

Jane turned on her side, facing Claire. "What? How?"

"The DNA testing may tell a lot about them, including their hair color, eye color, and skin tone..."

"No way!" Jane exclaimed.

Claire gave a nod. "Yes, way. I've been studying it... For instance, the MC1R gene can tell if Cara had freckles. It can tell us their approximate age... gender."

Jane's eyes grew wide, and her mouth fell open.

Claire chuckled. "When are we getting the DNA and radiocarbon test results?"

Jane quickly grabbed her phone and began sifting through her emails.

"Here it is... We should receive it this week!"

Claire smiled at Jane, then reached over and turned off the nightlight.

"Get some rest. We've got a busy day ahead."

Jane let out a groan. "All right… Party pooper."

Claire laughed. "Do you realize we've been going to bed after midnight almost every night?"

"Um, I think your watch is broken… But don't worry, I'll buy you a new one."

The following morning, Jane woke up to find Claire already gone.

Claire had made pancakes and placed a plate covered with plastic wrap on the coffee table, along with a note: "Good morning! There's coffee in the pot."

Jane's face lit up with joy as she unwrapped the pancakes and took a bite. She glanced at the clock on the dresser. It was 8:30 a.m.

Technically, she didn't need to be at the dig site; her job was to crunch numbers and supervise others, but she was caught up with her tasks, so she devoured her pancakes and washed them down with coffee. She then sprang to her feet and hurried to brush her teeth and get ready.

Claire called it a premonition—she felt something big was about to happen. Whatever it was, she was spot on.

She took the trowel from Sharon and gently scraped away the dirt from the top of the object, revealing a section of its smooth, shiny surface. She brushed her fingers across it and paused, glancing up at Sharon with a beaming smile.

"Do you know what this is?"

Sharon shook her head. "What is it?"

"It's a marble sarcophagus." Claire gently swept away more dirt from its lid. She grabbed a tape measure and measured the length. "It's 243.8 centimeters long."

"That's eight feet!" Sharon exclaimed, her eyes widening.

Claire nodded. "That's right."

"Do you think there's a body in there?"

Claire shrugged. "We won't know until we open it, will we?"

Sharon continued to scrape away the dirt from the top of the sarcophagus and paused when she saw markings on its side. She gave Claire a questioning look.

"What are these?"

Claire traced her fingers over the indentations on the lid and said, "They're Greek letters carved into the marble." She then reached for her phone and took pictures of the letters, murmuring, "I can't read Greek... But I know someone who can."

"Let me guess… Damian?" A voice chimed in.

Claire turned and saw Jane standing in the sun. She raised her hand to her brow to shield her eyes from the bright sunlight. "Good morning, Jane! Yes, Damian Kostas. How did you know?"

"Good morning! I've heard you talk about him... He went to Oxford, right?"

Claire nodded. "He graduated the same year I did. He got his graduate degree in Greek language and literature."

Claire pulled Damian up in her contacts and, with Jane peeking over her shoulder, texted him the picture with the caption, "Solve this Greek riddle and win a trip to beautiful Santorini!"

Jane let out a chuckle and placed her hand on Claire's shoulder. "Wait, do I get a trip to Santorini if I figure out what it says?"

Claire laughed. "Sure, Jane, I'll even come with you."

Damian Kostas's eyebrows shot up when he saw the text. He pushed aside his plate of food and stared at the image on his phone. Then he noticed the caption and laughed.

Instead of responding to Claire's text, he dialed her number.

Claire immediately answered. "Hello, Damian!"

"Hi, Claire! How are you?" he asked.

"I'm fine, thank you! How are you?" she replied.

"I'm well, thank you. I'm really glad to hear from you—glad and surprised! It's been a few years."

"I'm sorry I haven't kept in touch, Damian. I've been super busy."

"I know; I read the newspaper articles—congratulations!"

"Thank you, Damian! So, where did you go after graduation?"

"I went nowhere."

"I mean, where did you move to? What are you doing now?"

Damian chuckled. "I didn't go anywhere, Claire. I live in Oxford and teach at the university. You know, our alma mater."

"Gosh, Damian! That's wonderful! It all makes sense now. You always liked teaching... I remember you were always tutoring students."

"Well, yes, I do enjoy teaching. And I had no interest in a regular desk job."

Claire sighed. "I'm truly happy for you, Damian—really, really happy!"

"And you, Claire—you are a renowned archaeologist. I'm jealous!"

Claire laughed. "I spend all day playing in the dirt, Damian." "And excavating ancient artifacts... Speaking of which, Claire, have you opened the sarcophagus yet?"

"No, I haven't. I saw the carving—the Greek letters—and immediately texted you... Were you able to translate them?"

"Yes, I was. The letters are in ancient Greek; they read, 'A queen... A warrior... A goddess.'"

Silence.

"Claire? Are you there?"

"I'm sorry, Damian... Yes, I'm here..."

"Do you realize the significance of those words?"

"I think so... Am I..." Claire stammered. "Am I staring at Cleopatra's sarcophagus?"

Jane's mouth fell open. She turned to Sharon, whose eyebrows shot up, her hand clamping over her mouth.

"You might be, Claire," Damian said, his voice crackling from poor phone reception. "Are you able to see any carvings on the side of the sarcophagus?"

"Not yet. We've only uncovered the top of it. How about I call you when we've fully excavated and opened it? It should only take a day or so... Are you available later?"

"Claire, this could be the most exciting thing I've ever laid eyes on in my life! Of course, I'll be available later. Call me the moment you open it."

"I will, Damian. Thank you!"

"And Claire..."

"Yes, Damian."

"Send pictures—pictures of the sides of the sarcophagus. That'll tell us a lot about the piece. And, of course, what lies inside."

"I will. I promise."

"I'll let you go then. Best of luck, Claire. I'm so excited for you..."

"Thank you, Damian! Goodbye for now."

"Goodbye!"

Claire immediately called Stewart and asked him to stop what he was doing at the new site and come over to help her. Minutes later, he arrived. With Stewart and Sharon working on one side and Claire and Jane on the other, it took only a few hours for the main body of the sarcophagus to slowly begin to surface.

Eve and the rest of the crew helped remove buckets of dirt from the pit, their eyes fixed on the stunning white marble emerging from the dark soil around it.

A relief appeared on the marble, depicting the tops of palm trees, followed by the crest of a helmet and a rider on horseback.

Alongside the rider, a female companion wearing a long robe with royal insignia rode on a horse. Claire took a picture of the relief and continued to remove the dirt until it was fully uncovered.

She took a step back, staring at the relief and shaking her head in disbelief. She noticed the expressions on Stewart and Sharon's faces as they gazed at the relief on the opposite side of the sarcophagus.

"This is amazing," Stewart exclaimed, scratching his head. "But I don't get it."

Claire circled the sarcophagus and stood facing the opposing relief. She raised an eyebrow. "I can see why!"

She took a picture of it and knelt beside it, resting her chin on her hand as she contemplated the image before her.

Sprawled across the side of the sarcophagus was a depiction of the Roman Senate, which wasn't unusual. What was highly unusual, however, was that while the Roman senators sat on one side of the Senate floor, a female figure was seated on a throne opposite them—a female figure wearing the headdress of the Egyptian goddess Isis.

"So, what am I looking at, exactly, Claire?" Stewart asked, his brow furrowed in confusion.

"Well, if I'm right in my assumption, Stewart, this is Cleopatra on the throne of Rome," Claire replied.

"On the throne?"

Claire nodded and pointed to the figure on the throne, holding a scepter and wearing an Isis headdress. "This relief portrays Cleopatra as Rome's sole ruler."

"Do you mean as a queen?" Jane asked.

"Why not?" Claire directed her attention at Jane, smiling. "After all, she ruled Egypt with enormous success."

Claire then walked around to the other side of the sarcophagus and waved for everyone to follow her. She paused and gestured toward relief. "Can anyone tell me what this scene is about?"

"Is it Alexander?" Jane asked.

Claire nodded. "Yes, Jane… Well done!"

"Who's that next to him?"

"My guess is Olympias, Alexander's mother... a queen herself."

Claire traced her finger along a symbol on the rider's robe. "This is the Vergina Sun—a Macedonian royal insignia."

Jane cocked an eyebrow. "But how do you know it's Olympias?"

"If this is not Olympias, then it must be another Macedonian royal. But who? Which other Macedonian royal female would accompany Alexander on the march?"

Claire pointed to other aspects of the relief. "This shows a large army—Alexander's entire phalanx—following behind him and his cavalry. They are riding away from the sea, which I presume is the Mediterranean, and towards a temple in the desert."

"Towards the temple of Zeus Ammon," Jane said excitedly.

"That's spot on!" Claire placed her hand on Jane's shoulder. "Exactly what I was thinking."

Jane wrinkled her brow. "So what's she doing marching in the desert with Alexander?"

"That's a great question, Jane." Claire gazed at the relief for a moment. "I believe she's accompanying her son to the temple of Zeus Ammon... to watch him be declared a god."

Claire circled the impressive sarcophagus, lost in thought. She delicately brushed away more dirt while her team watched. Jane stepped closer and stood beside her.

Claire turned to Jane and smiled.

"Let's open it... Carefully!"

Jane returned Claire's smile and nodded. She gestured to Stewart and the rest of the team to open the sarcophagus.

A wax or resin layer sealed the lid to the sarcophagus, presumably to protect its contents from the elements. It took about an hour to carefully run a thin, tapered blade along the sealant to loosen the lid.

Claire took a deep breath and exhaled. She motioned for her team to remove the lid.

"Please be super careful!"

Despite its broken seal, the sarcophagus lid made a faint hissing sound when it was lifted off as if cautioning the intruders to beware. The team then lowered it onto a protective tarp and covered it up.

Claire's heart pounded like a battle drum inside her chest. Approaching the sarcophagus, Jane looped her arm through Claire's while others watched. Claire and Jane craned their necks, looking over the top, brimming with anticipation.

As they peered inside the sarcophagus, a heavy, musty scent filled their nostrils. Jane turned to Claire and made a face. Claire nodded and scrunched her nose, mirroring Jane's expression, before shifting her attention to what was inside.

She squinted, trying to figure out what she was looking at.

A look of disappointment washed over Claire's face; she'd hoped to find the remains of Cleopatra or perhaps Olympias inside.

"What are we looking at?" Jane asked, looking confused.

"Hmm… I'm not quite sure," Claire replied, leaning closer. "I see a bundle of scrolls."

"Scrolls?"

"Scrolls, tablet… And I see pouches—lots of them."

Sharon approached to peek inside and turned to Claire.

"Do you want to take pictures before we take these to the warehouse?"

Claire nodded. "Yes, please. And then let's send them out to the conservation lab."

"I've got some good news for you," Jane interjected. "I researched and found a mobile conservation lab that can come to us instead of us transporting the artifacts to them. It'll save time and money, and we won't risk damaging the artifacts during shipment."

"That sounds fantastic, Jane, but is there a downside?" Claire asked.

Jane shook her head. "None! I looked into it." She grabbed her phone and opened her notes app. "Here, let's see... They said they have XRF analyzers and FTIR spectrometers. They said they can do anything our lab can do, and they can do it on-site!"

Claire nodded in approval. "Wow, Jane! That's wonderful... It always stresses me out when we ship things out. These artifacts are priceless." She paused, then added. "I bet we'll save on insurance as well."

"We will!" Jane smiled triumphantly. "I checked—we'll save a ton."

Claire resisted the urge to hug Jane in front of the team. Instead, she gave her a warm smile and a grateful pat on the arm.

"That's brilliant, Jane! Truly, well done!"

Sharon and Stewart carefully held the wooden tablets while Claire took pictures of them. The scrolls were rolled up and too delicate to unroll; they would need to go through a preservation process that could take weeks or even months to complete. However, there were enough tablets to keep them busy for quite a while.

When they opened the first leather pouch, Jane let out a loud gasp; it was filled with gold coins. She shot Claire a quizzical look as she held one of the coins in her palm.

"What's this? I haven't seen one like it!"

Claire extended her hand, and Jane placed the coin in it.

Claire knew instantly what she was looking at: "This is a Cleopatra tetradrachm."

"A tetra what?"

Claire chuckled. "It's a Greek coin. Cleopatra probably minted these coins to assert her authority and her legitimacy, among other reasons."

Jane glanced at the pile of bags inside the sarcophagus. "Well, she certainly minted a lot of them." She turned her attention to Stewart. "Are all the bags filled with gold coins?"

Stewart nodded. "They sure are." He and Sharon had opened all the bags and examined their contents.

Claire opened the Photos app on her phone, selected the images of the legible tablets and the reliefs on the sarcophagus, and texted them to Damian.

Hello Damian. Please see pictures of the sarcophagus reliefs and tablets we found inside. Let me know your thoughts. Thank you again and I hope I'm not imposing.

She grinned as she added:

BTW Cleopatra wasn't inside!

Jane sat by the trailer window, nursing her wine glass while Claire uploaded the pictures she'd taken on her phone to her laptop.

Suddenly, she saw a shadow dart across the excavation site and quickly vanish behind staff trailers. She sprang to her feet and set her wine glass on the coffee table. Grabbing a flashlight, she dashed out of the trailer.

In a panic, Claire closed her laptop, slipped on her sneakers, and ran out after her.

Claire saw Jane crouching next to one of the trailers and followed her. Jane cocked her head and saw Claire approaching.

She pressed her index finger to her lips, gesturing to Claire to be quiet. Claire nodded in understanding as she silently moved closer behind Jane.

Jane then stopped and turned off her flashlight, her back pressed against the trailers. She stealthily peered around the corner. Claire walked up behind Jane and looked over her shoulder.

"Did you see something?" she asked as her vision adjusted to the dark.

Jane nodded, her eyes fixed ahead, peering out into the darkness. A chill wind blew, sending shivers down Claire's spine.

"Follow me," Jane said as she turned the corner and continued along the length of the trailer, with Claire trailing behind. She paused and let out a frustrated sigh.

"I could swear I saw someone out here."

"Oh, I believe you," Claire murmured. "But I wonder who it was."

Jane pulled out her phone from her pants pocket and texted Peter.

Peter! Where the hell are you?
Our stalker is out again!!!

38

"Are you fuckin' kidding me, Peter?" Jane scoffed as she read Peter's text reply.

"What did he say?" Claire asked, her brows furrowing at Jane's reaction.

"He's giving me lip service. He's telling me he can't be in two places at the same time. He should've hired the extra security guard when he started working here—not wait until the last minute!"

"Mmm…"

"We've got this slasher creeping around this place at night, and he's nowhere to be found!"

Claire chuckled. "Slasher?"

Jane rolled her eyes. "Who knows? Slasher, stalker… What's the difference? And on top of that, he's got an attitude about it!" She paused when she noticed she had new emails. "Wait…"

"What is it?"

Jane glanced up from the phone screen. "We got the DNA and radiocarbon test results."

Claire, who had been reclining on the bed, stood and walked over.

"What does it say?" Claire asked.

Jane shrugged. "There are lots of technical terms: 'Carbon C-14,' 'Accelerator Mass Spectrometry'... Here, take a look," she said, handing her phone to Claire. "The summary conclusion narrows the time period to around 120-130 AD... The DNA analysis is in the next email."

Claire took the phone from Jane and scrolled through the emails. "The DNA analysis is also pretty technical," she commented as she studied the report. "But here's a snapshot composite..." Jane leaned in next to Claire, peering at her phone screen. Claire continued, "This suggests that Cara likely had fair skin, blue or green eyes, and red or blonde hair. It seems she carried the MC1R gene; she probably had freckles. This is consistent with her Celtic origins. Her ancestry shows she was primarily of Northern European descent."

"And Lucius?" Jane asked.

"Lucius likely had dark olive skin and brown eyes. His ancestry shows Southern European, mostly Italian, with a sprinkling of Spanish and Greek."

Claire strolled over to the window, with Jane following closely behind her. She gazed out at the River Tyne in the distance. "This is what we've been waiting for—confirmation of what we've suspected all along." She pointed toward the river, meandering across the plains, its water glimmering under a starlit sky. "Imagine Roman ships sailing up the river. They spot this location and decide to build a fort or settlement here... They've been ordered by Emperor Hadrian to build a wall here. At some point, Lucius ventures out to meet the local tribes, and along the way, he meets this exotic-looking girl."

"And he falls head over heels," Jane chimed in, beaming.

Claire nodded. "Uh-huh... But remember, this is the early second century... Roman soldiers were prohibited from marrying local women."

"But he doesn't care... He loves her and decides to marry her..."

"That's right... and over the years, their bond grows stronger, as we see in their letters."

"And he's always bringing her gifts," Jane added with a playful tone.

Claire chuckled. "Yes, and he travels a lot... He has lots of adventures..."

"And he captures pirates and brings back lots of pirate booty!" Jane quipped.

Claire nodded, trying to hold back her laugh. "And here we are, almost two millennia later, digging it all up!" She turned and faced Jane. "But remember, he's also on the cusp of changing history—with the sarcophagus reliefs, the scrolls, and Alexander's breastplate with the Medusa emblem confirming his deification. He may have inadvertently rewritten centuries of ancient history."

"Greek history?"

"Greek and Roman."

Claire returned to the bed and opened her laptop. She gestured for Jane to sit beside her and pulled up the picture of the sarcophagus relief. "Look at this image. It shows an Egyptian queen seated on a throne, addressing the Roman senate. I'm waiting to hear back from Damian—I need to know who this person is—this could be big, Jane!"

Isabel didn't know what to expect when she walked onto the dig site; she had a vague idea about archaeology, but she wasn't prepared for what she was about to encounter.

She walked along the excavation site, where the crew was busy removing layers of dirt from the newly dug squares. As she passed by, she exchanged waves and smiles with them.

She noticed a bench displaying familiar household items: combs, leather shoes, brooches, and pottery. Jane spotted her and waved enthusiastically.

Claire was working inside a recently excavated square when she glanced up and saw them. A smile spread across her face as she watched Jane gleefully show Isabel around and introduce her to all the staff.

Something about Isabel moved Jane—it was as if she was reunited with a friend she hadn't seen in years. By the time Jane brought her to Claire, it was late afternoon. Isabel had seen the entire excavation site and learned about their discoveries.

"Hello, Claire!" Isabel waved and smiled. "It's great to see you again!"

"Hi, Isabel! Likewise, it's lovely to see you again as well." Claire greeted Isabel with a warm smile. "So, how do you like our little dirt pit?"

"I…" Isabel stammered. She threw her hands up. "I'm blown away! It's out of this world."

Claire laughed. "Well, in a way, it is out of this world—a world that's now almost two thousand years old."

Isabel nodded. "I know… It's amazing!"

"I'm glad you like it here."

"Why don't you go hang out with Sharon and Eve?" Jane interjected. "Maybe help them out a little. I've got to go over something with Claire... I'll catch up with you later."

"Can I? Really?"

"Of course! Go have fun."

"Thank you, Jane! I will!" Isabel waved to Claire and Jane, then spun around and dashed toward the square where Sharon and Eve worked.

Claire followed Jane's gaze as she watched Isabel stroll away. "You like her, don't you?"

"She's really sweet," Jane nodded, her eyes still fixed on Isabel. She turned to Claire and asked, "Don't you think so?"

"I do!… I think she's wonderful. She's an excellent bartender... She was very attentive and professional when she served us."

"About that," Jane said. "She's not very happy at her job... She was hoping to make a change."

"Oh?" Claire responded, curious.

Jane nodded. "Crappy customers stiffing her... and creepy guys with their foul mouths and wandering hands..."

"Mmm... I see... That's terrible."

"Isn't it?"

Claire knew where Jane was going with this. She grinned and said, "Why don't you offer her a job?"

Jane hesitated. She gave Claire a questioning look. "Seriously?"

Claire nodded. She gestured around them. "Look around… With our expansion, we'll need all the help we can get."

"I agree. I think Isabel is going to be a hard worker… and she seems to like it here—a lot!"

"I'm glad. Let's have her start right away!"

Claire didn't have to ask; she could read it all over Jane's face. For some reason, Jane was genuinely eager to have Isabel around.

Claire didn't know why, but she knew it would make her happy. Jane had consistently worked long hours, even on weekends, without ever complaining. On most nights, she'd even shared a bed with Claire, who'd never formed a stronger bond with anyone else.

Jane wasn't just an integral part of Claire's company—she was an integral part of her life.

39

Claire hurried up the mound, frustrated with her phone reception. Jane ran after her. When Claire reached the top of the mound, she held up her phone and saw solid bars appear.

Opening her call log, she gasped at the sight of three missed calls from Damian.

Jane walked up to her, panting. She leaned in to see what Claire was doing.

Claire turned to Jane with a look of disappointment. "I missed his calls..."

"Whose calls?" Jane asked, trying to catch her breath.

"Damian's."

"Oh."

"Yeah… Oh…. Let's see, here... He left a message on the last call."

Claire opened her voicemail, found Damian's message, and pressed play. She put the phone on the speaker and held it up so Jane could hear.

"Hello, Claire. So sorry I couldn't get back to you sooner; I had to finish some work before I could delve into this... So, here it is in a nutshell..." Damian lowered his voice to emphasize his words. "These tablets, Claire... I believe they are written testaments in Cleopatra's own handwriting. They reveal her intentions… her ambitions to expand her realm—to conquer Rome herself. According to her own words, she did not find Caesar or Anthony captivating; they were merely pawns in her grand scheme. Cleopatra aimed to extend her empire… from India in the east to the Atlantic in the west. She envisioned a realm far beyond Rome's boundaries; she knew Alexander had a dream to conquer the known world, and she wanted to revive it. That's what the relief tells us: Cleopatra is proclaiming herself queen of Egypt, queen of Rome. In the other relief, you see Alexander marching towards his destiny, to the Siwah Oasis and the temple of Zeus Ammon, to be proclaimed god. Next to him is his mother, Olympias, queen of Macedonia. She is about to become a mother to the son of Zeus, the son of Ammon. She encouraged and supported her son. She wanted to see him surpass his father's ambitions... And Cleopatra revered Olympias. She wanted to follow in her son's footsteps… To pick up Alexander's mantle and march towards his unfulfilled destiny."

Damian took a moment to collect his thoughts before concluding. "Right then, there you have it, Claire. Call me when you find time in your busy schedule. And I'll crack on... there's more... I've barely scratched the surface."

The voicemail message ended.

Claire glanced at Jane, who stood with her mouth open, speechless. "What did he mean by 'There's more?' What more could there be?"

Claire shrugged. "I can't imagine what else there could be. This is colossal!"

Claire tried calling Damian, but he didn't answer. She smiled at Jane and said, "Let's go back. I'm sure he'll call again." She let out a long sigh and gestured toward the sprawling excavation site below. "To use Damian's words, we've 'barely scratched the surface.' We have so much more to dig up. God knows what else is buried right here beneath our feet."

Claire typed an email detailing her newest discoveries to Callum. Based on Damian's translations of the Greek tablets, she explained the significance of the sarcophagus reliefs and gave Callum a brief summary of the voicemail message he'd left.

She felt a breath on her neck, and the smell of perfume filled her nostrils. She let out a giggle. A glass of red wine appeared next to her head. Reaching for the wine glass, she tilted her head back and smiled at Jane.

Jane grinned and scrunched her nose. "I opened a Merlot... getting tired of Chablis."

Claire gave a nod. "I'm not picky; I'll drink whatever you've got."

Jane moved closer, focusing her gaze on Claire's laptop monitor.

"What's this?"

"I'm sending a quick email to Callum to update him about the sarcophagus and what Damian said in his message."

Jane swept her hand over her head. "This stuff goes right over my head! I'd just gotten used to the Roman history; now I've got all this Greek and Egyptian history swirling around in my head."

Claire laughed. "It's not that complicated."

Jane rolled her eyes. "Wait... Hold your horses... Let me see if I've got this; you've got a Greek queen, who's also Egyptian, and who wants to rule over the Romans—am I right so far?"

"Yes, that's right."

"But that's not enough for her; she wants to go even further and rule the rest of the world."

"You got it—that's Cleopatra!"

"I love her! You know who she reminds me of?"

Claire shook her head. "Uh-uh... who?"

"Our own British girl—Boudica!"

"You amaze me, Jane!" Claire exclaimed. "Yes! ... our Celtic queen... They were two of a kind. Both of them defied Rome! But Cleopatra apparently had far bigger plans than Boudica—far bigger than history tells us if we were to believe her writings."

Jane threw her arms up. "I get all that, but Cleopatra's story is much more complicated. There are so many moving parts. It's hard to keep up."

Claire closed her laptop and sat cross-legged on the bed. She shifted to face Jane and smiled. "I agree... Here, let's start at the beginning with Alexander."

Jane sipped her wine and smiled. "Yes—let's."

Clair tilted her head and closed her eyes. Picturing herself in the ancient capital of Macedonia, Pella, she opened her eyes and began.

"Imagine you're a 20-year-old boy. Your father has just been assassinated by a jealous young man who, according to some historians, may have been his lover—someone who was more than half his age. You're now heir to the throne of Macedonia and in charge of the greatest army ever. You are surrounded by people who want you dead: political rivals, enemies... You get the picture?"

Jane nodded and arched her brow as she sipped her wine.

Claire sipped hers and continued. "Dangers lurk in every corner of the palace... and many of your father's Macedonian veterans don't like to take orders from a kid. They are your father's age. You have a few friends who follow you, but only a handful."

"Wow, now I feel awful for Alexander," Jane commented.

Claire nodded in agreement.

"It's a tough time to be a kid at the Macedonian court. You're exposed to a great deal of violence, both physical and sexual. You often witness scenes of heavy drinking and, at times, even bouts of fornication or rape among the Macedonian adult males."

"Ew!"

Claire arched her brow. "Yeah, ew!" She paused and studied Jane's face. She didn't want to go too far, but Jane seemed engrossed in her story. She continued.

"But your mother, Olympias, is very protective of you. From a young age, she has instilled a sense of greatness and destiny in you. And eventually, you consolidate your power and invade and conquer Persia—the greatest empire that ever existed... But here's where things get interesting..."

"Interesting?" Jane interrupted. "You mean so far you were telling me the boring stuff?"

Claire chuckled. "No, what I mean is that now we depart from historical accounts."

Jane quirked her lips, confused. "Depart?"

Claire nodded. "You see, history tells us Olympias stayed behind in the capital when Alexander embarked on his Persian campaign."

"Yeah, so?"

"So, why is she depicted on a sarcophagus, riding alongside his son in Egypt, on her way to witness his deification?"

"Hmm."

Claire got out of bed and walked over to the window, gazing out into the dark.

"And Alexander… He never returns to Macedonia. He dies in Babylon. He is 32. His empire is divided up between his three generals... One of them is his childhood friend, Ptolemy. Cleopatra was descended from Ptolemy. She was descended from greatness... She knew she had big shoes to fill."

A bright light flashed in Claire's eyes, temporarily blinding her. She raised a hand to shield her eyes from the glare.

Jane rushed to the window, peering out to see where the light came from.

"He shows up, finally!" She scoffed.

"Who?"

"Captain wonderful!"

Claire chuckled. "Peter?"

"Yeah, can't you see him announcing his presence to the whole world with his torch?"

The beam of light vanished behind the staff trailers.

Jane gestured toward it. "Let's go see what he's doing."

Claire rolled her eyes. "Oh, Jane!"

Jane pouted her lips. "Please?"

Claire knew resistance was pointless. She caved. "All right, let's go."

They exited the trailer and headed for the spot where they saw the light.

Jane let out a giggle. "Hey, we're getting pretty good at sneaking around at night. If archaeology doesn't pan out, we can always become cat burglars."

"You're going to make me pee my pants," Claire snorted, struggling to contain her laughter as she followed Jane.

Sharon, Eve, and Isabel also saw the flash of light; they ran into Claire and Jane as they exited their trailer.

"It's a party now," Jane whispered. She pressed her index finger to her lips. "Shhh... Keep it down... We're chasing a stalker."

Isabel gasped. "Really?"

Jane shook her head. "No, dear. I'm only joking. It's just our fearless security guard, Peter."

"Honestly, Jane?" Isabel seemed shaken.

Jane ran her hand along her arm. "Honestly! We saw someone roaming around a few days ago, but I'm sure it was one of our own guys. He probably stepped out to pee. You know, men like to pee outside... It's their caveman instinct."

Isabel smiled nervously and nodded. "I get it."

"Here, let's go find our brave security guard," Jane murmured. She motioned for everyone to follow her.

They didn't have to walk far. Rounding the corner past the last trailer, they saw a uniformed figure standing in the shadows with his back to them. He was oblivious to their presence.

"Hey, Peter," Jane said.

Startled, the man turned around to face Jane. He pointed his flashlight directly at her face, temporarily blinding her.

"God, Peter, turn that thing off," Jane yelled as she covered her eyes.

"I'm so sorry, Miss Claire," a voice said sheepishly.

"Wait! You're not Peter," Jane said.

"No, ma'am. My name is William... But you can call me Billy."

"Can you turn that damn thing off, Billy?" Jane sounded agitated.

"Yes, of course, ma'am." Billy quickly switched off the flashlight and tucked it into his holster.

Jane approached Billy, studying him closely. Claire and the rest of the crew stood behind her, watching. Billy looked young with a disarming smile; he was in his late teens or early twenties.

"Hi Billy, I'm Jane. Where's Peter?" Jane asked, sounding calmer.

"He's at the storage facility, ma'am. He sent me here. He told me to secure this place... He told me to stay here and keep guard all night."

"Mm-hmm..." Jane gestured toward Claire. "Billy, this is Claire, my boss... and yours."

Billy extended a hand to Claire, flashing a smile. "It's a pleasure meeting you, ma'am."

Claire smiled and shook Billy's hand. "It's wonderful to meet you, Billy... Welcome aboard!"

Billy gave a polite nod. "Thank you, ma'am."

Jane motioned toward the rest of the crew and introduced them: "Billy, this is Sharon, Eve, and Isabel."

"Hello, everyone," Billy said, waving at them. "I'm sorry I gave you all a start. I was just trying to familiarize myself with the area."

Jane saw the embarrassment in Billy's face. He looked intimidated, surrounded by five women at night in an unfamiliar place. Feeling sorry for him, she softened her tone and said, "Well, Billy, we'll let you get back to work. We're glad you're here to protect us... and keep your eyes open for our camp stalker."

Billy nodded. "Peter told me about that... Don't worry, Miss Jane; I'll take care of it—you've got nothing to worry about!"

Jane smiled at him and patted him on the arm. "I'm sure we're in excellent hands... We'll talk again soon, Billy. Goodnight!"

"Thank you, ma'am. Good night!"

Jane watched from her window as she sat listening to Claire read to her about Lucius's campaign in Gaul and his return home across the North Sea. She saw the light beam flashing across the dig site as Billy surveyed the area.

She smiled and said, "I like Billy. He's a good kid. I'm watching him march back and forth, keeping a lookout. He hasn't stopped once... I'd rather have him around than Peter."

Claire chuckled. "Why don't you come sit here and relax? And bring some wine... I'm reading something interesting."

Jane sprang out of her chair and hurried to the kitchen. She returned with two glasses and a bottle of Chablis. "We've only got Chablis."

"Chablis is fine." Claire smiled and patted the bed beside her. "Come sit."

Jane poured herself a glass and downed it. She poured another glass and handed it to Claire, who shook her head. "Why did you gulp down the whole glass like that?"

Jane smirked as she sank into the bed beside Claire.

"I want to lay down next to you." Jane curled up beside Claire with her head propped on her hand. "I didn't feel like holding the glass."

Claire chuckled and began reading.

"Lucius wrote this while sailing back from Gaul. He's writing about some Germanic tribes he encountered on the North Sea, or Mare Germanicum, as the Romans called it. The Romans referred to them as Germani, but I picture something different when I read his description of them."

"What? What do you picture?"

"Vikings… But Vikings didn't appear on the scene until the 8th century when they first raided the Lindisfarne monastery just up the coast from here..."

"Well…"

"Well, the description of their boat and their appearance is almost identical to the Vikings."

"Hmm… Maybe history has it wrong," Jane chimed in. "Maybe they were around much earlier than history tells us."

Claire quirked her lips and nodded.

"Think about it," Jane went on. "It's not like the Vikings just appeared out of thin air in the 8th century... I mean, look at what we just learned about Alexander and his mother. History tells us she stayed behind in her palace, but the sarcophagus relief shows she was on the march with her son." She sat up, topped off Claire's glass, and refilled hers. "The Vikings were probably there all along, and..."

"And history only noted their presence when they attacked Lindisfarne monastery," Claire interjected, finishing Jane's thought.

Jane shrugged. "Hey, it's just a theory."

"But a highly plausible one." Claire smiled at Jane. "Kudos, Jane… You're a smarty pants!"

Jane chuckled. "I mean, if it quacks like a duck and walks like a duck, then it's... a Viking!"

Claire was sipping her wine and nearly spewed it out laughing.

"Oh, Jane!"

Jane smirked. "So, does Lucius attack them?"

Claire shook her head. "He trades with them. He says they were friendly."

"So not like those nasty Vikings," Jane said with playful sarcasm.

Claire chuckled and closed her laptop. She placed her wine glass on the nightstand and turned off the nightlight.

"Why did you turn off the light? Are you upset with me?"

"Not at all... We need to get some sleep."

"You're a party pooper," Jane sulked.

"We're partying every night." Claire yawned. "It's catching up with me. I'm getting bags under my eyes. You're perfect—you don't have that problem."

"No, I'm not. And I've got bags too."

"No, you don't... You look like a fashion model."

"I do… I do have bags; they're just on the inside."

Claire burst out laughing.

Jane chuckled. "Are you going to finish the story?"

"There's not much else... They entered the Tyne estuary and sailed up the river to the settlement—to this place. He was home… The end!"

"And he made passionate love to Cara as soon as he walked through the door."

"Good for them." Claire laughed. "And now it's time for us to go to sleep."

"I'm not tired."

"I know... That's also why you don't get bags under your eyes." She paused, then said. "I figured it out: You're a vampire. A beautiful, timeless vampire."

Jane let out a faint laugh. She curled her lips, flashing her teeth. "Yeah, check out my sharp fangs."

"You also have beautiful teeth."

Jane curled up next to Claire, mumbling softly, and quickly drifted off to sleep.

40

Callum Mackenzie arched his brow as he read Claire's email. He tried calling her, but there was no reception. He left a message, telling her he'd be in his Edinburgh office all week, and asked her to call him.

He rose from his chair and walked to his office window, which overlooked Edinburgh Castle, perched on a hill in the distance.

It had rained all morning, but the downpour had stopped. He opened the window and deeply breathed the fresh, dewy air. He reached into his pocket, retrieved his cigarette case, and took one out. Placing it between his lips, he lit the cigarette and took a deep drag, contemplating Claire's email.

He knew full well the significance of what he'd read. Smothering his cigarette in the ashtray, he returned to his chair; he had a full schedule and hoped to speak with Claire soon.

What he didn't know was that Claire and Jane were already on their way to see him—she'd listened to his message and wanted to surprise him. But first, she planned to stop in London; she wanted her father to meet Jane and update him on the progress of the excavations.

She'd coordinated the trip with her father to ensure her mother would be away during the few hours they were visiting. She wanted to shield Jane from her mother's scrutiny.

They arrived in London the night before and stayed at a hotel. In the morning, they took a cab to Claire's parents' house.

As Claire had expected, Jane stole the show; her father hardly stopped talking to her. After giving her father a detailed update on her progress at the excavation site, Claire took Jane on a tour of her childhood home and introduced her to the household staff.

It was early afternoon when Claire said goodbye to her father, and she and Jane left to spend the rest of the day at Jane's flat, where she checked her mail and watered her plants before leaving for the train station.

Jane had reserved a first-class cabin with a double bed and en-suite shower. They arrived early, unpacked their clothing, and got dressed for dinner.

Jane wanted to stay in the city for dinner then head to the train station, but Claire had another idea: dinner in the first-class dining car. Once seated in the dining car, Claire and Jane gazed out the window at the bustling crowd as passengers boarded their trains.

Jane ordered two mini bottles of Merlot. When the server returned with their drinks, she poured them, and they clinked glasses, toasting their trip.

A young girl in a red overcoat stood on the station platform with her mother, about to get on the train. She waved at them, and they responded with a wave and a smile.

The train lurched into motion, slowly gliding along the tracks as it left the station.

"Aren't you glad I made you wait to have dinner on the train? Isn't this nice?" Claire murmured.

Jane nodded.

Claire noticed tears welling up in her eyes as she looked away, sniffling. She reached across the table and took her hand, slightly squeezing it. "Hey, you... What's the matter?"

Jane shook her head. She took a tissue from her purse and blew her nose.

"Come now... Please talk to me," Claire persisted.

Jane shook her head again, her eyes down. "Mm-um... It's nothing..."

Claire paused, then said, "It's all right, Jane. We don't have to talk about it... Let's just enjoy the trip... All right?"

Jane nodded. Claire poured another round for them and raised her glass.

"To my best friend."

Jane cracked a smile and raised her glass.

Claire drew closer, looking at Jane. She smiled and said, "There she is... the smartest, most gorgeous girl in town."

Jane laughed. She rolled her eyes. "Not even!"

Claire took Jane's hand again. "Yes, even! You are gorgeous. And you're my best friend." She sighed, then added, "No, you're much more than that... You're my sister... You're the little sister I ever wanted and never had."

Jane got choked up. Her eyes welled up with tears again. Seeing this, Claire rose from her seat, came around the table, and sat beside Jane, putting her arm around her.

"What's the matter? You're breaking my heart."

"It's nothing... I just..." Jane stammered.

"You just what? Talk to me."

"I guess I miss my parents."

"I'm sorry... I know it must be hard, losing both parents... But you've got me. And I'm not going anywhere. So chin up."

Jane smiled and nodded, her eyes down.

Claire slid the menu toward Jane. "Here, let's get some supper... That'll make you feel better. I know it'll make me feel better. I hear my stomach grumbling, saying, 'Feed me, feed me... Don't just drown me in alcohol.'"

Jane laughed. "All right."

Claire drew closer to catch her gaze. "There's her lovely smile."

After a couple of drinks, Jane seemed to settle down and relax. She smiled and nodded as Claire shared stories about her trips on overnight trains, weaving through the picturesque English countryside.

Claire suggested they return to their cabin and slip into pajamas. She raised her hand to wave over the server; she wanted to order drinks to go. Jane took Claire's hand and lowered it, shaking her head.

She opened her purse and tilted it toward Claire—just like on previous trips, she'd come prepared.

Claire's mouth flew open as she craned her neck to look inside. "Where did you get all that?"

Jane scrunched her nose and gave a slight shrug. "I had a few bottles left over from the last trip."

Claire grinned and whispered, "You naughty girl!"

Jane nodded. "I forgot I even brought them." She pointed to the wine menu. "Look at these prices; they are insane... From now on, I'm bringing my own stash!"

"I don't care if I spend a few dollars more, Jane. I'm here with you. We're having fun!"

Jane rolled her eyes. "Save your money. We'll spend it on shoes instead... I need more shoes."

"But your closet is bursting at the seams with shoes."

"Hey, bite your tongue! You can never, ever have too many shoes... You have too few shoes. I'm buying you more... We'll save money and buy more shoes!"

Claire's lips parted to raise an objection, but she hesitated when she saw the spark in Jane's eyes. Instead, she said, "You know what?"

"No, what?"

"I agree! We'll go shoe shopping when we're in Newcastle or when we return to London!"

Jane narrowed her eyes. "Are you messing with me?"

Claire chuckled. "Absolutely not! I don't muck around about shoes."

Jane laughed. "Look out now, but you almost sound like me."

"Good... I want to sound like you," Claire said sincerely.

"Aw..."

"I mean it. If shoes will cheer you up, we're going shopping... Jane, you're the sweetest, kindest person I know. It hurts me to see you upset."

Jane lowered her gaze. "Thank you, Claire. This means a lot to me—your words." She let out a deep sigh. "Let's go back to the cabin... Will you read to me?"

Claire smiled. "Of course I will."

The first-class cabin had a cozy double bed with a luxurious en-suite bathroom. Kicking off her heels, Jane hurled herself onto the bed. She opened her third mini bottle of gin, gulped it down, then patted the bed beside her and said, "Story time!"

Claire chuckled. "All right, let me change first."

"No, don't change... You're perfect," Jane said, slurring her words.

Claire grinned. She saw Jane was tipsy, so she grabbed Jane's purse and stowed it in the storage compartment.

"Hey... Why'd you do that?" Jane protested.

Claire sank onto the bed and propped her head on her hand. "You want me to read to you, right?"

Jane gave an exaggerated nod of her head. "Uh-huh, but it's more fun when I drink, so kindly gimme back my purse..."

"Your eyes are glassy. One more drink and it's lights out for you."

"No way," Jane argued. "I can listen just as well with the lights out." She reached above her head, flicked off the light, and whispered, "See? I'm fine."

Claire chuckled. "That's not quite what I meant."

Jane rolled onto her side, facing Claire. The moonlight streamed through the panoramic window and onto her body, accentuating her curves.

She was as beautiful in the shadows as she was in daylight. Claire never understood why she was single. She wanted to ask about her past relationships but didn't want to pry.

She knew her waters ran deep, but it wasn't the right time to probe—not when she'd been drinking. It seemed too intrusive to question her in her present condition. She wanted Jane to offer up her past willingly—if and when she was ready.

Claire glanced at the moon, peeking through the clouds at them.

"I've got an idea."

"Mm."

"Let's sit by the window, and I'll read to you. We can't miss the view."

"Mm-hmm."

"Are you all right?"

"I'm better than all right… I'm perfect!"

Claire sat at the edge of the bed, gazing out the window. Snuggling close beside her, Jane rested her chin on Claire's shoulder. The silvery moon's rays poured over the hills, the lake's waters shimmering beneath the starry sky.

Jane let out a gasp. She pressed her hand to her chest and pointed at a lone stag standing on a hill, head raised, proudly displaying its antlers. Their eyes remained glued to the majestic beast until it slipped into the shadows. Obediently following its tracks, the train rocked from side to side, putting them in a trance.

"It's magical," Claire murmured.

"Breathtaking," Jane whispered. "And this rocking motion... It's the most relaxing thing I've ever felt."

"Do you still want to hear a story?" Claire asked as she opened the tablet images on her phone.

Jane gave an exaggerated nod. "I do."

Claire smiled at Jane and began reading from one of the tablets. "So, in this letter, Lucius talks to Cara about their daughter…"

"Wait!" Jane interrupted. "They had children?"

"Uh-huh… They had three—all girls."

Jane chuckled. "I bet Lucius was freaking out when he was away, constantly worried about them!"

Claire laughed. "Indeed, he was… Cara wrote to him about their youngest daughter, Cassia. She was sixteen."

"Cassia… What a beautiful name!"

"Yes… and she was Lucius's favorite."

"Daddy's girl!"

"Mm-hmm... And apparently, she'd met a young boy…"

"Uh-oh!"

"Yeah, uh-oh—he went ballistic! He asked who the boy was…"

"Who was he?"

"A boy from another tribe. He forbade Cassia from ever seeing him again. She was devastated. In her letter, Cara was pleading with him not to overreact."

"I'm sure. It must've been tough having a Roman soldier for a father. So what does he do?"

"I don't know. I haven't gotten that far."

"Hmm… I picture her in my mind."

"Cassia?"

"Mm… She had long, wavy red hair and freckles… she got that from her mom, but she got her olive skin from her dad. She must've been beautiful."

"I'm sure."

Claire yawned, her eyelids growing heavy. She lay back down on the bed. Jane followed suit and lay beside her, facing her.

Claire caught a whiff of alcohol on her breath.

"Did you have fun tonight?"

"Mm… The most ever," Jane murmured as she drifted off to sleep.

Claire smiled and whispered, "I'm glad," before closing her eyes.

Jane was sitting cross-legged at the foot of the bed with a cup of coffee in her hand when Claire opened her eyes.

"Good morning!" Jane smiled and offered Claire a steaming cup of coffee. "You've got to taste this. It has to be gourmet!"

Claire curled her body forward, propping herself on her elbows. She smiled and took the coffee from Jane.

"Good morning… Wow, you got up before me!"

Jane nodded, smiling. "I've explored this entire train. Did you know they serve breakfast here?"

Claire laughed. "Of course I did. I planned to surprise you and take you to it."

"I strolled through the dining car. I was staring at everyone's breakfast, licking my lips, and sniffing the air," Jane beamed. "I got a few strange looks."

Claire laughed. "Give me a tiny minute, and we'll go together. There's nothing better than breakfast on a train."

Jane traced circles on her belly with her palm. "Yum, let's go! I'm starving."

The dining car was filled with hungry passengers. Claire and Jane followed the hostess down the aisle to be seated. Walking behind Jane, Claire couldn't help but grin when she noticed a woman glaring at her husband, who was clearly stealing glances at Jane as she passed by.

Oblivious to it all, Jane looked around at everyone's breakfast and tilted her head back, saying, "Can we order a few plates and sample them all?"

The hostess chuckled at Jane's request. Claire laughed. "Sure, we can order whatever you want!"

"This view is spectacular," Claire said as she gazed out the window at the scenery. "It's not as enchanting as last night's, but it'll do."

"Mm…" Jane murmured, taking a bite of her eggs. "Last night felt like a dream... like a fairy tale. And the bed was so comfy... with the rocking back and forth... My God!"

"I'm really glad you enjoyed this trip," Claire said, sipping her Darjeeling tea. "I wanted us to get some rest. We've been working so hard... and the rest of the crew... We'll take them out to Newcastle next weekend. They all deserve it. But mostly you... You've been working non-stop."

Jane shrugged. "Yeah, but I also have the biggest perk..." She took a sip from Claire's tea and said, "I get to sleep with the boss!"

Claire's face turned a bright shade of pink, and she put her hand over her mouth, trying to suppress her laughter. She heard the sounds of forks and spoons clattering on plates and the murmurs of the other women. She caught glimpses of heads turning and staring at them.

Jane scrunched her nose and grinned, completely unbothered by the attention.

A voice over the loudspeaker announced their arrival at Edinburgh Waverley Station. Claire followed Jane as she walked down the narrow corridor toward the exit. Stepping onto the station platform, Jane turned and faced the train.

She sniffed the air.

"What is that smell?"

"Do you like it?" Claire asked, closely observing Jane.

Jane nodded. "I do."

"Me, too. I love the smell of trains. My dad told me it was the smell of diesel from the train's engines... But I think there's something else."

Jane waved and blew a kiss at the train. "Bye, train… I'll miss you!"

Claire let out a giggle. "Don't worry, you'll see Mr. Train again."

"I hope so!"

Standing by the curb, waiting to hail a cab, Jane clutched Claire's arm.

Claire turned to look at Jane, who nodded at a girl in a red overcoat standing with her mother further down the street—the same girl they'd seen at the train station in London.

"She's our good luck charm," Claire said, smiling. At that exact moment, the girl spotted them and gave them a big smile. They smiled and waved at her.

"She sure is," Jane beamed.

41

Marcel stood behind the punching bag, holding it steady for Amelie. He'd been bringing her to his martial arts studio several times a week to teach her the basics of self-defense.

It comforted him to see her able to defend herself, and it kept Madeleine from freaking out every time Amelie left the house, even if it was just to go to the corner market.

Naturally athletic, Amelie's body was flexible, and she was in excellent shape from her dancing days. It didn't take long for her to get bored, so Marcel took her training to the next level—from self-defense to pure offense.

"I want you to practice your spinning back kick," Marcel said, holding the bag. "I want you to turn that hip as you kick. Keep your guard up, cock your head toward the target, turn your hip, and kick... Snap that kick!"

Marcel motioned to his eyes with two fingers. "Remember, focus!"

He held the bag tightly, bracing it against his body. Amelie spun around and delivered a kick, her heel landing in the center of the bag and knocking the wind out of Marcel.

Amelie let out a giggle. "I'm sorry! I didn't mean to kick so hard."

Marcel shook his head and laughed. "That was the best kick I've seen in a long time!" He wrapped his arms around the bag and said, "Let's do it again, princess!"

"Are you sure?"

Marcel nodded. "Sure, I'm sure. And don't hold back—give it all you've got!"

Amelie's eyes locked on the bag. She took a deep breath and exhaled slowly. She bent her knees, lowering herself into her fighting stance. Then her eyes widened, and her brow furrowed into a fierce gaze.

Marcel swallowed hard as she exploded into a spin, her hair swirling in the air and her heel landing in the center of the bag. This time, Marcel flew backward and fell to the ground.

Amelie heard clapping. She turned and saw Marcel's instructor in the corner.

"Bravo! That was beautiful," he yelled. She smiled and waved at him, her face flushing.

Other students also clapped. She gave a polite nod of her head and waved at them.

"Can we get out of here?" she whispered to Marcel.

"Sure, princess," Marcel murmured, smoothing out his shirt. "You are amazing! Now, let's go grab some lunch."

The small, mom-and-pop restaurant on the Seine was Amelie's favorite hangout spot.

Marcel would take her there to see her girlfriends from Montreal or to catch up with Luc on the rare occasions she could locate him. But today, it was just the two of them, and they were famished.

Amelie smiled at Marcel as she took a bite of her food. She didn't speak during lunch; there wasn't much to say, so she just gazed at him and smiled. He knew the look—it was a look that said, "I love you."

She wore her designer jeans, white high tops, and the T-shirt Madeleine bought her, which read "I love Titou" on the front.

A group of young men close to her age walked past them, smiling at her and muttering in French.

Marcel winked at her. "Would you like to go talk to them?"

Amelie smiled and shook her head while sipping her soda.

Marcel heard his phone ping. He glanced at his phone's screen and saw a text message from Marek.

Hello Inspector. Please call me.

"I have to make a call," Marcel said, holding up his phone. "I'll only be a minute—I promise!"

Amelie gave him a smile and nodded.

Marcel stepped away from the table and called Marek. He quickly answered.

"Hello, inspector! Thank you for calling me back."

"Hello, Marek! How are things in Prague?"

"Oh... Prague... Well, sir, Prague is beautiful... but I get to see its other side."

"Hmm... I can imagine. I got a glimpse of it myself... So, any news about our suspect?"

"Yes, of course... our suspect." Marek paused. He cleared his throat. "Well, inspector, I interrogated him myself... as soon as he was out of surgery and able to communicate."

Marek sounded nervous. Marcel kept quiet, allowing him to gather his thoughts.

Marek continued. "He wasn't talking at first—he was very stubborn. I tried to convince him but couldn't get anything out of him..."

"How did you try to convince him?"

Marek cleared his throat again. It seemed to be a nervous tick. "When I was alone with him in the hospital room, I..."

"Yes?"

"I made sure no one was around. I covered his mouth and pressed my finger into his bullet wound... He was in a lot of pain..."

"Hmm... Good... But let me guess, he didn't sing."

"No, he didn't... But finally, when I told him he was going to prison for the rest of his life, he started to talk. I offered him a plea deal, and he took it. He told me he'd only been on the yacht once. He had two new girls with him. He told me they were taken to the yacht by a speedboat at night. He didn't know his whereabouts. He only remembered that the yacht had dropped anchor near an island; he couldn't identify the island… He said it was dark and cloudy."

Marek paused, then added, "I'm very sorry, Inspector, that's all I could get out of him."

"No need to apologize, Marek," Marcel said. "You did just fine. Please stay in touch with me if anything comes up."

"I will, sir."

Marcel hung up the phone, thoroughly impressed by Marek. He felt he couldn't have gotten any more information even if he'd personally interrogated the suspect.

It was another dead end—another low-level criminal scraping a living, coaxing young girls into the dark web of human sex trafficking. The thought of it turned his stomach.

However, he'd discovered a new piece of information that gave him some consolation: the yacht was likely anchored near an island somewhere.

He returned to the table with a furrowed brow, his head down, deep in thought. Amelie had seen the intense look before—she'd seen it when he dismantled Ivan's gang in Montreal.

He looked up and saw the concerned look on Amelie's face. He smiled and said, "I don't want you ever to worry again... or be afraid. I will never let anything happen to you—never!"

Amelie set her fork down, rose from her chair, and threw her arms around Marcel. She planted a gentle kiss to his cheek and whispered, "I know."

<h1 style="text-align:center">42</h1>

Callum anxiously paced back and forth in his office. He'd left Claire another message but hadn't heard back. He was beginning to worry—not about the project but about Claire.

He hoped everything was all right. It was already 10 a.m., and he contemplated sending her a text; he thought perhaps she was more accustomed to getting texts.

With an exasperated sigh, he opened his text app and found her in his contacts. It took him a while to key in the letters, but he eventually made it and hit send. Almost instantly, he heard a chime. He furrowed his brow, confused: the chime came from the office reception area just outside his door. Then he heard a knock on the door.

"Come in," he said.

The door opened, and his secretary, Dorothy, walked in. "Sorry to bother you, sir, but you have company."

"Who is it?"

Dorothy smiled sheepishly. "They told me not to say, sir."

"What in heaven's..."

A face appeared over Dorothy's shoulder.

"Surprise!" Claire exclaimed as she and Jane emerged from behind Dorothy. "I hope you don't mind, Callum... We wanted to surprise you!"

Callum flashed a big smile. "Oh, for heaven's sake, my dear... I've been trying to call you," he said with outstretched arms. Claire stepped into them and hugged him.

Following her, Jane approached Callum. "Hello, Callum... It's wonderful to see you again."

"Dear Jane, how lovely to see you!" Callum gave Jane a hug. "Claire is constantly raving about you in her emails."

Jane smiled, her face flushing. She glanced at Claire. "Claire is too kind... I'm just the paper pusher—the bean counter."

"No, she's not," Claire told Callum with a dismissive wave of her hand. "She practically runs the entire operation." She returned her attention to Jane and said, "Jane, you're my right-hand person. Without you, I'd never be able to keep up."

"Why don't you both have a seat?" Callum said, motioning to his couch. "I've been looking forward to talking to you. The extent of your progress is truly remarkable!"

He took a cigarette from his pack, then paused and said, "I hope you don't mind."

Claire shook her head. "Of course not; please go ahead."

Jane raised a hand. "Can I bum one?"

"Please... be my guest, Jane," Callum said, holding out his cigarette pack.

Jane walked over to him and took the pack. She flicked the pack, coaxing out a cigarette, and pulled it out with her lips.

Callum flicked his antique lighter and held the flame close to Jane's lips. She lit the cigarette, her eyes fixed on the glowing ember.

He opened the window, and Jane released a stream of smoke into the cold spring air.

She gave him a smile. "Thanks, Callum."

"You haven't had a cigarette since we got on the train," Claire commented.

Jane gave a slight nod as she took a drag. "I guess I didn't need one... I was having too much fun to think about it."

"I must say, ladies, I'm so glad you came to see me," Callum said. "Allow me to begin with your most significant discovery..." He paused to gather his thoughts. "Your biggest..."

"Alexander's armor..." Claire interjected, completing his sentence.

Callum nodded. "And the sarcophagus reliefs." He put out his cigarette, returned to his desk, and sank into his chair. "Please don't mind me sitting—too much excitement for a lazy spring morning."

"Not at all," Claire said. "Please be comfortable. I'll start at the beginning and give you all the details."

Jane approached Callum's desk and smothered her cigarette in his ashtray before returning to sit beside Claire.

Claire gave Callum a detailed account of her discoveries, Damian's message, and his translation of the Greek tablets. Callum listened patiently, occasionally nodding in acknowledgment.

The expression on his face said it all: he was still grappling with the enormity of the situation. When Claire finished filling him in on all the recent events, she paused and waited for him to respond. But Callum said nothing. He stood and returned to the window. He lit another cigarette and gazed out with a distant look on his face.

Callum motioned toward Edinburgh Castle, perched on a hill in the distance. "You know, I look at this castle every day. I can't avoid it. It's right in front of me every time I look out the window. Some say it dates back to the 12th century. Others say it goes back far earlier. Many dynasties were associated with it in some shape or form. Now, imagine how many were associated with your site, which dates back almost two thousand years. As you've already indicated, your new site may date back to the time of Emperor Honorius." Turning to face Claire and Jane, he said, "I wonder how many generations have left their mark on your site. My gut feeling—and in my old age, I rely mostly on my gut—tells me you'll be busy with that site for months, perhaps longer, which brings me to my current dilemma."

"What's that?" Jane asked, her curiosity piqued.

Callum sighed. Taking another puff from his cigarette, he blew the smoke out the window and said, "My dilemma is twofold: first, I need to secure more funding for you... Secondly, I urge you to travel to Alexandria to assist our team."

"But, Callum..." Claire interrupted, a look of surprise crossing her face.

"I know..." Calum raised a hand, gesturing for Claire to let him continue. "I know I can't ask you to do this now... But I was hoping at some point in the future, you may be able to take a trip—an all-expenses-paid trip—out there on an advisory basis. What you've discovered is going to turn centuries of history on its head. You're about to rewrite history, can't you see? We must inform both the academic community and the general public. We need to set up a public exhibit and showcase your profound discoveries." He paused, took a deep breath, and lowered his voice to emphasize his words. "Centuries of Greek and Roman history, our entire understanding of Alexander's life and his mother's role in it—and subsequently, Cleopatra's—will change. Just imagine what she would have done had she and Anthony defeated Octavian at the battle of Actium. She might indeed have sat on the Roman throne, just as it was depicted on the sarcophagus reliefs."

"Gosh, Callum, I have no words!" Claire exclaimed.

"Look, dear, this is an excellent way to secure more funding, which you're going to need for ongoing projects. You don't have to make a decision now. Take your time; think about it."

"All right, I will—I promise!"

Callum smiled and nodded. "Let me finish by saying how proud I am to be your partner. You have no idea what's in store for you. You're going to become a celebrity in academia... You'll be asked to lecture at some of the most esteemed academic institutions. Perhaps you could even become the preeminent Alexander scholar. Remember, my dear, history is dynamic and interconnected. You began your work in a remote corner of the Roman Empire, but you've ended up with pieces of a much larger, much more significant historical puzzle spanning centuries. I've spent my entire life working in this field... I have dedicated my entire life to this field. I have never encountered anything this significant." He drew closer and said, "How about we have a party? Let's showcase what you've discovered—what do you think?"

"Of course," Claire replied without hesitation. "Where and when would you like to have this party?"

Callum pressed his palm to his forehead, deep in thought. "It must be in London. People from around the world will fly into Heathrow to attend this event. The last thing we want is for them to have to take a connecting flight to a less desirable location."

"I agree. So, when do you think we should have it?"

"As soon as practicable, my dear... Tempus fugit."

Claire laughed. She looked at Jane, who cocked an eyebrow. "It means time flies," she explained. "Well, what do you think, Jane?"

Jane clicked her tongue and winked. "I'm on it! What's the budget?"

"Use your discretion, dear," Callum answered. "I'd like to say spare no expense, but that could be limitless in London... Let's just say we aim to dazzle the audience."

"I can dazzle," Jane quipped.

Callum laughed. "Of that, my dear Jane, I have absolutely no doubt!"

43

The trailer door swung open, and Jane hurried towards Claire, who stood beside Sharon and Eve, gazing out at the excavation site. Claire saw her approaching and smiled.

"Guess what?" Jane said.

"What?" Claire asked, eager to hear what had Jane so excited.

"I found the perfect venue for our event!"

"That's wonderful!" Claire said excitedly. "Where is it?"

Jane handed Claire the reservation confirmation. "It's called Wellesley Manor. It's just outside London. Wait till you see the pictures!"

Claire beamed. "I'm so glad you took care of it quickly. Callum is going to be thrilled!"

"Why don't you take a break and come have a look? I have it up on my computer. You've got to see the pictures."

Claire turned to Sharon. "Do you mind if I take off for a few minutes?"

"Go ahead," Sharon insisted. "I've got this covered. I'll let you know if we dig up anything exciting."

Claire sat behind the computer as Jane leaned over her shoulder, scrolling through the photos of a nineteenth-century Tudor manor on a sprawling hundred-acre parcel of prime English farmland.

The estate had 20 bedrooms and employed live-in staff who catered to guests around the clock. A crushed-stone driveway circled a fountain in front of the manor, with a statue of Poseidon as its centerpiece.

The estate also included a working farm with cattle, sheep, horses, and other domestic animals.

"So, what do you think?" Jane asked, eager to hear Claire's perspective.

"I have no words, Jane! This place is stunning," Claire raved.

"Isn't it?"

Claire nodded vigorously. "I can't believe you found this place!"

"They said the estate fell on hard times. They had to do extensive restorations... Lots of capital expenses, not enough revenue."

"So, they have money problems..."

"Cash flow problems—that's the proper term," Jane said.

Claire tilted her head back and smiled at Jane. "Gosh, you're so smart!"

"Well, thank you! And you're the most amazing boss a girl could ever have—and you're incredibly beautiful!"

Claire scoffed. "Oh, come one! You've got the monopoly on looks. I always watch men give themselves a whiplash walking past you."

Jane pulled a face. "Ugh! I hate that!" She continued browsing through the photos. "I wish they'd just fuck off."

Claire giggled. Deep down, she sympathized with Jane; she'd never liked unwanted attention herself.

Glancing at her phone, Claire noticed she'd missed a text from Arnold. She opened it and read it out loud.

Hi Claire! Please call me ASAP! I'm getting lots of blips.

She tried calling Arnold, but she had no reception. She looked at Jane. "I'm going down there to see him."

"I'll come with you."

As they approached, Arnold and Stewart were gazing at the GPR screen with their backs to Claire and Jane.

"Whatcha got there, Arnold? This better be good!" Jane teased.

Arnold laughed. He raised a hand and waved without taking his eyes off the screen.

"Hi, Jane! It is—I promise!"

Stewart tilted his head back. "Come check this out. He's right… This could be big."

Claire and Jane drew closer and peeked at the GPR screen.

"These are walls," Arnold said, tracing his finger along the linear shapes on the screen. "And this appears to be a platform of some kind." He rubbed his chin, then added, "It looks like an altar... This structure could be a chapel or church."

Claire arched her brow. "Well, if it is a church or chapel—and it dates back to the time of Emperor Honorius—that would make it the oldest in Britain; it would make it older than St. Martin's church, which dates back to the 6th century." She took a moment to study the images on the screen. "But we're not in the business of speculation. Let's find out what it is. I'll stay and help you out."

Excusing herself, Jane returned to the trailer; she had to coordinate the guest list with Callum and arrange the catering.

Claire felt Stewart's eye on her. She stole a glance at him, and he smiled back at her. Her skin tingled with excitement, and goosebumps formed on her arms.

She regretted staying, but it was too late. She said she'd stay and help out. Having already banished him to the far corner of the excavation site, she couldn't leave now without insulting him or risking losing him—she'd kept him at a distance out of fear of losing control.

The thought of another failed relationship terrified her, especially since he was her employee. Stuck in limbo, she couldn't be near him, yet she didn't want to lose him. But something had to give; she'd fallen for him and could no longer avoid him.

Stewart stood close beside Claire as the excavation team began to remove the top layers of the earth, allowing them to get in and use their hand tools to finish digging up the structure. Claire texted Eve and Isabel and asked them to come and help speed up the process—and create some space and distraction between herself and Stewart while she sorted out her complicated feelings.

By sundown, the tops of the walls emerged, revealing the outlines of the ancient edifice.

Sitting behind her computer and finalizing preparations for the upcoming event, Jane caught a glimpse of Claire lying on the bed, staring at the ceiling.

She'd never seen her lie there idly, lost in thought. "What's up, buttercup?" She quipped.

Jane's voice jolted Claire from her daze. She sat up and smiled.

"Sorry, I was just thinking..."

"I can see that. What were you thinking about?

"Oh, I was just thinking about the dig."

"Hmm… How did things go today?" Jane asked as she typed an email to Callum.

"It went really well, actually. We were at it all day. You can see the outlines of the walls now."

Jane finished her email and clicked the send button. She turned off her computer, walked over to Claire with a smile, and said, "Can I get you some wine?"

Claire returned her smile and nodded. "Yes, please."

"Chablis?"

"Anything you've got."

"Chablis, it is, then," Jane said with a wink as she opened a bottle of wine.

She sensed something on Claire's mind as she poured the wine. She looked at her and smiled disarmingly.

"Is everything all right?"

Claire nodded quickly—almost defensively. "Of course. Why wouldn't it be?"

Jane noticed Claire swallow hard at the question, signaling something was clearly off, but she didn't want to press the issue.

She smiled and raised her glass. "To my best friend."

Claire raised hers, and they clinked glasses together.

Claire felt her eyelids grow heavy before even finishing her drink. Pointing to the nightlamp, she said, "Let's go to bed; I can't keep my eyes open." Jane nodded and turned off the light.

Even with the lights off, Jane could see Claire's eyes wide open as she lay beside her. A wave of worry washed over her. She gently ran her fingers along Claire's arm to soothe her.

Claire rolled over and faced her with a smile. "I'm really looking forward to the event; it's going to attract a lot of interest in our work."

"And funding," Jane added.

"And funding," Claire chuckled. She ran her fingers through Jane's hair. "Don't worry, I'm perfectly fine. I just have a lot on my mind."

"Well, I'm here... Lay some on me."

"I do—every day. I hired Stewart as my assistant, but here you are, still carrying all the weight while he's out there in the dirt with Arnold."

Jane laughed. "Good. Leave him out there. We don't need any men—they'll just screw things up." She grinned, then added, "In fact, I'll go out and fire him in the morning."

"Oh, no!" Claire chuckled. "Don't do that... We still need him."

Working alongside Stewart, Claire's excitement grew with each passing moment. Every subtle glance and touch made her heart race with anticipation.

Despite having mixed feelings about the whole situation, she found herself swept away, fully immersed in the possibilities—both personal and professional.

Busy with final arrangements for the event, Jane saw less and less of Claire in the following days, as Claire was occupied working at the new site. Often at night, she found herself tending to Claire's sunburns from the long hours in the sun.

Jane had many questions swirling in her mind, but a voice inside her told her to keep them to herself; she'd developed a strong bond with Claire and didn't want to compromise her relationship. She'd spent entire days and nights with Claire, so hardly anything about her ever remained a mystery.

Claire's team reached the structure's foundation in no time, and it became increasingly clear that they'd unearthed an ancient church. But she had to stop and take a break—the big day had finally arrived.

<h1 style="text-align:center">44</h1>

The guest list was long and distinguished, including notable university presidents, celebrated historians and archaeologists, politicians, and even entertainers.

Claire welcomed guests at the entrance while Jane led them to the main hall, where the exhibits were displayed inside temperature-controlled, sealed glass containers.

Late from his flight, Callum was one of the last guests to arrive. He exited the cab and approached Claire with his arms outstretched.

"Hello, my dear!"

Claire hugged him and smiled. "Hi, Callum… It's wonderful to see you. I'm so glad you're here to hold my hand."

Callum waved his hand dismissively and scoffed. "You've got this under control, my dear. If anything, you should consider chaperoning me." He took a moment to take in his surroundings. "This mansion is enormous. I'm liable to get lost in this place."

Claire smiled warmly and looped her arm around his. "It would be my pleasure!"

Jane spotted them and came over. "Hi, Callum! How are you?"

"I'm peachy, my dear," Callum replied, his eyes twinkling with amusement. "Now that I'm here with the both of you, I'm peachy!"

She wore a black V Bias Twist maxi dress with a front slit that complemented her hourglass figure, paired with silver stilettos and matching white gold earrings and bracelet.

In her hand, she held a silver leather clutch bag—an evening ensemble Claire had put together for her.

Claire had on a champagne sequin halter jumpsuit with a cowl neck and backless design, paired with strappy heels and gold jewelry, along with a crossbody bag.

Callum leaned back slightly, shaking his head. "Dear Lord, you ladies are going to steal the show... Who's going to be interested in Alexander's armor when they can look at you?"

Claire and Jane laughed. Claire motioned towards the main hall.

"Shall we?"

Callum extended his elbows, linking arms with them as they entered the main hall. He froze, gasping at the sight before him—a circular display case housing Alexander's breastplate, illuminated by circular track lighting, with a plaque detailing its historical significance.

A crowd of guests surrounded the display, murmuring in admiration. One of the guests spotted them and began to clap, prompting others to join in.

Callum gestured toward Claire and Jane, and they began chanting, "Bravo!"

Jane smiled and nodded while Claire waved and mouthed, "Thank you."

Other artifacts, including the golden bust of Olympias, Cleopatra's sarcophagus, tablets, coins, and household items, were arranged in separate displays around Alexander's exhibit.

Claire's team interacted with guests, providing historical context and describing the displayed objects as the household staff moved about the room, serving beverages and hors d'oeuvres.

Jane drew Claire aside and whispered, "Come, I want to show you something."

Claire arched an eyebrow but followed. "All right."

Jane took Claire's hand and led her to a private corner under the staircase. She opened the photo app on her phone and faced the screen toward her.

"I wanted to surprise you."

Claire's eyes widened, her lips curling into a broad smile. "You took these?"

Jane nodded. "With Arnold's help—we took these at sunset!"

She scrolled through pictures of the church's walls silhouetted against the sun as it retreated beneath the horizon. They reminded Claire of Hadrian's Wall at sunset, an image they'd marveled at on countless occasions as they sat by the fire, relaxing after a long day's work.

Claire looked up at Jane and said, "They're beautiful." She threw her arms around her, holding her tightly. "You're amazing... Thank you, Jane!"

Jane put her lips to Claire's ear and whispered, "I've prepared a slideshow if you don't mind me showing it... It's part of the surprise, but only if you're okay with it."

Claire pulled back and looked into Jane's eyes. "Of course not! I love you for doing this. You're so thoughtful, Jane!"

"There's more... other pictures... But I wanted to surprise you later during the slideshow—do you trust me?"

Claire flashed a big smile and nodded vigorously. "I do. I absolutely do!" She paused and asked, "You don't have nude photos of me, do you?"

"You'll never know," Jane winked.

Claire laughed and gently squeezed Jane's hand. "Oh, Jane!"

Jane smiled triumphantly as she tapped the rim of her champagne flute with a fork.

The room quieted, and all eyes turned toward her.

"May I please have your attention?"

The crowd quickly gathered around her, whispering to each other—they sensed she was about to make an important announcement.

"Thank you, ladies and gentlemen!" Jane began. "Would you please follow me to the media room? We have an impromptu presentation for you." She grinned and added, "Don't bother looking at your event programs; you won't find it there. It's a surprise. Even my boss didn't know about it until a few minutes ago. I hope she won't fire me."

Claire smiled, her face flushing. She looked at Jane and mouthed, "I won't."

The audience roared with laughter.

Jane smiled and went on. "Please feel free to bring your drinks or food plates... We've got a fun evening planned for you!"

Jane shot a look at Claire before hitting the Start button on the presentation remote. Claire smiled and nodded in response. Jane returned the smile and pressed the Start button.

Claire's mouth dropped open, and her hand flew to her chest. On the screen was an image of a woman—a striking, fair-skinned Celtic woman with red hair standing alongside a Roman warrior.

Claire couldn't believe her eyes; it was as if she was gazing at her reflection. Turning to Jane, her eyes welled up with tears. Jane walked over and threw her arms around her.

A soft chorus of "Aw" filled the room.

Jane whispered something to Claire, and she nodded. Then, Jane returned to the podium and continued with the presentation.

"Ladies and gentlemen, I would like to introduce my favorite couple: Lucius and his lovely Britannic bride, Cara. This is where it all began—with them. Their story is the greatest love story ever told." She glanced at the guests' faces; they looked captivated as they stared at the eerily lifelike renderings. She continued, "I know; I've read their love letters." She clicked on the next slide, which displayed the tablets. "Here they are—two-thousand-year-old love letters. These tablets offer a detailed account of their love and their life together. You might think I'm exaggerating; after all, who can read these ancient scribbles?"

"I can read it," a male voice called out from the crowd. "It says, 'Te desidero, te amo'; it means 'I miss you, I love you.'"

Jane chuckled, her eyes scanning the audience for the source of the voice.

"I'm impressed! May I ask your name, sir?"

"Andrew… Andrew Kowalczyk."

"Would you mind telling us which institution or university you represent?"

"Cornell University."

"Wow… an American!"

"Guilty as charged."

Jane waved to the crowd. "Thank you, Andrew! Even though I can't see you, I appreciate your contribution. We're grateful you hopped across the pond to be with us."

Andrew's voice carried through the room, amused. "You're quite welcome—I wouldn't have missed this for anything!"

Jane nodded politely and continued, "Two lives intertwined—two lives from distant parts of the world and different cultures. Two people who spoke different languages. However, Cara, as we've seen, learned to read and write in Latin; all her letters are in Latin." She paused to study the faces of her guests. "The things we women do for love."

The crowd burst into laughter.

Jane smiled and went on. "It was during his travels that Lucius encountered pirates, and after defeating them in battle, he seized most of the treasures displayed here tonight. We may assume that the pirates didn't realize the significance of what they possessed and how it could rewrite history; to them, it was loot. It was pirate booty. But for us, this is a pivotal discovery: we now know that the ambitions of Alexander, his mother Olympias, and Cleopatra were far grander than their historical portrayals. You'll find our detailed analyses and findings on our website. The link is on your event programs.

Now, I've rambled on long enough." Jane made a sweeping motion with her hand toward Claire. "It's time for me to let my wonderful boss take over... She can tell the story far better than I can."

The crowd erupted in applause as Jane handed the remote to Claire. She quickly adjusted Claire's microphone, offering her an encouraging smile before stepping aside.

Claire turned to Jane and smiled. "That was a wonderful surprise, Jane... a beautiful presentation... Thank you!"

Jane smiled and blew Claire a kiss. Claire then directed her attention to the audience. "She's a tough act to follow, but I'll do my best."

She pressed the Next button on the remote to continue with the slideshow. The first image from the church appeared on the screen.

"There's a lot to unpack here. This second site took us by surprise. First, we discovered the coins from the reign of Emperor Honorius, an entirely different period in Roman history; then we stumbled on this church. This was quite a surprise, to be honest." She clicked through the remaining images of the church. "We have to conduct radiocarbon dating to ascertain that this church dates back to the early 5th century... If so, this would make it Britain's oldest church, older than St. Martin's church, which dates back to the late 6th century."

Claire paused, shifting her gaze to Jane. "Returning to our favorite couple, the DNA analysis revealed a wealth of information about them, including their appearance. You'll find all that information on our website and in upcoming publications. It was through their letters and journals that we learned so much about them. Through Lucius' campaigns and travels and what he confiscated from the pirates, we learn about the ambitions of Alexander, his mother, and, centuries later, Cleopatra. We learned about Lucius' skirmishes in Caledonia and his encounter with a seafaring tribe in the North Sea he called the Germani, whom I believe greatly resembled early Vikings." Claire glanced at Jane and smiled. "As Jane so eloquently put it, 'If it quacks like a duck and walks like a duck, then it's a Viking.'"

The audience laughed heartily.

Jane returned to the podium, and Claire stepped aside.

"And with that, ladies and gentlemen, we'll conclude our presentation," Jane announced.

"Please follow me to the dining hall. We have an exquisite dinner prepared for you."

Claire and Jane had just settled into their seats after directing the guests to their designated places when Claire spotted a man across the dining hall, smiling and waving at her.

Jane looked at Claire and motioned to him with her eyes. "Do you know that man?"

Claire smiled and waved at him, her mind racing to figure out who he was. "I'm not quite sure," she murmured.

The man began to walk towards them. As he drew closer, realization dawned on her. "Damian? Is that you?"

The man grinned and nodded, running a hand over his beard. "I grew this a few months back."

Claire threw her arms around him. "Gosh, Damian, I didn't recognize you with the beard!"

"I know; I'm not too crazy about it either. I'm probably going to shave it off."

"No, it looks good on you! You should definitely keep it."

Damian chuckled and nodded.

Claire turned to Jane. "Damian, please meet Jane. She's my indispensable right-hand person."

Damian extended his hand. "It's a pleasure to meet you, Jane!"

"Likewise, Damian," Jane replied as she shook his hand. "I've heard a lot about you."

"Good things, I hope?" Damian quipped.

"Wonderful things," Jane shot back with a smile.

Damian glanced at his watch and turned to Claire. "I'm sorry for being late. I had to take the train from Oxford and..."

"Don't worry about it; you're here now." Claire interrupted, brushing her hand along his arm. "I'm just glad you made it. It's wonderful seeing you again!" She dropped her voice and asked, "So, what do you think of the exhibits?"

"Oh, Claire, I don't know what to say," Damian said. "This is the most impressive collection of artifacts I've ever seen... I..." He stammered. He was about to finish his sentence when a press photographer interrupted him.

"I'm sorry to interrupt," he said. "May I take a quick snapshot of the three of you?"

Claire smiled and nodded.

"Please come closer together," the photographer instructed, motioning with his hands.

Claire stood at the center, with Jane and Damian beside her.

"That's perfect!" The photographer called out, giving a thumbs up. "Now, everyone, a big smile!"

He took the shot, pulled it up on his display screen, and turned it toward Claire. With a Cockney accent, he asked, "It's gorgeous, innit?"

Claire smiled and gave a slight nod. Jane and Damian leaned in to take a look.

"You ladies look great," Damian raved.

"It better look great," the photographer said. "It's going to be on the front page of the paper!"

Claire noticed Callum talking to another man. She called out to get his attention and waved him over. After politely wrapping up his conversation, he strode toward them.

"I'm sorry, dear. I was chatting with an old colleague. He's likely going to contribute to our future ventures," he explained.

"That's wonderful!" Claire grasped his arm playfully. "But for now, we just need you to smile for the camera. This is going to be on the front page of the paper, so please give us your best smile."

Claire positioned Callum between herself and Jane, with Damian at her other side.

The photographer took another picture and showed it to them. "This one's even better than the last."

45

As the evening began to wind down and guests started to leave, Jane focused on securing the artifacts and arranging their shipment back to the warehouse.

She'd assigned Peter to oversee security for the event and to ensure the items were returned safely. Spotting him, she saw him coordinating the details with Stewart and the crew.

Jane then scanned the room for Claire but couldn't find her anywhere. After a short search, she discovered Claire standing alone by the entrance, sipping her wine and gazing out into the darkness.

"Penny for your thoughts," Jane murmured as she approached from behind.

Claire tilted her head back slightly, smiling. "Oh, hi, Jane."

"Hi, why are you standing here all alone?" Jane asked, placing her hand on Claire's shoulder.

"Oh, no particular reason. I'm just looking at the stars and saying goodbye to the guests as they start to leave," Claire replied.

"I know! Did you see the expressions on their faces? They looked amazed!"

Claire's lips curled into a smile as she gazed up at the stars. "I did… We dazzled them!"

"And remember, we've got this whole place to ourselves tonight. It's all paid for until tomorrow."

"Yay! We get to sleep in a mansion tonight."

"That's right… We get to be princesses for the night."

Claire laughed. "Maybe you… You're the one who looks like a princess."

"Oh, come on!" Jane said with a playful tone. "You're the real princess. Remember, I saw the house you grew up in."

She looped her arm through Claire's and gave it a gentle tug. "All right, let's go."

"Where are you taking me?" Claire chuckled.

"We're going to the bar. The bartender took off already, and I saw lots of unopened bottles. I'm going to have Isabel make us some drinks—it's all paid for, so..."

"That actually sounds great," Claire beamed. "I could use a drink."

"Or five," Jane joked as she led Claire towards the bar. On their way, she spotted Isabel and signaled for her to follow them.

Jane gasped when she entered the grand suite and caught sight of the antique four-poster bed with its draped canopy.

She took off her heels, nearly spilling her vodka spritz—it was her third drink, and she felt quite tipsy as her eyes scanned the spacious bedroom with its luxurious en-suite bathroom.

She paused to gaze at the paintings of the manor's past inhabitants adorning its walls. It felt as if they were staring at her, studying her. She made a face, feeling a bit creeped out.

An old Georgian-style stone mantel framed the fireplace, and in front of it, two antique sofas and a loveseat encircled a carved walnut coffee table covered with history books.

Two large windows, draped in French pleated curtains, looked out toward the front of the manor with London's lights shimmering in the distance.

Jane collapsed onto the bed, sinking into the plush mattress with a contented sigh. She patted the space beside her.

"Come sit with me," she invited Claire. "You won't believe how comfy it is."

Claire sipped her Margarita and placed the glass on the nightstand. She climbed onto the bed on her knees and then fell beside Jane. "Oh my god, this is so cozy!" She raved, clawing at the comforter. "This must be goose down... or something else that's insanely soft."

Jane grabbed the remote and pointed it at the big-screen TV on the wall. "What do you think?"

Claire shook her head. "It'll ruin the ambiance. We don't get to stay at a mansion often. Let's enjoy this place... I hate TV."

"Agreed!" Jane quirked her lips, looking around the room, searching for ideas. "Hmm… Let's see… What can we do?"

"I've got an idea," Claire said.

"Good… What?" Jane perked up.

"We can do our nails."

"We can do each other's nails! But wait, we don't have nail polish…"

Claire grabbed her bag and opened it. She reached inside and fished out a handful of bottles. She smiled and said, "Pick a color."

Jane gaped at the assortment. "You carry nail polish in your purse?"

Claire nodded smugly. "Think about it… Why would I do that?"

Jane took a moment to think about the answer. Then, her eyes widened as if a lightbulb went on in her head. She clicked her tongue and said, "I got it—you mess up your nails because you're always digging in the dirt!"

"Bingo!" Claire held her hand out to Jane, her fingers extended. "See? My nails look atrocious!"

"No, they don't... They may be a little chipped, but we can easily fix that. Got a nail file?"

Claire pulled a file from her purse and smiled. "What color do you want?"

Jane ran her fingers across the bottles spread out on the bed. "I'll take the nude."

Claire chuckled. "Fine, I'll take soft pink."

Claire began to unscrew the nail polish cap, but Jane clasped her hand.

"Wait," Jane said in a suspenseful tone. "We're missing something. Let's go downstairs for a minute."

"Why? What do you need downstairs?"

Jane raised her hand to her lips, mimicking holding a shot glass and pretending to take a swig.

Claire shook her head and laughed. "You've had three drinks already."

"Oh, come on! Don't be a...

"I know," Claire cut in. "Don't be a party pooper."

Jane nodded and pointed her finger at Claire. "Yes, exactly."

"Fine, let's go," Claire caved. "But keep it quiet. I don't want the staff to see us and think we're a couple of drunks."

Jane pressed her index finger to her lips and mouthed, "We'll be very, very quiet."

Claire began to laugh, but Jane pressed her palm to Claire's lips and whispered, "Shh… Be very, very quiet."

Claire nodded, struggling to contain her laughter.

The heavy bedroom door slowly swung open with a loud creaking sound. Jane let out a chuckle, and Claire snorted, sending echoes through the hallway.

"Shh…" Jane whispered again. Claire covered her mouth to stifle her laughter as she clung to the back of Jane's shirt, following her into the dimly lit hallway.

Tipsy from the drinks, Jane couldn't remember how to get back down to the main floor.

"Hey, I don't remember these paintings," she said, glancing at the walls.

Claire gave a quiet chuckle. "That's because we didn't come this way."

"What? Why didn't you tell me?" Jane whispered.

"Because we're exploring the manor. Why spoil the fun?" Claire said with a grin.

Jane laughed. "Look at you! Miss Audacious!"

Claire snickered. "It's the Margarita!"

"Good! I'll pick up tequila and triple sec and make you some more when we get back—I love this version of you!"

Eventually, Jane found a staircase that brought them down to the first floor, but they still couldn't figure out where they were.

"I think we're lost," Claire said.

"I know; don't rub it in," Jane snorted.

Jane noticed a light coming from the wall ahead. They drew closer and discovered a knight's alcove—a wall niche housing a full-length suit of armor gripping a gleaming sword in its hand.

"Oh, I love these things," Jane raved. "I think they're the coolest."

Claire got closer, examining the armor. "You know what?"

Jane arched a brow. "What?"

"I think this is the real thing... I don't think it's a replica." Claire pointed to the coat of arms. "That's the symbol that represents the house or family."

"That's so cool!" Jane beamed as she leaned in, her fingers gliding across the grip of the sword.

Suddenly, the smile faded from Jane's face, and she recoiled in horror as the sword broke free from the armor's grip and came crashing onto the floor with a deafening clang.

Jane shrieked, pressing her palms to her face. In a panic, she picked up the sword and propped it against the wall. Then, she took Claire's hand, and they ran down the hallway, laughing hysterically.

As they rounded the corner, Jane suddenly stopped. She turned and raised her finger to her lips, gesturing for Claire to be quiet. Peeking around the corner, Jane checked the hallway to see if anyone was following them, but there was no one in sight.

"They're probably all passed out," Jane murmured. She surveyed her surroundings and realized they were standing at the grand entrance. "I know where we are now... Let's go this way." She led the way, with Claire trailing behind as they entered the grand hall.

"There's the bar," Claire said.

Jane didn't respond—she gave Claire's arm a squeeze. "Check this out," she said, motioning toward a dark corner of the room.

Claire shifted her gaze to the spot where Jane was pointing. "What am I looking at?" She murmured.

Jane took Claire's hand, and they stepped forward into the shadows. They heard snoring.

"It's Peter." Jane shook her head. "There's our security expert." She looked around and saw that the artifacts were boxed up and ready for shipment. "At least they managed to get everything packed and ready to go."

"Well, that's a good thing, right?"

"Yeah, but with this Keystone cop passed out in his chair, anyone can just stroll in and steal everything."

"It's all right," Claire said, tugging on Jane's hand. "You worry too much. Let's grab a bottle and go back to the room. I'm sure everything will be fine."

"Mm-hmm… All right, let's go. I hope we can find our room."

"I know how to get back from here," Claire chuckled softly. "Let's just get out of here."

Back in the suite, Jane kept spilling her drink as they sat on the bed, painting each other's nails. It was the most intimate and enjoyable time Claire had ever shared with Jane.

Claire couldn't stop laughing at Jane's antics as she fumbled with the nail polish, leaving smudges on her skin.

Then, suddenly, Claire's smile vanished, and her heart sank.

She saw shadows peeking from beneath Jane's skirt as she sat cross-legged in front of her—matching bruises on her calves shaped like fingers.

46

Claire glanced nervously at her watch; the train was set to leave in five minutes. She scanned the station platform through the window, searching for Jane.

Suddenly, a loud thump startled her from behind. Turning around, she found Jane standing next to her, grinning.

Jane's eyes flickered toward the newspaper on the table. Claire didn't need to pick it up to see the cover story—it was glaring at her.

HISTORY RETOLD

Two women, united by a grand ambition, sought to revive Alexander The Great's dreams of world conquest—dreams that were cut short by his untimely death.

An archaeological dig at Hadrian's Wall has uncovered remarkable artifacts: letters written in Cleopatra's handwriting, revealing her grand ambitions—ambitions that may equal or even surpass those of Julius Caesar—as she aspired to become Rome's sole ruler and queen.

Additionally, a royal sarcophagus features a carved relief depicting Olympias, queen of Macedonia and mother of Alexander the Great. She may have been the true source of inspiration for one of history's greatest conquerors.

Finally, there are clues pointing to Alexander's final resting place, which has eluded historians for centuries.

Explore the intimate letters and correspondence between the Roman soldier and his Britannic bride, which bring these stories to life.

Claire sucked in a sharp breath and slumped into her chair, pressing a hand to her chest. Jane sat beside her, facing her. "You so deserve this. I'm so proud of you." She reached to her side, picked up a bundle of newspapers, and laid them on the table one by one.

Taking Claire's hand in hers, she said, "You're on the front page of every major newspaper in England—congratulations!"

Claire smiled and squeezed Jane's hand, her eyes welling up with tears.

"Thank you, Jane."

Jane shook her head. "No, thank you for letting me be a part of this—part of your life!"

"You're welcome... You know I can't do this without you."

Jane lowered her head on Claire's shoulder. "You exaggerate, but I appreciate it. By the way, you are featured in every major publication worldwide, including Europe and America. I just couldn't carry any more newspapers; my hands were full. And I checked online; all of our social media are blowing up!"

Claire leaned her head on Jane's as it rested on her shoulder. She was thrilled about the acclaim she'd received, but her joy was overshadowed by what she'd seen the night before. She decided to bring it up again, hoping Jane would open up to her.

"Can I ask you a question?" Claire asked in a hushed tone.

"Sure—anything!" Jane said.

Claire hesitated, trying to choose her words carefully.

With her head still on Claire's shoulder, Jane picked up on her unease and said, "What's the matter? Is something wrong?"

Claire sighed. "Well... I was going to ask you the same question."

Jane lifted her head slightly. "What do you mean?"

"Last night... I saw bruises on your legs... I'm really worried about you!"

Jane gave a dismissive wave. "Oh, it's nothing. I bump into things all the time. And I've been in and out of the pit, working next to you all day. It's probably from sitting on my legs... you know, from all the little rocks and pebbles."

Claire studied her, unconvinced. "Hmm."

"Really—you've got nothing to worry about!"

"You'd tell me if there was anything wrong, right?"

"Of course I would!"

Claire's voice softened. "You know you can share anything with me; I'm always here for you."

"I know that. Please don't worry. Everything is fine."

"All right."

"Remember, we're going to town this weekend."

"Good. We can all use a break."

Claire turned her head and gazed out the window, swallowing her pangs of doubt and holding out hopes that Jane would one day open up to her.

47

Jane lit a cigarette, took a deep puff, and exhaled a stream of smoke through the crack in the trailer window.

She opened her email and began scrolling, her eyes skimming over subject lines stacked in bold.

After taking another drag from her cigarette, she scratched her head in thought. She counted the unread emails, then hesitated before going back to the first one and clicking it open. Her brow furrowed in disbelief as she smothered her cigarette in the ashtray and dashed out the door.

"I don't know how I'm getting so many pebbles in my shoes," Claire vented to Sharon as she loosened the laces on her ankle boots. She took them off, flipped them upside down, and shook them.

Tiny stones clattered onto the ground. "It seems like there are less pebbles on the ground than in my shoes!"

Sharon laughed. "Tell me about it. I can feel at least three of them in my shoes right now. I've just learned to ignore them until I can't ignore them anymore, and then I take my shoes off and toss them!"

"Hey, that sounds like fun," Jane chuckled as she approached them. "Are we having a shoe-tossing contest? What are the game rules?"

"Hey, Jane!" Claire shot back. "How are things going?"

"That's all right... Go ahead and change the subject." Jane playfully rolled her eyes as she stepped inside the excavation square. "I can see I'm not invited to the game."

"We were complaining about pebbles in our shoes," Claire laughed. "Trust me, you don't want to be in this game."

"Sure," Jane said with playful sarcasm. She took her phone from her pocket, opened her bookkeeping app, and held it in front of Claire.

Claire's eyes widened. "Am I looking at..."

Jane nodded. "Uh-huh."

Claire traced her finger over the screen. "Am I seeing..." She stammered. "Am I looking at seven figures?"

Jane nodded again. "I know; I had to rub my eyes and check twice myself... The numbers are correct. And you know what else?"

Claire shook her head. "What?"

"I haven't checked all the emails... They keep coming—donations, pledges, contributions. Our biggest contributor is the Dimitriou Foundation."

"Never heard of them... Greek?"

"Mm-hmm... And guess how they found out about us?"

"Let me guess—Damian?"

Jane clicked her tongue and pointed at her. "Damian!"

"Gosh, I've got to call him and thank him. You know, he told me he's still working on translating the rest of the tablets."

"Mm... I know; he's a great guy. I gave him some free advice: I told him not to shave his beard."

"What?" Claire laughed.

"Yeah," Jane replied. "I saw his picture online before he grew his beard. While we were taking pictures at the event, I leaned over and whispered, 'Don't shave your beard.'"

"Really?"

"Yeah... He laughed and said, 'Thank you—I won't.'"

Claire and Sharon burst into laughter.

48

Back at her favorite spot in town, nursing a pint of ale, Jane sat at the table with Isabel, listening intently as Isabel shared her life story. From across the bar, Claire watched them closely. Although she nodded in response to Stewart's words, she didn't hear what he said; her entire focus was on Jane, who seemed captivated by Isabel, her brow furrowed and her gaze attentive.

Claire had noticed Jane spending more time with Isabel at the dig, showing her the ropes and making sure she was well-adapted to her new job. But that wasn't all; it was her inexplicable yearning to be around Isabel. Claire had seen Jane display similar behavior with Eve, treating her like an older sister, but there was something different about her connection with Isabel—something deeper.

A light touch on her arm startled her. She flinched.

"I'm sorry, I didn't mean to make you jump," Stewart said.

Claire managed a nervous smile. "It's all right... I'm sorry, Stewart, I was distracted. I better go and see how everyone's doing."

Stewart smiled and nodded. "Of course."

Claire had kept Stewart close, but not too close. There was always a gnawing hesitation inside her, knowing that she couldn't—and shouldn't—take this fantasy of hers any further.

Stewart was her employee, and her gut told her that any workplace romance with a subordinate could negatively impact her other employees, particularly Jane.

As she walked toward Jane, Claire felt Stewart's gaze on her. Her impulse to join Jane overcame her desire to stay and talk to him. There was no competition, no hesitation; when it came to Jane, everything else faded in comparison.

The feelings were mutual. Jane's furrowed brow relaxed, and she smiled when she saw Claire approaching.

"Hi, Claire," Jane beamed. "Isabel and I were just talking about her childhood. Why don't you join us?"

Isabel smiled and waved at Claire. "Hi, Claire! Can I get you a drink?"

Claire sat in the chair next to Isabel's. She smiled and placed her hand on Isabel's. "You know, I'd love that, dear."

"What would you like?"

"Surprise me!"

Isabel nodded and grinned. "I know just the thing," she murmured before heading towards the bar.

"She's really sweet," Claire said, turning back to Jane.

"Isn't she?" Jane said.

Claire nodded. "How are you doing?"

"I'm fine… Why? Do I look…"

Claire shook her head. "I didn't mean it like that. You just had an intense look."

Jane gave a slight shrug. "I'm all right. Isabel was telling me her life story. "

"You don't have to explain," Claire interrupted. "As long as you're having fun."

"I am—lots."

Isabel returned with drinks for Claire and Jane, placing them on the table.

"Here you go. I think you'll like these."

"Thank you, Isabel. Which one's mine?" Claire asked.

"They're both the same." Isabel flashed a smile. "Pimm's Cup... It's a gin drink with fruit and some other tasty stuff." She gestured toward Sharon and Eve, sitting at a nearby table. "I'm going to go sit with them for a bit if you don't mind."

Claire waved at Sharon and Eve, who waved back. Turning to Isabel, she said, "Of course not. Have fun!"

"Mmm, I love this Pimm's Cup," Claire raved. Jane nodded in agreement as she sipped hers.

"I've got an idea." She leaned in, putting her lips to Claire's ear. "How about we go mingle with the gang for a bit, then sneak out and go shopping?"

Claire drew back, raising a skeptical brow. "Really? Are stores still open?"

"Uh-huh. It's still early. I found a swanky one—I could use some retail therapy."

Claire chuckled. "Gosh, me too. All right, let's go!"

Claire laughed when the cab pulled up in front of the shoe store.

"I should've known," she muttered as they exited the cab. Jane giggled and muttered under her breath, "Shoes!"

Sitting beside her, Claire watched patiently as Jane tried on pair after pair of shoes. Claire had picked out her own shoes within minutes and was intrigued as Jane joyfully sorted through the pile in front of her, searching for the pair she really liked.

Claire considered asking Jane about Isabel, but before she could, Jane spoke first.

"So, I noticed you've been spending more time with Stewart." Jane let her words hang in the air, hoping Claire would fill in the blanks.

Claire felt her heart thumping inside her chest. The question caught her off guard—she certainly wasn't prepared to answer it. Still, she felt compelled to respond.

"There's nothing there if that's what you were thinking... I just didn't want him to feel neglected," Claire said, forcing a hard swallow. "... or feel ignored."

Jane clasped the ankle strap of the platform heels she'd picked out. She looked up at Claire and grinned widely. "What do you think? Do you like these?"

Claire smiled and nodded. "I love them."

She knew right then that she had to create some distance between herself and Stewart. She didn't want any more speculation or raised eyebrows about her personal life—especially not from one of the most important people in her life.

On the way back to the hotel, Jane didn't speak much, and there were no follow-up questions about Stewart. She simply smiled, resting her chin against the window as she watched the city pass by.

"I'll have Sharon work at the new site with Stewart and Arnold," Claire murmured, trying to break the awkward silence. "She'll take Eve with her."

Jane turned to face Claire, closely studying her. She moved closer and lowered her head on Claire's shoulder. As usual, her body language communicated everything; no words were needed. She was clearly satisfied with Claire's idea.

49

She sat on the bed with her knees tucked into her chest, staring at the painting on the wall. Her fingers curled around the necklace Amelie had given her, comforting her.

She recalled how the painting had once terrified Amelie, causing her to curl up and tremble in her arms.

Tears welled up in her eyes as she ran her hand over the empty space where Amelie used to lie. Shaking her head defiantly, she wiped her tears away, a frown wrinkling her brow.

Her gaze was drawn back to the painting, focusing on the boat bobbing in the surf with the lighthouse in the background. She hated the painting because of what it represented, yet a smile spread across her face—it reminded her of Amelie.

Standing in front of the mirror, running her fingers through her wavy blonde hair, she heard heavy footsteps approaching. Heart racing, she dashed to her nightstand, grabbed a vase, and pressed herself against the wall next to the door. She watched as the doorknob turned, and the door slowly swung open.

With both hands, she raised the vase over her head and took a deep breath.

"Celine! Where the fuck are you, you little bitch?" A voice growled.

She immediately recognized the voice—it was Armand, one of Henri's sadistic goons. The moment his feet crossed the threshold, she brought the vase down with full force onto his skull, and his body crumpled to the floor.

Without thinking, she bolted through the door and down the hallway, her heart pounding.

Turning the corner, she ran straight into Gabriel, the yacht's chief engineer.

"Hey, Celine! Are you all right?" He asked, clutching her arms.

Celine gave a vigorous shake of her head, terror etched in her wide eyes.

"What's the matter? Tell me!"

Before she could speak, Armand came hurtling through the door, his face twisted with rage. The second he spotted Celine, he lunged at her with his arms outstretched.

Gabriel's eyes blazed with anger. He'd witnessed Armand's cruelty toward Celine before, and he wasn't about to let it happen again. As Armand reached for her, Gabriel grabbed his arms, spun him around, and slammed him against the wall with a loud thud.

Gripping his collar, Gabriel peered into his eyes. "I'm warning you, Armand! If I catch you touching her one more time, I swear I'm going to throw you overboard! Do you hear me?"

Visibly shaken, Armand nodded.

Gabriel saw the fear in his eyes. He loosened his grip, and Armand pulled himself away. He straightened out his collar before quietly slinking away.

Gabriel turned back to Celine and held out a hand. She hesitated before taking it. He smiled at her and said, "You can come hang out with me for a while. I'll teach you to operate a yacht... Would you like that?"

Celine smiled and nodded. Gabriel saw an object in her free hand.

"What's that in your hand?"

Celine raised her hand, holding a slender chain. She let a pendant drop from her fingers, allowing it to dangle in front of Gabriel. It was a silver crucifix.

She smiled, gazing at it. "Amelie gave it to me."

"It's beautiful! Why don't you let me put it on you?"

Celine's smile faded. She shook her head. "I don't want to lose it!"

Gabriel frowned. "Why would you lose it by wearing it around your neck?"

Celine gave Gabriel a look as if she expected him to know better, but he returned a perplexed expression.

"I don't want one of these creeps to rip it off my neck," she clarified.

Gabriel was a member of the hired crew, and he had his suspicions about what was happening, although he didn't know the full extent of it. The crew was intentionally kept away from the girls and was generously compensated for their silence.

Now, Gabriel had the perfect opportunity to learn more from Celine—but only if she would be willing to open up to him.

50

Sharon nodded in acknowledgment, her gaze lowered, hands planted firmly on her hips. "Whatever you want, Claire," She said as they stood on top of the mound, gazing down at the new site. "I think it's a good idea for me to work on the new site for a while. Things'll probably move faster if I'm on top of them."

"I think so, too." Claire agreed. "And if the guys ask, just say I needed to be close to my trailer and my computer." She paused before adding, "I think I was part of the problem—too much chitchat and all."

Sharon furrowed her brow and scoffed. "Well, that's not going to happen now. You're way too nice, Claire—the party's over. We just got back from town, and they've had plenty of rest. Time to go to work!"

Claire laughed. "Just take it easy on them."

Sharon chuckled. "Easy?" Sharon raised her hand and brought it down swiftly. "I'm going to crack the whip!"

"Don't forget the leather straps," Jane said, approaching from behind.

Claire and Sharon spun around and burst into laughter.

"Oh, Jane!" Claire exclaimed.

Jane stood beside them, tilting her head toward the sun, her eyes shut, and her lips curled into a smile. She knew what was happening; she'd only come over to be near Claire.

Sharon wasted no time. She quickly mapped out new grid squares around the old church and started digging.

Before long, a cemetery from the reign of Emperor Honorius began to emerge from the earth. Each day brought new finds— early Christian relics like crucifixes, mosaics, and various religious artifacts.

But it was the discovery of Anglo-Saxon relics within Christian burial sites that truly captured the world's attention, providing compelling evidence that some Anglo-Saxons converted to Christianity well over a century earlier than previously thought.

Jane kept up with Sharon and regularly posted new images and details about the dig on social media, igniting a flurry of interest and attracting donations from religious and charitable organizations around the globe.

"This deserves a toast!" Jane exclaimed, raising her glass as the flames danced and shimmered, casting a golden glow on the swirling whiskey inside.

Claire mirrored her gesture, clinking her glass with a smile. "It certainly does."

A chill wind blew, sending orangish-red embers soaring into the night sky.

"It doesn't get any better than this," Jane beamed, holding her hand against the warmth of the flames. She glanced across the dig site at the crew, who were gathered around their own campfire, their laughter drifting over. She waved at Sharon, who waved back.

"Sharon's doing a fantastic job," Jane commented.

"She's amazing," Claire agreed without hesitation.

Jane sipped her whiskey and closed her eyes, feeling the warmth of the fire on her face. A slight smile appeared on her lips.

Suddenly, her phone pinged. Raising it to her face, she opened her eyes just enough to glimpse the screen. Her heart pounded fiercely, and her eyes flew open, locking onto the text message displayed.

Claire felt a wave of concern wash over her. She sprang to her feet and leaned in to see what Jane was looking at.

Jane turned her phone screen toward Claire, her hand trembling. Claire steadied it instinctively, her pulse quickening as she read the message from Peter.

Sorry to bother you but we have an emergency. Please call. We had a break-in.

<h1 style="text-align:center">51</h1>

The Inspector was in the vicinity when he got the call from dispatch and was the first to arrive at the crime scene. He didn't announce his presence; he wanted to survey the crime scene and gather evidence before interviewing anyone.

He noticed signs of forced entry at the rear entrance to the warehouse: gouges and scratch marks on the door frame and lock. He was examining the door and jotting down his observations in his notebook when he heard footsteps approaching.

"Can I help you?" A female voice called out from behind him.

The inspector turned around and saw Jane and Claire standing in front of him. "Yes, thank you. I'm Detective Inspector Javan Siddiqui of the Northumbria Police Department. I apologize; I'm not in uniform." He reached into his coat pocket, took out his ID card, and showed it to Jane. She glanced at it, then looked into his eyes, studying him closely, before handing it back to him.

"Thank you, Inspector. My name is Jane Morgan," she said, gesturing to Claire. "And this is my employer, Claire Langford."

The Inspector smiled and extended his hand. "Hello, Miss Langford!"

Claire returned the smile and shook his hand. "It's a pleasure to meet you, Inspector. Thank you for coming—I realize it's late."

"Not at all, ma'am. I'm used to it."

Jane, arms crossed, wasn't in the mood for pleasantries. "So, what is your assessment, inspector?" she asked, cutting straight to business. "I noticed you were examining the door."

"Yes, ma'am," the Inspector said in a calm tone. "My assessment—my initial observation—is that we need to conduct a proper investigation to find out how someone gained entry into your facility. That'll help us identify our suspect."

Jane gave a puzzled look and pointed to the gouge marks on the door.

"I understand your confusion, ma'am," he continued, "But whoever broke into this place may have had a key, picked the lock, or had someone open the door from inside; he could've mucked up the door to create the impression that this was a break-in."

"So, you think it could be an inside job?" Jane asked in a tone that was impatient, bordering on irritation.

"It's always a possibility, ma'am... but I'd prefer to wait until I've conducted my investigation and my interviews before jumping to any conclusions."

"Well, Inspector, the only people who stay at this site are our nightwatchman and our security person, Peter. The rest of the crew work and stay on-site in company trailers."

"I understand, ma'am. I'll start with the personnel here and then come to your worksite to continue interviewing the rest of the staff. Meanwhile, my partner will take fingerprints and collect other forensic evidence."

"Yes, we just met her. She's at the front entrance, taking a statement from Peter now."

The Inspector nodded. "That would be Detective Sergeant Emily Walker. She's very thorough." He underlined something in his notebook, then continued. "Now, let's start with what's been taken."

"They took some gold coins," Jane said, casting a sidelong glance and clenching her jaw. She lit a cigarette and took a long drag, holding it in for a few seconds before releasing the smoke into the crisp night air.

"What quantity and value would you say?"

"The coins were in pouches," Jane said, nervously tapping her feet. She took another puff from her cigarette. "I am assuming somewhere between fifty and a hundred coins."

"And the value?"

"Value?" Jane scoffed. "They're priceless, Inspector—they're ancient Roman coins..." She paused and then added, "Luckily, they took nothing else."

"Why do you think that is?"

"I don't know... Maybe they didn't have enough time to take anything else. We'd just returned from an event in London where the artifacts were exhibited, and some of the items were still in boxes and crates."

"Does the general public know about this place?"

"No, only my employees," Claire answered. She could see Jane's mounting frustration and took the reins before her F-bombs started flying. "I've intentionally kept this location private for security reasons. As you can see, all the windows are barred, and we've had around-the-clock security."

"Yes, I can see that, ma'am," the Inspector said, shifting his gaze to Claire.

Claire watched as the Inspector made his final entries in his notebook. There was a calmness about him, a confidence, and his eyes seemed to conceal his thoughts as if he already had the answers. It made her feel safe and protected; her worries washed away in his serene gaze.

He looked up from his notes and smiled at Claire. She noticed he was left-handed as he clicked his pen closed with his thumb and tucked it into his shirt pocket.

She smiled back at him, her face flushing. She'd checked for a ring on his finger and saw he wasn't wearing one.

"Do you have any final thoughts, Inspector?" She asked.

"Yes, ma'am. I'll put a call out to the local foundries in case they try to melt the gold coins. I'll also call the local antique dealers and ask them to contact us if they come across the stolen items... or if they hear anything." The Inspector saw the worry in Claire's eyes. He hesitated, then added, "You know, ma'am, I don't want to give you false hope, but I have a feeling about this— I think we'll be able to recover your items!"

Claire nodded, a glimmer of hope in her eyes. "Thank you, Inspector!"

"My pleasure, ma'am!"

It was nearly 3 a.m. when Claire and Jane got back to the trailer. Jane went straight to the liquor cabinet in the kitchen and poured herself a double shot of whiskey.

Claire collapsed onto her bed and opened her laptop. Rubbing her tired eyes, she typed out a brief email to Callum, detailing the night's events, then closed her laptop with an emphatic thump—she was done with this night.

Jane returned from the kitchen and handed Claire a glass of wine.

Claire gulped it down and let out a satisfied "Ahh."

Jane sank into the bed beside her and moaned, "I second that!"

"Mm."

"What a fucked up night!"

"I second that!"

With her eyes closed, Claire's fingers searched for the light switch on her night lamp and clicked it off.

"Are you going to sleep in your clothes?" Jane whispered, turning to face her.

"Mmm…" Claire hesitated, then unzipped her jeans and peeled them off. She then took off her shirt.

Jane giggled and followed suit.

A few moments later.

"You awake?" Jane whispered.

"Mm-hmm."

Jane hesitated before asking, "Do you think the investigator can get our coins back?"

"I do… I've got a good feeling about him."

52

Amelie gently stroked her pendant between her fingers and smiled at Dr. Tussaud, who crossed her legs and smiled back.

Dr. Tussaud wasn't going to break her silence; she was waiting for Amelie to respond to her question—why did she keep dreaming about Celine?

Amelie finally spoke up. She lowered her gaze to the ground and said in a hushed tone, "I dream about her because I love her... because I miss her... I'm worried about her."

Dr. Tussaud jotted down notes in Amelie's file and continued with her questions, deliberately avoiding eye contact. She didn't want to signal anything that could sway Amelie's response.

"I'm going to ask you a question. You don't have to answer if you don't want to, but if you do, it's very important that you're honest with me, all right?"

Amelie looked up, her expression cautious. She paused for a moment, then nodded.

"You'd mentioned that Celine would sneak into your cabin, and she'd cuddle with you to comfort you…"

Amelie nodded again.

"Did things ever get intimate between you?"

Amelie knitted her eyebrows. "Intimate?"

Dr. Tussaud pressed her index finger to her lips, searching for the right words. She didn't want to be vague. "Did you ever have sex with her?" She stopped to remind her, "Remember, you don't have to answer if you're uncomfortable, but if you do, please be honest."

Amelie turned her gaze toward the window. She shook her head.

"It wasn't like that."

"What was it like then? … How did she comfort you?

Amelie continued to gaze out the window—she felt embarrassed and tried to avoid eye contact as she responded.

"She was much stronger than I was. I felt protected when she was with me. Comforted… I slept better when she was with me. I didn't have nightmares."

Dr. Tussaud's voice softened. "And you believe she also felt comforted when she was with you?"

Amelie took a deep breath and sighed. She looked directly into Dr. Tussaud's eyes.

"Yes!"

"Did she say so?"

"No… Not exactly… Not in words."

"How then?"

Amelie's eyes clouded with emotion. "She held me... and played with my hair. She came to me every chance she got. She could've gone with the other girls—they were always together, drinking, playing cards, or watching movies. But she wanted to be with me. She didn't hold or touch any other girls."

"And you worry about her..."

Amelie nodded, her eyes closed. "I'm worried because she always fought them—fought him. I'm afraid he may really hurt her."

"Henri?"

"Yes… She hated him! He was cruel to everyone, but especially to her, because she wouldn't obey him." Amelie took a deep breath and exhaled. "But as I said before, Marcel is going to find her—he promised he would!"

Amelie became anxious, chewing on her nails and clutching her knees. Dr. Tussaud decided to move on to another topic, one that she knew would instantly cheer her up.

She smiled gently. "How is Titou?"

Amelie's eyes widened, and she grinned widely. "I love Titou. He's the best!"

Dr. Tussaud laughed. "I knew that would cheer you up!"

Amelie took her pendant between her fingers, caressing it. "He always cheers me up."

"How are things at home? Are you happy?"

"Very. Things are great."

A knock at the door interrupted them.

Dr. Tussaud walked over and opened it, letting out a startled shriek as a small, furry creature dashed inside, leaping into Amelie's lap and licking her face.

Marcel stood at the entrance, smiling.

"I'm so sorry, Jacqueline! They told me at the reception that your session was over. I asked if I could come back here and say hello. They said yes. I'm taking Amelie and Titou to lunch."

Dr. Tussaud waved her hand dismissively. "Oh, it's quite all right... We were busy chatting and lost track of time. Funny enough, we were just talking about Titou, and then... voilà! Here he is!"

Amelie approached, carrying Titou in her arms.

"Thank you, Dr. Tussaud."

"You're very welcome, Amelie! And please say hello to Madeleine for me. Tell her I miss her and would like to take her to lunch."

"I will."

Marcel stepped closer and gave Dr. Tussaud a hug. "Thank you for everything, Jaqueline."

She smiled warmly. "You're most welcome."

Dr. Tussaud waved at Marcel and Amelie as they walked away, with Titou trailing behind.

53

Claire forced her eyelids open and quickly covered her eyes with her forearm, shielding them from the sunlight streaming through the window blinds. Blinking against the brightness, she glanced over and saw Jane sprawled on her stomach next to her, fast asleep.

The aroma of freshly brewed coffee wafted through the air, enticing her out of bed. She padded into the kitchen, poured herself a cup, and brought it to her lips—but then paused.

Looking out the window, she noticed a familiar figure standing across the dig site, talking with Sharon.

Her heart raced with anticipation as she slipped into her jeans.

"Good morning! Did you get any sleep, Inspector?" Claire said, announcing her presence.

The Inspector looked up from his notes and smiled, his eyes heavy with exhaustion. After leaving the warehouse, he'd gone straight to the police station to file a report before heading to the dig site to continue his investigation.

"Good morning, ma'am... Actually, no, but I'm all right. Thank you for asking."

Claire stood holding two steaming mugs of coffee. She offered one to the Inspector. "It's strong, and it's freshly brewed."

"Thank you, ma'am. You're very kind!" The Inspector took the mug from Claire and read the words printed on it: "I dig dirt!"

Claire tugged on the hem of her shirt, motioning toward the identical phrase printed across the front. Then, she grinned and said, "And please, call me Claire."

The Inspector managed a tired chuckle. "Of course, Claire! You can call me Javan."

"Thank you, Javan! It means a lot to me that you're here so early... but I feel awful that you didn't get any sleep!"

Javan exhaled, running a hand through his hair. "I understand how important this matter is to you, and I want to solve this case as soon as possible. To be honest, I don't follow the news much, but some of the lads at the station knew all about you..."

Claire raised an eyebrow, smiling playfully. "Oh, I see—I'm notorious."

"You're celebrated—respected!"

"Well, that's nice of you to say, Javan!"

"Of course," Javan smiled, his gaze lingering on hers. "Now, I better get a move on. I just finished interviewing Miss Sharon. Next, I'll be interviewing the rest of your employees."

"Thank you, Javan," Claire said as she ran her hand along his arm.

"My pleasure, Claire," Javan said with a comforting tone. "And please don't worry. We'll get this all sorted out for you!"

Claire sighed and nodded, watching him as he turned and walked away.

A warmth settled over her as she sat inside the square, scraping away layers of earth and stealing glances at Javan from a distance.

She barely knew him, but there was something familiar about him—it was as if two old souls had reunited.

She felt drawn to him. He was exotic-looking; his darker complexion and dark hair inherited from his Pakistani father, paired with the striking contrast of his grayish-blue eyes from his English mother, made him immensely attractive.

But it wasn't just his looks. There was a depth of character— a seriousness and maturity about him that made him much more attractive—something that resonated deeply with her.

He reminded her of her father.

An image flashed before her eyes. She blushed at the thought of herself in a flowing wedding gown, her father walking her down the aisle, and Javan waiting at the altar, his gaze filled with anticipation. She'd never felt this way about any other man.

She felt a hand on her shoulder and a warm breath against her ear.

"I can read your thoughts," Jane whispered, stepping inside the square and kneeling beside her.

Claire chuckled, her cheeks heating. "You can, huh?"

"Uh-huh… And I think he's hot, too… He's hot, but he doesn't know it. That's the best kind of man. I hope he's a decent cop."

"I think he is—I have faith... How did you sleep?"

Jane groaned. "Ugh! I had nightmares all fuckin' night."

The voicemail message was brief: "Hello, dear, call me, please... It's urgent… Please call privately."

Callum's tone was more ominous than his message, and it made Claire's heart race.

She removed her gloves to access her phone and dial his number. Turning to Sharon, she gestured to her phone.

"Shar, I've got to make a call. I'll be right back."

"Take your time," Sharon said, waving a hand. "It'll all be here when you get back."

Claire gave her a smile and started walking towards the top of the mound, where she could get reception.

Callum picked up on the first ring. He sounded out of breath, speaking between exhales as he took puffs of his cigarette.

She didn't know what to think; her mind was mired in a haze of confusion.

She listened and paced back and forth, trying to comprehend the seriousness of the situation.

Callum explained why he'd asked her to quietly print her business bank statements and mail them to him. He told her what to do, but her mind rejected the notion.

She returned to the dig site and kept to herself all day, mindlessly scraping away at the dirt with her trowel. She tried to reconcile what she'd heard with what she felt, but something didn't make sense, and she didn't want to jump the gun.

Her gut feeling told her something was wrong—awfully wrong.

Sharon watched Claire repeatedly run her trowel over the same patch of dirt, her thoughts clearly a thousand miles away. "You trying to dig to China? Because that's where you'll end up if you keep digging in that same spot."

Claire forced a smile and paused.

Sharon drew closer and took Claire's hand in hers. "I know you're worried, sweetie, but your handsome Inspector will get it all back... Please try not to worry."

Claire nodded. She didn't want to say what was on her mind; it certainly wasn't the coins, and she didn't want to worry her crew.

They'd already dealt with enough during the investigation.

By sunset, Claire was emotionally drained. She abandoned her work and joined Sharon and Isabel for a drink in their trailer. She smiled and nodded at the small talk, but she knew she'd eventually have to do what needed to be done.

She'd racked her brain all day, trying to come up with an explanation, an answer, but she hit a wall—there were none.

54

Javan froze when he saw the image appear on his computer screen. He couldn't believe his eyes. Immediately, he picked up the phone and dialed the number displayed.

Sergeant Walker watched him nodding vigorously and taking notes. Even though she couldn't hear him from behind his office window, she could tell it was an important call—she had never seen him so worked up.

He looked up and noticed her watching him. After he hung up, he waved for her to come in.

It was dark when Claire set out for her trailer. Each step felt heavier than the last as doubt and apprehension churned inside her. She struggled to find the right words to initiate the conversation.

She gazed up at the stars, searching the heavens for answers, a sign from above—anything. But the stars offered none; they just twinkled at her.

With her head bowed in resignation, she arrived at her trailer and paused. This was the moment of truth. She reached for the doorknob but hesitated.

Suddenly, a scream shattered the stillness. Her heart sank.

She peered through a gap in the curtain, and her breath caught in her throat.

Jane's face was pressed down against the table, her eyes wide with terror as she gazed back at Claire. She struggled to shake her head to warn her.

Then, Claire saw fingers clawing through Jane's hair, lifting her head and slamming it back down on the table.

Claire's eyes flew open, her veins surging with adrenaline. She grabbed the door handle, yanked it open, and climbed into the trailer. Horrified, she gasped at the sight.

Jane lay bent over the table, face down, with her jeans pulled down to her ankles. Stewart stood behind her, forcing her head down while fumbling with his belt. He was bleeding, and there were scratches all over his face and neck.

There was no thought, only the impulse to act—to defend Jane.

A high-pitched, guttural shriek pierced the air. It took a moment for Claire to realize that the sound was her own scream echoing inside her head.

She lunged at Stewart, her fists flying as she clawed and struck him with everything she had. He began to slump backward as he fended off her blows.

Then she saw the back of his hand; a flash of light erupted, a ringing in her ears, and she collapsed to the ground. Above her, Stewart stood panting, snarling like a wounded animal, his eyes burning with rage. Blood streamed from his face and brow.

Dazed but aware, Claire's eyes followed the flickering images in the background, catching a glint as Jane lifted Stewart's handgun from the table.

A deafening roar suddenly pierced the momentary stillness, a warm splatter of blood spraying her face.

Stewart staggered, his eyes filled with shock as he looked down at his abdomen, his hands trembling as he pressed them against the gaping hole where the bullet had struck. His knees buckled, and he collapsed beside her.

Claire's chest heaved as she looked up at Jane, who stood behind him, her hands steady, the barrel of the gun still smoking, her eyes burning with fury.

She extended a hand to Claire, helping her up. They cautiously retreated, settling onto the couch behind them as Jane firmly held the gun steady, her gaze locked on him.

Moments later, Javan burst in with his gun drawn and Sergeant Walker right behind him.

He caught a glimpse of Stewart on the floor—he was conscious but bleeding.

Sergeant Walker cuffed him, then slowly rolled him onto his back and began applying pressure to his wound as Javan read him his rights.

55

The interview room at the police station felt cold and impersonal. Stewart's haunting likeness sent shivers down Claire's spine as she gazed at the image. She shook her head in disbelief as she read the name at the bottom of the composite sketch: "Henri Bouchard."

A wave of nausea surged inside her. Standing up, she rushed toward the trash can in the corner, gripping it tightly, preparing to vomit. But the urge subsided as a cascade of emotions poured in: betrayal, disgust, resentment—she was furious with herself for letting him into her life—for opening her heart to him.

She returned to her seat, arms crossed defensively, and stared at the bare walls, devoid of color or emotion.

Javan entered, carrying a steaming cup of hot cocoa, and offered it to Claire. She smiled and shook her head, politely declining it.

He pulled out a chair and sat across from her.

"I'm so sorry you had to go through all this, Claire," he said, his gaze filled with sympathy.

Claire sighed and nodded.

"But I've got good news for you…"

Claire glanced up at him, her eyes filled with curiosity.

Javan smiled and continued, "We've recovered your gold coins. All are accounted for."

Claire's lips curled into a slight smile. "Thank you… That's a relief."

"You're quite welcome!"

Javan expected a more enthusiastic reaction, maybe even joy, but Claire's response was subdued. Something else was weighing on her.

Noticing the disappointment etched on his face, she said, "I'm sorry, Javan. This is great news, and I'm truly grateful for your efforts..."

"There's more, Claire," he added, sensing what she really wanted to hear.

Claire paused, studying him closely with a skeptical expression.

"She provided us with her statement," he went on. "I believe it would be best for you to hear it directly from her—it'll explain a lot." He hesitated, then added, "She'd really like to speak with you."

Claire let out a deep sigh. "I'd like that."

"Would you like me to stay in the room or let you speak with her privately?"

"Privately—if you don't mind."

"Not at all!" Javan stood up and walked to the door, reaching for the knob but paused before turning back to her. "Claire, I want you to know that her statement is fully supported by corroborating evidence." He paused to study Claire's reaction; she smiled faintly and nodded. Then he opened the door and said, "She's in the interview room down the hall with Sergeant Walker... I'll go and fetch her."

"Wait!" Claire raised a hand. "May I ask how the coins were recovered? Did she have anything to do with it?"

Javan shook his head. "No, she had no involvement in the theft of the coins. That scheme was hatched by Henri and your nightwatchman..."

"By Richard?" Claire snapped, her voice laced with frustration.

"By Pavel..."

"Who?"

Javan hesitated. He smiled at Claire and said in a calm voice, "Your nightwatchman's name is not Richard. His name is Pavel...

and he's not from Manchester, as he put down in his employment application—he's from the Czech Republic."

"Czech…" Claire stammered. "He's from the Czech Republic?"

Javan nodded. "Yes… and he's an accomplice of Henri Bouchard. He applied for the job before Henri, who orchestrated the entire plan; he wanted someone on the inside."

"And the break-in?"

Javan shook his head. "It wasn't a break-in—it was a diversion. I suspected it from the start. Pavel simply opened the door for Henri. The break-in was staged."

"But how did you find out?"

"When we ran a background check on Richard, we found no records… Well, no records of a living person, to be precise. Pavel assumed the identity of a deceased person. So did Henri. He took the identity of a Canadian…"

"Wait!" Claire cut it, color fading from her face. "Is Henri Canadian?"

"Yes, he's a Canadian citizen."

"He said he was from Indiana," Claire murmured, shifting her gaze to the bare walls, her voice tinged with defeat.

"I understand your disappointment," Javan said in a sympathetic tone. "And I realize this must feel like a betrayal…"

Claire scoffed and rolled her eyes.

"But it's not," he continued. "A betrayal is personal; this is a crime… these people are criminals. They have no sense of loyalty. When I discovered Pavel's true identity and told him he was about to go away for a long time, he sang like a canary—he gave up the location of the coins and everything he knew about Heni… You know what they say, 'There's no honor among thieves.'"

Claire sighed. "How exactly did you link him to stolen coins?"

Javan flashed a sly smile. "We have him on CCTV footage from the street corner; it's all there. He let Henri in… We obtained a warrant and got his telephone call records. He's been in regular contact with Henri, including on the night of the robbery. Is there any specific reason he would be in contact with Henri?"

"No, not at all. He's just a nightwatchman."

"He's much more than that, Claire. He's a dangerous criminal on the run. He's wanted in France and the Czech Republic."

"Hmm… what about Jane?" Claire cast a sidelong glance, avoiding eye contact as if she feared the response.

Javan hesitated, his gaze locked on Claire's. He mulled over the words about to escape his lips, but there was no way to soften them.

"Celeste… Her real name is Celeste Moreau."

Claire's eyes grew wide, tears pooling in them. She became still, letting the name sink in.

Javan saw the devastation in her eyes. It was as if her entire world, her entire reality, had been turned upside down.

He lowered his voice and continued. "As you know, she has redeposited all the money back into your account… It was all him—he forced her to do it…"

Claire nodded, her eyes down. "I understand."

"And you can still press charges if you wish."

Claire looked up and met Javan's gaze. She furrowed her brow and shook her head emphatically. "No, I do not!"

He gave her a reassuring smile. "Well, you'll be happy to know that the Crown Prosecution Service has decided not to file charges either… She's a victim herself, Claire. I can share the rest with you, or you can hear it directly from her. It's quite sad, actually… and once Henri is out of surgery, we should be able to get a confession from him and organize the immediate rescue of her sister."

Claire paused and leaned in, placing her hands on the table, her fingers splayed as if trying to anchor herself.

"Her sister?" she asked, her voice trembling, her eyes locked on his lips.

He nodded with a faint smile. "Her younger sister… Celine."

Celeste's face was a mask of pain and remorse. She entered the room with her eyes downcast and sat at the table facing Claire. She tried to speak, but only a faint whimper escaped her lips.

The sight of her melted Claire's heart. She struggled to find the words. She took a deep breath, trying to calm her nerves. "Please tell me about your sister, Celine."

"She's only 19..." Celeste stammered, then broke into quiet sobs.

"It's all right," Claire said softly. "Take your time."

Celeste nodded, unable to look Claire in the eyes. "She was taken..."

"By Henri?"

"Yes..."

"Did you know Henri?"

"Mm-hmm... He was my... my boyfriend." Celeste choked, her voice quivering. She cleared her throat.

"He was your boyfriend... Please go on," Claire encouraged, trying to help her find her words.

"I met him at a bar in Paris... when I was out with my work friends... I didn't know him long. I didn't know he was..."

"A criminal?"

Celeste nodded. "He was kind to me at first... Then he changed."

"Did he become physically abusive?"

"Yes... He beat me... And one day..." Celeste stammered. She wiped the teardrops streaming down her cheeks with the back of her hand. "One day, he went after Celine."

Claire's heart sank at her words. She wanted to stop, yet she pushed forward. She needed to hear Celeste's story. Even amidst all the chaos, she'd never felt closer to her.

"I'm so sorry, Celeste... Did he hurt her?"

Celeste looked up at Claire. It was the first time she'd heard her say her real name. A slight twitch at the corner of her mouth hinted at a smile. "He tried... but Celine grabbed a kitchen knife and threatened to stab him if he ever touched either of us again."

Claire gestured toward Celeste's body. "Did he give you those bruises? ... The ones you kept getting all over?"

Celeste gave a slight nod. "Every time he found me alone, he grilled me about money... He wanted to see your bank statements, and if I didn't give them to him, he'd hurt me."

"Is that what happened last night?"

Celeste shifted her gaze to the blank walls and nodded, her lips twisting as she fought back another wave of tears. "I couldn't..." A whimper slipped through. "I redeposited the money back into your account. He followed me to the trailer... I argued with him. He was furious... When I opened the door, he pushed me in and shut it behind him."

"Bastard!" Claire seethed, her voice dripping with anger. She could see that these events had deeply traumatized Celeste—she grew more agitated as she recounted them, wringing her hands and biting her nails. Claire couldn't bear to watch her fall apart. She said softly, "You don't have to continue. We can talk about it later."

Celeste shook her head, her eyes scanning the walls, avoiding Claire's. "No, I want to."

Claire nodded. "All right..."

Celeste let out a sigh and continued. "One day, when I was at work, he took Celine... and I haven't seen her since. Later, he told me he had her... He told me what he did for a living."

"Human trafficking," Claire interjected.

"He called it his gentlemen's club."

"Yeah, right!" Claire snapped angrily, narrowing her eyes.

"Every time I tried to leave him or call the cops, he'd threaten to have her sold..."

Claire's brow furrowed. "Sold?"

"Sold into sex slavery. He said I'd never be able to find her or see her again. He said as long as I cooperated, she'd be safe."

"Scum!" Claire growled, standing abruptly and pacing the room, arms folded across her chest, breathing heavily.

"We had an apartment in Paris," Celeste continued, her eyes following Claire. "I was working for a company that sold excavators. He always made me bring home the company bank statements. He asked me to take out money or transfer it to his account, but I couldn't; I didn't have access. The owner's son handled the finances." Celeste took a deep breath to calm herself. "One day, your order for excavators came in... He noticed the large money transfers..."

"And then he started to look into my company," Claire cut in, filling in the gaps.

Celeste nodded. "He searched online and found you. He looked up your company, your parents..."

"Let me guess..." Claire raised a hand. "He said, 'Pack your bags; we're going to England.'"

"Interpol was investigating him—he said we needed to get out of France, fast! We moved here a few weeks before I applied to work for you, and he had us change our names." Celeste paused before adding, "After that, he took a few days to learn a little about Roman history, create a fake resume... fake references, and apply for the job."

Claire took a deep breath, her fingernails digging into the seat cushion. She took a moment to compose herself. "Tell me about your parents."

"They both passed away. I told you the truth about them; she died of cancer, and he died in a car accident... I raised Celine."

"But your parents weren't Welsh?"

Celeste's face flushed a bright pink. "No... They were French... I was born in Giverny, just outside Paris."

"Home of Monet!" Claire smiled, a lightness breaking through.

"For a time." Celeste smiled back.

Claire was reluctant to go back to work. She decided to take a few days off and return to her flat in London with Celeste. She yearned to spend time with her and learn more about her—about her past and her sister, Celine. It felt as though time had frozen; everything around her seemed to come to a standstill, leaving only her feelings for Celeste at the forefront of her thoughts.

Meanwhile, her sister, whom she had never met, was out there somewhere, with monsters lurking around every corner.

56

Marcel looked down at his hands in the crimson glow of the helicopter cabin lights; they were trembling, driven by fury, not fear.

He'd flown out on the first flight from Paris the moment he heard about Henri's arrest; he insisted on being there for the interrogation.

Images of the hospital emergency room flashed before his eyes. He recalled Javan's arms reaching from behind, yanking him back before his fingers tightened around Henri's neck, smothering his breath.

Javan asked him to leave the room. He assured Marcel he'd get a confession and the yacht's location out of Henri before the day was done. In the end, he got both through a plea offer he arranged with the Crown Prosecution Service.

The good cop, bad cop routine had worked flawlessly.

Henri was facing a laundry list of charges: kidnapping, extortion, human trafficking, assault, and battery. He quickly caved and took the deal.

Marcel lowered his night vision goggles from the top of his helmet and peeked out the window; there were only small vessels and fishing boats. He raised the goggles, settled back into his chair, and closed his eyes.

As if he were watching a double feature in a theater, new, vivid images flickered to life in his mind. A smile tugged at the corner of his lips, imagining Madeleine's palms cradling his face and her lips on his—her last kiss before he left. He could still smell her on him.

He recalled the quizzical expression on Amelie's face as she watched them. She had sensed something was up. Something big. She could read it on their faces.

Her gaze shifted to the duffel bag on the floor beside him and the tactical watch on his wrist. He opened his arms, and she stepped into them, her cheek against his chest.

He lowered his lips to her ear and whispered, "You're going to get a wonderful surprise, my dear." She pulled back and gazed at him, her heart racing. Even Titou seemed to sense the excitement; he kept sniffing the duffel bag and barking.

The crackling voice on the radio roused him, and his eyes snapped open, his smile fading.

"Five minutes, captain."

"Copy that," Marcel said, pressing the mic key on his radio. He paused, then pressed the mic key again. "Team, keep your eyes peeled, don't fire unless necessary, and be careful you don't accidentally shoot the girls."

Marcel could see Corsica's coastline. According to the intelligence extracted from Henri during his interrogation, the yacht was anchored in a small cove along the island's southern tip.

He had pinpointed its exact coordinates during the mission briefing. He felt confident, having assembled the same team as before. The only thing that worried him, as always, was the unexpected.

"Descending to 100 feet," the pilot announced over the radio. "Be ready to rappel down in about 60 seconds."

"Listen up, team, just like on our last mission, we may be rappelling under fire," Marcel said. "Keep sharp, and don't forget the most important thing: I don't want the girls hurt."

"Roger that," his partner Jean replied, trying to lower the intensity. "But wasn't there a bonus... Something about you buying us a few rounds if we ace this mission?"

Marcel chuckled. "Jean... we get home safe with the girls, and I'll be buying drinks all night long."

"I'll hold you to that!"

"You got it, Jean!"

Celine's eyes sprang open when she heard the popping sounds. A lump formed in her throat, and she swallowed hard as she sat upright in bed.

She glanced at the clock on her nightstand: it was 4:30 a.m. Her heart pounded inside her chest. She peered out the window, but all she could see was darkness.

She heard a whirring sound. Her pulse spiked as she leapt out of bed, hurriedly slipping into her jeans and T-shirt.

More popping sounds erupted, sharper, closer. Shouts rang out. Screams of pain.

She started to panic.

A knock on the door made her jump.

"Open up! It's me, Gabriel!"

Celine rushed to the door and opened it. Gabriel quickly entered and shut the door behind him, propping a chair against it. His eyes were blazing with excitement. He hurried to the window and peered out, but he saw nothing.

Celine followed him to the window. "What's going on?"

Gabriel spun around and gazed into her eyes. "You're getting rescued!"

"What?"

"The police are here. I saw them on the stern deck… I ran here to get you!"

Celine shook her head in disbelief.

Gabriel took her hands and muttered calmly, "Trust me!"

The popping sounds stopped. Everything grew silent. Gabriel pressed his ears against the door, straining to listen.

"Can you hear anything?" Celine murmured, standing behind him.

Gabriel shook his head. He paused, then said. "We need to go… We need to go now!"

He removed the chair he'd wedged against the door. He listened once more for any sounds before slowly opening the door and peeking out to check the hallway.

"It's clear!" He reached behind him and took Celine's hand. "Let's go… We need to find the police!"

The stillness was disquieting. There were no voices, no sounds—only eerie silence. Gabriel stealthily followed the narrow hallway toward the stern deck, Celine trailing behind.

They tiptoed slowly to the corner at the end of the hallway when a voice suddenly called out, "Celine!"

As they turned to locate the source of the voice, a click sounded behind them. Gabriel felt the cold barrel of a gun pressing against the back of his head. At that moment, a loud bang shattered the silence, followed by a bright flash ahead.

A loud thud echoed behind them. They turned around to find a man on the ground behind them, a hole in the center of his forehead and a cocked pistol in his hand.

It was Armand, her tormentor. Celine lunged forward, kicking him as he lay unconscious on the floor.

Gabriel seized her and pulled her away while she kicked at the air, screaming.

Amid her screams, she heard the voice echoing: "Celine! Are you Celine?"

Eyes locked on the heavily armed man approaching, Celine stopped struggling in Gabriel's arms and nodded in confirmation when she read the word "POLICE" on his helmet.

The man lowered his gun as he drew close and said, "My name is Marcel Fornier, Celine. I'm here to take you home!"

57

Claire lowered her nose to her teacup, inhaling the aroma of her morning Darjeeling as she gazed out at the sycamore tree outside her window.

She smiled when she spotted her old companion, the goldfinch, perched on a branch. He wasn't alone; there was a female and three juveniles.

Settling into her living room couch, she crossed her legs and raised the teacup to her lips. Just as she was about to sip her tea, her phone chimed. Reluctantly, she placed her teacup in its saucer on the coffee table and picked up her phone.

She quirked her lips as she stared at the image on her screen, wondering why Javan had texted her a photo of Celeste—and why so early in the morning. Her gaze shifted to the time on her screen: 6:30 a.m.

She expanded the photo with her fingers, studying it closely. Suddenly, it struck her that she wasn't looking at a photo of Celeste; the woman appeared younger and had slightly different features. Before she could fully process it, her phone pinged with another text message from Javan:

"Isn't she beautiful? A carbon copy of her sister!"

Claire let out a startled gasp and quickly covered her mouth with her hand. As she tiptoed into her bedroom, a smile spread across her face. Celeste had curled up on Claire's side of the bed, hugging her pillow tightly.

She approached Celeste slowly and knelt beside the bed. She held her phone screen facing her while gently caressing her arm. A contented moan escaped Celeste's lips as her eyelids fluttered open. Still half-asleep, she met Claire's gaze with a soft, drowsy smile.

Claire returned the smile and then nodded toward her phone. Celeste's eyes shifted to the screen. She grasped the phone with both hands and brought it closer, squinting as she tried to bring the image into focus. She froze. Then her eyes snapped open, and she let out a scream, kicking her feet in the air in joy.

Meanwhile, in Paris, Madeleine was startled by a piercing scream followed by the sound of barking—both coming from Amelie's room. She leaped out of bed and raced toward her room.

Throwing the door open, she found Amelie sitting up in bed, her face glowing with a smile, tears of joy glistening in her eyes. "It's Celine!" She beamed, holding up her phone. "Marcel just texted it to me!"

Madeleine rushed to her side and took the phone from her. She pressed her hand to her chest and sighed. "She's beautiful!"

Amelie nodded, her smile stretching even wider. "She's wearing the crucifix I gave her!"

58

Claire was thrilled that her mother had agreed to host the girls' reunion at their home. According to her father, she was "delighted" about the idea. It was yet another opportunity for her to throw a party and invite some of her "posh pals," as he referred to them.

The idea was to host the party in London; Marcel, Madeleine, and Amelie were flying in from Paris, and Sharon and the rest of the team were taking the train from Newcastle.

The girls were coming in from all over. Celeste suggested keeping things casual—most girls were in their late teens or twenties.

"I still can't believe how much Celine looks like you!" Claire exclaimed, sitting on the porch steps beside Celeste as they watched the girls mingle in her parents' enormous backyard.

"I could say the same about you and that redhead," Celeste grinned, pointing to one of the girls chatting with Amelie and Celine. "She's Scottish, and her name is Ava. From a distance, I wouldn't be able to tell you apart." Her smile faded as her expression turned serious. "Those bastards took these girls from all over. I've been going around meeting them all… Ava was on vacation in Paris when they took her."

"Hey, look on the bright side," Claire said softly as her hand gently caressed Celeste's back. "You've got your sister back…"

"I know, I know," Celeste nodded. "I should count my blessings." She sighed, then went on, "All right, Miss Sunshine, here's a silver lining on my otherwise black clouds: Celine said Marcel and Madeleine asked if Amelie wanted to live with them permanently. They want to adopt her formally… She said yes!"

"That's wonderful!" Claire beamed. "See? Things always work out. You've got to have faith!"

Celeste pulled a face. "Mm… Faith… Yeah, anyway, I caught up with Marcel earlier at the bar; I hugged and thanked him for everything he's done. He said Celine and I are always welcome to stay with them when we go visit Amelie."

"That's excellent news! I'm so glad you and Celine will be able to stay in touch with them."

Claire had a nagging question she wanted to ask Celeste but never did—she was unsure how she'd take it and didn't want to risk offending her.

Her tightly pressed lips and her silence were telltale clues for Celeste. She pulled out a twenty-pound note and held it up between two fingers. "Twenty pounds for your thoughts!"

Claire laughed. "I believe the expression is 'Penny for your thoughts.'"

"I didn't want to be stingy with my best friend… So, what's on your mind, bestie? Or do you need more cash?"

"No, I'm fine, thank you!" Claire chuckled. "All right, I'll tell you." She took a deep breath to gather her thoughts and then said, "I noticed that you were keeping close to Isabel and Eve. I wondered if it was because you missed Celine. They were young, and they reminded you of her… Did you feel like you needed to be an older sister to them?"

Celeste gave a slight shrug. "I don't know… I guess… I was also very worried about them."

She cast a sidelong glance and sighed. "I caught Henri spying on them. He had a picture of Isabel on his phone. He took it at the bar where she worked—it's a popular spot. He must have gone there when we were in Newcastle. That's why I wanted to hire her: to keep her close. She was his type. Eve, too… I was worried he might have his people take them… I was keeping an eye on them."

"Do you think he was our camp stalker?"

"I know he was! I saw him creeping around the night before he attacked me. I was too afraid to say anything. I know he spied on me to see where I kept the company files... You know, your bank statements..."

"I know."

Claire stood at the main entrance with Celeste, introducing her to her mother, when they spotted a man in formal attire approaching. He stopped to shake Marcel's hand before turning to walk toward them.

"Now, there's a well-dressed young man!" Claire's mother exclaimed, her eyes sparkling with admiration. "See, ladies, he's so handsome! I've never understood the casual look."

"Agreed!" Celeste chimed in. She leaned in and whispered in Claire's ear, "He does look pretty hot! Anyone we know?"

Claire squinted, trying to make out the man's face. A telling gasp escaped her as she recognized him. "That's..." She stammered. "That's Inspector Siddiqui... It's Javan!"

Claire's lips parted to say something when she glanced to the side—she found Celeste had vanished, and her mother was chatting with a guest. Panic set in. She rose to her feet and put on a bright smile, her cheeks flushing pink.

"Hi, Javan!"

"Hello, Claire!" Javan said, flashing a smile. "It's wonderful to see you again! I'm sorry if I'm a bit overdressed... Celeste said it was casual, but when I told my mum, she was horrified." He motioned to his outfit. "She had other ideas, as you can see."

Claire laughed. "Your mum should meet mine. They'd agree!" From the corner of her eye, she caught sight of Celeste grinning and winking at her. Claire playfully narrowed her eyes at her.

Claire felt an undeniable magnetism towards Javan. It was his traditional family values that attracted her; she envied his close relationship with his mother, something she had always lacked in her own life.

Time stood still as she stood beside him, captivated by his life story. Everything he spoke about revolved around his family, siblings, and friends.

Celeste felt a warmth wash over her as she watched Celine mingle and laugh with her friends; she was particularly close to Amelie, rarely leaving her side.

Celeste's gaze then shifted to Claire and Javan as they joined Marcel and Madeleine.

Standing in the dining room, she sipped her margarita and listened to their infectious laughter echoing through the open window.

She caught a glimpse of Claire's hand grazing Javan's and noticed the telling smile on her face as his hand ran along her arm.

Despite her lingering skepticism, she thought it was a perfect ending to her story.

Then, dark clouds rolled in—she recalled the sinking feeling in her stomach when she came home to find Celine gone. How would she take care of Celine now? Could she trust herself with that responsibility?

Sitting at the bar, she ordered another drink—something bolder: a double scotch and soda. She stared at it, swirling the ice cubes inside, searching for answers.

A folded fifty-pound note materialized over her right shoulder as a whisper brushed against her left ear. "A fifty for your thoughts?"

She let out a laugh. She reached over her shoulder and took Claire's hand.

Claire lowered her lips to Celeste's ears again and whispered, "Don't overthink it—have faith!"

Celeste nodded, her eyes misting up, and whispered back, "Faith!"

59

The station was bustling with passengers waiting to board the train. Celeste watched as families embraced their loved ones, their eyes following them as they climbed aboard.

With her arms wrapped around Celine and her head resting on her shoulder, Celeste smiled at Claire and scrunched her nose playfully. Humming, "Au Clair de la Lune," she gently brushed a strand of hair behind Celine's ear. It was a melody their mother sang to them when they were young.

Suddenly, Celine's body stiffened as she heard a voice. She wriggled out of Celeste's arms and spun around to look behind her. Letting out a scream, she dashed towards the voice—it was Amelie, with Marcel and Madeleine following closely behind her.

Celeste shot a glance at Claire, who grinned and shrugged. Overcome with emotion, Celeste threw her arms around her, pressing her lips close to her ear. "I love you, Claire! Thank you for doing this!"

Claire nodded and whispered, "Like I said, 'Have faith!'"

"I will—I promise!"

"Good! I spoke to Marcel and Madeleine. They're okay with Amelie staying with us for a few weeks to catch up with Celine. Madeleine thought it was a fantastic idea. They asked if they could periodically visit, and I said, 'Absolutely! We'd love that.'"

"That's…" Celeste stammered. "That's so nice of you. Celine is going to freak out!"

"You're welcome! It'll be fun having both of them around."

Celeste laughed. "I don't know—you may regret it later."

"I doubt it… They're so sweet." Claire turned to look at Celine, who was animated and laughing while talking to Amelie and Madeleine.

After sharing hugs and tearful goodbyes, they boarded the train. Claire had reserved two connecting cabins for the four of them. As the train jolted into motion and started rolling along the tracks, they waved through the cabin window at Marcel and Madeleine.

Madeleine followed the train, waving and blowing kisses at them until she reached the end of the platform and faded from view.

Celeste moved closer to the window, absorbing the vibrant countryside that whizzed by in a blur of green and gold as the sun began its retreat behind the horizon.

Her lips curled into a smile as she shifted her gaze to Claire, who was sitting silently across from her and smiling back.

Then, it dawned on her that they were on a night train. She had been so overwhelmed with emotion—so absorbed in the moment—that she never stopped to consider why.

"You know, we could have reached Newcastle by now if we had taken the fast train," she said, raising an eyebrow.

"Who said we're going to Newcastle?" Claire replied with a sly smile.

Celeste laughed, then narrowed her eyes playfully. "What are you not telling me?"

Claire gave a mischievous grin and shrugged. "It's a surprise—ask me another question."

"Hmm… All right, miss smarty-pants!" Celeste pressed her fingers against her lips. After a moment of thought, she said, "I've got another one: What were you and Javan talking about at the party? Do I hear wedding bells?"

Claire's mouth dropped open, and she laughed. "Really? That's your question?"

Celeste gave a vigorous nod. "Mm-hmm… Spill the beans—all of it! I want to hear all the juicy details."

Claire's cheeks flushed as she struggled to suppress a laugh. "I'm sorry to disappoint you, but there's very little to tell…"

Celeste rolled her eyes playfully.

"All right, if you must know…"

Celeste nodded. "I must."

"Fine, we talked about family… mostly his family. He's very traditional."

"Good, we like traditional—go on."

Claire went on, stammering her answers. "He quit his job… He'd like to start a family… He asked me out…"

"Whoa, whoa, whoa!" Celeste threw up a hand. "Wait— what? In what order?"

Claire burst into a hearty laugh. "He quit his job because he doesn't think his work hours are conducive to family life."

"He's right—go on!"

"He asked me out…"

Celeste made a rolling motion with her finger, urging Claire to continue.

"He said he'd like to take me to the British Museum… He said he's been there many times with his parents, and he loves ancient history."

"Classy… I like him a lot. Keep going."

"He'd like to start a family."

"When? Before or after the date?"

"Oh, Celeste!"

Celeste stood and moved to sit beside Claire. Leaning in, she whispered, "Can I be your maid of honor?"

Claire chuckled. "Of course you can! I'd insist on it. But aren't you putting the horse before the cart?"

"It's, 'Aren't you putting the cart before the horse?' You had it backward. Just remember not to make that mistake with Javan: the date comes before starting a family. I'll make a note to remind you."

"Hahaha… Did you bring any of your illegal contraband?"

Celeste's eyes widened, and she flashed a mischievous grin. She turned her purse upside down, letting a handful of mini alcohol bottles tumble onto the seat between them.

"Take your pick!"

Celeste grabbed a vodka while Claire took a gin. They opened their bottles and were about to clink glasses when Claire drew back her hand.

"By the way, it was pretty cute how you took off and left me alone with Javan at the party… Don't think I didn't notice."

Celeste giggled. "Just remember: date first, start a family after. In that order—don't ruin my plans!"

Claire laughed and clinked glasses with her. Celeste switched off the lights so they could sit and gaze out the window at the twinkling city lights as they sped by. She lowered her head to Claire's shoulder and let out a contented sigh. Then, a scream followed by laughter echoed from the cabin next door.

"Don't worry, it's Celine," Celeste murmured calmly. "I know her laugh... She can't sit still. We're probably going to be listening to them all night. I think she's pillow fighting with Amelie."

"I'm not worried at all," Claire whispered. "I'm so happy they're having fun."

A thump followed by an "Ow!" resounded through the thin cabin wall.

"Yup! They're definitely pillow fighting."

Celeste was the first to fall asleep, her head resting on Claire's shoulder. She was completely exhausted from the emotional roller coaster she'd been on for the past few days.

Claire smiled, listening to her snoring, and nestled comfortably against the backrest, trying not to wake her.

She let out a quiet chuckle when she heard, "Ow! You cheated!"

Celeste awoke to the gentle caress of Claire's fingertips on her arm and her whisper, "You need to get up now, sleeping beauty… I let you sleep in... I'm glad you got a decent night's rest."

Celeste yawned and stretched her arms, forcing her eyelids open. "Mmm… That felt so good… What is that smell?"

"We got you some sausage, bacon, eggs, and toast, Aunt Celeste," a soft voice said.

Celeste sat up and rubbed her eyes, trying to shake off the sleep. "Is that you, Amelie?"

"Yes, Aunt Celeste," Amelie answered, raising a hand. "I hope you don't mind me calling you that."

"I told her she should call you that," Celine interjected, stepping out from behind Amelie. "I said, 'She'll like that.'"

Celeste rose to her feet and threw her arms around Amelie. "I would love for you to call me 'Aunt Celeste!'" She gushed, her heart melting.

"Why don't you eat so we can get going," Claire suggested.

"Where are we?" Celeste asked as she peered out the window.

"Edinburgh… Callum wants to see us."

60

Callum paced eagerly, his shoes sinking into the plush carpet, leaving imprints behind. His heart raced with anticipation as he contemplated his next steps.

After lengthy discussions with Claire and Javan about the recent incidents and Celeste's involvement in them, he concluded that she was an innocent victim.

This realization filled him with confidence in what he was about to propose. He took a cigarette from its case and placed it between his lips. As he flicked his lighter, ready to light the cigarette, he heard a knock on the door.

"Come in," he called out, quickly putting away the cigarette.

The door slowly creaked open, and Claire stepped through, followed by Celeste, Celine, and Amelie.

"Hi, Callum!" Claire waved. "Your secretary said we could come in. She said you were expecting us."

"Yes, of course! Come in, come in, please!" Callum said, directing them inside with a warm smile. He motioned to his office sofa. "Please have a seat. Thank you for coming!" He paused, shaking his head in amazement. "My goodness! I've never seen such beautiful ladies all in one spot, let alone in my office!"

A giggle came from his secretary, Dorothy, who was at her desk outside his office.

Callum pointed in her direction. "See? Even Dorothy agrees!"

The women erupted into laughter, prompting Dorothy to join in.

When their laughter subsided, Callum said, "I don't wish to keep you long; I'm sure you've got better things to do than sit in my dingy office all day." He gazed out the window and sighed. "It's such a beautiful day… What I wouldn't give for another twenty years." After a pause, he turned his attention back to the women before him, smiling. "How would you ladies like to go on a grand adventure?"

Celeste turned to Claire, a quizzical expression on her face.

Claire smiled and said, "Callum has invited me to join his team in Egypt… at the ongoing excavations at the temple of Zeus Ammon. He'd like for me to lead the expedition…"

She paused to study Celeste's face, then added, "I'd really like for you and the girls to come with me."

Celeste let out a gasp, clutching Claire's arm, her words struggling to escape her lips.

Claire chuckled, placed her hand on Celeste's, and whispered, "Just nod."

Celeste gave her head an exaggerated nod, and a slight moan escaped her lips. "Mm-hmm." She turned to look at Celine and Amelie, who were barely holding back their grins. They were in on the secret; the only one left in the dark was Celeste—this was meant to surprise her.

"Marcel and Madeleine are completely okay with Amelie going," Claire continued. "I already spoke with them; they think it would be a great experience for her."

Celeste shot a glance at Celine, who nodded, her eyes brimming with excitement. "I'd really like to go!"

Celeste turned back to Claire and threw her arms around her, her cheeks damp with tears.

"Thank you," she murmured.

"You're so welcome!" Claire whispered back.

"Ladies," Callum said, drawing attention to himself. "You're about to embark on the greatest expedition of your lives: to find the final resting place of Alexander the Great!"

61

Claire initially wanted to fly directly to Alexandria, but Celine and Amelie pleaded with her to stop in Cairo first. "We have to see the pyramids," they insisted. She couldn't refuse.

Waiting to board their flight, they sat slouched over at the airport terminal, browsing different hotels on their phones and sending their top picks in a group text to Claire and Celeste.

What they didn't know was that Celeste had already made reservations at one of the top hotels in Cairo, waiting to surprise them. They were having a great time scrolling through hotel pictures, and she didn't want to spoil their fun.

Celine looked up and saw a man approaching. She immediately recognized him. He was wearing the same black leather jacket he had on when he welcomed her at the airport following her rescue. She remembered him guiding her through security to Celeste and Claire, who were waiting for her with bated breath.

She sprang to her feet and waved at him. "Hi, Javan!"

He waved back enthusiastically and smiled. "Hi, Celine!"

Celeste shot Claire a surprised look, cocking an eyebrow. "You invited him to come along?"

She chuckled and gave a nod. "I did better—I hired him… You're looking at your new head of security… among other things."

Celeste's eyes grew wide, and her mouth flung open. She clutched Claire's forearm, sinking her nails into her in excitement.

Claire winced, then laughed. "He'll be joining us on our trip… for security reasons, of course."

"Of course," Celeste repeated with playful sarcasm, pushing into her. She shot a sidelong glance toward him and murmured, "Here he comes… I hear wedding bells!"

Claire rolled her eyes but couldn't help smiling.

It was a five-hour flight from London to Cairo. Celine sat by the window while Amelie took the aisle seat. Celeste sat behind Celine, and Claire sat behind Amelie. Javan took a seat on the opposite row across the aisle, keeping a close eye on them.

Before long, they all dozed off.

A sudden shake jolted them awake. Celeste let out a shriek. Javan's eyes snapped open, and he quickly unbuckled himself. He got up and leaned in across the aisle to check on her.

"Are you all right, Celeste?"

"Sorry!" Celeste blushed, looking embarrassed. "Yes, I'm fine. I'm afraid of flying."

"Just a bit of rough air," Javan reassured her calmly. "Nothing to worry about."

He realized he was standing too close, hovering over Claire. She looked up and smiled at him, secretly savoring the scent of his earthy cologne.

"I'm so sorry!" He exclaimed as he drew back. "I didn't mean to crowd you, Claire!"

"Not at all," she said with a sly grin. "You're fine!"

Beneath the blanket covering their legs, Celeste found Claire's hand and gave it a playful squeeze. Claire pressed her lips together, fighting back a nervous laugh.

Suddenly, Celine's head popped up above them, her blonde hair spilling over her face.

"Look out the window! Pyramids!"

Celeste let out a loud gasp as she gazed through the window—there they were: three diamond-shaped structures rising from the earth, casting long shadows across the plateau, their tips kissing the crimson sunset sky.

Celeste was excited to see the surprise on Celine and Amelie's faces, grinning as she opened the hotel room door. They squealed with excitement and hurried inside, jumping up and down and pumping their fists in the air.

Opening the sliding glass door, they stepped onto the balcony, the warm desert air caressing their faces.

Celine grabbed her phone, opened FaceTime, and flipped the screen to face them as they stood with their backs to the Giza plateau.

Sharon's face appeared on the screen, with Eve and Isabel beside her, craning their necks to fit into the frame, waving and cheering.

Celine and Amelie waved back, beaming. "Hi, guys! Check this out!"

Celine positioned the camera to capture the scene behind them, bringing the background into focus: silhouetted against the red haze of dusk, three pyramids stood in the shadows, with a setting sun nestled between them.

Celeste wiped the tears from her cheeks with the back of her fingers. As she watched, Claire felt her own eyes well up. She gestured toward their luxurious bathroom with a giant Jacuzzi bathtub in its center.

Celeste smiled. "I told you we should bring our swimsuits, and you gave me a look and said, 'Why would we wanna bring our swimsuits to the desert?'"

Claire chuckled. "As always, you're right... Now, let's go before they find out about the tub."

Sitting in the tub with bubbles rising all around them, they raised their champagne glasses.

"Here's to us... and to finding Alexander the Great!" Claire toasted, their clinking glasses echoing softly in the tub.

Even with the sound of the jets spewing bubbles all around them, they could hear the girls laughing and chatting on the balcony. Javan's voice floated in from the adjacent balcony, mingling with the girls' laughter; he'd booked the room next to them to keep a close watch.

Relaxing in their lounge chairs on the balcony and nursing their morning coffee, they marveled at the grandeur of the pyramids, thousands of years of history unfolding before their eyes.

But it was time to leave—they had a rendezvous with destiny.

62

Callum wasn't taking any chances; he'd arranged for two SUVs, accompanied by local security personnel, to escort them safely to their destination. Following the lead car, they wound their way along the stunning Mediterranean coast for a few hours before veering southwest into the arid, scorching desert—a nine-hour journey across a vast sea of sand.

In the third-row seat at the back, Amelie excitedly shared her experiences with Claire, scrolling through pictures of Titou on her phone. Claire gasped in delight when she saw a picture of Titou in Amelie's arms, licking her face.

Javan caught Claire stealing glances at him in the rearview mirror and smiled. She returned his smile, her face flushing.

He'd offered to drive so he could take evasive action in case of a security incident. He remained vigilant during the drive, surveying his surroundings throughout the entire trip.

He'd brought a satellite phone and kept a semiautomatic rifle with him at all times. When they stopped to stretch their legs, he remained on the phone the entire time, gesturing with his hands as he spoke.

Sitting in the middle row, Celeste gazed out the window at a caravan of camels gliding gracefully across the shimmering dunes. Her mind transformed the image into a mirage of Alexander's invincible phalanx marching relentlessly through the desert.

She closed her eyes and let the hot desert wind dance through her hair as she held Celine's hand, their fingers intertwined.

It was pitch dark when they arrived at their final destination, with the only light coming from their campsite. Weary from the long drive, they unloaded their belongings and were directed to their tents by the crew—a stark contrast from their well-equipped trailers.

Celine and Amelie didn't bother to unpack; exhausted, they collapsed onto their cots and were out cold within minutes.

Celeste picked up two mini bottles—one vodka and the other gin—and clinked them together to grab Claire's attention. Claire glanced up from her unpacking and chuckled softly.

"Let's take a walk! It'll be fun," Celeste urged with a playful wink. "We can unpack tomorrow. I feel like procrastinating... and my ass is sore from sitting in the car all day!"

Claire nodded in agreement and pressed her palm to her lips, trying to stifle her laugh.

Celeste watched as Claire's face turned a bright shade of crimson—she didn't want to wake the girls sleeping nearby.

Perched on a citadel, the temple of the oracle rose a few meters above its surroundings, set against a velvety black sky dotted with sparkling stars.

They opened their bottles and raised them in a toast to the girls and the success of their venture. As they sipped their drinks, they climbed the centuries-old steps to the temple entrance. At the top, they spotted a stone platform where they sat down, soaking in the tranquil stillness around them.

"Listen… Can you hear that?" Celeste murmured, cupping her hand around her ear.

Claire took a moment to listen, then shook her head.

"I can't hear anything."

"Exactly! Isn't it amazing? Not a sound!"

Claire let out a deep sigh. "Hmm… it is. It's beautiful out here." She felt the weight of the moment settle around her and pointed to the temple entrance. "Just imagine Alexander walking past us and into the temple… Imagine the oracle proclaiming him the Son of God."

Suddenly, Celeste noticed shadows in the corner of her eye— they moved stealthily and then vanished into the darkness. Her heart raced as she grasped Claire's hand and raised a finger to her lips, signaling for her to be quiet.

Silence.

In an instant, the calm was shattered by bright flashes of light erupting beyond the rocks ahead, followed by muffled popping sounds. They then heard whispers and radio chatter, more flashes and pops, and then, abruptly, silence.

Paralyzed with fear, Celeste and Claire clung tightly to each other, their eyes fixed on the pitch black ahead. They heard the sound of tires crunching on gravel but saw no lights. Then they heard car doors opening, followed by the sound of them closing.

They froze, bracing to run, when rustling sounds broke the silence. A ghostly figure emerged from the darkness. "Wait! Don't be afraid... It's me!"

"Javan?" Claire murmured, craning her neck, her voice trembling.

"Yes," Javan replied, peeling off his black mask. He was dressed in a black tactical outfit and carried an assault rifle. "I'm so sorry I frightened you!"

"What's..." Claire stammered, her words caught in her throat.

"Let me explain," Javan said in a reassuring voice.

"Please do, Javan," Celeste snapped, folding her arms across her chest. "You scared the shit out of us! What's going on?"

"I truly apologize..."

"Stop with the apologies—please just explain!"

"All right!" Javan exclaimed, raising a hand in surrender. "We've been followed... They've been tracking us since we arrived in Egypt."

"Who? Who's been following us?" Claire asked, alarm flashing across her face.

"The same people who kidnapped Celine and Amelie..."

"Wait! What? I thought Henri was in jail," Celeste interrupted, throwing up her hands in frustration.

"He is..." Javan replied to Celeste, then turned to Claire. "And he won't be getting out for a long time, Claire!" He noticed she was shivering, goosebumps rising on her arms. He took off his jacket and draped it over her shoulders, continuing, "But we're talking about a vast criminal network. Henri only ran the European side. But now the Asian ring is trying to fill his void."

Claire looked stunned, at a loss for words.

"As head of your security, I've been working closely with Marcel and Peter to monitor their operations and ensure your safety." He paused, then added. "... and the security of the girls, of course."

"Peter?" Celeste cut in, confused.

"Yes," Javan said. "We've cleared him—he's not a suspect, and he has extensive security and military experience... He's an asset, and I don't want to lose him!"

"Hmm... all right... Were they here tonight?" Celeste asked, her tone softening. "I saw two shadows moving together..."

"You only saw Marcel and me... He flew in with his team from the south of France to Cairo, then followed us closely by car. This was the same team that rescued Celine. But don't worry; they've already cleaned up and left."

Celeste stepped forward and threw her arms around him, her lips curling into a warm smile. "Thank you, Javan! Thank you for everything... for watching over us!"

Claire met Javan's gaze over Celeste's shoulder and smiled. She then approached and wrapped her arms around them both.

"Remember, mum's the word," Javan whispered, lowering his lips to their ears. "Nothing happened here tonight!"

"See no evil, hear no evil," Celeste quipped. "I didn't see anything... Did you, Claire?"

"Nope!" Claire murmured, burying her face in his chest.

Epilogue

A month later…

Celeste burst into the tent, breathless and shaky, pointing with a finger toward the temple. "I've found something—I think!"

Claire's heart slammed against her chest. She snapped her laptop shut and sprang to her feet, gripping Celeste's shoulder to steady her. "What? What is it?"

Celeste took a deep breath before continuing, "We found a hidden chamber!" She shuddered at the thought. "Ew! And there are spiders every-fuckin-where in there!"

She let out a hysterical shriek, imagining a black spider crawling up her shoulder.

Claire laughed, plucking a piece of lint from her shirt. "It's just lint," she said, bringing it in front of her face.

With a sigh, Celeste sank into Claire's chair, taking a deep breath. She pulled out her phone from her pocket, her hands shaking. Struggling to open her photo app, she went on. "We came across the chamber by accident—almost missed it. It's a tiny chamber. We had to crawl through a small opening."

She paused to shoot Claire a dramatic glare.

"Javan… I'm so mad at him…" She curled a corner of her lips, showing she was faking anger. "… he convinced me to follow him in, saying, 'It's just a couple of feet. I can see a chamber.' So I followed him in like an idiot!" She paused to bring up a photo and continued. "And then I saw this on the wall."

Claire took the phone from Celeste's trembling hands, her eyes wide and mouth agape as she stared at the image—a bearded man with ram's horns. She shot a glance at Celeste, her words stuck in her throat.

"Keep swiping," Celeste urged, nodding for her to continue.

With her thumb swiping on the phone screen, Claire brought up the next image: a narrow shaft with its cover moved to the side.

She gazed up at Celeste as if expecting a punchline. "What am I looking at?"

"Go to the next picture!"

Claire swiped to the next image and paused. Suddenly, she let out a scream and sank to the floor, one hand propping herself up while the other rested on her thumping heart.

Celeste jumped out of her chair and rushed to sit beside her. "Is it…?"

Claire gave a tentative nod, unsure. "I think… I hope!"

At that moment, Javan flung open the tent flap and charged in. "Are you okay, Claire?" he asked, concern etched on his face.

Claire smiled and nodded. "Yes, Javan. Thank you!" She returned her gaze to the phone in her hand.

The screen displayed a picture of Celeste's hand holding a flashlight, its beam directed down a narrow shaft in the ground. At the bottom, a broad stone slab was visible, with the letters "ΑΛΕΞΑΝΔΡΟΣ" carved into its surface.

She looked at Celeste and said, "I don't know Greek, but I recognize the first three letters: 'Alpha… Lambda… Epsilon.'" She sounded them out: "A… L… E."

"Alexander!" Celeste exclaimed, color fading from her face.